Tower of Blood

MISTY THOMAS

TOWER OF BLOOD

COPYRIGHT

DEDICATION

To those with scars both seen and unseen.
    Wear them with pride.

AUTHOR'S NOTE

This story deals with many difficult themes and events including sexual and psychological abuse, mental illness, self-harm, and torture.

This story and characters may be fictional, but their emotions and the things they encounter are very much rooted in reality. If you find yourself struggling, please reach out for help

For a complete list of content warnings, please visit the author's website.

CHAPTER 1

Elora

The nightmare had woken Elora again last night, the remnants of it keeping her from falling back asleep. Echoes of teeth and hands and chains lingered long after she had darted up, panting so loudly she was sure one of the night nurses would come to check on her. The voice she heard in her dreams never fully went away, forever haunting her even in the light of day with two little words—little rose. It was a whisper spoken in her ear, a brush against her thoughts during group therapy or meals. The medication was supposed to help, but it did very little these days.

Not even the sunlight streaming through the line of tall windows in the dayroom of Blackwell Psychiatric Hospital could force the whispers away, could warm the lingering chill in her bones. Elora sat with her head resting against the back of the cracked leather armchair, knees pulled to her chest as she watched the other residents file into the room. Some took seats among the eclectic collection of wooden chairs that belonged in a dining room, armchairs like the one she sat in, and couches, while others lined up in front of the desk where the nurses prepared the medication. None of the furniture matched and probably had decades of wear and tear. Chipped wooden tables, slightly burned couches, torn rugs, and an ancient television that only played a handful of shows, forever repeating the same episodes over and over populated the space where they spent most of their time.

Elora assumed the dayroom could be charming if one didn't look too hard. It had the traditional color palette she had expected to see when she arrived five years ago. Pale blue walls with pastoral paintings in frames that held no glass. There were no curtains for the windows since they were too much of a hazard when fifteen people with violent tendencies, either to themselves or others, spent most of their time in there. On the bulletin board were drawings done during weekly art therapy, an alleged peek into the healing soul.

A small snort fell from her chapped lips. Healing was an interesting word to use and inaccurate as well. They were all here against their will, participants in their involuntary hospitalization, forever kept behind locked doors until some higher person decided they were well enough to leave. Her first hearing had been one year into her sentence where her primary psychiatrist insisted Elora wasn't ready, that her delusions still made her a danger to herself and others. Elora's hand curled into a fist at the thought, at the memory of Dr. Montgomery's smug smile even after half an hour of begging, promising, and negotiating.

Slowly, chattering filled the room, a mixture of comments about the weather they would only experience for an hour when they went out to the courtyard for recreation time, gossip about one of the nurses, and whispers of protests in the streets just beyond the walls of the facility. The television didn't get the news channel, either by design or a twist of fate, but visiting family members and nurses talked.

Elora tuned out the gossip, the tales of piles of burning bodies, of groups of people storming grocery stores, stealing food they could never afford. Nothing she would contribute to these conversations would end well for her. At best, it would be an argument with another resident, screaming back and forth about who was right and who was crazy. At worst, it would be a stay in the green room, a space for isolation and thinking about one's actions before meeting with their head psychiatrist.

"Elora Reynolds. Morning meds. Let's go."

The nurse's voice rang out, crowding out the various conversations, the sounds of the television, and scooting chairs as the therapist rearranged the room for group therapy after breakfast. Elora stood, arching her back to chase away the stiffness that always came with a lack of sleep, with the way her body tensed and her muscles clenched during her nightmares. At one point, Dr. Montgomery had been concerned it was seizures causing it, but several exams and tests later, she had tossed out that theory. Now it was just sedatives and mild muscle relaxers at night and a complicated cocktail each morning. Mood stabilizers and anti-psychotics. She didn't bother to remember the names or doses.

The nurse, a young man in blue scrubs and shaggy brown hair, waited at the desk, a tiny paper cup in one hand and a plastic cup of water in the other. The residents stood to the side, waiting their turns as they watched Elora inch closer and closer. She didn't rush or dart to the desk, but made eye contact with each resident, giving them a small smile before taking her place at the front of the line.

"Good morning, Viktor." Elora's voice was cheery, and the nurse nodded before looking her over as she took the two cups. With a grimace, she dumped the pills into her mouth before she swallowed the them with the cup of water. She took a moment before she opened her mouth and lifted her tongue, noting the hint of exhaustion in Viktor's face. The normally bright amber eyes were dark, with no hints of the gold flecks she was so used to seeing.

"Thank you." Viktor gestured for the next resident to step forward, and Elora shifted to the side, resting her palms on the cool surface of the desk. Her eyes trailed over the files, the random pieces of paper, and the checklists. With each resident who swallowed their meds and lifted their tongues, Viktor initialed the paper in front of him before moving on. Slowly, each resident took their cups and completed the morning ritual.

"Did you do anything fun yesterday?" Viktor gave her a quick glance, eyes moving over her barely brushed red hair and the shadows under her eyes.

"Unfortunately, not. You know this place is my life." He initialed on the last line before shoving the paper into a file and locking it away.

"I hope we are at least entertaining if you are dedicating your life to us." He gave her a sly grin, eyes twinkling with mischief.

"It's more entertainment than I can handle most days." Viktor took a moment to look over the room, noting where residents had retreated to now that medication was handed out. Most were waiting by one of the two locked doors, impatiently tapping their feet as they waited for it to be opened. The ward ran on a strict schedule, with consistency being considered one of the best medicines for unstable minds. Medication, breakfast, group therapy, outside recreation time, lunch, art therapy, quiet time, then dinner to end it all. When this was broken or hindered, the results were volatile.

Elora pushed off the counter, fingers sliding along the post-it notes with nothing of concern written on them. An update in therapy time, a missed call for a resident, and canceled individual therapy. She took a moment to adjust her shirt, pulling the sleeves down so they covered her wrists and fixed the collar, so it hid everything below her neck. People stared. Not just the residents who always had questions and theories, but the nurses. They were worse than Elora's fellow patients, who at least understood that sometimes things left scars and they were all well versed in that. The nurses, however, either looked at her with pity or thinly veiled disgust, assuming she had done them to herself to feel something or as a cry for attention.

"Line up for breakfast." Viktor finally came around the desk along with the other day shift nurse. Both walked to the door and stood in front, patiently waiting for everyone to line up. The residents chattered, debating what breakfast would be or taking bets on whether group therapy would descend into chaos. Elora knew it would. It always did. A resident would say something, a single innocent comment, which would trigger a memory or emotion and it would crash from there.

Elora stood in the back, hands in her pockets as watched them all shuffle through the door, pushing and shoving to get to the cafeteria first. As with every meal and journey to the cafeteria, she hesitated, staying in the back so she was last to go through the door. The nurses thought it was another quirk, like when she yelled at the characters on television or asked them about their pets. An innocent habit of an otherwise violent person. The residents, on the other hand, had noticed her aversion to their close contact, her shrinking away when they got too close. Each time they would mutter a curse word, or call her a stuck-up bitch, before screaming that she was no better than they were, that they were all locked up here together.

How was she to explain that being near them made her body ache, made her stomach clench with such intensity it forced the breath from her body? How was she supposed to explain that underneath the layer of bleach and disinfectant, she could scent their blood, and feel their pulse?

Viktor smiled grimly at her as the muttered curses echoed in the empty hallways, bouncing off the grey and black linoleum tiles as she inched forward, careful not to get too close. The door slammed shut behind her and Viktor moved to lock it before starting down towards the cafeteria.

"I watched most of a movie last night. Until I crashed and fell asleep." Elora giggled even as a tinge of jealousy hit her. It was always difficult to hear about the nurses' day-to-day lives and the way they left the hospital and did normal things. Shopping, cooking, bathing without someone in the next room.

"Oh? What was it about?" They trailed behind the last of the residents, the first nurse leading them, while Viktor made sure no one tried to leave.

"A new vampire one." He hesitated, chewing his cheek as he focused on the crowd approaching the open doors. For a moment, neither of them said anything, the taboo topic stretching between the two of them like a string pulled too tight. Viktor shrugged slightly, as if to brush off the awkwardness.

"The usual, of course. Sunlight, silver, crucifixes, and is irresistible." Elora huffed a laugh at his summary.

"None of that is even true. It is horrible how wrong they get it." Viktor said nothing in response, but his shoulders tensed.

"Elora," he warned, and her mouth snapped shut, regret coursing through her body. "I'll have to report that. I'm sorry." Elora darted a glance up at him, taking in the stiffness of his otherwise soft face, the hard line of his lips.

"I'm sorry," she whispered, hands clasped in front of her. Viktor shook his head as they approached the door, steps slowing as the residents entered and picked their tables to sit at. Most sat in small groups, two or three for each one. She shook her head, forcing the thought of the upcoming consequences from her mind. It would do her no good now.

~ ~

CHAPTER 2

Elora

*T*he bedroom was as familiar as the body next to her. Four walls and
two small windows with the curtains pulled off to the side. There was
one bed meant to hold two bodies, a closet, and a desk that held two back-
packs, and two sets of homework. The sleeping girl's blond hair was pulled
into a braid so that the other figure in the bed couldn't roll over onto it as
easily while the two of them slept side-by-side. The girl's too-thin body,
wrapped in a nightgown, was pressed against Elora, her arm around the
girl's waist as she slept. But Elora couldn't. The gnawing in her chest and
stomach kept her from falling into oblivion, kept her thoughts and breathing from calming.

Elora pushed a loose strand of hair away from the girl's neck and
stared at her, the way her skin was pale under the light coming through
the windows despite its normal olive color, the way every muscle in her
body was relaxed as she slept. Carefully, so carefully, Elora touched her
skin, fingers lingering where she could feel her pulse beating slow and
steady.

After readjusting, Elora pushed herself up on her elbow, keeping her
other arm around the girl's waist as something dark and angry and ur-
gent took over her. She nuzzled her face into the girl's neck, relishing the

feeling of her pulse against her mouth even as the sleeping girl stirred slightly, and a soft noise escaped her lips.

But the sleeping girl didn't wake. Not yet.

Slowly, carefully, Elora opened her mouth wide, feeling her heart beat faster, pounding so hard she was surprised the girl could not feel or hear it.

Her teeth and lips grazed the girl's neck, prepared for what was coming.

A scream forced Elora to pull back, her brow furrowed in confusion while her eyes frantically searched the room for the source of the noise. She glanced down to see the girl still asleep; her face the very image of innocence and peace, pulse still soft and steady.

Another scream, long and piercing. A scream of pain, of fear.

Her scream.

With a cry that echoed throughout the silent room, she lurched awake, painfully aware of the weight on top of her, holding her down, crushing any chance to draw a breath. With frantic clawing and screams against the large hand covering her mouth, Elora thrashed, desperately trying to take in a breath. The body on top of her compressed her ribs and her lungs as she tried to force out another scream. The tugging at her neck forced out another cry just as a large hand gripped her chin, jerking her head to the side, exposing the flesh there. A moment of shock hit her and froze her in a suspended state of confusion in which her limbs refused to move, and her mouth refused to make a sound.

Questions raced through her head as she tried to make sense of the body on top of her, the scent of cheap cologne mingling with the disinfectant. Was this all still part of the dream? There were no whispers of the nickname, no chains. A scream ripped from her throat once more, even as the large hand clamped down on top of it.

"Shut the fuck up." A rough voice rang out over her muffled cries, his lips, and the scruff of his beard against her neck, against her ear.

Elora threw her body on the bed, thrashing as she flung her arms around, trying to kick him, knee him, anything. She grunted as she missed, hitting only the mattress and the wooden bedframe. His body completely covered her, his thighs holding hers down, his chest on top of hers, rendering her unable to take a breath. Large, calloused hands pinned her arms to her side as she tossed her head from one side to the other. His breath was on her face, her neck, the smell of beer, and something else, something familiar.

Briefly, hazily, Elora recalled the rumors of attacks by staff members, that were told by other residents. Nothing was ever proven and until this moment she had always dismissed them as that, pure gossip among people who had nothing to discuss beyond their own trauma. Now, the stories told about female and male patients who woke up with bruises and bite marks, claiming they couldn't remember how they got them, held some validity.

Pain radiated through her neck, a burning so reminiscent of the many times she was sedated, so close to the feeling of a syringe piercing her skin as she thrashed in the intruder's arms. She closed her eyes, tears falling freely down her cheeks as the sensation of pulling against her skin grew. Elora let out a sharp exhale at the realization she knew this feeling, something akin to what she felt in her nightmares when there were teeth and hands and pain. Blinding pain.

A groan sounded from the body on top of hers and Elora's lungs expanded, letting air in with a rapid flush as the body retreated slightly, jerking away from her neck and skin.

"What the hell?" His whisper was harsh against the silence of the room, only the sound of her own panting breaths. Instantly, she could recognize him — one of the nurses. Not Viktor, but the other one whose name she could never remember. Quietly, he released her hands and stood before the bed, watching her as if she was some creature to be studied.

"Quiet." He forced the command out, cupping her chin so she was forced to meet his gaze as he gave the order. Compulsion. She met his glare and tugged her chin out of his punishing grip. There would be bruises tomorrow where his fingers had dug into her cheeks. But nothing else happened. She didn't fall to his demands and didn't feel the overwhelming desire to please him. Confusion was etched across his face as another whimper seeped from her mouth and he repeated the order with a harsher tone.

Still nothing. Then, the screams raged from her mouth so loud and forceful she could feel her throat tearing itself apart. The door opened and closed in a mess of slams and bangs, barely audible above the sounds of Elora's cries. She squeezed her eyes shut, pulled her knees up to her chest, and rolled onto her side. And she did not stop screaming. The feeling of his mouth, his hands on her wrists, the smell of his breath, the sound of his voice was ever-present.

Silence fell over the room as Elora felt another puncture in her upper arm, suddenly pulled out of her thoughts long enough to realize she was no longer alone.

"Shush, Elora. It's okay. Just another nightmare." The sedation was already taking effect as Elora tried to open her eyes, the sensation of her blood slowing, her thoughts disappearing and fading away one by one. Dr. Montgomery's face was full of concern, dark circles under her pale blue eyes.

"No," she murmured, throat raw. "It was a man, a nurse, or someone. He attacked me. My neck." The words started rushing out, slurred and stammered, getting worse with each one that passed her lips.

"It was just a nightmare. Sleep, Elora. Just sleep." Dr. Montgomery stood and walked back, hands clasped behind her back.

Not a single glance was given to the figure on the bed as orders were barked at the night nurse.

"That should be enough sedation to last until morning. I want her to be moved into the green room for the night, just in case she wakes. We can't be sure what her reaction will be. It will be safer for her and everyone else."

The nurse agreed with the doctor, but the words sounded as if they were coming from underwater. Her eyes flickered closed before she forced them back open, everything blurry through the tears soaking through the pillow. She wanted to yell at them, to tell them it wasn't a nightmare, that it was real. But once more, her eyes flickered shut and only this time, they did not open again.

CHAPTER 3

Elora

The green room was dark except for the fluorescent lights built into the ceiling. The walls were covered in a pale sickly green fabric and the floor was a soft material meant to absorb impact. A single body lay in the middle of the floor, with her crimson hair in a tangled mess around her face. Slowly, Elora opened her eyes. Even the dim light was painful as she tried to sit up, wincing from the feel of the padded floor. She hadn't been back in this room for almost a year, not since she hit the nurse, thus extending her stay. The idea was to give the patients a place to stay while they calmed down from an outburst, and hers had been legendary. New nurses and staff were warned about all the residents and given dossiers with just enough information so they knew who they were taking care of. Elora's was simply a list of topics to avoid, comments not to make, and a warning that she could get violent if pushed.

Slowly, Elora sat up, extending her legs out in front of her as she moved her head one way and then the other, stretching the stiff muscles.

"Good morning. Someone will be there to get you in a minute."

Elora's hands reached up to her ears, pressing her palms over them in hopes it would block out the sound of their voice, and stop the way it reverberated throughout her head. The sensation was akin to someone hitting her head with a bat with each word spoken, and she groaned before letting her hands fall into her lap. The sedation always had lingering effects. Slight memory loss upon waking. Headaches. Light sensitivity. Elora squeezed her eyes closed once more, using her forearm to shield them while waiting for the door to open, piecing together the night before.

She had woken up screaming and her throat felt the aftermath now, the raw burning sensation each time she tried to swallow. As she chewed on her lips, Elora recalled the nightmare, the feeling of a body on top of her own, not being able to breathe, and a burning in her neck as a vampire fed from her. At the memory, the room grew smaller, the walls shrinking, the air growing stale as she struggled to take in a breath. Her hands tried to clench the fabric on the floor, grab anything to anchor herself as she found herself drowning, unable to feel anything but sheer panic.

Elora's hand hesitantly made its way to her neck, gingerly touching the wound that someone had bandaged. Pain radiated from the spot as she prodded the injury with her fingertips, almost like a bruise, but she remembered the puncture of his teeth entering her skin, of the pulling sensation as he fed from her. Bringing her hands down, Elora looked over the body parts she could see, wincing as she studied the black and blue marks around her wrists. Slowly, she twisted her hands to judge the damage done and nearly cried out as pain erupted from her hand and arm.

She recoiled slightly as the door opened, not sure exactly who it would be or what their treatment would involve. Sometimes the nurses were kind, gentle hands escorting her back to her room or Dr. Montgomery's office, murmuring words of comfort. Other times, it was disinterested cruelty. It was watching as she fell against the wall, dramatic sighs of annoyance as she stumbled down the hallway. It depended on what time it was, and if it was the day shift or night shift. Viktor's grim face came into view, and she exhaled, her body relaxing despite the aching soreness. He didn't say anything even as his jaw ticked, eyes tracking each and every bruise visible on her body. After a long moment, he jerked his head and waited for Elora to stand, her legs jelly and knees buckling underneath her.

"I can't—" Her words faltered as she crawled to the wall and used it to push herself up. Her fingernails dug into the fabric, trying to find some type of hold as she forced herself to stand and remain there. For a moment, she simply waited and closed her eyes before opening them to discover if the room was still spinning.

With a pointed glare at the nurse waiting for her to make her way to the door, Elora pulled herself along, one shaky foot in front of the other.

"Are you going to help?" Viktor averted his eyes, staring at something on the wall behind her.

"As soon as you are out." She groaned, biting her tongue against the retort she wanted to hurl at him, against the desire to tell him what she thought about that particular piece of protocol.

As if I have the strength to overwhelm him, take his keys, and lock him in here, she thought bitterly, gritting her teeth as she stood to her full height, all five foot seven inches, once she was in front of him. With each step, she felt the aftereffects melt away, each step stronger than the one before, and now she simply met his gaze, panting slightly. A large hand grabbed her biceps, gripping tightly enough to keep her from falling over.

"Where to first?" Her words were still stiff, as if they were stuck on her tongue for a moment before coming loose and escaping.

"Your room so you can change. Then the doctor and then food." She nodded, now noting the hallway they were taking. The ward itself was shaped like a "V" with the nurse's station and door leading to the cafeteria and the doctor's office in the very center. From there extended two hallways with the one on the right containing only the day room and a collection of bedrooms and the left containing the green room along with more bedrooms.

Silently, the two passed the nurse's station where a young woman in blue scrubs sat working on something, and down the right-side hallway. Elora's room was the very last one, and the floor became increasingly cold beneath her bare feet as they got closer. The hallways were empty as Viktor escorted her, walking beside her, his grip on her arm gentle. The doors to the other rooms were open, providing glimpses into the chaos of the other residents—clothes and stuffed animals thrown around in some rooms, while others were spotless, with tightly made beds devoid of any identifying marks. In some rooms, Elora saw pictures on their desks, drawings on the walls held up with tape, stuffed animals, and other comfort items left over from childhood. Some even had their own blankets and pillowcases brought in by family members.

Her own room contained none of that. A single bed, nightstand, small desk, and a dresser filled the otherwise empty space. Standard-issued blanket and pillow. No pictures or trinkets. No stuffed animals. There was a single window along the wall, mesh included between the two panes to make it harder to break should someone want to escape. To the side was a bathroom connected to the room, the door just next to the dresser. A sink, toilet, and shower took up the meager space. The mirror wasn't technically a mirror, but a reflective piece of plastic. They couldn't have anyone breaking it to slit their wrists. Or at least that was the theory. Elora had found out it was breakable in the days following her first release refusal. After the meeting had ended and the papers were stamped and signed, she rushed back to her room and punched it hard enough that it had shattered. She had required stitches for the two slashes down her forearms. Dr. Montgomery had only looked at her with a mixture of sadness and disappointment.

Viktor waited outside the open door, back to the opening as Elora grabbed a pair of sweats and a long-sleeved shirt from the dresser and tossed them on the sink as she took in her appearance. There were marks on her neck, but they were not necessarily distinguishable as bite marks, at least not with that quality of reflection. The skin was black and blue, with some fading to green around the edges where it was already starting to heal. Her red hair was a tangled mess as she tried to move a brush through it, wincing as it hit each knot and tangle. There were more dark shadows than normal under her green eyes and her thin lips were cracked, along with a bruise on her right cheekbone.

She didn't even remember him hitting her.

As she set the brush down, hair finally tamed, Elora noticed the bruises on her wrists. She froze in her examination and held her arms out in front of her as if someone were gently holding her hands.

Little rose. There it was again, the whisper that traced its fingers along her ears, her jawline, a caress and a tease of something long since forgotten. Her body contracted as she curled in towards herself, pulling at the clothing on her body. First, the shirt which was ripped along the sleeves, and then the pants, tossed into a pile in the corner where she could only hope they would disappear or burst into flames. Her breathing came in harsh pants and her heart raced, beating wildly against her chest as she looked down at her legs and torso, taking in the full extent of damage that is so familiar it hurt.

Bruises lined the pale skin that hadn't seen more than a daily hour of sun in five years and tears began to pour down her face, free and unrestrained as they hit her jawline, dripping onto her chest. Tears reminded her of the only lesson she knew, the only lesson she was taught before her memories were locked away in a vault, which was that her body was not fully her own and never would be.

"Elora?" The sound of her name pulled her out of the spiral, a rope thrown out to sea to drag her back to reality. She ran her hands along her face, wiping away the tears before throwing on the clothes she had gathered. Elora was silent as she left the bathroom and brushed past him, marching with steady steps to Dr. Montgomery's office. A hand gripped her arm, and she stopped. She knew better than to fight or try to rip it away.

"Are you okay? Were you crying?" His voice was soft, as if he didn't want to be overheard by any residents or staff. Elora drew a deep breath and held it tightly in her chest before letting it go, steadying herself in the process. Her heart rate slowed to an even pace and her body finally stopped trembling. For the first time since she woke, she turned towards him with a smirk plastered on her face.

"I'm fine. Let's get this over with." Viktor didn't look convinced, and his eyes narrowed as he tried to read her expression, searching for hints as to what happened. Elora relaxed her expression, letting it fall into a mundane look that would tell him nothing. But she couldn't hide the redness that mingled with the dark shadows around her eyes, couldn't hide the tears that were still there waiting to be shed. She knew he could see the absolute surrender as she walked toward her psychiatrist's office.

But he didn't say anything. Only squeezed her arm in a gesture that seemed more like reassurance than anything else. Viktor let his hand drop to his side and followed her, a stoic yet comforting presence. Silently, he unlocked the door that took the residents from the housing part of the adult ward to the therapeutic section. Viktor led her down a hallway that she could walk down blindfolded, without making a single mistake.

This part of the ward was small, with only a few offices, the art therapy room, and the cafeteria. Quickly, they both found themselves outside her office, along with the tiny white noise machine that sat beside the closed door. Dr. Montgomery had worked with

Elora since the first day of her psychiatric hold, which had turned into a court-mandated extended stay. She supposed it was better than the alternative, which was prison. Finally, Viktor rapped three times while Elora took a deep breath, prepared for the absolute disaster this meeting would be.

The door opened instantly, as if Dr. Montgomery had been standing on the other side waiting for her. The doctor's face was the absolute picture of both concern and irritation, each emotion carved into her otherwise pristine face marred by only a few wrinkles. It made figuring out her age nearly impossible. After a quick glance over at her patient, Dr. Montgomery's eyes locked with Viktor's, glaring at him before she dismissed him with a gesture.

"I'll call for you when we are done. It shouldn't be more than an hour or so." Viktor tensed beside Elora, as if he were uncomfortable with leaving her, forcing her to wonder if maybe he knew something she didn't. He grunted slightly before his footsteps started to retreat down the hallway and Dr. Montgomery shifted her attention to her patient and stepped aside to let her in.

Her office always gave Elora a sense of familiarity, as if she knew it before the confines of the hospital walls. The enormous desk that contained a computer and stacks upon stacks of papers and files sat in the middle of the room. Behind it were shelves, filled to the brim with various versions of mental illness manuals and workbooks. When Elora had perused those books years ago, there were only medical texts, nothing of interest to a regular person stuck in a psychiatric hospital. The wood that made up the shelves and furniture was dark, almost black, and the curtains covering the windows were a pale cream color, giving the room a balanced appearance. Most rooms in the hospital aimed for pale colors and pastels that were meant to put the troubled mind at ease. This room did the opposite; it was dark. Foreboding. Ominous. Or Elora was simply scared and nervous, seeing demons and monsters in any and all shadows.

Elora strolled over to her favorite spot, a lush black armchair across from the desk, and pulled her feet underneath her as she sunk into the leather. After a moment of wiggling, she leaned on the armrest, praying that she looked as calm as she was pretending to be.

Dr. Montgomery gave her a small smile, the lines around her eyes and mouth becoming slightly more pronounced. Elora couldn't help but admire her beauty, admire how the grey and silver in her hair added an air of sophistication, how her pale blue eyes always made her feel like she was suffocating under their weight. Dr. Montgomery was a tall woman, thin to the point that Elora had always wondered if she was sick, some long-term illness or disease. During their first session, Elora had asked exactly that, hoping to annoy her or get under her skin, force a reaction from the woman who sat so stoic as Elora raged or cried or screamed. Instead of even the tiniest reaction, Dr. Montgomery smiled softly and shook her head.

"No, Elora. I am not sick. But let's talk about why you might think that."

Their conversations and Elora's questions were always treated this way, spun around, and directed back at her like a mirror reflecting anything and everything. Why did she think that? Why did she feel that way? How had she been feeling when she hit the nurse? Or when she refused her medication, resulting in some very unpleasant forced compliance?

Now, Dr. Montgomery lazily sat in her high-back chair and waited, her eyes watching more intensely than Elora would have liked. She wanted the doctor to make the first move and ask the first question. The beginning of each session was always a power struggle, a clash of wills to see who would cave first. During one session, neither of them had spoken, and it had ended with an increase in medication due to an increase in symptoms.

To Elora's great surprise, it was Dr. Montgomery who broke first.

"I think the first question to ask is how you are feeling after your night." Her fingers laced together, resting lightly on the desk in front of her. Elora squirmed a bit, readjusting her feet to ease some of the soreness in her hips and legs. With eyes trained on her lap, Elora pulled at her sleeves, yanked them down over her wrists, and held the fabric in her fists.

"Fine, I suppose. As much as I can be."

Dr. Montgomery nodded at the response and considered something for a long moment in which silence stretched between them. "I think we should tackle this head-on. We could do the usual approach where I ask you questions that you already know are coming, you answer, and we eventually get the full story. But I am just going to sit back and ask you to tell me what you think happened."

Elora's eyes narrowed as every ounce of her limited attention focused on the ending of her sentence. *Tell me what you think happened.* Dr. Montgomery was always careful with her words, choosing them with the precision of an expert surgeon with a scalpel. Elora considered rolling her eyes, refusing to tell the doctor anything since she had decided that whatever Elora said was a lie or a fabrication of her nightmares. But that would only lead to more time in the green room, more restricted privileges, more medication.

Elora took a deep breath, letting it out slowly, and looked Dr. Montgomery in the eyes.

"I was attacked by a nurse in my room. I woke up to him on top of me. He was pinning my wrists, and his mouth was at my throat." Elora pulled down the collar of her shirt and turned her head to give Dr. Montgomery a clear view of the marks there. She completed the tour of bruises and remnants of the attack by holding up her hands and turning her wrists to ensure the doctor could see the bruising in the shape of fingers.

Dr. Montgomery nodded once more and wrote something down quickly, the scratching of the pen the only sound in the room before she finally glanced back up.

"I screamed and then someone came. You were also there. I heard your voice. But I was sedated and woke up in the green room."

"Which nurse do you think attacked you?" Again, Elora latched on to the phrasing, the insinuation that none of this was real, that the attack was a figment of a traumatized imagination.

"Ryan. The one with longer brown hair, a bit short." She nodded again and made another note on her pad. Elora gazed down at her hands, picking at the skin around her nails, hissing in pain each time the cuticle tore too deep. It was a nervous habit neither she nor the other doctors had been able to break, and the torn skin and scabs told the world as much.

"Were you dreaming before you woke up?"

Elora scoffed. The question she knew would come was finally voiced into the space between them. It always came back to her nightmares, always came back to her mind somehow making things up. A defense mechanism is what Dr. Montgomery described it; a way for the mind to protect itself from particularly traumatic events. And to a certain extent, she was correct. There were too many memories, almost an entire life hidden behind a vault locked up tight, and Elora would break into a cold sweat every time one of the fragments came close to the surface, squeezed between the gaps in the steel walls.

Faced with the choice of either lying or telling the truth that would only make Dr. Montgomery shake her in disappointment, Elora decided to say nothing at all. After all, lying was pointless. Five years of therapy with this woman left them knowing each other better than anyone else. Dr. Montgomery knew the way her face shifted when she lied, the way her muscles tightened while she waited to see if she was believed. But telling her the truth would only result in Dr. Montgomery declaring the attack fictional, a hallucination of her guilt-ridden mind.

A beautiful and inescapable dilemma where both options were equally bad.

"Yes, I had been dreaming. Yes, it was one of the normal ones. This time was with her." Elora decided to face her directly, announce the truth, and demand that the doctor listen to her. This wasn't simply her mind trying to cope. There was a danger here, a nurse preying on the residents and attacking them in their medication-induced sleep.

"And you don't think the two are connected? The nightmare and the alleged attack?" It had been a few years since Elora had wanted to hit her psychiatrist, not since her second release hearing had come back with a denial due to her continuing to be a danger to herself and others. She had decided at that moment to show exactly how much of a danger she could be. Elora tucked her hands between her thighs, hoping that keeping them there would help with the overwhelming desire to jump across the desk and hit the woman with her own paperweight.

Dr. Montgomery leaned forward and rested her hands under her chin, studying Elora's expression like she was an interesting insect, a new species, and she wanted to see how it would react to stimuli. She was taunting Elora, and the gleam in the doctor's eyes made that much more obvious.

"No, I do not, Doctor. I think the bruises on my neck, the bruises on my thighs, the marks on my neck prove it was not a nightmare." There was an edge to Elora's tone, a venom to her words, a threat of violence that lingered below the surface.

"Then what do you think should happen next? If the attack is real, as you claim, and not a manifestation of your nightmare, then what should happen? What should happen to the nurse, for example?" Her voice was smooth and cool, like she was placating a toddler on the verge of a tantrum.

"Because the attack did happen. I want the nurse fired. I want him arrested. I want him to be unable to work in any place like this again." Dr. Montgomery leaned her head to the side.

"But if you are wrong, then an innocent man loses his job and is potentially arrested."

"I'm not wrong." Elora was suddenly on her feet, not remembering standing or even taking a step toward the imposing woman on the other side of the desk. Her hands were curled into fists at her side as Elora stared down at the doctor's unnervingly calm face. The room was suddenly far too warm.

"Considering your past, I don't think it is a fair course of action. We could be ruining that man's life." Dr. Montgomery raised an eyebrow as Elora took a step forward, no doubt reaching for the panic button just under her desk. They both knew it was there, waiting to be of use once more.

"Why don't you believe me?" Elora's voice broke as she forced herself to sit back down, balancing on the edge of the chair, hands grasping her knees. Dr. Montgomery tapped her pen on her desk and then looked down at her notes, pulling a file that was sitting to the left of her. With a leisurely pace, like this was nothing more than a meeting to discuss the paint color in the rooms, she flipped through the pages in there.

"It isn't that I don't believe you, Elora. I believe that you believe it happened. I know that your nightmares have been getting worse and more intense. I know that you hear voices sometimes. The nurses tell me you will hear someone call you a pet name and demand to know who said it." Elora took a deep breath as her blood froze and its progression through her body instantly stalled as the explanation washed over her.

"Forgive me, Elora. But a lot of this sounds like what you talked about when you were first admitted for long-term care. Back then, you talked about vampires running rampant in the city, controlling everything from the government to food supplies. And just now, you mentioned marks on your neck." Elora reclined back in her chair, face in her hands for a brief moment as she tried not to falter under the weight of such speculation, of such skepticism. She raised her face and stared at the carpet, noticing for the first time that it was more gray than black, like she previously believed.

"You don't understand. You can't understand unless you just believe me." The words came out broken, shattered like so many other pieces of her. For a single incredibly brief moment, Elora considered begging for her to listen, to suspend disbelief for a single second, just long enough to hear the entire explanation, and not only the bits and pieces dropped during therapy sessions.

Dr. Montgomery picked up her pen and started making notes again. Without looking up, she explained in a cold voice, "We are going to up your evening medication. It should help with the nightmares and the thrashing around that are causing your bruises."

"Fucking bitch," Elora muttered as she watched the doctor raise her brow at the language. She hadn't thought Dr. Montgomery would be able to hear her, but there wasn't anything that the doctor could do that she hadn't done before.

"I want you to know that there will be an investigation into what happened. It's hospital policy when something like this happens and when accusations are made." Elora sat up straighter at these words, hope sparking in her chest. Hope that Dr. Montgomery was quick to suffocate and kill. "This does not mean anything will happen or that the nurse will be fired. Please do not have any expectations or get too hopeful about it."

A gust of air brushed past Elora's face as the door opened, cutting off any chance for her to respond. She would have explained that even investigating it was a start, that it could yield results even if Dr. Montgomery suspected it wouldn't. Viktor marched into the room and to Elora's side without a single glance at anyone but the psychiatrist, who signaled for him to come back.

"Take her to cafeteria for lunch. I want to see her tomorrow morning after breakfast. Make sure she is given her increased dose tonight. I will send the orders over to the pharmacy now." Viktor nodded and looked at his patient, waiting for her to follow him. Elora glared at Dr. Montgomery for just a moment as she stood and smoothed down her shirt, considering for a brief moment whether it would be worth it to punch the psychiatrist and hit her with her own paperweight again.

A hand was suddenly gripping her elbow, and a voice whispered, "Don't." Viktor didn't look at the woman or the patient beside him, just stared at the door as he escorted Elora to lunch.

~ ~

CHAPTER 4

Damien

The dirty dive bar near the industrial district was crowded when Damien entered. People were pushing their way up to the bar while servers maneuvered gracefully between drunk or nearly drunk patrons playing pool or celebrating something like a new job or a promotion. He stepped further in from the door, rolling his sleeves up automatically as he felt the heat from so many bodies envelop him. The bar smelled of smoke despite there being no smoking allowed, even as it radiated off the various forms in the room. It blended with the immense amount of perfume and cologne blanketing the space, the smell of spilled drinks, and something more unsavory. Damien took a second to glance around, a small space for so many people to be crowded into, bodies touching and mingling as voices fought for supremacy. He scowled at the scene before heading to the bar, hoping a beer would dull the edge that came with this type of place, that came with his contact not being here yet.

Damien ordered a beer, just the cheapest they had on tap, and took a seat at the very end, leaving an open one to the right of him for his guest once they arrived. He didn't bother looking around at the various people crowding the bar. He ignored the snippets of conversation that he overheard since everyone was shouting over the music and each other.

He didn't like being around this many humans at once. Instead, he took a sip of the sour beer, definitely the cheapest they had.

Damien cringed at the feminine voice that screeched about how this was her last night of freedom. A bachelorette party. Another group started singing some type of karaoke song without the actual music itself. A man further down the bar was telling the incredibly busy bartender about how his girlfriend left him and he was fired for the stupid and unfair reason of drinking during a job.

A body settled onto the barstool next to him and Damien looked up, ready to tell whoever it was to find a different spot. Instead, he saw a short man with brown hair. His face was fleshy, like he never grew out of his baby fat and his eyes were glowing slightly, indicating he had fed recently. He was still in his blue scrubs, his badge bearing the name Ryan still hung from the pocket where the name of the hospital was embroidered. Damien could scent the blood on him, even over everything else.

"I think I found a lead for you." The newcomer said after ordering a gin and tonic. "A girl at the place I work at."

"And why do you think some crazy is a lead?" This had better not be a waste of his time. Already, Damien's hand flexed around the beer. There had been so many leads, so many dead ends. He wasn't sure he would survive another one.

"I tasted her blood." He raised an eyebrow at Ryan, who was nursing his drink, a look of hesitation on his face. "It wasn't human."

"So, a vampire ended up with humans in a psychiatric hospital. It wouldn't be the first time." He took a long drink from his beer as he debated whether killing this waste of time was worth it. Damien wondered for a brief moment if the girl in question had been a willing part of this whole feeding. His lips curled slightly with disgust, guessing that it probably was not fully consensual.

"No, no, you don't understand. It didn't taste like vampire blood, either. At least, not fully. I don't know how to describe it. But there is something different about it, something worth looking into." Ryan shifted on the barstool, downing the rest of his gin and tonic in one go before he signaled for another.

He ran his hand through his shaggy hair, face falling into an expression of bliss as he seemed to recall the experience. "Euphoric. Human blood is good, even if it can be bland. But this was borderline orgasmic." He held his hands up. "I know. I know. But even now I want it, crave it, and I only got a tiny taste."

He took a drink before he leaned closer to Damien. "And it's strange. I tried to quiet her. When she woke up, she started screaming, and I tried to force her to be quiet."

"You tried compulsion?" The vampire across from Damien nodded before darting a look at the rest of the bar.

"It didn't work. I held her gaze and did everything right, but it didn't work at all." Damien nodded, finally intrigued by the vampire's story, about the patient who tasted strange and could withstand compulsion. Even the weakest and newest of vampires were capable of using it on a human, so if she had been able to withstand it, that was something to look into.

"Fine. Tell me more about her." The bit about her blood was interesting, he supposed. It could mean something, and it could mean nothing. It could be the medications she was sure to be prescribed that were altering the taste. It was rare for that to happen, but not entirely unheard of.

"She has been there forever since she was around nineteen, I think. I only got a quick look at her file, but she came in about five years ago after attacking someone and declaring to everyone that vampires were real."

"She hasn't been released yet?" Damien tried to think through what he knew about the mental health system, which was little to nothing. But he knew that they normally didn't keep people unless they were dangerous and had proven themselves so. What had this woman done to keep her there, to have her release denied numerous times?

Ryan took a drink of his new gin and tonic and shrugged. "I guess she was deemed too unstable to be released. From what I understood, she has a hearing every year to see if she is fit to rejoin society. So far, it's been a no each time, and she's been there ever since."

"What's her name? Describe her." He stared at the empty beer glass in his hands as his palms slightly itched. This was a lead, a solid lead. It was probably the best one he had had in years. It had him on edge and he finally decided another beer was warranted, signaling to the barkeeper, who brought it instantly.

"Elora, I think. Longer dark red hair, green eyes. She is medium height, around 5 foot 7. Thinner. Pale skin. Normal features for someone who had been there that long. It's not like they feed them that well."

Damien took a deep breath. It was a pretty close description of who he was looking for, who he had been searching for. It had been four years since he was given that mission. The timeline didn't match up perfectly, but the basics of it were fairly close. The person he was searching for had been gone roughly a decade, ever since she ran away. He reached into his back pocket and pulled out his wallet, throwing some cash for the bartender before handing a small envelope of cash to the man sitting beside him.

"Here is how this will work. You are not going back to your job. You quit. Got it?" Ryan fingered the envelope in his hand, opening it just enough to peek at the cash inside. "And you are not to talk about this with anyone else. You do not mention it. If you do, I will find you. You know exactly who I am and what I would do to you if you even breathe a single hint of this."

Ryan just nodded, his hand reaching out for his drink after shoving the envelope into his pants pocket. A hand was suddenly attached to his wrist before he could grab his gin and tonic, squeezing until he finally cried out, the sound drowned out by the music and conversations all around them.

"Do you understand? I need verbal confirmation, Ryan."

Ryan's eyes bulged slightly as if he didn't think the man holding his wrist had known his name, as if he had forgotten he wore his name badge like a fool.

"I understand. Not a word." Damien released Ryan's wrist before standing up, straightened his shirt, and headed to the door.

The cold night air hit him in the face, and he breathed deeply, all too happy to be away from the humans in the bar. He pulled out his cell phone and dialed a number for the business office of his employer. He needed to get into the hospital, preferably as a worker of some sort. It should be easy enough for them to fabricate some training certificates, even a degree if necessary. His employer's power knew no limits, especially not when it came to finding the object of his obsession. Damien needed to take a look at this girl, smell her, maybe taste her. He couldn't just walk in and take her on the off chance she was who he was looking for.

A small conversation and a few minutes later, everything was set in motion. It would take a couple of days to get the paperwork in order, but he would be starting as a nurse at the hospital. But something told him that this was it. He would finally find her and take her home, complete the assignment given to him years ago when the daughter of the man he had come to call father disappeared and everyone else had failed to bring her back.

~ ~

CHAPTER 5

Elora

Two days later, the bruises were mostly gone. Only the most stubborn ones around her neck and wrists were still visible. Dr. Montgomery didn't mention the investigation again, claiming it was illegal to discuss it before it was finalized. Elora had argued it was strange no one had asked her any questions, no one had asked her side of the story, but Dr. Montgomery had shaken her head and assured her all would be well. And now Elora sat in the cafeteria, morning medication taken and her body begging for food of any type. Unfortunately, it was her least favorite. Instead of powdered eggs and turkey bacon, they were given whole wheat bricks of cereal with watery milk and canned fruit.

Elora rested her forearms on the table, hunched over her bowl of cereal as she debated whether she could force it down, whether it was even worth it to do so. With a soft curse, she grabbed the mug of tea, sweetened it with sugar, and sipped it slowly despite it having gone cold. Hot tea could be a weapon, so they were given lukewarm beverages at best. Cereal and milk truly were the worst of the breakfast rotation options. It also meant that today's lunch and dinner would consist of a turkey burger for the former and chicken breast and root vegetables for the latter. It wouldn't be so bad if the cook seasoned anything. Everything followed a routine, a rhythm to keep the city of Carvesk from imploding, though if rumors were to be believed, it was only a matter of time. The vampire hold was weakening, and the human population was finally tired of the government having a say in what they eat and what they could purchase.

The sudden hush in the normal breakfast conversation pulled Elora from her mug of tea as she searched for what had grabbed everyone's attention. The steady hum of gossip and dramatic retelling of childhood memories ceased in a single moment and the contained chaos of mealtime was eradicated. Each resident in the cafeteria always sat at one of the eight plastic tables and chatted to themselves or someone else, either another resident or a nurse. It was always loud, a dozen voices competing with each other as they tried to carry on, as if they weren't locked up for violence.

Each face was staring towards the corner where Viktor was standing with a man Elora had never seen before, not on the day or night shift. Not even on the weekend shifts when the part-time nurses worked to give the full-time workers a day off. Elora could hear the whispers coming from the nearest table: the new nurse. Ryan's replacement. On its own, this usually wasn't a reason for this type of silence, this type of undivided attention that only happened when they all watched cartoons in the afternoon after recreation time. New nurses and staff members came and went fairly quickly. No one wanted to corral crazy, didn't want to assure an old man that the voices weren't telling him the truth, didn't want to hear the residents swap stories about horrific childhoods. Maybe it was too depressing. Maybe it was too frustrating. Maybe the pay just wasn't good enough for what was required of them.

In this particular case, Elora could only surmise the undivided attention and silence was because the nurse himself was gorgeous in a way that seemed wrong and unfair. Beautiful in a way that wasn't fully human. Her breath hitched as she realized what he was, that what replaced Ryan wasn't any better or safer.

Elora's hand tightened around the mug as her lungs contracted and her breath got caught in her throat. With shaking fingers, she drew the mug to her lips, taking a deep drink to stop herself from choking on air. She looked up over the crowd, hearing the growing whispers as eyes darted to the vampire standing there, watching them all with a calculated expression. She took a moment to study him, to take in his dark hair that was shaved along the sides while remaining long on the top, falling in a haphazard way. His face structure was strong, with a sharp jawline and nose. Only his lips seemed soft, like the edges of his face didn't dare touch them. The dark blue scrubs that all the nurses wore were stretched across his broad shoulders. The short sleeves revealed toned muscular arms and there was a tattoo of what looked like a moth along his neck, on full display above the fabric. He gave Viktor a closed-mouth smile and then surveyed the room, eyes roaming from table to table, lingering on each and every face, until he reached hers.

Every instinct in her began to shout instantly for her to lower her eyes, to look anywhere else, to study the tea in the mug until she knew it as well as she did her own skin. And when his gaze finally shifted away, lingering on other faces brimming with smiles and darkened eyes, the moment of agonizing fear was replaced by an overwhelming need to leave the cafeteria, to lock herself in her room.

"Okay, everyone. Breakfast is over. Finish cleaning up and line up to return to the day room." Viktor's voice was loud, louder than it needed to be, considering how quiet it still was. Elora grabbed her tray carrying her bowl of uneaten cereal and fruit along with her now empty mug and left them at the window that led into the kitchen before heading towards the door. It was only then she realized her mistake. Only then that she noticed that the new nurse had not moved and was standing directly next to the entrance.

With her heart in her throat, Elora hesitated at the threshold, staring at Viktor, trying to wordlessly force him to look back at her.

"Come on, everyone back in the day room." Viktor never met her eyes as his own roamed over the cafeteria, noting each resident who was still finishing their food or taking their tray to the counter, following through on his job to make sure everyone left at the same time. Elora forced her legs to move, holding her breath as she moved past the two nurses, pushing her way through the residents to get as far away as possible from the new one.

I could go to Dr. Montgomery. The thought came unbidden, and she giggled a little at the absurdity of it. If she hadn't believed her about Ryan, she wouldn't believe her about a new nurse. No, it would be no different.

I could tell Viktor. This thought had more promise, and she considered it for a moment, letting it flit around in her head as she thought about each angle and avenue of it. Elora furrowed her brow at the painting on the wall, a landscape complete with a bunny and flowers. Even if Viktor did believe her, what could he do? He wouldn't be able to just fire the new nurse since he had done nothing wrong and informing everyone that he was a vampire would be met with laughter and higher medication dosages. Maybe even a short stay in the green room for good measure.

Elora stood in front of the locked door to the ward and played with her sleeves as she waited for Viktor to catch up. All the doors were locked so the patients couldn't wander around on their own. There wasn't enough shared trust for that, no matter how long a patient had been there or how well-behaved they were. Elora fidgeted with the collar of her shirt, pulling slightly at the elastic, and tugged at the loose thread near her neck. The shirt covered the healing wounds, but only barely. The scars were more difficult to cover, to hide since they went up along her neck where nothing, but a turtleneck would work.

"Excuse me." The voice behind her wasn't one she knew. It wasn't the deep warmth of Viktor or the smoker rasp of the other daytime nurse. Elora froze, unable to move, her feet rooted to the ground, sinking further and further into the linoleum floor until she wasn't sure she would ever be able to move again.

"Excuse me." He was closer as he leaned down enough that Elora could feel his breath on her ear, jolting her from her co-matose state. She turned and glanced up through her lashes before moving to the side, maneuvering herself behind another resident in a futile attempt to hide.

With deft fingers, the nurse unlocked the door and pushed it open as he walked through and moved aside so the residents could follow suit. Viktor followed the back of the group, ensuring there were no stragglers. Elora forced herself through, keeping her eyes directly in front of her as she tried to blend in, telling herself over and over again that he had no reason to single her out, and that her fears were irrational. Five years of constant therapy, individual and otherwise, helped a person to recognize that type of thing. But knowing he was a vampire, knowing what he does, what his kind had done made her nervous, her entire body responding to the predator now in their midst.

What if I traded one vampire for a worse one? After all, Ryan hadn't actually fed from her. Instead, he had bitten her and then stopped, cursing as his attempt at compulsion failed.

Elora wandered stiffly to her normal armchair and curled up, legs tucked underneath her in a position that had become auto-matic. Softly, she snorted as she realized the television was not exactly on and no one had joined her for their usual routine of breakfast, followed by an episode before group therapy. Usually, it would be a baking show or some cartoon, just something to break up the monotony of almost inedible food, medication, and ther-apy. It seemed the majority of the residents had decided to take up board games or arts and crafts this morning, lingering in the areas closest to the nurse's station where they stayed when not herding them around like cats.

"Want me to turn it on for you?" Elora glanced up to see Viktor smiling broadly. She knew a laugh waited just beyond the amusement in his eyes. She chuckled at not only the fact the screen was blank, but that Viktor knew her schedule as well as she did, sometimes even better since he knew in advance if there was a surprise therapy session.

"Please. Just whatever comes on. I'm not picky."

"It's not like there are a lot of options," he quipped before bending over to push the button. "Isn't today an episode of the baking show?"

"Yup. We get to find out who wins. Again." The board members who ran the hospital refused to pay for a new television or anything that would give the residents more material to watch, claiming it was an unnecessary expense, and that the money could go to better things. Instead, the residents got reruns and the same three seasons of the baking show replaying, all of them blending together. On Monday, they would get an episode from season one, and then on Tuesday, they would get an episode from season three. There was no rhyme or reason for it.

Viktor just smiled as the episode came into focus and took a step back, waiting to see what it would be. It appeared it would be the finale of season two.

"If I remember correctly, I think the one named Robert wins. He ends up having the best cake of the final three." Elora grinned at Viktor as he continued to watch the screen, periodically surveying the room to check on the residents who hadn't moved away from the nurse's station as they pretended to play checkers or cards.

"That sounds right." He winked at her before heading back to the nurse's station. Her eyes followed him and the warm feeling in her chest grew. She had never liked any of the nurses. They were usually either quiet or rude. The quiet ones weren't too bad.

They just simply ignored you and anything you may say to them. They just took you through the day. The rude ones, however, were something else entirely. It started with pinches on your arms here and then refusing your privileges there. It was rude comments and outright hostility. They assumed they could get away with it because it was the resident's word against theirs.

They were right to assume so.

As Viktor approached the nurse's station, the new nurse was leaning against the desk, eyes sweeping across the room, taking in the odd nature of a psychiatric facility: mismatched furniture, a couch with teeth marks on the armrest, tables covered in paint and other stains long past the hope of being cleaned. And then his gaze found Elora and his lips thinned slightly, a hard look flashing in his eyes before a sense of nonchalance washed over him once more. It felt like a brick had dropped heavily in her stomach and she pulled her legs closer as if they could protect her, rendering her invisible. Elora shuddered as an undeniable suspicion that he knew her raged through her, that he knew who she was beyond the walls of the facility that had been her home for five years. Even if she didn't know.

~ ~

CHAPTER 6

Elora

"I don't like him, Viktor." Elora's voice was hushed as she leaned over slightly towards the only person she had considered a friend in years, the only person who was even slightly deserving of the term since her foster sister. Viktor's hands were busy attempting to open the door to escort the residents to dinner while the new nurse was back in the dayroom, rounding up the patients who were still preoccupied with their games and conversations. One of them was simply refusing to come to dinner at all, declaring that it was garbage and not worth eating. They weren't necessarily wrong.

"Who?" Viktor didn't spare her a glance but took his time to find his badge that acted as a key to the doors. With a scowl on his face, Viktor dug into the various pockets of his blue scrubs and pulled out pens and rolls of elastic bandage wrap.

"The new nurse. I don't know his name."

"It's on his badge." His lip quirked as he spoke, and Elora rolled her eyes.

"It's not like I've looked or cared. Have I ever cared about the nurses' names?"

"You learned mine." Elora lowered her head, hoping he didn't see the way her cheeks reddened slightly. She didn't respond, unable to think of anything to say. For a long second, he didn't say anything either until finally, he nodded. Elora huffed a sound of frustration at him for not declaring the nurse a problem, not agreeing that there was something wrong with him.

Why would he? You're another resident. Crazy and still here five years later. Elora wrapped her arms around her chest as if it would protect her from her own thoughts. Her sleeves had ridden up past her wrists and she winced, looking anywhere but at the scars that lined the skin there. Most people were eventually released into treatment homes where they got help to find jobs and paying bills and all of that. There were only two other people who had been here longer than her. One of them had been released once and ended up killing their neighbor, and the other had never said a single word to anyone.

"I'll look into him." He studied her for a moment, eyes dark as he finally pulled his badge out of his pocket. "And his name is Damien. Just in case you need to know."

Elora stepped forward, her smile wide across her face, stretching her features. Her green eyes lit up, relief and something like excitement making them brighter, more alive than they had been in days. At least since before the attack by Ryan. For a moment, she almost pulled him into an embrace, arms extended and outstretched. With a single step forward, she would have. With a slight shake of his head, Viktor retreated, and his jaw ticked, the only sign of any emotion. He knew as well as Elora that physical contact like that was disastrous. Touching wasn't necessarily wrong, but it would depend on the type. Hugs weren't on the list of approved types.

"What happened to the last nurse? Ryan or whatever his name was." Viktor raised a brow at the question, his mouth twisting as if picking the right words to use.

"He quit the day after you came out of the green room. A better job with better pay from what I heard." Elora laughed, the sound strange in the space between them. A confused look crossed Viktor's face.

"It's a great cover story. That's all."

"What do you mean?"

Elora glanced behind her, watching for a moment as the residents cleaned up the puzzles and board games and pushed in their chairs as they started towards the door.

"He was the one who attacked me. All the bruises were from him. They were investigating it." Viktor's mouth thinned into a sharp line; jaw clenched as his fist tightened around the badge in his hand. Violence, pure and beautiful, erupted in those normally welcoming eyes.

"They should have told me." Elora shook her head and questioned whether she should have opened her mouth.

"I'm fine now. At least he is gone, even if Damien doesn't seem much better." Viktor's focus switched to Damien, who was kneeling next to a resident, talking quietly, apparently unaware of the conversation occurring about him.

Viktor gave Elora a small smile that was absent of every bit of warmth, of any lingering affection, before announcing to the room: "Let's head over for dinner."

The residents made a mad dash for the doorway before being forced into a single-file line so they could leave. Elora stayed off to the side, not wanting to get crushed by their craving for whatever was being fed to them that night. She wasn't sure Viktor believed her about Damien, that there was something wrong with him. And Elora didn't mention the whole vampire aspect of it, didn't figure it made sense to push her luck. Viktor and Elora had never discussed her reason for still being here, never discussed vampires in general, though she was sure he knew enough based on reading her file and what he picked up during his time.

How do I tell him Damien is a vampire? That the city is run by them and has been for at least a century? She chewed on her cuticle as she considered her options, considered whether Viktor would be able to do anything, even if he found out about Damien. Now that she thought more about it, she wasn't sure she wanted Viktor to investigate him. There were too many variables and too many things that could go wrong. What if the vampire figured out Viktor was doing that? Would he retaliate? Elora realized she didn't want anything to happen to the one person who seemed to be on her side.

Instantly, nausea swirled in her gut as she watched the last resident walk through the gateway. Had she just put Viktor at risk? And to compound her anxiety and overwhelming fear, Damien's cheery voice rang out as he joined Viktor at the gate.

"Well, you two seem close. Is this standard protocol?" The coolness with which he said it didn't hide the underlying threat of his observation.

Elora spun around, facing Damien, chin lifted and eyes blazing. "You should know protocol, shouldn't you? And waiting to leave hardly counts as closeness."

Damien's smile fractured for just a moment. The mask of cool amusement slipped to reveal something darker, something closer to disgust as he met her defiant gaze. Her heart raced in her chest, beating furiously against her ribs and she was sure Damien could hear it, could sense the pulse in her neck, the harshness of her breathing. He inclined his head so subtly that it was almost missed by Elora.

"I know it when I see it. Consider it a talent, a natural ability if you will." Elora took a step back.

"Then you would know you are currently too close to me." She turned, nodding at Viktor as she followed the last of the residents, head spinning at the unspoken accusation, the dangerous nature of it should the rumor be passed around. Relationships between residents and nurses were forbidden, and the nurse had the most to lose. It was a fireable offense, resulting in an investigation and normally the loss of their license if the conversations around the nurse's station were to be believed. During Elora's first year there, she heard a story about a nurse and resident becoming close. There were lingering hands as meal trays were passed, hands on their face when the nurse made sure the resident took their meds. Then, later, the nurse would disappear for chunks of time during the night. It continued for months until one of the doctors saw the nurse exiting their room. Suddenly, that nurse was gone, and the resident was placed in the green room for days while she alternated between screaming and being sedated. She had yelled, pleaded, screamed, and pulled out her hair as she demanded to see the nurse again. Then, she disappeared into the maximum-security ward, never to be seen again. The rumor was of medication amounts so vast that the resident was a shell, drooling and staring at the ceiling.

Or that was the rumor, anyway.

Elora could hear them speaking, voices low as she walked away. She clenched her hands into fists, forcing her fingernails into her palm and counted the tiles with each step she took.

One. Two. Three. Four. Onwards until finally, her breathing evened out, the anxiety and impending panic attack retreated into their place nestled in her breastbone where they created a lingering ache that never seemed to fully go away.

~ ~

CHAPTER 7

Damien

One thing that Damien realized quickly while working his shifts was that Viktor was close to the girl he needed to investigate, making him wonder if the human could be useful and help him. Viktor could feed him information or provide some type of insight into who was and what her history was. Damien had read her file over and over, shocked that was so sparse. There was information there, but nothing concrete, vague references to therapy sessions and medications. Strangely, a girl who had been here for five years had so few pages of doctor's notes, therapy notes, and recorded history. Instead, it was bare basics with a small bit of information about where she came from and why she was here now.

Damien settled into a chair, resting his feet on the edge of the desk currently covered in loose paper and old coffee cups. It was curious that the nurse's station was so disorganized, considering they were tasked with taking care of a dozen or so patients, all with violent histories. With a brief glance down both hallways, Damien opened the file on his legs, trying to ignore the feel of the scrubs against his skin. It reminded him too much of what he wore as a child, cheap material that had probably been used before by someone else. The embroidered name of the hospital went through the fabric, irritating the skin on his chest as he adjusted his position.

Elora Rebekah Reynolds.

The patient was admitted after attacking her foster sister, Elizabeth Weaver. The patient attacked her sister during the night, around 2 a.m. The patient bit her foster sister, who was asleep at the time. The foster parents were able to intercede, and police were called.

The patient was in a state of duress and attacked multiple officers. It took four officers to subdue the patient and then sedate her to take her to the emergency room. After an intake evaluation, she was admitted to the hospital under the care of Dr. Montgomery.

The patient was put on a tranquilizer and an antipsychotic at the time of admittance.

With a groan, Damien ran his hands through his dark hair and frowned. It had taken four full-grown police officers to subdue her. Normally, that wouldn't be too impressive. Human police officers were notorious for being under-trained and weak. It was why vampires tended to have their own units within the various precincts throughout the city. He considered briefly finding the officers who had responded to that call, had been inside the home, and subdued her enough to take her to the emergency room. He wanted to assess them himself, decide if an eighteen-year-old female could have beaten them so easily. But that had been five years ago. They might not even be working anymore or could have been transferred. And what would he even actually learn? That they were poorly trained? That she had been stronger than she looked at the time?

He let out another noise of frustration as his eyes darted to the figure standing in front of the desk, palms flat on the surface, as they watched him.

"Viktor. How is everyone? All accounted for?" Viktor glared at the nurse sitting before him, a file in his lap that had a picture of Elora paper-clipped to the inside. It was from her first day and was taken as part of the admission process. Her hair was a wild mess of crimson, and her eyes were distant and haunted. The scars along her neck were in clear view, still red and raised against golden skin that had since gone pale.

The silence between the two of them was punctuated only by the clock on the wall, each tick forcing the smile on Damien's lips to grow wider and Viktor's glare to grow more intense. It was individual quiet time for the residents, leaving the day room empty, which gave it an eerie feeling like there were echoes that latched onto the furniture, the walls, and the windows. Damien hated it there. The smells, the noises, the dead expressions on everyone's faces. Everything. But to complete the job that so many other vampires had been killed for, he would deal with it.

Slowly, Damien closed the file and set it on the desk, removing his feet from where they rested, and sat up. Viktor stood to his full height and squared his shoulders. Damien assumed it was an attempt to be physically intimidating. Viktor was a large man, tall with broad shoulders, the kind that puts on muscle without really trying. Damien had known humans like him growing up, men who thought that their size gave them power over everyone else.

But Viktor's face always betrayed a softness that was at odds with his build. It wasn't in the bone structure or anything like that, but in the way he looked at the world. Damien had seen it when he interacted with the residents or when he interacted with the girl. But none of that softness was there now. No, at the moment, Viktor just looked pissed. He knew exactly what file Damien had been reading since this was the third time he had caught the newer nurse with it, almost like he was studying it. The angry and disapproving looks had only gotten more intense each time he caught Damien.

Viktor didn't say anything as he walked around the desk with heavy steps on the chipped floor, and grabbed the file from where it sat on top of post-it notes and sign-in sheets. Damien grinned as he watched him, amused at his attempt to put him in his place. For him, it was entertaining, and he loved nothing more than pushing him, seeing exactly how much Viktor would take before he snapped.

"I'm curious. What is her deal?" Damien gave the file in Viktor's hands a pointed look and leaned back in the chair.

"Why do you care? Why not ask about Marie? Or Joseph?" Damien shrugged lightly before answering, meeting Viktor's hesitant eyes.

"I already know about Marie and Joseph. She is here because she killed her daughter and was diagnosed with postpartum depression. Her sentence is almost up. And Joseph talks a lot to his dead wife and thinks he is a dwarf. His file claims standard delusions and hallucinations." Damien pointed to the file as Viktor sank into one of the other chairs. "Her file says absolutely nothing concrete. An attack on a family member and delusions."

"Again, why do you care?"

"Call it curiosity and a desire to know who I am working with." Viktor froze at the explanation, searching Damien's face as if his expression would give away the lie he was sure the nurse was telling. Damien grinned under the scrutiny, careful not to show too much of his teeth, not wanting to risk the human questioning the shape of his canines or asking questions.

"What do you want to know? The file is sparse because she doesn't remember very much. A mental block is what her psychiatrist called it from what Elora has said."

"You two talk about her therapy sessions. Interesting." Viktor shook his head at the comment and Damien watched him, noting the way his hand flexed in his lap, the way his eyes darted down the hallway toward her room. Damien wanted to add more, explain how he had been watching, how he noticed the looks, the touches, and the banter the two of them had.

"We talk, as I do with many of the residents. If you paid attention to anyone but her, you would have noticed." Damien waved his hand, dismissing the insinuation. Of course, he kept his eyes on the girl, kept his focus on what she did and said. He needed to know if she was who he had been looking for ever.

"You still haven't told me anything I don't already know." The human was stalling or trying to distract him. It was clear he didn't really want to answer, didn't want to explain what the girl had done to end up here. Damien had checked Viktor's file after noticing how close they seemed to be in an effort to know exactly who he would be working with. He didn't want any surprises, like another vampire sniffing around or just hoping for an easy meal, like Ryan, who had been another example of someone trying to get around the Accords. The laws developed by humans and vampires stated feeding directly from humans was forbidden, punishable by death in the right circumstances. And a human who couldn't consent? A human whose sanity was already at least partially in question? Damien felt bile rise in his throat at the thought, at the forced nature of it.

I should have just killed that disgrace, he thought bitterly as he waited for Viktor to finally speak again. Viktor had been there for roughly four years, appearing shortly after the girl had been admitted by court order. From what his file said, he had transferred from another city, but there hadn't been any record of which one or what facility he had worked at. And his personal life was ever more mundane. No family. No partner. No real friends outside of drinking buddies who also worked there.

Damien had spent several days doing surveillance, and it had given him nothing.

Maybe it's the fact Viktor had been working here so long and taking care of the girl that accounts for the relationship, he considered. But that didn't sound completely right. Either way, he knew he needed to figure out what it was, needed to know if Viktor was going to be a problem.

"She attacked her foster sister from what I have gathered. She doesn't really talk about it, but it was fairly bad. The sister was disfigured by it. Elora—" Viktor hesitated, his mouth twisted, and his eyes stared off into the distance. "She bit her, tried to drink her blood. She claims vampires are real and that she was one, that they exist and run the city." Viktor shrugged.

"So, delusional?" Damien sneered, and Viktor's eyes hardened.

"That's a fucked-up thing to say. She is confused. Her life before her foster family was hell, but that is not something for me to talk about. That is her story. At least what she remembers about it." Viktor ran his hands through his sandy blonde hair and sighed.

"Look, she doesn't like you. I don't know why. I just know she doesn't. Keep your distance from her."

"Are you telling me to avoid a resident?" Damien struggled to keep the surprise from his face. He had known she had noticed him, but most residents were annoyingly attentive towards him. The prey recognized a predator but was unable to stay away. Viktor met Damien's eyes once more and the smile on his face faltered and disappeared in a single instant. He had been ready for a face of frustration or even anger. Instead, Damien noted the concern, the exhaustion, the fear for the girl. He had always been able to read people, vampire or human, with little effort. Growing up, reading people meant getting fed, meant knowing who to steal from, and who to beg from. Older women made the best targets. Mothers were second best, their desire to help a child in need overriding any logic or rational thought they may have had before he approached them.

Viktor's expression was different. There was too much there to pinpoint a specific emotion.

"Elora has been through enough, especially lately. Let's just leave this alone." It was the statement of a man who protected someone he cared for, someone he saw as important to him. Damien wanted to comment on the relationship, a quip about the potential unprofessionalism of it. But something stopped him.

"What do you mean? Like before she came here or after?" Damien leaned back in the chair, hands clasped in his lap as he waited for the human to explain.

"About a week ago, Elora was attacked in her room. Another nurse — the one you took over for, actually — attacked her while she was sleeping. He –" Viktor stopped, and Damien just watched as torment flashed over the human's face.

"He hurt her. I'm not sure of the extent of it. I'm not allowed that information and not even she would give me details. But I know what she looked like the next morning. She was covered in bruises; her hair was a mess. She wasn't even able to talk because she had screamed so loudly that her throat was torn up." Again, a pause as Viktor bent forward with his forearms resting on his knees.

"The doctor didn't believe her, but I saw the bruises. And then the nurse just happened to quit a few days later. So, yeah, she has been through enough." Damien shifted slightly in his chair as unease raced through his veins. The only thought in his head was that he definitely should have just killed Ryan.

Damien didn't say anything for a long moment while an irritation — no, anger — flooded through him. He wasn't sure which part was so problematic for him. He had known Ryan attacked her, and tried to feed from her, so that part wasn't surprising. Was it the fact no one had taken her seriously? Vampires feeding on humans was a dirty secret and not a well-kept one. No matter how much blood was pumped out into the city and to the vampire population, there were always those who preferred it straight from the source. And since vampires were a secret, there weren't any willing participants, unless they were employed, sworn to secrecy under the pain of death. You can't consent to someone you don't know exists.

But to take it from someone who was confined like this, drugged to sleep through the night, that was different somehow.

Maybe I am going soft, he mused before discarding the thought.

Viktor must have taken the silence as the end of the conversation because he stood, remembering to grab the file once more. Damien didn't say anything, despite the fact he was painfully away that he wouldn't be able to find it again and this place was so outdated and underfunded that none of the files were digital. Maybe that was by design, to keep the information contained and controlled. Viktor once again stopped at the doorway.

"So, just leave her alone. She deserves a friend, someone who listens to her. Don't ruin that for her." His words were rough. A plea, Damien realized and suddenly found himself unable to deny either of them that, deny them using one another for companionship in this place. Thinking back to the kids he ran with as a child, he could understand the need Viktor had to help the girl, to protect her.

Damien tried to think of a witty remark, something that could defuse the tension left behind, something that made him seem uninterested in the girl and whatever was going on there. But for once, his mind was blank and refused to process thoughts or produce words. Instead, he just nodded and watched him walk away.

~ ~

CHAPTER 8

Elora

It annoyed Elora greatly that it wasn't Viktor who would be taking her to her appointment with Dr. Montgomery that morning. Usually, Viktor would wait for her to finish breakfast and then walk her over while the nurses took the residents back to the day room for group therapy. But as she dropped her tray off at the kitchen window, Viktor caught her eye and jerked his head toward Damien, an apologetic expression on his face.

She considered for a moment refusing the escort, or specifically the choice of escort, but that would be pointless and stupid. It wouldn't change anything, except for maybe a stint in her room without any privileges or a short stay in the green room. Instead, she squared her shoulders and ignored the pit in her stomach, the tiny voice whispering that damn nickname in her ear and walked to the door. Her steps were confident, and her head held high, eyes staring directly ahead at something on the wall. A flower in the painting? Or is that a stain? With a cool indifference that she did not feel, Elora brushed past him by a few steps and then stopped, waiting for him to follow. When he didn't, she turned around and stared at him, glaring daggers at his smiling face, which were still looking out over the cafeteria.

"Dr. Montgomery doesn't like for me to be late." For just a heartbeat more, Damien looked at the room before turning to her. His face was empty, almost like a statue she had seen at the art museum she visited when she was in school. But his eyes, dark brown to the point they were almost black, betrayed his amusement.

"Well, we wouldn't want that." Even his voice sounded entertained by the entire exchange. Elora refused to give him any hint of frustration or irritation or even a sarcastic retort. Instead, she simply spun on her heel and started walking, feeling him fall in step behind her.

At least he didn't feel the need to hold on to her arm like she was going to run. Most of the nurses did that, tight grips that felt more like exerting their control than anything else. Viktor held her arm sometimes, but that always felt different to her. Protective. Comforting. He knew that these meetings always went one of two ways. Either horribly, with some type of punishment that was referred to as homework or positively when she confessed some memory or revelation, both of which were at least partially made up.

"Is it true you've been here for five years?" His question caught her off guard, since she knew that Damien was aware of the answer. Nurses looked over all the files to get the basic information about the people they would be taking care of. How long they have been there, why they are there, and what type of risks they pose. All in the name of being better prepared to do their job.

They just like the gossip, she thought bitterly as she recalled the way the nurses sometimes whispered around the desk, eyes darting to various residents or their fingers pointing in their direction. It was usually followed by dramatic gasps or giggles, depending on the story.

"Yes," Elora responded after a moment, the answer pushed through gritted teeth.

"When will you be released?" Elora stopped and turned to look at him, annoyed that he was asking, annoyed that she did not know the answer.

"When I am better. When Dr. Montgomery says I am better." She spun back around and started walking a bit faster, for once desperate to get to Dr. Montgomery's office.

"You seem fine enough to me. They could just release you now." Elora stopped once more, eyes glaring at the vampire towering over her. He no longer looked amused or curious. Instead, that blankness had returned, his face and eyes betraying nothing. And suddenly, she couldn't breathe, hearing only the whisper of *little rose* in her ear. Her hands itched, desperate to force them over her head and block out the sound that was coming from inside her mind, a lingering echo torturing her at every moment, surprising her at the least opportune moments.

"You are far too interested in my release." Damien let out a laugh, the sound like winter, like ice cracking and falling to the ground.

"Trust me. I'm far more interested in you than you think." Elora shivered as his assertion reached her, a soft caress along her cheek.

"That sounds like your own problem." She began marching ahead once more, steps hurried, and the sound boomed in the hallway until she reached the door. She let out a soft sigh, feeling the muscles in her stomach relax, her shoulders lower. He was much too interested, and it was unsettling. Nurses talked to them, made conversation, and made small talk to make things seem more normal, and to socialize them in case they were released. On the surface, they could all pass for sane, whatever that actually meant.

You attacked your foster sister. Sank your teeth into her neck and ripped her skin. You dug your nails into her face like a rabid animal, she reminded herself, feeling the expected guilt and shame fill her whole body once more. Sometimes she could forget about it, could exist without its crushing weight.

You don't even know if she is alive. Another reminder and one that made her hand hesitate before she knocked. Dr. Montgomery wouldn't tell her if she was alive or dead. Whenever Elora asked, she simply shook her head before returning to the topic at hand, which was usually her delusions that she refused to abandon, refused to refute even if it meant being released. It felt like a betrayal to deny it, something in her twisting and turning at the thought.

She knew without a doubt that vampires were real, that they ran the city and farmed the humans for blood. Usually the poor. A grand complicated system that kept the poor in decent health to keep their own food supply at the highest quality. For Dr. Montgomery, the vampire theory, as she called it, was a product of a very traumatized mind, a mind that hid memories and conjured fantastic stories in order to cover up emotions. But that was where the psychiatrist was wrong. Elora always felt them. They surrounded her like old friends and family members, her only constant companions.

She had long since decided that remaining at the facility was punishment for what she did. For the night that she ripped into her sister's throat with her teeth and drank. She could have revealed all of this to Damien, who watched her with an expectant expression, as if he were owed her story, her darkest secrets and thoughts. But the words stuck to her tongue, anchored in a way that promised they would not come loose anytime soon. She raised a brow at the vampire nurse beside her and knocked, fingers playing with the long sleeves of her favorite blue sweater.

"Come in." Dr. Montgomery's voice rang out, muffled by the door and the white noise machine. Damien nodded slightly before he opened the door and stepped aside to let Elora enter. He did not follow behind her as she slammed the door, the sound echoing in the massive office.

Her doctor was not at her desk as Elora walked in and was instead at one of the bookshelves that lined the wall, head cranked to the side as she pursued the titles, seemingly looking for something specific.

"Take a seat." Elora was already on her way to her chair when the request filled the room. She took a moment before sitting, noting how dark it felt in there today, as if a lightbulb were dead or wasn't working. It made the shadows more pronounced, and the edges of the walls and furniture sharper. The room had never been comforting, but this put her on edge as she finally sank down into the chair and assumed her usual position.

Dr. Montgomery sighed and shook her head before she walked back to her desk, rifling through some papers and sitting. She interlaced her fingers and rested them under her chin, staring at her patient with an unreadable expression.

"Elora, you have been my patient the longest out of any resident who has ever stepped foot inside these walls. I thought our treatment plan would eventually yield some progress, but it unfortunately has not." She stopped as she watched her patient's face, searching for any sign of a reaction. Elora schooled her expression into a look of neutrality, trying with every ounce of self-control she had to not give her one.

She just shook her head once more and continued. "It is time to switch tactics and try a different therapy type, one I've tried only a few times with select patients. We are going to try exposure therapy."

"Which is what?" Elora scolded herself for asking as a strange smile spread across her psychiatrist's face.

"In simple terms, this therapy type forces the patient to face what is tormenting them. For people with a phobia, they face it. Hold a spider for arachnophobia and so on. For someone who is using shame and guilt to feed their delusions, it means facing the source of said emotions."

The room was suddenly shifting, the air thinning and thickening all at once. Elora's brain started screaming the word 'no' over and over again, the sound so loud she wondered if the psychiatrist could hear it. Dr. Montgomery had never even told her that her foster sister was alive. She had, instead, hinted that she may have lived, but refused to give any details, claiming it was all for the healing process. It had been a control tactic, and they both knew that.

But if this was the new course of therapy, as she called it, then that meant she had survived the attack.

Suddenly, questions flooded Elora's mind, each one attempting to leap from her tongue, explode past her teeth, and pill out onto the rug between her and her psychiatrist. Her body lurched up slightly, the urge to ask them forcing her to move, the words waiting on her lips. Instead, Dr. Montgomery lifted her hand, silencing her.

"I will not tell you details, Elora. Your mind has created an immensely powerful shield, and I do not want to give it time to construct something that would render this approach pointless before we even begin." Her voice held a strange edge like she was enjoying this, soaking up this moment like it was the finest wine money could buy. There was ecstasy shining in her eyes, and Elora fought the urge to vomit onto her stupid rug.

She had never meant to see any of them ever again, never meant to see her foster sister.

Elora leaned back in her chair and nodded, still holding Dr. Montgomery's gaze despite the burning of tears in her eyes, refusing to cry in front of a woman who hadn't earned any of them. Quietly, vehemently, Elora vowed the woman would never get that satisfaction.

"Part of exposure therapy can sometimes be the element of surprise. Being able to prepare for it helps the patient build walls that can protect them and their fear or delusion. Just know that at some point very soon, your new therapy will begin. And let's hope it is successful this time."

Elora stood, legs shaky underneath her, and started heading for the door, reminding her of the one time she had gotten drunk. A boy had broken up with her sister and to deal with the heartbreak they had stolen a bottle of wine from the street market, drinking in the park like cliche teenagers. Elora had held her sister in her arms and brushed away her tears as she cried over a boy whose only redeeming quality was his ability to play sports. Then later, they took turns holding each other's hair while they vomited the red liquid up, vowing to never do so again.

"Elora?" She stopped, keeping her eyes on the door as if it could help her not collapse into a heap on the floor.

"Do you even remember her name?" Elora didn't answer, refusing to answer her because Dr. Montgomery knew that she didn't. So many details had been lost over the years—where they lived, who she was running from, her foster sister's name. Before Elora could burst into a thousand tiny little shards spread out all over her office, she left, slamming the door behind her.

~ ~

CHAPTER 9

Elora

It had been three days, and nothing had happened. Elora hadn't thought whatever Dr. Montgomery had planned would occur immediately, but with each passing day, the knots in her stomach grew tighter and tighter. Food made her feel ill. The very smell wafting from the cafeteria three times a day made her gag. Sleep eluded her since the nightmares had returned with a vengeance as if she needed to be reminded of what she had done in preparation for whoever would be waiting in that room.

Or maybe there was no meeting, no new therapy type, and this was what Dr. Montgomery had planned for. A paranoid thought entered Elora's head: *Maybe she was planning to make me so unstable and weak I would break, having only her to put the pieces back together. Maybe to fix something, you must break it first.*

It was torture. Every door that opened or shadow in her peripheral vision could be them, could be her.

Elora jumped as Damien knelt beside her in the dayroom. She was in her usual seat and usual attire of sweats and long-sleeve shirts. Luckily, someone had turned on the television, but she hadn't even noticed the noise of the ridiculous reality show, too lost in her fear to hear anything but her own heartbeat.

"Come on. You have an appointment." Elora didn't look at him, just pulled her knees in close to her as she realized she wasn't sure she could stand. She scolded herself softly, words dripping with self-doubt and shame about how she didn't know with any certainty that this was anything other than a usual appointment. Yet, she knew that it wasn't. For a moment, she took in the tugging feeling in her chest, just beneath her left breast. The air felt heavy, as if it would squeeze her, crush her beneath it. Somehow, Elora realized that *she* was in the building. Somewhere among the chipped paint and locked doors, her foster sister was waiting for her.

Damien waited for just a moment before he let out an annoyed grunt and grabbed her arm, his fingers somewhat gentle despite the hard grip, and lifted her to her feet. Elora jerked her arm away from his hands before marching over to the doorway. If she was going to do this, she wouldn't rely on him to walk her over like a good puppy.

She wouldn't show Dr. Montgomery what she wanted to see: fear, apprehension, hesitation, and shame. Elora knew the doctor wanted to see her break, each fragment falling to the dirty floor. Instead, Elora decided she would confront her guilt, her family, and her sister. She would speak with them, plead for their forgiveness, or whatever else they wanted. She would listen as they screamed or cried, or both. They would get whatever they wanted from her. They had earned that much.

Dr. Montgomery had not earned anything from her. She wouldn't see the hesitation that tried to halt her steps, the fear that etched itself into her flesh, the shame that curled itself into her core and made itself at home. The doctor had heard about that over the years, and it hadn't been enough.

Damien unlocked the door and let her pass through, her steps louder than normal on the linoleum tiles.

"Stop at the elevator."

Of course, we aren't going to her office.

Elora knew Dr. Montgomery wouldn't risk anything happening there. She would want a more controlled environment. Probably one of the interview rooms on the first floor, usually reserved for the police to talk to residents who had been involved in a crime.

She speared Damien with a dark look as he pushed the downward-pointing arrow and then stepped back. A sharp ding rang out in the otherwise silent hallway and the doors opened to reveal yellow wallpaper and a silver rail lining the back. With a deep breath, Elora stepped in, followed by Damien.

"Excited?" She scoffed at the question.

"For what? A new therapy type she wants to try? Or meeting the one person in the world I never wanted to see again?" She forced her gaze onto the elevator door even as it shifted to Damien's reflected image. His focus was solely on the patient beside him, hands clasped behind his back, his dark hair a disheveled mess around his face.

"I suppose both, in a way." He was quiet for only the briefest of moments. "Your foster sister, I guess. Though some might think it's strange you don't want to see her, would say it is a chance to apologize."

"Some? And what do you think?" The elevator dinged, and the doors slid open to reveal a long hallway lined with rooms. The building was older in this area, and it showed. The cream paint on the walls needed a new coat, and the plaster was peeling in some places. The hallway was punctuated with steel doors with small horizontal slots every six feet or so, and the fluorescent lighting felt like it could go out at any moment.

Damien shrugged as they both stepped out, eyes on her face.

"I would say I understand not wanting to see your own darkness. The worst moment of your life reflected in such a physical way. I would say it makes sense to be scared, to not want to see the consequences of your actions, no matter how many bodies pile up." Elora's focus snapped to him, recoiling from the rage and disgust she saw burning in his eyes.

"Are you talking about you or me, nurse?" Damien leaned in close, his breath warm on her face even as she tried to back away.

"We are always talking about you." His words were lined with a promise of violence and wrath, of disdain and hate. Elora's hands squeezed into fists, and he glanced down at the movement, a cruel smile on his lips.

"Seems I struck a nerve. How fun." Damien grabbed her arm, fingers digging into the flesh there. He steered her to a room at the end, positioning her in front of it, where the psychiatrist yanked open the door. Dr. Montgomery nodded to him and then entered the door beside it. Elora's theory was that there was some type of camera or two-way mirror that would allow her to watch everything.

Damien pushed the door wide, allowing her to walk in alone. Elora hesitated as her lead feet sank into the floor and she became rooted to the spot.

"You need to go in." She could feel his breath as he whispered in her ear, nudging her softly into the room.

"I can't do this." It was an admission she hadn't planned on making. Not to him, anyway. Elora never wanted anyone to see her weaknesses, her fear that did more damage than anything else. She didn't want Dr. Montgomery to see or know that her therapy was indeed having results.

"Yes, you can." His voice was stern, as if he was tired of waiting for her to do something so simple.

"You can face this. I promise." Her eyes snapped to him. He stood so much closer than she had originally thought. Only a couple of inches separated him from her as he leaned down slightly to whisper. She had thought to find irritation on his face, mild annoyance. Instead, his dark brown eyes were soft, a small smile on his full lips.

His eyes flashed, a sheen taking over. Elora recoiled, understanding hitting her in the gut.

He's trying to compel me.

Her hand reared back before hitting him with every bit of strength she could summon. Her palm collided with his cheek, a faint stinging lingering on her hand, radiating slightly up her arm. His normally blank face betrayed him, revealing the plethora of emotions fighting for control of his features. Rage and surprise seemed the most poised to win and Elora decided the others were not worth dissecting.

Instead, she took one step and then another, and then three more before she found herself inside. A single metal table dominated the center of the room. There were two chairs opposite each other, and someone was already sitting in the one closest to the door. Elora glanced up into the corners of the room, taking in the cameras before staring directly into the two-way mirror lining the wall behind the body in the chair. It would give the best vantage point, a perfect view of her patient. Dr. Montgomery was being very thorough. Whether it was to protect the woman sitting in the chair or to protect herself should anything happen, Elora wasn't sure. She just knew it was not for her, that she was just the entertainment, the experiment.

The door shut behind her and she walked over to the far chair, perching on the very edge of the cold metal. Her eyes refused to look up from her hands where they lay in her lap. She knew who was sitting across from her. Her skin burned as she felt the woman stare at her and study her. Elora could feel her like a smooth caress against her bare skin, as if the woman were touching her.

"Hi, Elora." Her voice was the same despite five years having passed. The same girlishness underlined the lyrical quality as Elora closed her eyes and shuddered at hearing her name from those lips once again.

Elora still didn't look, counting her breaths, tracing swirls and scars that lined her hands.

"Please look at me, El." In response, Elora's focus stayed down even as she screamed at herself to raise them, to look her foster sister in the eyes. But the desire to remember her exactly how she had been before the attack and before Elora's teeth sank into her skin was winning. She wanted to remember how her foster sister looked at the Winter Gala in her silver dress with one slit up her right leg, her hair in a complex up-do and perfect make-up, the very portrait of simple elegance. Elora wanted to remember her in a beanie and sweater, drinking coffee before school in winter, cheeks flushed from the cold.

"Please." Finally, it was the plea in her sister's voice that shattered whatever hold her mind had over her body and her eyes rose, moving from the metal table to her hands clasped in front of her, to the long-sleeve shirt to her scarred neck, to her lips, her eyes. A silence enveloped them as they studied one another, taking in each scar, each blemish, each change since the last time they saw one another. Elora's breathing hitched as she scanned her sister, still beautiful despite the scars along her cheek and neck. Indeed, they only added to her beauty, adding a fierceness to her otherwise soft features. Her blond hair was pulled back into a braid, just as it was that night. Two ice-blue eyes roamed over Elora's face while her full lips were pulled into a frown. Emotions flickered quickly across her face, their disappearance instant, leaving Elora to wonder what she saw there other than complete despair.

Elora's eyes rested on the scars on her sister's neck, a mixture of long, thick lines and puncture wounds.

"I'm sorry," she croaked out even as her voice broke, and she felt the tears on her cheeks. She wasn't sure when she started crying. Had it been when she walked in, the anticipation eating away at her resolve to never show tears to Dr. Montgomery? Or was it when she saw the damage she had wrought to the girl who was her sister? The girl who defended her at every turn, no matter who Elora lashed out at. The girl who had held her as she sobbed for days after being dropped off at the people who would become her foster family.

"I know." The woman's voice was a whisper, and all Elora wanted to do was wrap it around herself, a jacket to keep out the world. After a moment, Elora's sister sat back in her chair, hands moved into her lap.

"You know, I was angry with you. Obviously, I was angry with you. As the stitches healed and the stares from the other kids turned into taunts, I was so furious. I even tried to visit you. Did you know that?"

Elora shook her head and forced herself to maintain eye contact, even though she wanted to look anywhere else to not see the pity on her sister's face.

"They wouldn't let me. You were dangerous. And I wasn't technically family anymore, so I just kept my anger to myself. I watched everyone live their best lives, going to dances and on dates while I stayed home because my scars were just that repulsive." Her hand moved and settled on her neck, fingering the scars, tracing them one by one.

"Mom and Dad tried to find creams and other treatments to make them less noticeable. But they were scared and didn't know what to do. We couldn't afford any type of surgery to make them disappear. Honestly, I think they felt guilty since they were the ones to take you in. They probably thought that if they had refused to take you that day, then this wouldn't have happened to me. And maybe they were right." She shrugged her shoulders as if none of what she was saying mattered. Elora's blood stopped at her sister's words, noting the one clue that would answer her own questions.

Past tense. It was all past tense. *They thought. They were right.*

"What happened?" Elora's words came out so low she wasn't sure her sister heard her until a cold smile stretched across her red lips.

"They passed. A few months after you were sentenced. It was very sudden, at least to me. Apparently, it was some type of poison mixed in with their wine. We had saved up to buy some to celebrate my acceptance to Brightman University. Full scholarship. I'm sure talking about my scars in my scholarship letter helped quite a bit."

The air in the room had become charged, like a storm was brewing within the confines of these four walls. Her voice had taken on an amused tone. There was no softness left, no more of the girlishness from the beginning. No, there was only cold rage.

"The guilt was too much. The three of us shared a glass to toast my future and then they took the bottle, poured the poison in, drank, and went to sleep. I found them the next morning, curled up together on the bed. Now that I could leave and make my own life, they figured they could just succumb to their guilt."

"I'm sorry."

"I know, Elora. Trust me, I know. I am sometimes, too." She stood suddenly, the move surprisingly graceful and fast. For a moment, she turned from Elora, staring into the two-way mirror. The button-up shirt was tucked into a long black skirt that shifted as she moved and her braid reached down her back, hitting just above her tailbone.

Elora counted her breaths, quietly instructing herself to inhale and exhale as she wiped away the tears that ran freely down her face. There was no hiding it. She had always held out hope that they were fine, that they had taken care of her sister, and had done well despite her actions. Not even once had Elora thought they might feel guilty for what happened, though she could understand it. It was a feeling was intimately familiar with.

They were her foster parents for three years, and she had grown to love them both fiercely. Without a single question, they had taken in the sixteen-year-old girl who was brought to their doorstep. They had clothed her, fed her, and sent her to school. They had dried her tears and grounded her when she failed her English class. They had loved her like their own, never asking where she came from, never asking why she cried in her sleep, why she had nightmares about chains on her wrists, about pain, and crushing weakness.

"And after all that time, after their deaths, my disfiguration, I was brought here to see you because you need my help to get better." The disgusted amusement was clear in her words, in her tone as she scoffed softly.

"Is that what Dr. Montgomery told you?" Irritation rose under Elora's skin and her body felt too warm. Of course, that was how her doctor would present this.

"She told me you are still struggling, that you can't handle your guilt about what you did to me." She turned from the window, her blue eyes hard.

"And I will tell you what I told the doctor. I don't care about your guilt or your grief. I was angry for so long before I realized what you did was a gift. Sure, I got the scars and the dead parents, but it was a blessing. And I agreed to be here simply to thank you for it."

"What?" Elora pushed the chair back a little away from the table, needing to be further away from the woman in front of her. For a moment, there was a crackle in the air.

"I heard that you do not even remember my name. Is that true? That you blocked out a lot of what happened before you came here?" Her long pale finger traced the edge of the table as she made her way around to Elora, who leaped to her feet, her eyes darting to the two-way mirror. Something was off. She was off.

"I don't –"

"Do you remember their names? Mom and Dad?" Her voice had gone harsh, as if she was barely restrained.

"Brian and Leslie. Their names were Brian and Leslie." Her lips turned up into a smile, and Elora backed away a few more steps until she was standing in front of the chair, her hand resting on the back as she sucked in a breath. She hadn't remembered their names until this moment.

"But not mine? The person you sank your nails into. The person you bit. The one you left with all of this."

Elora shook her head. There was nothing for her to say, nothing to promise and explain. She tried to take in a deep breath, but the act was becoming increasingly difficult. The room started to close in around Elora, or she was growing larger. For a heartbeat, she was unable to tell as she struggled to grab hold of a single shred of reality and force herself to stay inside her body. She retreated once more until her back collided with the wall. Faster than Elora thought possible, her foster sister was in front of her, hands on either side of her chest.

She leaned in and Elora shivered as lips brushed along her neck, the familiar voice whispering. "Elizabeth. My name is Elizabeth."

After a moment, she moved back and away from Elora, meeting her eyes. "But you called me Lizzie, just like mom and dad did."

Elora lurched forward, slapping her palms on the table as she struggled to stand. Her legs felt boneless, and she realized she wasn't sure could keep doing this. Talking and remembering, each moment was a stab of pain in her chest.

Yes, that was her name. She recalled calling after Elizabeth as they pulled her away and how her voice had broken through the cries of their parents and the commands of the emergency personnel. Elora sank into the metal chair, her hands still pressed flat against the cool metal as if it would anchor her.

"Say it." Elizabeth stood beside her, a sold yet terrifying presence. Her hand rested next to her sister's. Elora didn't move. She wasn't even sure she could speak.

"Say it!" Elora could feel her hands on her shoulders as her fingers dug into her flesh. Elora flinched, desperately straining to twist away from the woman who felt wrong. Not older or angry, but different in a way that was familiar and dangerous. The hand on the table grabbed Elora's other shoulder and yanked her body from the chair. Elizabeth forced her to stand before her, grip tightening as she held her in place. Red cheeks and black eyes met Elora's while Elizabeth's barely restrained fury lingered just below the surface, swimming within what used to be blue pools.

"Elizabeth. Your name is Elizabeth." Fingers detached themselves from Elora's body and fell to Elizabeth's sides, flexing in the folds of her skirt. Silently, with a small smile on her lips, Elizabeth nodded.

CHAPTER 10

Elora

Elizabeth returned to her original chair and settled back into it. She crossed one leg over the other while Elora watched her warily as she sank into her own seat and rested her trembling hands on the table. Elora looked down at her nails while her brows furrowed and waited for Elizabeth to speak.

"To be perfectly honest, I am not sure how I am supposed to help you get over your guilt or grief. But I saw this as an opportunity to see you, tell you what happened to Mom and Dad, and thank you. Like I said, I may not have seen it before, but what you did was a gift."

"How?" Elora's voice shook as she asked her question, trying to hide the growing fear of being trapped there with her sister. Something about her was not right and Elora knew it, noting each way that Elizabeth wasn't the same girl or woman she had known before. The same girl who had cried about a captured squirrel who had made a nest in the attic before being trapped by the landlord. The same girl who had drunk coffee like water and saved her money to buy chocolate despite how expensive it was for people like them. Instead, there was a cavalier attitude to how she spoke about the attack, about her parents. At first, Elora thought perhaps it was just grief or shock at seeing her attacker after so long.

"The doctors at the ER weren't really sure what to do with me when I came in. I got very sick afterward. The doctors thought it was some type of infection brought on by either you or just a general mishandling of the wounds themselves. So, they gave me medicine, and it cleared right up. I was able to go home."

Elizabeth leaned in close, her smile making Elora's breath stop momentarily as pieces started to find each other.

"Your bite did something, Elora. And for a while, the medication worked. It kept the urges at bay. But eventually, I couldn't afford it. And that is when the fun began. And the first time I brought someone back to my bedroom, our bedroom, I understood completely why you attacked me. It was divine."

She flashed Elora a large, toothy smile, and she finally saw them. The sharpened canines. Elora's eyes were drawn to them, tracing them as Elizabeth ran her tongue over them. Her sister's grace and speed instantly made sense.

Elora's chair hit the floor with a resounding metallic thud as she stood up and backed away from her until her body hit the wall. She watched Elizabeth make her way over to her, steps low and languish as if she had all the time in the world. Elora's panicked gaze darted to the two-way mirror and camera.

They will stop this. Either Dr. Montgomery or Damien. Someone will stop it. Her hands clenched and unclenched at her sides as her breathing became harsh and haggard. Elizabeth finally rounded the table and stood in front of her. Elora's eyes squeezed shut as Elizabeth's finger traced her jawline and then dropped to her neck.

"I can feel your heart racing, Elora. You tasted me. It's only fair I do the same." Her lips were on Elora's neck, her blood pulsating in her veins.

Maybe this is fair, Elora mused as Elizabeth inhaled sharply, tongue darting out and licking along the column of her neck.

A groan escaped the vampire's lips, even as a shudder radiated through Elora's body.

If I made her what she is now, then this seems fair, Elora rationalized. *She can get her pound of flesh, or blood, in this case. Will that absolve me of my sins? Of my guilt? Maybe she can succeed where I have failed.*

Elora tilted her head to the side slightly, granting her sister better access, welcoming the feel of her grin against her skin.

And then burning radiated through Elora's body from two sharp points in her neck. The fire raced through her veins as her pulse quickened. Elora cried out, and the sound reverberated through the silent room. She knew this pain, knew it before Ryan and before Elizabeth.

Elizabeth drew from her in a deep drink and then another, and Elora lost herself in the rhythm of it. She gasped slightly as the vampire reached out and tangled her fingers into her hair, grasping a handful of it tightly as she maneuvered Elora's head into a better position.

This was not the absolution Dr. Montgomery planned for her, not the exposure therapy that was supposed to happen. She was meant to confront her guilt, not succumb to it.

A door slammed open, the sound distant yet echoing throughout the tiny room. Neither Elora nor Elizabeth moved. They did not pull away from one another, teeth did not leave the flesh. Loud, heavy footsteps made their way towards them and then there was nothing. Elora shivered at the icy coldness left in her sister's wake as she collapsed to the ground while blood still flowed from the puncture wounds on her neck.

A scream filled the room, and she knew without a single doubt it belonged to her foster sister. It may have been five years since Elora had heard Elizabeth scream, but she remembered it like it had happened yesterday. There was a scuffle, bodies hitting the walls, and a chair fell to the ground. A voice demanded that someone restrain the screaming figure, followed by Elizabeth sobbing while repeating the word "no" over and over.

And then whispers that seemed to come from nowhere and everywhere all at once.

Little rose. My beautiful little rose.

Elora tried to raise her hand and push against the bleeding wound on her neck. She could smell the metallic tang laced with something else, something floral. Lavender maybe. With a small groan, she attempted to raise her head. It felt heavy, like it had been filled with bricks and concrete as she frantically searched for Elizabeth, her eyes washing over the room, searching for a hint of her blond hair.

She shook her head, forcing out the whispers as her eyes closed for a moment and weakness settled over her limbs and thoughts. All she could think was that Elizabeth needed to finish what she started, that she had earned this moment from her. Elizabeth had earned it with every cry of pain, every scar, every taunt from her peers. Earned it with the death of her parents.

"Get her out of here." Elora vaguely recognized the voice and struggled to place it as her eyes opened once more. Damien was kneeling in front of her, and his eyes stared intently at her neck. Her mouth moved to form words, to tell him that it burned, that her whole body could feel it. But nothing came out. Behind him, Dr. Montgomery was shouting orders at whoever was standing in the doorway, her hands moving in rough motions that were so at odds with the composed professional Elora was used to.

Her vision grew hazy, the corners of her sight going dark.

"She'll be okay. We should get her to a bed so we can better assess her wounds." Damien's voice commanded the attention of the room and Elora allowed herself to fall into it, finding comfort despite not understanding why.

Something cool touched her neck, and she closed her eyes, welcoming any sensation that could cut the fire ravaging her body. An arm wrapped around her waist, lifting her slowly as if she would break if they her moved too quickly. Another arm went under her legs and Damien cradled her against his chest, hands holding her tightly.

Her head fell against him, feeling the rough fabric of his scrubs, the hard threads of the hospital name sewn onto it. She struggled to keep her head up for only a moment before she collapsed, allowing her eyes to close. The warmth of his body enveloped her, fighting with the coldness that now spread from the loss of blood.

"It's okay. I got you. It's going to be fine." Elora managed to open her eyes long enough to glance at him, take in the tightness of his jaw. His lips thinned into a line across his face. She considered asking him why he thought that, why he cared enough to say it. But forming words felt beyond her ability as her thoughts became thick and slow.

A scratchy pillow was beneath her as Elora was laid down on the gurney waiting in the hallway, blood-red hair spilling out over the white fabric. Damien's eyes searched her face, returning over and over to the wound on her neck. He slipped his hand into hers, squeezing tightly.

"You should have let her finish." He stared at her, anger and something else flaring in his eyes. A hand reached out and pushed a strand of hair away from her face and she closed her eyes, finally knowing only darkness and nightmares.

* * *

"Hold her down." The voice was coming from the corner of a room Elora only vaguely recognized, knew only that it wasn't her room at the hospital or even the bedroom she shared with Elizabeth. This room was barely lit by the small light fixtures along the wall that were covered in what looked like paintings. Or maybe framed photos? She could make

out a large chair with lush cushioning standing before the four-poster bed, which contained only a pillow and a black silk sheet. Attached to each of the bedposts were silver chains with cuffs at the end.

No, this was somewhere else.

She screamed as two sets of hands latched onto her. One grabbed her arms while the other grabbed her ankles and dragged her onto the bed. With a sharp cry, she thrashed in their grip, and they held her tighter, forced her in place as the metal cuffs clamped around her wrists.

"Are you going to place nice tonight, little rose?" She spat towards the voice, a voice she recognized even though a part of her wasn't sure why. The scene, the voice, and the hands on her body felt intimately familiar, like she had lived this before, like it was routine.

A hand caressed her cheek, their knuckles moved towards her lips before running their thumb along them. Elora turned her head away and the owner of the hand chuckled before he leaned in. His weight made the bed groan as he kissed away the tears that had formed and started streaming down her face before moving to her ear. She could hear him, feel him, but couldn't see him. His face was a blur, a blended mess of color where his features should have been.

"You know I prefer it when you fight, anyway." Bile rose in her throat as she yanked her arms, trying in vain to break the chains that held her in place. He laughed softly before kissing her neck. Without a single thought, Elora brought her legs up, kicking him awkwardly in the side, and he laughed at the effort.

"Chain her legs as well." There was amusement in the voice, and she grimaced. As his hand settled on her stomach. She bit her tongue, knowing that screaming would mean nothing. No one would come for her. No one would save her as the hands started to roam, her clothing the only barrier between him and her flesh.

He stood slowly, gracefully, and moved away from her. "I think we will leave you like that for just a bit. Don't worry, little rose. I'll be back for you."

And she screamed as she woke.

~ ~

CHAPTER 11

Damien

He couldn't help but believe that the so-called emergency meeting was a waste of time as he sat at the long conference table.

Cheap conference table, he thought as he shifted in the chair. After exhaling loudly through his nose, Damien glanced at the large figure to his right. Viktor sat with his arms crossed over his chest, a deep scowl on his face. Damien didn't bother looking at the other nurse to his left. He hadn't even bothered to learn their name. His eyes swept over the three people across the table, but only one of them mattered at all in this whole meeting. Dr. Montgomery sat in the chair, squirming slightly while two other doctors sat beside her. All eyes were on the man standing at the front of the table. Damien recognized him as the chief board member for the hospital and an instrumental part in getting him a job there. He had been present for many meetings between his boss and the man in front of him. The short, balding man dressed in a suit too small for him stared daggers at Dr. Montgomery.

"What the fuck happened, Dr. Montgomery?" Despite his small stature, the man was bold and loud as he demanded answers.

"Elizabeth attacked my patient during an approved therapy visit. The goal was for Elora to meet with Elizabeth to confront her past. Her progress has become stagnant. By facing the person she attacked, Elora was forced to face what she did and finally take responsibility." Dr. Montgomery faced the man, her chin high and eyes defiant, and Damien almost respected her for it. If she wasn't unintentionally keeping him from taking the girl, he would have probably liked this woman.

"The girl attacked your patient! Do you have any idea of the nightmare we will face if this gets out? The rest of the board wants to remove you from her case and is considering petitioning for you to lose your license."

Damien's gaze moved from the board member to Dr. Montgomery, whose face had paled.

"You can't take me off her case now, Richard. Yes, she was attacked under my supervision. I take full responsibility for that. But we have an opportunity here to finally make progress. Elora showed signs of progress just during that meeting. Her therapy will move forward very quickly now. I am sure of it."

Richard ran his hand over his bald head and then sat back in his chair, looking at each person at the table in turn, before he returned his stern gaze to Dr. Montgomery.

"Here is what is going to happen. You will continue your care of the patient. But I want her released. You say her therapy should move quickly now after the attack. Good, the board wants her gone. You have one month to approve her release."

Dr. Montgomery's hands slammed down on the table as she half stood, outrage clear on her face.

"You can't demand progress like that! Elora is my patient. She will be released when I say so."

"We can and we do, Doctor. Either you approve her release, or we terminate you and release her without your say. She has been your side project for too long. We were accommodating when you wanted to continue her care. We allowed you to continue your research with her. But she has not proved to be a risk to anyone and so we can't hold her anymore. You know this. Your time is up."

Damien studied the woman across from him as her eyes settled on the table, shifting rapidly from left to right. Probably trying to work through the ultimatum to find some type of loophole.

Why does she want her here so badly? Is the girl really that dangerous? Damien considered the girl, the aftermath he saw in that room when Elizabeth attacked. The girl didn't seem like much of a fighter. If anything, she seemed to give up at that moment, giving into Elizabeth as if she had been compelled.

And what did Richard mean by research? Was it a simple case study? Something more?

No matter the answers to any of these questions, Damien knew one thing. He needed to get out of that room with its horrific pale blue wallpaper with tiny white flowers and portraits of past board members. The questions could be answered later if they needed to be. But the hunger gnawing at his stomach was becoming a problem. It had been too long since he fed and the number of humans in the room was tempting. He could hear their pulse and smell their blood. It was intoxicating. Distracting.

His hand went to his pocket where his pilfered vial of blood sat, assuring himself that it was still there. It was not how he had planned on getting it, having assumed he would need a much more complicated plan that included mild sedatives and a syringe. His plan, or the bones of one, had included being gentle enough not to wake her as he gathered her blood and to prevent any issues or mistakes. Her blood had a strange effect on vampires, according to Ryan. Elizabeth herself was another mystery.

"I understand, Richard. I will continue to work with her and have her ready for release by the end of the month." Her voice was an icy wrath coated with bitter resignation. Damien almost smiled before he stopped himself. That little development would be incredibly helpful if the girl turned out to be who he thought she was.

Richard clapped his hands together before continuing. "Fantastic. Now, let's keep the attack under wraps. We do not need anyone outside this room and the board knowing about it."

Damien nodded slightly along with everyone else who murmured their agreement. Richard waved his hand, and the dismissal was clear. One by one, they filed out of the conference room. Dr. Montgomery raced down the hall towards her office, no doubt panicking about the limited amount of time left with the girl. Damien simply headed towards the doors in the lobby when a voice stopped him.

"Were you there when she was attacked?" Damien had just been grabbing his keycard to unlock the door when Viktor's question reached his ears. He turned slightly, just enough to see the human in his peripheral vision. Viktor just jerked his head towards the door and followed him. They let the doors shut behind them and stepped down the few stairs leading to the entrance before Damien responded.

"I was outside the room, but yes." Damien watched with fascination as Viktor's eyes flashed and his jaw clenched so tight he wondered if the human's teeth would crack from the force.

"And you didn't stop it?" Damien had expected something along these lines and had known the human would be angry that his precious resident was hurt. For Damien, it simply further cemented his theory about the two of them being closer than what was appropriate for a patient and a nurse. He hadn't noticed the attraction between the two of them at first, but he also hadn't been looking for it. Not until after Viktor's reaction to finding Damien with her file once more. He took a second to make a mental note to pay better attention.

What Damien didn't expect was his own surge of frustration at the insinuation that he had just allowed the girl to be hurt.

Even if he despised her, he wouldn't have just let her be bitten and drank from. One part of this was that Damien's boss would rip out his throat if he found out Damien had stood aside while she was harmed. She was a waste of space, but she belonged to his boss. If she was who he thought she was, that is.

"Stop it how, exactly? I was placed outside the door. I couldn't hear or see anything that was happening. I didn't know something was wrong until Dr. Montgomery ran out of the other room and demanded my help." Damien raised a brow as Viktor's shoulders slumped, his anger at his perceived lack of action gone.

"Someone should have been in there." Viktor didn't look at the vampire, just at his shoes as they walked towards the parking lot.

"I agree with you there." Damien was quiet for a moment, eyes on the perfectly manicured hedges that lined the sidewalk, the trees and grass that surrounded the older brick building. The only signs that the people inside were potentially dangerous were the reinforced glass and bars on some of the windows in the older wings.

"What do you think about her being released?" Viktor's eyes darted up at the question, his mouth opened slightly as if to answer.

"I have no opinion. It isn't my place." Damien scoffed at the response.

"Personally, I think it's for the best. She doesn't seem violent. Maybe she deserves a chance at a normal life. A job. A relationship. All the things that come with it." Viktor grunted slightly at Damien's words.

"I'm not sure about that. It may be best for her to stay. She is safer here than anywhere else." Damien stopped in his tracks even as Viktor kept walking towards the rows of cars. He didn't stop and didn't expand on his statement. Instead, he left Damien behind to try to figure out what had meant.

~ ~

CHAPTER 12

Damien

The building in front of him never failed to make him nervous. Ashcroft Tower, the home of anyone who was part of the vampire family by the same name, was a tall, sleek building made primarily of reflective glass. It was a myth that vampires couldn't be in the sun, but a myth they perpetuated and used in their favor. No human would guess that the most powerful vampire in the Ashcroft family, Killian, lived in a building made of mostly windows.

The Tower was located in the area of the city reserved for the very wealthy. The city of Carvesk was home to four vampire families that were all part of the Council, a group made up of one representative from each vampire family, the human mayor, and the human governor. The job of the Council was to uphold the Accords while keeping vampires fed and humans safe.

The increase in illegal feeding had caused some tensions between not only the Council members but also the vampire families, which explained the increased security at the building. Farmed blood wasn't as satisfying as it had been, according to the growing number of vampires who tempted the wrath of the head vampires by drinking directly from humans.

But the increase in feeding from humans had led to other problems — humans who knew vampires existed and actively fought against them. They considered themselves a rebellion and freedom fighters. Mostly Damien had considered them a nuisance, ungrateful children who didn't understand how well they were taken care of. Something the girl would have in common with them if it turned out she was who his boss was looking for.

But his lack of interest in the group had disappeared the moment piles of vampire bodies had been lit on fire like funeral pyres across the city. Ever since, they started attacking vampires, destroying blood banks, and actively preventing people from donating blood. Now they were pests to be eradicated if the vampire heads got their way.

The lobby was a large room, a crescent-shaped desk off to the side where two vampires sat and waited for visitors. There were numerous leather couches in the space, each with a small side table. Tall plants lined the back wall, lending the room an earthy smell that almost covered up the scent of blood. Directly before the doors were metal detectors and three guards, each clad in vests with a gun at the hips. Damien bypassed security, the few guards there nodding at him as he made his way to the elevator and pushed twelve. Subtle music played. It was some orchestra music that paired well with the simple design of the space. Dark wooden paneled walls and a white marble floor rendered the space elegant without being gaudy, as it was with the rest of the Tower.

The first thing Damien noticed as he stepped off the elevator was that the secretary was gone from her desk, which was devoid of anything. No decorations, pictures of family, or tiny knick-knacks. Not even a pen or notepad. Only a phone and a closed laptop sat on top of the pale wooden desk. Either she had been fired, yet another one, or she didn't expect to last long enough to bring in anything personal. It was a smart assumption to make if Damien was honest. The head of the Ashcroft vampires had a habit of firing most secretaries and assistants after a few months. The lack of a secretary presented a small hiccup in his plan. He had hoped she would have to call into the office and inform his boss that he had arrived. It would have given Damien a moment to collect his thoughts and consider how he was going to present his findings and the vial of blood in his pocket.

It wasn't that he was necessarily afraid of him or how he would react to the girl being attacked. It was more about the weight that came with a mission nearing completion. He had been working on finding the girl for years and now there was a very real chance he had found her. He expected to feel relief or pride at the accomplishment, but no such thing existed for him. If the girl was who he had been looking for, who his boss had been searching and killing for, what would that mean? Damien scoffed at the thought. It meant that she would be taken care of. Food, a house, security, protection — all the things she ran away from, discarded while others were left to fend for themselves.

Once more Damien felt for the vial in his pocket before he knocked on the door with two sharp raps. It was quiet only for a moment before a voice responded.

"Come in."

Damien pushed the door open and entered, taking easy steps until he stood in front of a large desk in the center of the room. His boss wasn't sitting there as he usually did during the meetings when Damien would tell him which enemy he had dispatched or the Resistance hideout he had destroyed. Instead, the head vampire was pouring himself a drink at the small bar located along the far wall to Damien's right. Bottles of what looked like expensive liquor lined the shelves along with a collection of glasses, each a different shape or size to accommodate various drink types. Damien didn't know which one was meant for which liquor. To him, any of them would work. To Damien's left was a long line of shelves filled with books, statues, and other trophies from past enemies—enemies he had taken care of, carefully picking each item to bring back for display.

Killian, his boss and the head of the Ashcroft family, was a tall man, lean in a way that could lead some to think him weak. They would be wrong. He was lean, sure, but Damien had seen him work, had seen him snap bones without exerting any effort at all. Killian's long white hair was left loose around his shoulders today and was messy, a sign he had been running his hands through it in agitation. The fact that Damien was late for this meeting was probably part of the cause. Keeping the head vampire waiting was never a good choice. But his placement in the psychiatric hospital had required his attendance and so now here he was, thirty minutes late.

With a soft grunt, Killian sank into his chair and motioned for Damien to do the same.

A smirk was on his lips as Damien pulled the vial from his pocket and set it directly on the desk in front of Killian. Only then did he follow Killian's request for him to sit. Killian's pale gray eyes widened as he reached out and snatched it like he was dying, and this was the only way to prevent that.

"It's about fucking time." Killian's voice was gruff as he held the vial up to the light, tilting it one way and then the other, watching as the blood moved accordingly.

"It was harder than expected. The girl had been attacked by a nurse before I infiltrated the ward, so there were a lot of eyes on her."

"I hope you took care of him."

"I sent him on his way, but nothing else. Would you like me to take care of that?" Damien met Killian's gaze, struggling to not recoil from the malice lining the head vampire's face.

"I will take care of him if this girl is who we hope she is." Killian let his words hover in the air before he continued. "How did you get this?"

"The girl was hurt during an experimental therapy session." Killian's eyes locked onto Damien's, demanding more information. Damien refused to look away or show weakness to this vampire. Killian would never respect someone like that.

"Her primary psychiatrist brought in the girl who was attacked, which was the reason she was sent there in the first place. The girl, Elizabeth, attacked her and bit her neck. Apparently, she is one of us. While she was bleeding, I just filled up the vial." Damien shrugged, as if the whole narrative was of no consequence. And it really wasn't. In the end, he had gotten what he wanted and needed.

The girl would obviously be fine.

"How opportunistic. Do we know anything about this girl who attacked her, the one named Elizabeth?"

Damien shook his head before he realized that Killian's gaze had returned to the vial, an odd reverence in the way he watched the blood flow one way and then the other. "No, nothing beyond the basics. Elizabeth was attacked by the girl. After that, she spent time in the hospital getting stitches and healing from what the human doctors called an infection."

"Hmm. But she is one of us? She was turned?"

"It appears so, yes."

"Interesting." Killian palmed the vial before walking over to the bar again, grabbing a clean cup from the cabinet. Damien understood why Killian found that piece of information so interesting. It was something he had considered himself after the attack, after learning what Elizabeth had said during the session. It took more than a simple bite for someone to turn. Damien had questioned whether there was more to the story, more that the girl either didn't remember or refused to talk about.

"Do you think this is the girl we've been searching for? That you've been searching for?" Killian slowly opened the vial, inhaling it briefly as if it was a fine wine and he was searching for the underlying notes.

"I think this is the closest we have ever been."

Killian turned to him; his eyes hard. "That doesn't answer the question."

"Honestly Killian, I'm not entirely sure. I do think this is the best bet we have had. But there is a lot that doesn't add up."

"Such as?"

"The fact she doesn't feed is the big one. I went through her records as vague as they are and there isn't a report of her attacking a resident or that she is being given blood. She also doesn't have fangs, so I'm not sure she could feed." Damien stopped for a moment, thinking through everything he had learned about her, every piece that didn't fit together.

"But she is also immune to compulsion. I've tried, as did the nurse who attacked her in the first place. And there is what he said about her blood."

"He tasted her?" Killian's eyes darkened as hatred and murder flared.

"Barely, from what I gathered. Just enough to know she was different, that her blood was euphoric, as he called it." Killian made a noise as if he were considering each fact, also trying to figure out how everything fit together. All the pieces were there, but they weren't fitting. It was like a puzzle that had been altered slightly, just enough to render it wrong.

"But yes, I think this is her." A smile spread across Killian's thin lips, making it look more like a grimace than anything else, as he poured the blood into the cup.

"Let's find out." He knocked the cup back, his eyes closed. For a long moment, he was quiet, and Damien shifted in his chair nervously. If he was wrong, Killian's wrath would be devastating. There had been so many hopeful leads, so many failures, so many bodies left in the wake of failure. He wasn't sure Killian would allow him to survive another one.

But as Damien watched Killian lower the glass, he couldn't tear his eyes away from his boss's: bright and hungry. Hopeful. Excited. A tinge of red covered his lips.

"We found my little rose." The smile on the vampire's face made Damien squirm more. He knew he should be flushed with pride or relief or both. Instead, he only wanted to flee from the room, from that smile.

~ ~

CHAPTER 13

Elora

Her entire body was screaming as she tried to open her eyes, the feeling akin to being ripped apart and poorly stitched back together. Her mouth tasted horrible, and she realized she desperately needed something to drink. She would even take what passed for the orange juice that was given with breakfast. Anything to take away the feeling of sand.

With a groan, Elora attempted to move her head before understanding that it hurt to move, to think, to breathe. She tried to turn her head, but she felt the tugging of bandages on her skin. Another groan escaped her lips as she opened her eyes, despite how heavy they still felt.

I must have been sedated. Heavily sedated, she realized.

Her eyes scanned the room, taking in the familiar desk and bare walls. The lights were off, but the sunlight coming from the partially closed curtain illuminated everything. She pushed herself up onto her elbows, cursing loudly as pain radiated through every part of her body. Finally, after a few moments of exertion that left her panting, she was sitting up, her back against the paper-thin pillows. She closed her eyes and laid her head back on the headboard, trying to catch her breath.

Elora's hand reached up and touched her neck, feeling the bandages taped to her skin. She cursed softly at the sting as her fingers wandered over the area, knowing that if she looked in the mirror, it would be horrifically bruised.

"Are you awake?" Viktor stood in the doorway, a cart with a tray of food and medical supplies beside him. Elora met his eyes, which were full of something she couldn't fully understand, and smiled softly.

"How are you feeling?" He pulled the cart into the room, leaving it beside the desk as he dragged a chair next to the bed.

"Exhausted. Weak. And everything hurts."

"So, like you spent the night drinking and woke up with a hangover?" He grinned as she scowled at him, face contorted in faux annoyance.

"And you would know what that feels like?" He shrugged as Elora leaned back against the headboard and he grabbed the glass of water off the cart. Elora took it gratefully, hands wrapping around it as she brought it to her mouth, drinking greedily. Words were difficult, but talking with Viktor was easy. There was no picking the correct words, no second-guessing intentions or underlying meanings.

"I would. I've woken up with more than one." He held up a hand, lightly touching her wrist. "Slow down. You'll make yourself sick, and that's the last thing we need." Elora began drinking again, this time more slowly. She really didn't want to vomit, since she could only imagine what it would do to her already sore and aching body. After she took the last drink, she handed the glass back to Viktor, his careful gaze fixed on her face, trailing slowly to the bandage on her neck.

He set it back on the cart before he turned back to her, his hand raised towards her neck.

"I need to check the bandages. Can I do that?" Elora nodded while an overwhelming sense of gratitude washed over her. No one asked to touch them, to touch her. They roughly handled them, moving them one way or another, poking and prodding them like dolls.

His fingers touched her jaw and her eyes fluttered closed of their own accord. Lightly, gently, he pushed her face to the side, exposing her neck and the bandage. Elora played with the sleeves of her shirt, pulling them down and twisting them in her fingers. She forced herself to sit still as something in her stomach did flips, like there was a circus in there doing an entire performance. His hands moved from her jaw to the bandage and began to pull the tape up. A sharp hiss fell from her lips, and she felt him wince, muttering an apology as he continued until the bandage came un- done.

"How does it look?" Her voice was hoarse, and she wasn't sure it was from the lingering dryness. She tried to turn her head to look at him, to try to read his expression, but he cupped her jaw in his palm, holding her in place.

"Not as bad. The stitches will probably be able to come out in a few days. But I will check with the doctor on call to make sure."

"At least I added to the collection," she joked, a harsh chuckle filling the room as she glanced down at the scars covering her arms and chest, even if they were currently covered by her shirt. Viktor didn't laugh as a muscle in his jaw feathered and a cold liq- uid touched her neck, causing her to recoil.

"Just some antiseptic. To help prevent any infections." His now gloved fingers rubbed the gel across the bite marks. Despite the la- tex barrier, she still felt the warmth of his hands. Elora clamped her mouth shut, refusing to make the slightest noise, afraid he would feel guilty for the fact it hurt and pull away.

"How long was I out?" It seemed odd to her that the wounds were that far along in the healing process if the attack was as se- vere as she remembered it being. His hands left her skin, and she heard strips of tape being ripped apart, followed by the tearing open of a package. Elora resisted the urge to turn her head, to watch him as he prepared what was needed, to study his face along with whatever she might find displayed there. The large bandage covered the bite marks, and he pushed them down lightly before he added the tape.

His hand didn't leave her neck, but moved up to her jaw, turning her face towards him. She sucked in a breath, not prepared for the honesty she found in his eyes. Desire. Concern. Fear. Elora smiled sadly at him as his finger stroked her cheek. They had grown close over the years. Most nurses didn't last much longer than six months at a time, but Viktor had never left. She had never asked why, afraid of the answer, that she was the reason. Her heart leapt into her throat in response to the thought and she felt her body grow tingly, her blood heating under a gaze that had turned regretful. Her hand reached towards him, unsure and hesitant.

"Your bedside manner is impeccable. Very cozy." Viktor's hand dropped from her face as he jumped to his feet in response to the voice coming from the doorway. Neither of them had noticed Damien's approach, hadn't heard him standing there while he watched the two of them at such an intimate moment.

How long has he been standing there watching us? She glared at the vampire in the doorway, the knowing smile on his lips proof that he had seen enough to understand what had been occurring.

"When I touch her or try to help, I get slapped." Viktor said nothing, but Elora could see the way his body stiffened, how his hands tightened on the cart handle. He busied himself by collecting the dirty bandages and depositing them in the biohazard bag at the bottom of the cart. He took the tray of food and set it on the desk, not once looking at her.

While Viktor worked, Elora glared at Damien, whose smirk made her want to launch herself off the bed and claw at his face, hoping that maybe this time she would do more damage, even if she did end up sedated in the green room. Damien studied her for a moment, and she resisted the urge to shrink under the weight of his eyes, not wanting to give him that kind of power or satisfaction. There had been plenty of nurses like him over the years: men with over-inflated egos who enjoyed the position of control they had been given over other human beings. Nausea swirled in her gut at the idea of a vampire in that position. Indeed, a building full of controlled humans made for a verifiable feast for a vampire like Damien.

"The doctor wants to see her. Now." His voice echoed his amusement, almost like a laugh was lingering just below the surface. It gave it a music-like quality that would be appealing if he wasn't a horrible person and a vampire.

"She hasn't eaten yet," Viktor growled at him, eyes brimming with hatred. "I'll escort her once she eats."

Damien raised an eyebrow, the amused look on his face slipping for just a moment. A hint of annoyance flashed before a bored expression took over.

"Oh, I'm sure you would. But I have my orders. She wants to see her. Now." Viktor took a step towards him as Damien leaned against the door frame on his shoulder, arms crossed against his chest. He watched Viktor like a child watches a gift being handed to them at a party, excited for what could be, what could happen.

Elora pushed herself up and swung her legs over the side of the bed, gripping the frame as she prepared to stand. Her legs shook slightly as she pushed herself up, grabbing the back of the chair to hold herself steady. The room spun and for a moment she felt weightless, as if she was floating in the tension that filled the room.

"It's okay. I'm not really hungry yet." Viktor's shoulders fell, visibly relaxing as the tightness disappeared from his face.

"Let me help you." Elora waved Viktor's request away with a gesture and let go of the chair completely. With a slight whimper, she stood straight up with her hands at her side. Everything shifted once more, and she felt herself reach out, hoping the chair was still there. An arm wrapped around her waist while another grabbed her forearm and she glanced up with an embarrassed smile, expecting to see Viktor. Her breathing hitched when she found Damien instead.

"Get a wheelchair," Damien ordered over his shoulder. His eyes did not leave hers. Elora glowered at him, trying desperately to push him away even as his grip tightened. He shook his head slightly, face unreadable.

"Now." Elora realized with a start that Viktor hadn't moved from his spot behind Damien. His hands were fisted at his side, his face murderous as he stared at the spots where Damien's hands touched her. Elora nodded, trying to tell him that she was okay, that she would be fine during the time he stepped out of the room. After a long moment, he turned and marched out the door.

"You can let go. I'll hold on to the chair until Viktor gets back."

Damien smiled, leaning in close. "I think I prefer this."

She rolled her eyes but didn't move, knowing that even if she was in full health, she wouldn't be able to do much. His vampire strength greatly surpassed hers, capable of breaking her bones with a simple twist of his wrist, a tightening of his grip. They lapsed into a tense silence during which she watched the door while Damien watched her. She fidgeted slightly under his gaze, under the feel of his body so close to hers.

"Aren't relationships between residents and nurses forbidden? It feels very much like a conflict of interest." Elora's eyes shot up to his. There was a hardness to Damien, as if this whole interaction, the fact he was touching her, was deeply unpleasant for him, beneath him. She shifted again, trying to wiggle out of his grasp once more.

"There is no relationship," she snapped at him, her resolve to not respond to anything he said breaking apart at his question, at the insinuation.

"Not officially, of course. But do you want to know what I see?"

"Not really. But I'm sure you will tell me, anyway." He smirked at her before bending towards her.

"I see a man taking advantage of a young woman trapped in a psychiatric hospital. I see someone using her isolation and desire to be touched, to be loved." His voice was an annoying purr in her ear, his breath warm on her cheek before he leaned back.

Elora's hand extended before she realized what had happened, her body no longer under her control, and it collided with his face. The sound of the impact filled the room. His head snapped to the side from the impact, frustration and fury clear in his eyes when he stared back at her. She took advantage of his shock and pushed him away. Damien staggered back a step, his arms disappearing from where he held her. A cruel smile spread across his face as she collapsed to the floor, knees hitting the ground with a distinct thud that forced a cry of pain from her mouth.

"Fuck." The curse was out before she could stop it and she reached for the chair, struggling to pull herself back up.

"What the hell, Damien?" Viktor's voice seemed to bounce off the walls as he left the wheelchair in the hallway and rushed to her side. With only a few large strides, his arm was around her waist as he pulled her up. With a soft exhale, she sunk against him. Any remaining strength she had was gone between slapping Damien and trying to regain her footing once she hit the floor.

The vampire didn't say anything, just watched as Viktor led her to the wheelchair and lowered her into it. None of them said a word as she was wheeled away from the room and from Damien.

~ ~

CHAPTER 14

Elora

Dr. Montgomery had abandoned her desk today. Instead, she sat beside Elora in another large armchair. This deviation from their usual dynamic was anxiety-inducing, forcing Elora's hands to clutch the frayed sleeves of her shirt. Elora considered looking anywhere but at her psychiatrist, who was currently studying her like one would study a particularly strange painting, trying to discern what all the sharp edges and smooth shadows meant. Elora struggled to meet her eyes, looking around the room at nothing in particular until returning to that penetrating gaze that had been turned on her so many times, prying out secret after secret until there was nothing left to give. Finally, Dr. Montgomery sighed softly and leaned back in the chair, pinching the bridge of her nose as she closed her eyes for a moment.

"I have news. I'm not entirely sure how you will react to it. I have a nurse waiting just on the other side of the door in case this all goes badly." Elora noted the strain in the doctor's voice, the way each word felt forced out through gritted teeth. She didn't say anything, just watched as Dr. Montgomery smoothed the fabric of her skirt and adjusted slightly, turning more towards her patient. Thousands of options ran through Elora's mind, crashing into one another like tiny bouncing balls. She couldn't latch onto just one as all of them shifted and turned away before she could get a grip on them.

Elora had planned on questioning her psychiatrist about Elizabeth, about what had happened during the meeting, and what had happened to her foster sister. Had she been arrested? Or was this another situation where there would be an investigation that she would be told nothing about? Elora was willing to believe it would be the latter. She rubbed at her chest, at her sternum as she felt the strangest sensation that Elizabeth was nearby, that her sister was there with her.

"You are being released." Elora's brows darted up as her eyes widened in surprise. This had not even been a consideration, not even included in the dozens of possibilities that had flooded her mind.

"Why?" She wanted to recoil from how hesitant her question sounded, how her voice cracked as she asked. Dr. Montgomery took a deep breath and shook her head.

"People more powerful than me have deemed you fit for release. I am to get you ready to meet the outside world and transition."

"But I don't remember anything other than my foster family. Nothing before that. How can they release me?" Her eyes darted back and forth, her breathing becoming more rapid as she sat there trying to understand what was happening and why. None of it made sense to her. Not her release. Not Dr. Montgomery's explanation for it.

"Your memory, or lack thereof, isn't truly a problem as long as your therapy continues, which it will. The concern is whether you are a danger to yourself or others. And they do not see you as such."

"Do you?" Elora leaned forward and watched the psychiatrist for the tiniest sign, the smallest flinch that would reveal everything she truly thought.

"No, I don't. But it doesn't mean I necessarily agree with the decision." Elora nodded at Dr. Montgomery's words.

"And what do they make about my so-called continued delusions, the symptoms of the psychosis-based diagnosis?"

Dr. Montgomery shifted slightly in her chair, allowing her hands to rest in her lap as her gaze moved away from her patient's face, lost deep in thought, as if she was considering the question for the first time.

"I'm not sure that is being taken into account. But again, you will continue to see a professional. Not me, but someone who does outpatient work."

"When?" Elora wasn't entirely sure that she was ready to be released, was ready to enter the real world again. She had dreamed about it, about walking in the city to a coffee shop or buying art supplies at the craft store. She had imagined exactly what her apartment would look like, down to the tiny animal figurines on the shelves and the books lining the walls. She would have plants along the windows where the light was best and would probably remember to water them, but would forget sometimes and then feel guilty, apologizing profusely as she gave them more than they needed. Her clothing would be of her own choosing along with the food in the refrigerator, as long as she could afford it on the pay of wherever she worked. She always wanted to work with animals and had imagined a life taking care of dogs and cats.

But now, with freedom looming just within reach, she hesitated. Fear forced her body to clench, and her fingers dug into her wrist as she imagined getting lost in the streets she once knew, not being able to find a job or a place to live. Not being able to afford her medication, which would lead to an incident that would result in her coming right back here.

"By the end of the month." Dr. Montgomery's lips pursed together, her anger making her features sharper. "But I need you to help me understand something, Elora. I think that this will be an important element for us to understand, especially since my time with you is limited and coming to an end."

Elora stared down at her hand, preparing for the questioning she knew was coming. The answers formed themselves in her head, scripted responses that had become second nature during her time. She didn't want to give them any reason to keep her, despite her fears about being released. Even if she struggled, it would be better than here where a vampire was always haunting her steps, his sneer ever present no matter where she turned.

Dr. Montgomery cleared her throat before beginning.

"Elizabeth bit you. I watched her do it and I have it recorded. But if she is a vampire, and she bites you, does that make you one as well?"

"I don't know."

"Okay. Well, in that case, who turned Elizabeth into a vampire? If it was you, then why haven't you bitten anyone else?"

"I don't know." Elora winced as her voice got smaller and lower with each response, as she folded into herself. Her shoulders hunched inward, and she pulled her legs closer as if it would allow her to escape this line of questioning. The last time they had done this, Elora had thrown a paperweight at the doctor and ended up in the green room overnight to think about why she had reacted in such a violent manner.

And the answer was simple, despite Dr. Montgomery never accepting it—Elora didn't actually know. It was the same response she gave over and over again, without fail. The night she had attacked Elizabeth, the desire to bite her and drink had been overwhelming, the hunger taking control of her every limb, her every thought. A puppet to her base instincts to survive and drink her fill. In her dreams, when she remembered each and every moment of that night, Elora could hear herself screaming, feel her throat go raw from the sound tearing at her throat. But it hadn't stopped her. Elora's teeth had still sunk into her flesh, still drank until hands ripped her away.

But had she turned her sister into a creature? Elora didn't think so, but she couldn't be sure. From the bits and pieces, she remembered, there was more to the process than a simple bite. If that was all it took, the vampire population would vastly outnumber the human one in a matter of months.

After that night, she had never had another desire to feed. The hunger had worn off, the gnawing in her stomach dulling into an ache until it disappeared completely. Elora had also never exhibited any other signs that she somehow knew set vampires apart, even if she couldn't pinpoint exactly why she knew it, something that had driven her and Dr. Montgomery crazy in the early days of her therapy. Elora didn't have fangs, accelerated healing, and could eat human food.

It had been the only reason she had even entertained Dr. Montgomery's theories about her guilt and shame manifesting these delusions that she was severely mentally ill and in need of intense treatment.

"Hmm. Maybe that should be your homework until tomorrow morning? Consider those questions and we can discuss what you come up with." Elora's face fell at the assignment, a suggestion that was more of a command from Dr. Montgomery's lips. It was always the same with a suggestion that she think about why she held the delusions she did, why she behaved in a specific way, and what traumatic event her actions and fears could be traced back to. It was, at its core, a game of hide and seek where Elora never won, only gained more questions and more nightmares. More than that, homework was a sign of disappointment, a signal that Elora did not accomplish what she was meant to during the session itself. She didn't answer something correctly or respond accordingly. Despite this, Elora nodded and accepted the repetitive monotony that came with homework.

"What happened to Elizabeth after all that?" Dr. Montgomery raised her brows, surprised by the question.

"She is now a patient here. In the maximum-security ward." The door opened and a nurse Elora didn't remember walked in, pushing an empty wheelchair.

"That will be all for today. Our work truly begins in earnest now, Elora. I hope you recognize that." Elora didn't respond but slipped her legs out from underneath her. For a moment, she wondered whether she would be able to stand. Her legs were still weak and trembling under her weight. She gripped the arm of the chair, hoping the room would finally stop spinning, and that reality would settle once more into the familiar sight of Dr. Montgomery's office. Elora let out a sharp gasp and flinched as a hand grabbed her arm, fingers tight around her forearm, and led her to the wheelchair, removing her from the room.

~ ~

CHAPTER 15

Elora

Her sessions with Dr. Montgomery continued to follow a pattern for three weeks with a session every other day, as if to gain some insight that her years under the psychiatrist's care had yet to yield. She would ask the same questions, and Elora would give the same answers.

"Why did you attack Elizabeth?"

"Because I needed to. I was not in control."

"But you haven't attacked anyone else. Why?"

"I don't know."

"Do you think you are a vampire?"

"I don't know."

The constant refrain of "I don't know" repeated in Elora's head over and over until it became an echo in her mind, drowning out other thoughts and whispers that were her usual companions. Whispers like *little rose*, which had been a background sound for so much of her time in the facility. By the end of each question-and-answer session, Elora could see the irritation on Dr. Montgomery's face, the barely contained rage mixed with something akin to despair. Usually, at this point, she would call a nurse to escort Elora back to the dayroom, where her mind devolved into a swirling whirlpool of anxiety, fear, and unanswered questions. To a certain extent, Elora understood the woman's frustration, her desire to see some sort of progress before the deadline looming just around the corner came to pass. In a matter of days, Dr. Montgomery would have to sign the papers that officially stated she was no longer dangerous to herself or others.

Elora played with her sleeves as she rested in her usual chair and considered whether Dr. Montgomery's reluctance came from losing control over her patient or because she truly feared for Elora's well-being. Or the safety of those who would be subjected to her presence. Dr. Montgomery never seemed like a woman who handled losing very well and that was precisely what had happened here. Someone else came in and declared Elora was ready to be released. At least it didn't really matter what Elora said to her psychiatrist now. Once she left, she would have a new therapist, who she would see once a week and a caseworker. Dr. Montgomery called them a care team, but the distaste was clear on her face as she spat the words. Apparently, Amy, the caseworker, had found Elora a spot in a transition home with other women in similar situations, along with a job at a coffee shop.

"You will start the job a few days after getting to the house. It will give you time to settle in and make friends with other women. It'll let you acclimate, you know?" Amy's explanation had made sense at the time, but Elora couldn't shake the rising fear that something would go wrong.

"Are you excited to be leaving?" Elora glanced up from the television that she hadn't truly been watching to find Damien sitting on the arm of the chair to her left, an old recliner with cracked leather that didn't recline anymore. It always snagged her clothes when she sat in it.

Elora shifted her focus back to the television, which was apparently turned to some wedding reality show. "Don't you have something else to do? Something related to your job?" The woman on the TV that was in a ballgown with her hair up in an elaborate style was suddenly incredibly interesting.

"I'm taking that as a no."

"Of course, I am. Why wouldn't I be?" Even though she didn't look at him, she could sense his smirk, the way his eyes crinkled slightly in the corner, the darkened amused glint in his eyes. It is amazing how much she really wanted to hit him again as her hand tightened into a relaxed fist.

"I understand that you wouldn't want to. It is safe here. You know what to expect. There is routine. That is all most people want." Elora snorted at his words, rolling her eyes as his face shifted from smug to confused.

"Adorable that you think it's safe here. We both know some nurses are not to be trusted." With a small grunt, Damien shifted on the arm of the chair, crossing his legs in front of him as Elora wondered if he understood he was part of that statement.

"Fair enough. But it doesn't change the fact it's clear you are afraid to leave, afraid to be on your own, having to live your own life and make choices outside this place."

"Excellent analysis. Maybe they should give you a promotion." She listened to him snicker slightly as the woman twirled in her gown and her friends started crying.

"You know, you will have to have a job and pay bills. Here, you just have to see Dr. Montgomery and keep pretending to be crazy. Sounds like a fairly good situation."

"Pretend to be crazy?" Elora repeated, glaring up at his smiling face. She would indeed really like to hit him again.

"It looks like you healed up well. Viktor must have taken excellent care of you." Apparently, he didn't want to clarify what he was referring to.

"Jealousy isn't a good look for you." Her eyes still shifted to Viktor, who was talking quietly to a resident towards the back of the day room by the windows. The bright sun that streamed through illuminated his golden skin, rendering him all light and shadows as he talked to the man who spoke to his dead wife. Grief had turned this man's head, leaving him with ghosts and whispers of her voice in his ear. Only now, the man seemed distraught, his hair pulled in all different directions, his face red and blotchy from crying. Sometimes he wasn't able to hear her voice because they got into an argument—the silent treatment from the ghost of his wife. Elora supposed it was romantic in its own way, the way love endured grief, through the finality of death.

"I wouldn't call it jealousy. Just a man trying to do his job."

"We both know only part of that statement is true." Elora left her statement hanging between them like something tangible, as if Damien could pick it up and dissect it. His eyes narrowed on her as his jaw hardened.

"Tell me, which part is true? The jealousy or something else?"

"Just stop." Elora ran her hand down her face before she glanced back up at him, her patience for this entire conversation gone in a single moment. With the nightmares and the constant therapy sessions, she had nothing left to give this vampire who wanted nothing more than to irritate her for some reason.

"Stop what, exactly? Discussing the relationship between the two of you, which is part of my job here?" His eyes had taken on a dark shine and a hardness that put her on edge. After taking a deep breath, she pulled at her sleeves, bundling the fabric in her fists.

"There is no relationship. Are you trying to get him fired? Is that what is happening?"

Damien leaned in towards her, inches away from her. All she could smell, even above the disinfectant and stale body odor, was his cologne, a scent that felt so familiar it squeezed her, forcing her stomach into knots upon knots until she was sure she would pass out. Elora fought the urge to pull back, to disappear into the chair she had spent so much of her time in.

"I know what a dedicated man looks like, what a man obsessed with a woman acts like." Elora scoffed, trying to brush off his words even though they filled her with something heated, like a small ember that warmed her from the inside out. She had known that for a while. Yet, she had ignored it every time and she rationalized it as caring for a resident, comparing it to how Viktor interacted with the other residents. But she had noticed it with how he cared for her wounds, how he made sure she ate, and that she didn't retaliate against Dr. Montgomery after some of the more painful sessions. How his gaze would soften when he saw her, how his hand lingered just a little too long, just enough to not arouse suspicion.

"I am his patient. Caring for me is part of the job, just like everyone else here." Damien's smile widened as if she said exactly the right thing.

"I highly doubt that, little rose." He reclined back with an expectant look on his face. Her vision darkened and her breathing hitched at the phrase she had heard whispered so many times. For years, the phrase had been there, lingering in the nightmares and waking hours, a soft call or plea in the stale air, a smooth touch across her skin. It always made her flinch and jerk away from the direction it came from, as if she was trying to avoid it or hide from it. If she could only disappear, it wouldn't be able to find her.

"What the fuck did you just say?" Damien's grin grew as her hands clenched into fists in her sleeves. He leaned forward once more, smiling widely for the first time, so his fangs were displayed only for her.

"I said, little rose, that I doubt that." Rage raced through her body, making her muscles constrict as if she were preparing for a battle, and for all she knew, she was. Damien's eyes revealed his surprise at the reaction for just a moment before he stood as well, staring her down despite being only a few inches taller than her. Elora stepped forward, embracing the tension that radiated off his body, knowing that he could, without a doubt, sense her own. She trembled as her heart raced, beating against her chest like it was just as angry, desperate to break free and seek violence on her behalf.

"Sit back down, Elora." Viktor's voice carried across the dayroom and several people glanced up from their puzzles or card games to see what the drama was. Apparently, it wasn't worth their focus as they shifted their attention back to their source. Despite this, Elora's eyes did not shift from Damien, while a smirk played on the corner of his lips.

"Damien, get back to the nurse's station and start prepping the evening medication. Elora, I said sit back down." The resident with Viktor started to cry, his wails filling the tense silence as the rest of the room decided Damien and Elora were indeed worth the attention.

"Do what your lover says, little rose." His words were soft and meant only for her.

Acting only on rage and instinct, Elora leaped at him, her body crashing into his as they both fell onto the grimy linoleum floor. Damien let out a rough curse, voice harsh and guttural as his head bounced, the sound echoing. His expression finally fell, the smug grin disappearing into surprise and then anger as Elora pulled her fist back and brought it down on his face, not aiming but seeking only to damage. Her breaths left her body in pants, desperate and brutal as she grinned at the feel of his cheekbone against her knuckles, growing wider as he attempted to squirm away. Once more, her fist met his face, this time hitting his nose and blood burst forth. It poured down his lips and then his chin while her fist was covered in gore.

An urge to lick it off pushed at her peripheral, a voice explaining the ecstasy she would feel, the beauty of the taste that would be beyond anything she had ever had before. Her mouth went dry as she hesitated, staring at the crimson that was stark against her sun-deprived skin. It smelled divine, she realized as heavy steps approached from behind. A hand clasped under her arms and yanked her away from the body on the floor. With one last burst, Elora's foot extended out, kicking Damien in the stomach before Viktor set her aside to assess the damage.

Elora didn't bother to wait to see if Damien stood up or if his nose stopped bleeding or if his face would bruise. Instead, she turned and raced down the hallway toward her room, feeling the floors shift underneath her feet and the wall shrink in on her.

"Elora, stop!" But she could barely hear Viktor call her name over the sound of blood rushing in her ears, over the sound of her own uneasy breaths.

The door to her room slammed shut behind her as she collapsed, her knees striking the floor with a harsh thud that should have elicited a cry of pain. But she was incapable of feeling anything other than fear or panic or whatever caused someone to feel like the world was ending in a single solitary moment, that the room was folding in on itself despite the fact it was also spinning. She tried to draw in a breath, but her chest felt compacted, as if there was a weight on it, rendering it unable to expand to allow for oxygen. Her eyes locked onto the floor in front of her, but it was blurry, undefined, and distant.

With a sharp exhale that was more of a whimper and a scream merged into one, she ripped at her sleeves, her fingers grabbing and pinching and holding the fabric. The shirt was too tight, the fabric burning her skin as she pulled at the collar and dragged it over her head, desperate to be rid of whatever was containing her, rendering her unable to move or breathe or scream.

Breathe. Just breathe. But the thoughts were lost in the haze of panic, tiny bubbles that giggled and popped each time she reached for one. She wanted to tell herself to stop clawing, that the hands were gone, that there was no one there, but the thoughts wouldn't formulate, and her mind wouldn't listen, an enemy set on destroying her. Only one sound repeated clearly in her mind, a whisper, a threat, a reminder: *Little rose.*

She knew that she knew the term, that someone had used it on her as a nickname, a term of endearment, even if it didn't feel right to call it that. For a moment she could almost hear their voice, a distant memory hidden under layer after layer of dirt.

At the sensation of something wet, Elora's breath hitched, and she glanced down, struggling to focus through the haze around the outer edges of her vision.

Blood. Sweet and bright, it called to her like a melody she knew in childhood, like a siren's call promising every hope and dream she ever had. And then she could only watch as her fingers dug into the skin, ripping back and leaving flesh underneath fingernails kept short to ensure this didn't happen. It wasn't scratches that appeared, but cuts, broken skin with red that seeped through, forming tiny drops before running down her arms, crashing to the floor beneath her. Over and over. Her nails dug in and pulled, yanked, ripped away more and more each time.

She could only watch, as if these were not her hands, her fingernails doing the damage of their volition. She was simply a marionette to her panic and the desperate desire to quell it by any means necessary. Pain, pure and clear, anchored her at the moment, and forced her back to reality as the door behind her burst open and slammed against the wall behind it.

She whimpered slightly at the sound, her fingers frozen above her skin of their own accord, as if the puppet master had run and hid from whoever was there in the darkness.

"Stop."

Massive arms enveloped her, holding her arms down so that the scratching and ripping stopped, leaving only her screams as they tore from her throat. She thrashed in their hold, throwing her limbs and kicking out in the hopes of hitting someone, anyone, as long as they let her go. As long as they didn't hurt her.

Not again.

"Elora! Stop! Listen to me." She stopped, recognizing the firm voice coming from in front of her, and she hung her head as her body went limp in response.

"Don't let them hurt me. Don't let them touch me. Please." Elora begged and pleaded with the person who held her. She just needed to know that they weren't there, even if she wasn't sure who they were. The boogeyman from her nightmares, the man sitting in the corner giving permission to the others.

"No one is here but me. No one but me." His fingers ran through her hair as she returned to herself and regained control of her body and thoughts and words.

"What the fuck?" Elora tensed as the other voice shattered through the briefest moment of peace. Viktor ignored him as he kept his arms tight around her torso, forcing her arms to remain at her side. She took a deep breath and relaxed into his grip, letting her head rest against his chest. She couldn't help but welcome the scent and warmth of someone so consistent. An anchor in a raging sea.

"Elora, I'm not going to sedate you. Okay? But I do need to get you onto your bed so we can look at your arms."

She didn't move, unsure that she even could. It was too hard, and her body was so heavy. Every breath was agony, and her arms were on fire now that reality had sunk back in. Now that she felt what she did, felt each cut, each scratch, even the developing bruises on her knees. Instead, she tried to nod before she closed her eyes.

Viktor stood and moved behind her. One hand gripped her upper arm and pulled her up enough for him to slip his other hand around her waist, lifting her to her feet. He held her steady for just a moment, eyes set only on hers as he waited for her to adjust. Gently, slowly, Viktor pulled her over to the bed since her feet had decided not to work. With a soft grunt, she fell into the thin mattress and rough blanket, barely recognizing that this meant blood would get all over the sheets.

With stilted movements, she lay on her back, arms on either side as she stared at the ceiling. She understood but couldn't care that she was on display before the two male nurses in just the hospital-issued bralette. Only the female nurses had seen her shirtless, when they were tasked to check for new injuries when she was first admitted and was still on suicide watch. The fact they were here now would probably be an issue further down the line, but her mind refused to settle on that or anything else. Only that her scars were there in all their shameful glory, each puncture wound, each cut and incision.

Elora tried to focus on the movement she could hear in the room. The whispers and angry mutters became her distraction from the pain that demanded that she cry, that she whimpers at their magnificence. After a moment, Viktor was back crouched beside the bed, and she could smell the cleansing pads before they even touched her skin. Slowly, Viktor cleaned the blood from her arms, the silence interrupted only by soft curses from his mouth each time she flinched.

Finally, he placed what felt like gauze along her arms in straight lines before he wrapped it in even more and taped it. He didn't move once he was done, and the moment stretched into what felt like hours, like a lifetime, in this room. Elora knew he wanted to ask questions about what happened. She knew they were there on the tip of his tongue and only his lips and teeth held them back. It would be pointless. The ability to speak had escaped her, leaving her mute before the two nurses.

She shuddered as his hand covered hers and her eyes closed, tears burning. She wanted him—or someone, anyone—to gather her in his arms and hold her, reassure her that no one could hurt her even if it was a lie. Without being able to explain it, she fell into the aftermath of the fear that had her in a chokehold so tight that she couldn't breathe or think or feel anything other than it. Her fear was greedy, desiring all her attention and willing to devour and twist anything else to make sure it happened. A toxic lover that never left.

"They can't get you here." His words were a whisper, an easy reassurance that she was not sure she believed.

His hand left hers as he stood and pulled the coarse blanket over her body, lifting her arms so they would rest on top.

"Sleep, Elora," he commanded softly before he turned and left, shutting the door behind him. She knew that she wouldn't, that the nightmares would come unbidden, ravenous like starved animals that fed on her cries of pain and terror. Instead, she stared at the wall and allowed herself to fall into her torment.

CHAPTER 16

Damien

To be perfectly honest, Damien wasn't expecting the fist that collided with his jaw after he and Viktor made it to the break-room, despite him knowing he should have. Instead, he had simply expected to clock out for the night and feed once he made it back to Ashcroft Tower. He had already been hit numerous times that day, plus kicked in the gut, and hadn't expected it to happen again.

His head jerked to the side, and he felt his lip re-split and bleed, the taste familiar and tangy on his tongue. It would swell, if only for a short time. He fought off the urge to smirk at Viktor standing in all his rage in front of him. It was a hard hit for a human, though not as hard as Elora's had been. Which was strange all on its own, but he would decipher that later. The hit from Viktor would do some damage and cause some pain, but in about an hour there would be no sign anything had hit him. He stifled a laugh as he rubbed his jaw before he met Viktor's red face and rage-filled eyes.

"What the fuck did you say to her?" Viktor's voice shook as he spoke, as if he was barely holding himself back.

Damien considered the question for a moment, despite know-ing exactly what had caused the scene they had just walked away from. But he wasn't about to admit that to Viktor, wasn't about to say it had been the use of a pet name. So, instead, he would go with the fact she had been irritated with him prior to its usage. It had been clearly written all over her face while he offered his insight into her leaving the facility as well as her relationship with the man standing just a few inches away from him, trying to intimidate him. Damien could admit he had been purposefully taunting her for no other reason than he was bored. Bored with the room filled with either tears and whimpers or dead silence. Bored with medication and the smell of bleach and despair.

But when he had used the pet name, something had changed. Her eyes had gone dark, not a single trace of that strange green remaining, and her body had tensed as if preparing for something horrific, preparing to defend herself against unseen assailants. Then she had stood and lunged at him, landing hit after hit once she had him shocked and confused on the ground. She was fast, her moves quicker and stronger than he had anticipated. He wanted to explain it all away as having been in shock or that he was maintaining his disguise as a nurse and that was why she managed to land so many hits, but that wouldn't be the full story. The truth was that her speed had left him at a disadvantage despite being a vampire and Killian's second-in-command, known for his violence and brutality.

Her file had stated that she didn't remember anything prior to living with her foster family, but if the pet name elicited that type of reaction, it had to be a lie. The only problem, he realized with a sinking feeling, was that now she knew Killian had found her. He had asked the head vampire why the girl had left, ran away and hid from anyone trying to recover her. It was incomprehensible that someone would leave a place where they were taken care of, their every whim catered to without a second thought. A place where they had been loved with such devotion. Killian had said she had grown rebellious, as most teenagers growing into their identity and power do.

It was amusing and infuriating all at once. Rebellion was something only the privileged had the capacity for. For others, it was about simple survival, whether that meant stealing food and other things or breaking into abandoned houses, so they had a place to sleep. Some people had to take care of those around them, people who needed their help to survive. To Damien, running away from warmth and safety was selfish and childish since he knew what the alternative was—alleyways, days without food, and shoplifting stuff to sell at the underground market that catered to those who wanted more illegal items.

He felt it as his lip started to curl into a sneer as he met the man's eyes.

"We were discussing you, actually. And her impending release. Just the usual gossip." Not a full lie, simply one by omission.

"Are you toying with her on purpose? With me?"

Damien didn't answer immediately because the answer would be a yes, and he wasn't sure that he would get a very positive reaction. It might even earn him another punch and he wasn't about to tempt that fate again in one day. Instead, his mind traveled back to what he saw when he followed Viktor into the room: her shirtless body kneeling on the floor, fingernails digging into her already heavily scarred skin. He could only wonder where they came from. Some of the scars had looked like puncture wounds, but that made no sense unless she had allowed vampires to feed from her while she was gone from Killian.

"Has she ever freaked out like that before?"

Viktor studied him for a moment, the desire for his own answer still obvious as he considered the question. Damien wasn't entirely sure the human would answer and that he would ignore it and walk away. He had expected her to have a negative reaction to the pet name and the taunting, but that was beyond anything he had thought possible. He hadn't thought she would attack him before she ran off. The blood and cuts on her arms had left him frozen in the doorway, simply staring because that was all he could do. It had been fear and rage and despair all mixed into one horrifying display.

Damien had never thought fingernails kept that short could be such an effective weapon.

After a moment, Viktor turned from him and opened his locker to collect the few things in there: a jacket, car keys, and a water bottle. He ran his free hand down his face, rubbing along the stubble on his jawline.

"Not in a very long time." There was a tinge of regret, of sadness in his admission.

"It's not in her file," Damien responded as he pulled his own car keys from his locker.

Viktor nodded in confirmation before he fell quiet for a long moment. If it wasn't in her file, then the details were in the portions Damien hadn't been able to get access to so far. Not even his connections through Killian's tech unit had been able to find it, and it had been frustrating, to say the least. Even backed by all the technology and personnel that the Ashcroft family had to offer, he hadn't been able to find even a trace of those files.

"I wasn't around for it. I was told about it after I started by Dr. Montgomery. There were two instances. One shortly after she arrived for the first time and the other was after her release was denied. The second was almost fatal from what I understand. After that, she fell into what you see most days."

No one had told Damien about this part of her history, and none of the nurses he had talked to had known about it either. It seemed like it was a well-kept secret that so far included Dr. Montgomery and Viktor, along with Elora herself.

"Why do you know about it? No one else seems to know anything about her." Viktor's brow raised as he stared down him.

"I think the better question is why you are so interested in her."

"Don't worry. I'm not trying to get involved in your patient. I'll leave relationships with women in psychiatric hospitals to the professionals." Damien could see the exact moment Viktor understood the implications of his words, the insinuation that Viktor was preying on someone who would seek a connection in any form. Viktor narrowed his eyes and studied Damien for a moment, a range of emotions flashing across his face—hesitation, anxiety, rage, and something Damien couldn't fully read.

"She also took a few nurses down with her the second time. Beat them up. None of them came back to this ward and actively refused to work anywhere near her." Viktor slipped his backpack over his shoulder before he grabbed his jacket and gave Damien a hard look.

"Just in case you are thinking about messing with her any more than you already are. But from the look of your face, maybe you already learned that lesson." He slammed his locker shut and stalked out of the room.

~ ~

CHAPTER 17

Damien

Damien knew before even he walked into the office that Killian was pissed. As he stepped off the elevator, he was welcomed by shouts and a sharp cry followed by muffled pleading. For a brief moment, no longer than a single heartbeat, Damien considered waiting to give Killian the news, to explain what happened at the hospital and his role in it. If the head vampire was already this angry, then how would he react to the girl's breakdown and everything that came with it?

Damien shook his head at the thought, forcing it from his head. That would be the worst possible approach. If Killian found out Damien had kept the information to himself, had delayed for even the smallest amount of time, there would be hell to pay. He would be the one screaming on the floor in the office. With a soft exhale, Damien pushed the door open after a brief knock. His eyes instantly found the man lying on the floor, blood dripping from split lips onto the carpet, his nose broken. Damien couldn't place him, but he took in the thinning hair and wrinkles around dull brown eyes. All he knew was that the man was human and probably worked under Killian in some capacity. Probably an informer or dealer in human recruits, who were usually people who were picked up from the streets and given the job of providing blood.

With a nod at Killian, Damien made his way to the bar and poured himself a drink before settling into a chair to watch the rest of the scene unfold. Normally, Damien would be here for any type of information gathering, especially from reluctant guests. It was his specialty, the very thing that gave him his reputation.

"Get the fuck out of here. Don't leave the building. I'm not done with you." Killian turned from the man as he scurried to his feet, half running, half crawling out the door.

Damien took a drink while Killian grabbed a bar towel and started to wipe the blood off his knuckles. It was always something that Damien respected about the vampire. He wasn't afraid to get his hands dirty and partook in punishments personally. And considering what Damien had seen in the past, the man had gotten off easy, considering he could still walk.

"Update?" Killian leaned against his desk as he studied his hands, which still bore traces of blood. His face twisted with disgust as he tried once more to get it off.

"The girl had a breakdown. Total and complete breakdown. She—" Damien hesitated, not sure how to phrase what had happened, what he had seen. Truly, he wasn't sure breakdown was a strong enough word to describe it. He had been able to smell the panic and fear in the room, a bitterness mingling with the sweet scent of her blood. Damien had tortured people, cut off fingers and ears when ordered to do so, watching each victim fall apart piece by piece. None of that had touched what he had seen when he followed Viktor through that door.

"She what?" Damien sat up a bit straighter. The bite in Killian's voice put him on edge.

"She hurt herself. Ripped up her arms with her nails. I've never seen anything like it." With a shake of his head, Damien drained his glass, unsure of what else to say. Killian didn't respond, just watched Damien for a moment before he strolled over and took the glass from his hand.

"We—" The glass Killian had taken from him shattered against the wall, tiny crystal fragments spread over the floor, settled into the grooves of the wood. Damien stilled, forced the surprise from his face, replaced it with a mask of pure obedience as he waited for what came next.

"What did you do, Damien? I told you she was not to be harmed! She was not to be hurt in any way! Period!" Killian was rooted in place in front of him, staring down at Damien's face with eyes that promised murder, promised a punishment like the one that left Damien with a broken wrist and jaw. Both of which had taken days to heal, even with his accelerated healing.

"I didn't do anything, Killian. We talked. I used your name for her. I wanted to see if she remembered who you were, to see if her memory loss was a lie. After I said that, she beat the crap out of me and ran off. When we found her, she was using her nails to cut her arms. We got her calmed down, and she was basically co-matose when I left." Hopefully, the explanation would help temper Killian's anger.

Damien ran his fingers through his hair before he ran his hand along his death head moth tattoo and the image of her in that room rushed back. Not that they were ever too far away. The vision of her shirtless, covered in not only fresh wounds, but hundreds of scars, was seared into his memory. He couldn't unsee it, was unable to push it away. At that moment, he had felt something for her beyond disdain and repulsion. He had felt fear even if he wasn't sure if it was on behalf of her or himself. A fear of what she was capable of doing or what Killian would do to him. Damien shook his head, not willing to pursue that line of thinking. She didn't deserve it, not when she had shown she was nothing but a spoiled child, throwing away every gift and opportunity given to her.

Killian stared down at him a moment longer, probably taking in the bruise along his cheek before he turned and poured another drink, ignoring the broken glass across the room. There was a brief flash of pride on his face as he took in Damien's healing injuries.

"We?" Killian's voice was calm, cold.

Damien cursed silently at his mistake. He hadn't meant to include the human when he debriefed Killian on what happened. Not out of any loyalty to Viktor, but rather because he was already a snag Damien didn't want to deal with. Putting him on Killian's radar would only further complicate things, since he would only see the human as a major issue, expecting Damien to deal with him as he had others in the past.

"Another nurse. His name is Viktor. A human." Killian nodded and handed him a new glass of whiskey.

"And was it you or him who was able to put a stop to her breakdown?"

"Him. I just followed him into the room and helped with the cleanup. They have a relationship, though it doesn't seem to be sexual in nature." Not sexual, but not exactly platonic.

"Hmm." Killian reclined in the chair across from Damien and crossed his ankle in front of him as he rested his arms on the sides of the chair.

"Your failure to keep her safe aside, Damien, you will still be charged with getting her to me. Despite this outburst, I will make sure she is still released within the week. I've grown impatient while waiting. Have you considered how you will get her here?"

Damien took a breath, only too happy to move on from the discussion of Viktor. If the human was lucky, Killian would forget he existed. He leaned forward and placed his forearms on his knees as he prepared to tell Killian his plan.

"I think the easiest time to move her here is when she is going to her transition home. She will already be in transit, so it is just a matter of making sure the right people are driving the car and are traveling with her."

"Anything you need from me for this plan to work?"

"Change the discharge papers if possible. If she doesn't show up to the original location, then someone will come looking for her or start asking questions, maybe even go to the police and file a missing person report. It wouldn't be a problem but would be a headache that is easily avoidable."

"Done. I will have the tech team change them the day she is released, so no one notices."

"I'm not sure if this is either already planned or done, but have rooms or a room set up for her. Doors that lock from the outside. Either no windows or windows with glass that won't break. Nothing sharp in there. Nothing that could be used to hurt herself. Not even a mirror."

"You think we need to furnish a prison for her? Another room like her current one?"

"I think she won't be happy about being tricked. She is already hesitant about being released and has shown she can and will hurt herself. Apparently, it has happened before." Damien took a deep breath before finishing and refused to look up and see the expression on Killian's face as he learned of her self-destructive nature.

"It's just better to prepare for it." Killian watched him, studying each feature of his face as if it would reveal something crucial that he was looking for.

Finally, he responded. "Her room will be prepared like you said. Though it is disappointing that she might not be happy about coming home."

Damien shrugged, finishing off his whiskey before setting the glass on the table and standing, prepared to finally leave. He hadn't fed before coming to Killian's office and the gnawing sensation was growing worse along with the other effects—weakness, irritation, a desperation that led to bad decisions. The hunger made it difficult to hold his tongue as question after question barreled through his mind. Basic questions he probably should have asked before, when he had first been given the job. He knew the girl had run away because of some basic rebellion, but why hadn't she come back? How had she managed to stay hidden for so long? Why had she wanted to? Was she really as young as she looked, especially considering how old Killian was? It was a human myth that vampires didn't age, that their aging process halted at the moment they turned. No, they aged, just slowly.

Damien would look twenty-four for decades before appearing to age even the littlest bit, even if he had been a vampire for six years.

But he didn't ask questions. He never did. It had only been a few years after he was turned before Killian brought him into this very office and gave him this mission. He had asked him, begged him to find his daughter when everyone else had failed and been punished for it. Most of them were dead now, a monument to what happens to failures. And those lives were stacked at the girl's feet.

Damien knew he should have been terrified of taking on a mission other vampires had died for. But he had been younger and relatively freshly turned since the settling process took up to a year for some. He had wanted to impress the vampire who had turned him, ripping him from growling stomachs and alleyway bedrooms. He didn't hesitate before saying yes, voice firm and unwavering.

And still, Damien did not ask questions. The answers would change nothing, would do nothing but assuage a curiosity he should not have. Harboring questions was dangerous. Asking them even more so.

Killian nodded at him, granting him permission to leave and he moved towards the door, already tasting the blood he would go straight towards.

"Damien." He stopped at the sound of his name with his hand on the door and cursed himself for not moving faster. His body clenched in response to the delay.

"The human will have to die. I won't share my daughter with one." Fuck. That was exactly what he had been afraid of.

CHAPTER 18

Elora

Elora tossed another long-sleeve shirt into the suitcase provided by the hospital, rethinking the final meeting with Dr. Montgomery that morning. The psychiatrist had expressed her disdain for Elora's release, citing her most recent outburst of violence as the reason why. Elora wasn't sure she believed her. The woman had seemed more stilted than before, more reserved, almost regretful during their meeting.

"I'm just worried about your safety." She had adjusted in her chair before she leaned forward, an earnest expression on her face.

"My safety or everyone else's?" Elora highly doubted the doctor was worried about her and was instead fearful her delusions would land her right back here, probably in this very room. Dr. Montgomery hadn't answered, just reiterated the plans for her release, her drive to the transition house, her new care team made up of a therapist, psychiatrist, and caseworker. Elora hadn't realized the therapist wouldn't be prescribing her medication since Dr. Montgomery had always handled both, but it was explained that was how outpatient treatment tended to work. Lack of professionals or something along those lines.

Elora didn't have much to pack. Her mostly blank journal where she was supposed to record her feelings, any memories she may recall, and her nightmares. Her collection of long-sleeved shirts, wireless bras, and underwear. There was some newer clothing added to the small bag. A dress, a button-up shirt, and a pair of slacks. For her new job, she figured. On top of the clothing laid a small pile of goodbye cards from the other residents, a tradition even if it wasn't one they partook in regularly. Anytime someone was released, the group made them cards as a way of saying goodbye and dealing with the crushing disappointment that it hadn't been them.

She was the first person to be released in roughly a year and, as the cards demonstrated, they were all horribly out of practice. The cards contained basic messages of good luck and dark humor mixed with a copious amount of glitter that would more than likely be on her clothes by the time she unpacked. Elora welcomed it on her socks and shirts. It was a reminder of the dysfunctional family that had been built through years of forced proximity and listening to each other's deepest fears, anxieties, desires, and traumas.

The psychologist in charge of group therapy on Thursday had asked how she was feeling about leaving and each pair of eyes had turned to her, waiting for her response. They sat in a circle on cracked plastic chairs, squirming as they tried to get comfortable, focus wandering over the room or anything else than the current one. Sun streamed through the windows lining the wall, a perpetual tease to what they only felt on their skin for an hour every day. Elora let out a breath, having prepared for this question, and gave them the same answer everyone gave when asked.

"Nervous mostly. I've been here forever. I don't know what to expect." The other residents nodded sagely, understanding better than anyone ever could that there was terror that came with this unknown. Elora had always thought that the line about being nervous was simply that—a line given to a group of people who were being left behind. That it was a way to lessen the blow that they were getting out and the rest were not. But no, the admittance of the all-consuming fear was very real.

Elora stood in front of the door to ward, bags packed, and good-byes said. Behind her was the world she had known for years. The cafeteria where they all took their meals, the day room where they watched the same shows over and over again, and the green room where they were placed when they needed to calm down. Underneath the medication, harsh caretakers, horrific food, and Dr. Montgomery, this had become her home. And now she was leaving it, not knowing how to feel beyond the strange pit in her stomach, the desire to turn around and shut herself in her assigned room.

Viktor came up behind her and stood there while they waited for the elevator to reach their floor. He didn't say anything, and she simply held her bag in a death grip, forcing back tears. The elevator finally stopped with a chime that seemed to echo through the empty hallways and both Viktor and Elora stepped on for him to use his keycard to access the first floor.

"A car is waiting for you. They will take you directly to your new house." Dr. Montgomery and the caseworker, Amy, had already explained all this to her. Multiple times, as if the anxiety of her release would allow her to forget. Viktor didn't need to explain it again.

"The house really isn't far from here. Maybe a couple of miles over towards Archway Park." Elora held in a breath as she remembered the park. She and Elizabeth had spent time there before everything happened. It was so close to the place she had begrudgingly called home.

"Maybe you can visit? We can get coffee or whatever people do outside of a hospital." His face scrunched slightly before it resumed his professional blankness. No response, no smile or hint of a grin. Nothing.

The elevator chimed again, and they were finally on the first floor, a space she hadn't seen in five years. When she was dragged through here the first time, she had been partially drugged, everything blurry, shadows of shapes. Now it was bright. So incredibly bright. Tall windows lined the wall in front of her, from the floor to the ceiling. The walls were painted a cream color and were filled with paintings of either board members or of the hospital at various points throughout its existence. To the right was the welcome desk, a long gray counter where a young woman sat in blue scrubs. She looked up briefly before turning back to whatever she was working on. Throughout the room were various chairs and benches where people could sit while they waited to be helped.

It was beautiful, elegant in a way that hid what the building was truly for. Nothing like the floor she had lived on. But she supposed if a person were expected to leave their loved ones in the care of the professionals here, they would want to give off the best possible first impression. And without cracks in the walls and floors, matching furniture without rips and tears, and wide-open spaces, they were successful in that endeavor.

Viktor and Elora slowly walked to the double doors, and she took a deep breath. *Inhale. Hold. One. Two. Three. Exhale.*

He held up his badge to the sensor beside the door before pushing it open once it beeped. Elora brought her hand up to shield her eyes. It had been bright in the lobby; the unfiltered natural light was foreign to her eyes at this point. She was used to fluorescent lights broken up by the obscured sunlight that came in through grimy windows and was partially blocked by the building surrounding the courtyard on four sides. Not a single beam of uninterrupted sunlight reached them, only shards that littered the concrete lined with boxes of half-dead flowers. Not even they could bloom in such a dark space.

The landscape of the hospital was, of course, perfect. Trees, hedges, and flowers surrounded the stone sidewalks and driveway that circled up to the lobby. It was strange to smell something other than bleach and sweat, body odor, and disinfectant. She could almost see the gates that waited at the end of the long driveway along with the road that lay just beyond that. She took in the flowers, the red and white of the rose bushes, the wild pink and yellow flowers growing in between them. With a deep inhale, she tried to shed the smell of the hospital, breathe it out like a toxin. Her eyes roamed over the space once more before they stopped at the large black car where Damien waited for her.

Instantly, Elora froze as every limb refused to move and her feet rooted themselves into the stone steps that she had been ready to walk down just a moment ago. Damien sauntered over, that smug grin plastered to his face, as he reached to take her bag from her. With panic etched across her features, she glanced up at Viktor, whose own expression was stern. Every smooth line deepened as the usual warmth shifted into a cold hardness that made her recoil.

"I'll take that." Without breaking eye contact with Viktor, she let Damien take the bag from her hand.

"Aren't you coming with us? I thought you would want to see me to my new home." Her voice was quiet. She couldn't help but be annoyed at how desperate she sounded. She had meant it to be teasing, a way to crack what she hoped was a façade.

"No. Why would I? My job is done." Elora flinched and took a step away, fighting back tears, each moment they had shared racing through her mind even though in this moment all she wanted was to erase them. Maybe then his words wouldn't hurt so much, maybe the confusion that filled her entire being would disappear.

"Understood. Thank you for doing your job, then." She kept her eyes straight ahead and stared at the large trees lining the driveway, counting each and every one until her heart started beating again.

The caseworker, Amy, leisurely exited the building, passed Viktor, and stood in front of Elora who met her gaze. The caseworker's black hair was cut short, stopping just at her chin, her eyes bright as they shifted between all the actors in this moment.

"How exciting! Are you ready?" Her voice was sickly sweet, high-pitched, and annoying, even more so than yesterday when she explained the process of Elora's release for the second time. Elora swallowed down the desire to tell her to shut up, that her voice made her want to stab both eardrums. Instead, she smiled at the case worker, forced and strained, and nodded.

"Oh, I'm sure you are nervous. But it is going to be okay. The other women at the transition house are wonderful, lovely people. I'm sure you will get along great!" She turned to Viktor and nodded quickly, as if this was already taking too long. He moved away from her and toward the car, where he opened the back passenger door and gestured for her to get in.

Her feet felt so heavy, like bricks were strapped on as she took one step and then another. He reached out his hand to help her into the vehicle, but she simply stared straight ahead and ignored it. His words echoed in her head, sharp and biting as they repeated on a continuous circuit. Yet it did nothing for the undercurrent of desperation to throw her arms around his neck and embrace him, ignoring the steady gaze of Damien and Amy as they watched, each movement and shift of emotion noted and studied.

Elora allowed herself to watch his face as she slid into the car, the leather seats so cold she could feel it through the jeans Dr. Montgomery had said would make the transition easier. She had argued that leaving in new clothes she hadn't worn since her admittance would highlight the new start, make it more real. The fabric, though, felt stiff and uncomfortable after years of wearing sweats. The band and button dug into the soft flesh of her stomach as she bent over or sat down.

Viktor's face didn't give anything away. Blank, expressionless, professional. Anyone who watched them would think he was just a worker escorting a young woman to her car. Not even his eyes, which usually revealed his thoughts, were empty as he looked down at her before he shut the door. The caseworker took her place in the front passenger seat while Damien got into the driver's seat.

But she can't look away from the nurse who had become her friend. A sharp pain stabbed through her chest, reminding her of the pain of losing yet another person. Her foster family. Elizabeth. Now Viktor as he stared at her like she was nothing, another resident who didn't matter. She had expected some sort of emotion on his face. Excitement. Pride. Longing. Anything would have been better than the ice she saw now.

Even a simple goodbye would have been enough.

~ ~

CHAPTER 19

Elora

The car door slammed shut, and Elora shifted her attention to the seat in front of her, studying the lines in the leather, the stitching along the sides. Anything to not have to see Viktor as he walked away and ignored the strange chasm in her chest where the hospital and a certain nurse used to reside.

"Are you ready? Sure, you got everything?" Elora realized with a start that someone was talking to her, the voice coming from beside her. She glanced over at the young man sitting opposite her. His long auburn hair was pulled back into a messy bun on the back of his head and his grey eyes were dark as he watched her. His blue scrubs were pulled tight, as if they were too small for him.

She nodded. "Yeah, I'm ready."

Elora stole a glance towards the front where Damien started the car and put it in drive, slowly making their way down the long driveway. Her hands curled and her nails dug into her palms as she forced herself not to look back, to keep her breathing even and steady. Amy turned her body as much as she could with the seatbelt, her head angled towards Elora despite still not being able to see her.

"The house is about 20 minutes away, so it won't be a very long drive. Do you have any questions?" Elora looked out the window at the passing landscape she could never see from the day room windows. The car slowed at the iron gates, and they passed through, turning onto an empty street.

"No, I don't." Everything had been explained numerous times, and Elora wasn't sure she could take another version of the same information.

"Well, if you think of any, just ask. That's what we are here for." She turned back around, and Elora let out a breath, grateful that the woman wasn't going to force conversation. Her thoughts were chaotic, a jumbled mess as her mind attempted to catch up with the fact she was no longer a patient at the psychiatric hospital, no longer with the only friend she thought she had managed to make while there. Even the other patients had avoided her, as if they knew something was wrong with her on a cellular level.

"You would think that you would be excited, but you seem terrified. I wonder why that is," Damien drawled after a brief, glorious moment of silence. The nurse beside her shifted slightly and sat up straighter.

"Didn't we have this conversation already? I believe I made my viewpoint very clear." Elora snapped in response and watched his smile grow as he peeked at her in the rearview mirror. Almost absentmindedly, his hand reached up and rubbed at his cheek. She smirked before turning her focus to her sleeves, pulling at a loose thread.

"Yes, yes, we did. But I never really got an answer. Do you want to go back?" She didn't reply, simply glared at him as she shoved her hands into her opposite sleeves, touching the scabs there.

"Does this line of questioning serve a purpose, Damien?" The caseworker seemed irritated, her voice taking on a hint of annoyance that seemed to be warning him to stop.

"Want to know what I think?" A moment of silence passed where all Elora could hear was the cars passing them on the road and the air conditioner forcing out cold air.

"I think you thought you were safe there. And now you're not."

"I didn't realize you were a psychologist. Maybe leave the psychoanalysis to the professionals." The sarcastic retort from the caseworker did nothing to deter him, only made his grin grow into a full smile that revealed his elongated canines. He had been so careful at the hospital, smiling but never too wide, never enough to show them off.

He turned his head and stared at the caseworker like she was amusing. A toy to be played with.

"Psychoanalysis has nothing to do with. I know her better than she thinks."

"What does that even mean? Your cryptic comments are getting annoying" Elora's words were out her mouth before she could stop them, and she felt the nurse beside her shift again.

"Let's just say I did my homework on you. Both while you were at the hospital and before that."

Elora's heart started to race, erratically pounding in her chest as she struggled to draw in a breath as panic rose, as the feeling of fingers appeared on her arms once more. She watched him closely, marking every movement of his eyes as they flicked between the caseworker and herself. The car slowed as he turned into an empty gas station, parking along the side away from the pumps. Elora pulled her hands from her sleeves and let them rest in her lap while she picked the skin around her cuticles.

"Why are we stopping? This isn't on –" Before she could finish her sentence, Damien darted across the space between the seats, something clutched in his hands. Elora screamed the caseworker's name as Damien grabbed her neck, large hands closing around the tender skin, and stabbed her with something. A syringe, Elora realized, as her hands searched for the door handle, not finding it in her panic.

Amy gave a sharp cry before she slumped down, the seatbelt the only thing keeping her sitting up. Finally, Elora's hands found the handle, and she started to yank on it. A cry of frustration erupted from her lips as it refused to open. Her eyes oscillated between the door and Damien as she searched for the lock, whimpering as it became clear that there wasn't one.

A hand latched onto the back of her neck, the touch scalding in the otherwise cold car, and she screamed before another hand went over her mouth. While she was focused on the missing lock and Damien, she had forgotten about the nurse beside her. With a muffled grunt, she threw her head and body back, hoping to collide with whoever the nurse was, twisting her body to the side, her back to the man.

"Shush, Elora. We aren't going to hurt you. Just calm down." She wanted to laugh as the nurse tried to console her, his voice low and calm. In response, she thrashed in his grip and smiled against his hand as she felt her head smack his face.

"Damn it!" Her smile grew as his curses and groans of pain reached her ears, but he didn't let go. His hold didn't loosen in the slightest amount as another hand cupped her chin and turned her face. Damien leaned over the seat, half his body in the front and the rest angled towards her. The excitement on his face was terrifying, the gleam in his dark eyes, the twist of the sneer on his lips. She stopped struggling even as Damien lifted his hand, another syringe held in his grip.

"We are taking you home, little rose. He's been looking for you for a very long time." There was something triumphant in the look Damien gave her, like he had won a grand prize. Elora's brows furrowed as she tried to understand who "he" was or why he had been looking for her. The only home she knew was the hospital, and it was clear Damien wasn't referring to that.

But there it was again. That nickname that made her blood seize and burn all at the same time, that made her want to curl up and hide in the darkest place imaginable, disappear into a void, be eradicated from existence so that no one would find her again. As the words left Damien's mouth, she braced her feet against the seat in front of her and pushed with everything her fear-addled body could muster as adrenaline raced through her. She collided with the nurse's body and heard the rewarding sound of him hitting the door, followed by a string of very loud, very creative curses. His hands fell from her body for just a moment, and she tried to scramble away, a flurry of hands and knees as she crawled across the leather. Damien grabbed the back of her neck, yanking her towards him with a snarl, his actions too fast for her to escape.

Now it was her turn to curse.

"Fuck! Let me go! I won't go back," she screamed, loudly and violently. She could feel the rawness in her throat as something pierced the side of her neck and a set of arms wrapped around her torso, holding her arms in place. A warmth spread from the injection site as it traveled through her body, each body part growing heavy. Elora didn't know where they were taking her, where she was going back to, but she knew it was dangerous.

"Don't let them touch me," she pleaded, voice low and shaky as her eyes drooped and thoughts slowed. Only the panic remained, dulling second by second as the area around her vision darkened, Damien's confused face becoming blurry.

The last thing she saw was Damien's expression, a mixture of confusion and triumph before she surrendered to the drug at last.

CHAPTER 20

Damien

"She broke my fucking nose, Damien!" The nurse in the back-seat unwrapped his arms from the girl and he clutched his nose as dark, almost black, blood poured out.

"It will be fine by the end of the day. It won't even look broken if you hurry up and set it, Lukas." Damien rolled his eyes and turned back into the driver's seat.

"Doesn't mean it didn't hurt. You could've sedated her sooner instead of letting her fight me back here. Or you could have compelled her. Either way, you owe me a drink."

"She's a human. There really wasn't much concern." At least Damien thought she was human. Other than the one attack on her foster sister, she didn't seem to feed or even have the equipment to do so. No other sign that she was anything but.

Damien sighed as he realized his response to his best friend was sharper than necessary. But with each word and complaint from his mouth, Damien felt his victory deflate just a little more. And the pleas from the girl hadn't helped in that regard. He wanted to bask in the glow of his success, and Lukas was ruining that.

"Plus, I'm not even sure compulsion works on her," he admitted.

"How is that even possible? You just said she's human." Damien shrugged at his friend's completely warranted question, as if it didn't matter.

"I tried to compel her before when she was struggling to attend a therapy thing her psychiatrist had set up. She was panicking, and I tried." He paused for a moment as he debated telling Lukas the reaction. "She slapped me."

Lukas's laugh rang out in the otherwise abandoned gas station parking lot and Damien immediately regretted his choice to tell him. He watched him, glared at Lukas as he cleaned the blood from his face. He didn't say a word after his laughter died. Instead, he repositioned the girl and arranged her so she could lie across the backseat. With a soft grunt, Lukas pulled out the restraints from their hiding place beneath the seat and closed them around her wrists. Damien watched each movement closely as the first one clipped into place and flinched slightly at the sound, hearing her pleas once again. Still, he watched, unable to look away as Lukas snapped the other one and grabbed the girl's shoulders to tug her further back into the seat.

Damien's eyes narrowed each time Lukas's hands touched her, grabbed, and pulled her body. Something in his chest twisted as he struggled to stop himself from ordering the other vampire from touching her, yelling at him that she was fine as she was and didn't need to be moved anymore. That she didn't need to be touched.

It's for Killian, he told himself, eyes still locked on the places where Lukas had touched her. *I am protecting her from Killian, protecting myself. He would kill them both if the girl was harmed now.*

Finally, after what seemed like an eternity, Lukas exited the car and made his way around, opening the passenger door to grab the caseworker, the collateral damage in this whole mission. With a harshness Damien wasn't sure was there when handling the girl, Lukas yanked the woman from her seat while he pushed the button to open the back. A loud thud sounded throughout the vehicle as Lukas dropped her body and slammed the trunk closed before slipping into the passenger seat.

Damien took a moment to look over his friend, the vampire he had hand-chosen for this little adventure, as Lukas put on his seatbelt. His auburn hair had come loose during the struggle and Lukas pulled the hair-tie from it, letting it fall down over his shoulders. His nose was still a mess, but at least it wasn't bleeding anymore. The nostrils were coated in dried blood, the area around his eyes appearing darker. It would be a black eye. Or two, more than likely. All the injuries would be gone by tonight, but she had managed to cause Lukas real damage, which didn't make too much sense if she were truly human.

So much of this didn't make sense.

Damien pulled out of the gas station and turned in the opposite direction of the transition house, heading instead for Ashcroft Tower roughly twenty-five minutes away. Only the Ashcroft vampires resided in the Tower, with the other families opting for their own versions. The Ravenwell vampires had a large manor on the outskirts on the other side of the city, while the Radcliff family owned a series of townhomes in the city center. No one knew exactly where the Corvin vampires resided. It was the greatest secret among the other three groups, with each one willing to give up almost anything to find out. Their secrecy granted them protection, which was highly coveted when feuds and rivalries ran high. The running theory that no one had been able to prove was that they lived in a collection of large warehouses in the Industrial neighborhood. But even that was a rumor. It drove Killian crazy that he didn't know where they stayed.

"Think they will stay passed out until we get there?" Lukas pulled his hair back once more and secured it with the hair tie before running his hand over it, checking for chaotic strands.

"Probably. I gave them a fairly hefty dose. I didn't want any delays in them passing out. No need to draw attention." And Damien wasn't sure how the girl would react once she woke up. The case-worker didn't matter, since she would end up being a snack or an addition to the private feeding rooms Killian kept. Either the head vampire would enjoy her himself or she would be sent over to the blood collection floor of the Tower.

But Damien had seen the girl break down and had seen her fight, a rage that brought forth fists and kicks that hurt more than any human he had ever encountered. Even when she had been almost too weak to stand, she had managed to knock him back before collapsing to the floor. He wasn't willing to risk Killian's wrath just because she woke up early and had a tantrum.

Lukas just grunted and nodded, twisting in his seat to check on the girl. A sarcastic comment about Lukas's concern for the girl waited on Damien's tongue before he swallowed it back, knowing that they were all on edge. Him and Lukas included. Everyone knew about the girl Killian had spent years looking for and knew the lengths he had gone to in order to find her. No one really knew why, only those who had been in the Tower and had survived his initial wrath.

Damien had heard the rumors though, the ones whispered in the corners of the feeding rooms, in the hallways and the lobby of the Tower. They all thought she was Killian's special toy, a human girl he had developed a taste for. But that would have made her a child when that special taste developed, which they all argued simply added to the delicious depravity of it. Others thought she was part of a rival family and would be used as collateral for more power and control. Vampire families were always trying to take over each other, consolidating power into fewer groups, hoping to become the vampire who combined them all into one. Currently, there was a truce as the vampires went to battle against the human resistance members, as vampire bodies literally piled up in public spaces, turning into pyres in a show of defiance.

Only a select few knew the truth, and Damien was one of them. The girl, in all her spoiled and selfish glory, was Killian's daughter, even if she truly didn't remember that little fact. Damien wasn't sure he believed her about that.

Most assumed vampires couldn't reproduce in a more natural way, like the way humans do. The only known method was to turn humans and claim them as their child. Killian had found a way, millions upon millions funneled into the science that allowed it to happen. Damien didn't know all the details and knew he probably wouldn't understand it anyway. His education as a human had been poor at best, even if he now spent his time attempting to rectify that.

Damien almost laughed at the whole situation as he turned onto a crowded street and stopped at the light. The only mystery in this was how the girl was both simultaneously Killian's daughter and a human. But he wasn't willing to ask questions about things that weren't his business. If he needed to know in order to do his job, Killian would inform him. After all, the head vampire would know, considering how long he had been around. He had been the head of the family for around a century but had been old prior to that. His real age wasn't really known. Only solid guesses based on the limited information other vampires had acquired over the years. Damien had a feeling Killian preferred to keep it that way. People fear what they do not know, and fear can be incredibly powerful to wield.

As they turned onto the street where the Tower loomed, standing out like the edge of a knife among the other skyscrapers, Damien let out a soft sigh of relief. Up and down the neighborhood, humans and vampires alike wandered along the sidewalks in suits and chic outfits, nary a hair out of place, appearances perfected. Cars drove along the streets while taxis parked along the sidewalk and waited for passengers. He pulled into the garage underneath the Tower, driving through the rows until he got to the very back where Killian's personal elevator was located. The girl was not necessarily a secret to be hidden away in the shadows of the parking garage, but Killian had been very specific about getting her into the building unnoticed to avoid questions before he was ready to address them.

He pulled up directly in front of the elevator and put the car in park while one of Killian's assistants waited. Damien took a moment to try to recall her name—Mary, if he wasn't mistaken. Since Killian had a habit of getting a new one every few months, Damien couldn't really be blamed for not remembering. This one had lasted longer than the others. Her copper hair was pulled into a low bun, and her dark eyes watched as he opened his door and stepped out. All he knew was he really didn't want to deal with her.

Her hands were clasped in front of her, resting against the black skirt, and the corners of her mouth were tucked down into a perpetual frown. It suited her in a strange way. Damien simply nodded before opening the back door and started reaching for the girl, grabbing her arms to pull her closer. Her body was entirely limp from the sedation as he wrapped an arm around her waist while the other went under her legs as he extracted her from the car. The girl's head fell to the side, resting against his chest, crimson hair splashed across her peaceful face while her arms hung by her side.

She fitted there perfectly, and Damien had to shake his head to force the unbidden thought away.

"This is her?" The assistant looked down at the girl in Damien's arms, lips twisted in disgust as she reached to move the hair from Elora's face. With a harsh movement, Damien moved away, removing the girl from the assistant's reach. Her hand fell to her waist, and she straightened her shoulders as she waited for an answer to such an obvious question.

"No, we brought some other random girl. You will need to send someone down to get the one in the trunk."

Mary raised an eyebrow and Lukas shrugged, shoving his hands into the pockets of his scrubs.

"The caseworker."

"Ah, yes. Forgot about her." Mary turned from them before she pulled out her cellphone and called security to retrieve the woman. Damien squashed down the feeling of discomfort at the fact she would be going to the third floor where Killian kept the humans who donated their blood, either by allowing its collection or live feedings. Usually, the humans consented to it for money and a place to sleep. That won't be happening for the caseworker. She would be given an upgraded cell, with a decent bed, a toilet behind a privacy screen, a sink, and a desk. Killian preferred for his meals to be taken care of with their very basic needs met. At least until the vampires grew tired of them or they feel too weak to continue.

Damien and Lukas entered the elevator together and pushed the button for the thirteenth floor, the one that held Killian's room. Damien's own room was on the floor directly below it, along with Lukas's. The building had a hierarchy ingrained in it. The top three floors belonged only to Killian. On the top floor were his entertainment rooms, where parties of all types were held. Below that were Killian's offices, along with those of his personal team: accountants, lawyers, and the computer scientists. Then there were Killian's rooms below that. After that, where a vampire was placed was directly related to where they stood in terms of Killian's favor. The further down from the leader's personal rooms, the less a vampire mattered to him.

The girl would be on the same floor as Killian. Directly across the hall from him, which was fitting, considering her relationship to the head vampire. Personally, Damien would have put her in one of the cells with the caseworker. The fact that she was being welcomed back with open arms, despite running away like a child, irritated him more than it probably should have. While she had been living a life of security and ease under Killian's care, he had been a human trying to survive in the industrial district, had been living with his mother in a small house with two other families with no water or electricity. His dad had been in and out during that time, only appearing if he needed money. Typical deadbeat behavior. Gambler and addict, the perfect winning combination. It was his fault Damien ended up turning.

Killian's smiling face was waiting as the elevator doors slid open with a loud chime. There was a light in his eyes Damien had only seen once before—when Killian sampled the blood he had brought him. Slowly, he stepped out of the elevator, the girl in his arms, and Lukas directly behind him. Killian's hand reached out and pushed the long strands of hair away from her face, tucking it behind her ear. The gesture was so gentle, so tender that it felt like Damien was witnessing something he shouldn't be, unintentionally privy to an incredibly private moment between father and daughter.

"Her room is ready." Killian turned and strolled down the hall, the stride of a vampire who now had everything he needed and wanted. A man rendered whole once more.

CHAPTER 21

Damien

Damien followed him into the room, careful to twist his body so that the girl didn't hit the door frame as they entered, and told himself it wasn't that he personally cared if she was hurt.

"On the bed." He nodded at Killian's command and laid the girl on the black silk sheets before he pulled the waiting thick blanket over her shoulders. He didn't spare her a second glance before he headed back towards the door. Killian simply stood in front of the bed like a man glued to the spot, a statue stationed before her while she slept. The light hadn't left his eyes, but it had turned to something darker, the normally pale grey eyes mere shadows of what they usually were. Damien glanced away, focus roaming over the room while he waited for Killian's instructions.

The room was larger than his own, almost double the size. The four-poster bed was large enough to fit multiple people and was flanked by two nightstands, each with a lamp and a stack of books. The door to the bathroom was off to the right and to the left was the door leading to what he assumed was the closet, full of high-end clothing, no doubt. As if Killian's daughter would be dressed in anything less than the finest that money could buy. There was a large desk that took up the corner of the room, along with a sitting area near the fireplace, two large armchairs, and a coffee table.

Drawings lined the shelves in the back corner, sketches of flowers mostly, beauty twisted into something sharp and dark. The bunch of daisies were slightly disproportionate, the petals jagged, lines dark and harsh. The roses were wilted, petals torn as they drooped and fell to the bottom of the page. They were at once both shockingly beautiful and disturbing. In the bottom corner of each one was a set of initials—E.A.

She didn't deserve any of it.

The room was silent. The only noise was the sound of the girl breathing. Damien wasn't entirely sure how long it would take for the sedation to wear off. He had been more interested in making sure they fell asleep quickly to stop any potential problems before they started. Killian turned to him, a smug and contented smile on his face, making him look younger. With a last look at the girl on the bed, Killian gestured for Damien to leave the room.

"Let her sleep. We need to talk."

Silently, they crossed the hallway into Killian's private rooms, a space Damien had only been in twice before. The first was the night he was turned, and the second was the night Killian had given him the mission to find the girl who was now sleeping across the hallway. A sense of triumph rushed through him, making him stand taller, shoulders back and spine straight.

Killian held the door open as Damien entered the sitting room. Off to the right was a door that led to the bedroom, while bookshelves lined the walls, filled completely with titles that seemed to be a combination of what Damien had read in school and non-fiction history. Some were plain, with no titles listed on the leather spine. Journals, he assumed. The head vampire took a seat in one of the armchairs and gestured for him to take the other. Damien sat on the edge, unsure of where this conversation was going and why Lukas wasn't there for it. The other vampire had left before they even got the girl in her bedroom to change from his scrubs, a disguise that had worked perfectly.

"Why are there two humans in my cells that I did not give authorization for?" Killian absently looked down at his hands, as if something in them was distasteful. Damien took a moment to gather his thoughts. To respond to Killian without carefully thinking it through was a sure way to incur his wrath. Plus, this was not where Damien saw the conversation going, which had been a mistake on his part. Killian wasn't going to thank and praise him for a job well done. In that moment, Damien realized exactly how much he wanted to hear those words, to hear that he had done the head vampire proud by bringing back the girl when so many others had failed.

"The case worker was with us during the abduction of the girl. I brought her here for you to decide what to do with her."

"And the other one? I remember distinctly telling you to get rid of him."

Viktor. Killian was talking about Viktor. Damien shifted in his seat, hoping for an air of nonchalance as he deliberated how to present this. It wasn't that he was against killing the human who had been a thorn in his side during the last month. Viktor had appeared at the worst times, blocking him from fully investigating the girl, protecting her. Or so it had seemed. Their interaction when she left had been a surprise, both to Damien and to her. He had heard every word, watched the pain flash across her face at the betrayal, the heartbreak. Damien had felt his hand turn into a fist as tears formed in her eyes, as he realized how right he had been with his assessment of the human. Yet despite that, Viktor could be useful as leverage. Feelings like the ones the girl held for him didn't disappear overnight. Loyalty like hers didn't go away. Especially not the face of torture should the need arise.

"The girl has a relationship with him. I thought he might be useful. Leverage, in case she misbehaves."

Killian made a noise, like he was considering the words, and then nodded.

"Smart, Damien. Very smart to use their relationship. Obviously, I am hoping my daughter behaves herself now that she is home. Hopefully, she has grown out of her rebellious phase." There was a tinge of rage sitting just below the remorse and disappointment.

Damien said nothing. After a moment, he asked a question, unable to contain himself.

"How do you think she will react?" Killian shrugged in response, motions jerky for the usually graceful vampire.

"It doesn't matter. Sooner or later, she will behave." Damien fought to suppress the shiver that threatened to run down his spine and returned the smile that Killian gave him, attempting to ignore the underlying threat in his words. It shouldn't have made him uneasy. No, he should have been content and happy that the girl was there, and his mission was complete. It was just the words of someone hoping to reign in a willful child. Or a young woman, as was the case now.

"I'm keeping you in charge of her. You were able to get her here without too much trouble. I want you to oversee her protection, both from herself and from others, if necessary."

A groan almost escaped his lips at Killian's command. Any hope that he was done with the girl vanished in an instant. He had wanted to go back to investigating the Resistance and shutting down their bases, the violent work that let him back out onto the streets where he felt most at home. Instead, he was stuck with her in all her irritating glory. She got under his skin like no one else. No fear of him. No hesitation when she punched him, kicked him, threw barbs and sarcastic comments his way.

"Wouldn't Lukas be a better choice? Then I could continue my investigation." Killian's eyes narrowed on him, lips thinning at the suggestion.

"No. You know her, have spent a month with her in that place, learning about her. You understand her and what she is capable of. Lukas does not." The finality of the tone was not lost on Damien, and he nodded, the order accepted as his mind latched onto something else Killian had said.

"Protection from others?" Damien knew that protection from herself made sense having seen what she could and would do under duress. Her mind was at once fragile and iron all at once, cracking under the weight while also fueling her impressive rage. It was confusing, whiplash in the form of a person. But others? Was Killian referring to the Resistance or other vampires? Both? Killian had no shortage of enemies, and it was usually Damien's job to take care of them. The relationships between the vampire families were as close to peaceful as possible, given the number of outside threats. But they were always there, lurking around and sniffing for weakness.

"Vampires. Humans. There are many who would use her. She is special. Not just to me, but to our people as a whole. To humans as well." Damien raised his brows, hoping Killian would continue. But he didn't. Instead, he stood and walked over to Damien's side, grasping his shoulder as he stared down at him. Killian's face was empty once more, eyes dark.

"Get some rest. We have a busy night ahead of us. You will be alerted once she wakes. I want us to visit and explain what is expected now that she is home. Then we have a meeting."

Damien nodded. "Of course."

"Oh, and I will send the caseworker up to you. You need to feed, and you earned it."

~ ~

CHAPTER 22

Elora

The room was familiar in a way that was terrifying, in a way that made her throat close up and her breath stop in her chest. The scents rushed to her first, blood and citrus and that cologne she had smelled on Damien every time she got close. She recoiled slightly from the feel of silk on her skin as the sensation made her want to pull the flesh from her bones in order to stop it from ever touching her again. She may not have understood her reaction, but her eyes opened anyway, and looked over the room. She only knew this was not where she was supposed to be, that this was not the transition house or the hospital. This place was dangerous.

Bits and pieces filtered back to her as she tried to fight off the aftereffects of the sedation she had been given. Viktor's cruel confession and refusal to say goodbye. Damien pretending to drive her to the transition home. He had used the syringe to puncture the caseworker's neck and then her own. Another vampire dressed as a nurse in the backseat with her. She cursed softly at her mistake of not recognizing him as what he was, at having been so distracted by Viktor that she hadn't seen the threat right in front of her face.

Elora dug her fingernails into her wrist, using the pain to anchor herself as she studied the room and the strange familiarity of it—dark paneled walls, the armchairs covered in plush grey fabric, the desk, the sketches along the bookshelf. It poked at something deep in the recesses of her mind, a memory buried away under dirt and brick and concrete. Protection from something awful, memories that would break her if released. Something horrible had happened in this room. Something horrible had happened here to her. Something she was not allowed to remember.

An unfamiliar fabric rubbed against her skin, and she jumped slightly, startled that she was no longer in her jeans and shirt. Instead, she was in a soft nightgown with thin straps over her shoulders. She cringed at how much skin was on display for searching eyes. With a slight whimper, she yanked the blanket up over her arms as her eyes searched wildly for something to wear—a robe, a jacket, something. Her body started to tremble. The feeling started in her fingers before traveling over the rest of her, leaving her violently shaking. She couldn't understand how the bed was not moving, rattling against the floor and wall. Her muscles painfully contracted only to release and then do it once more while her breathing became nothing more than harsh gasps.

"Breathe." The voice she unfortunately knew well came from the corner where the two armchairs were. One faced towards the bed, providing the perfect view of whoever was there, while the other faced away. Damien's hand sat on the armrest, fingers reaching towards the glass on the table beside him. Annoyance merged with her panic as she tried to do what he said and took in a breath, screaming at her body to do what she commanded. To calm down. To stop shaking. But it rebelled. The disconnect between her body and her mind was never clearer than in that moment.

Damien stood and made his way towards her; steps firm but unhurried as she tried and failed to pull in another gulp of air. He sat on the edge of the bed, and she recoiled and flinched as his hand rested on the mattress beside her. A sharp expression met her panicked one, eyes moving over her face to her arms wrapped tightly around her chest. They were no longer covered by the blanket, and his pupils widened slightly at the sight.

She could practically hear his thoughts. Scars. So many scars.

His mouth hardened and his hand cupped her chin firmly, fingers digging into her jaw, turning her face so she was once more forced to meet his gaze. Not that it would matter in a moment when she passed out.

"In." He took a deep breath and held it for a moment before he released it. "Out."

She tried to follow his lead, taking in a breath to fill a cavity that felt too small, threatened to cave in on itself. The breath itself was shallow, but her lungs expanded just a bit more.

"Again." His voice was firm, commanding with just a hint of reluctance and warmth, a balm for the terror. Elora did as he said and took another one, but deeper this time. The darkness around her vision was starting to fade away, the shaking easing into a dull ache from the way her body was contracting.

"Again." Once more and her thoughts had returned. She could breathe and think.

Her fist shot out before she realized it had happened, an automatic response to the vampire who sat beside her. Rage, like she had never known before radiated through her as Damien grunted and fell back on the bed, hitting his head on the corner post.

"Fuck!" He sat back up, hand stroking his jaw as he glared at her. No, not a glare. There was a promise of violence, of disgust, like he would destroy her if given the chance.

"Usually, people say thank you after getting help," he muttered as he watched her, taking in the fury in her eyes, the way her hand curled back up into a fist. Prepared, always prepared.

"Where am I?" Venom dripped from each word as she leaned back, putting space between herself and the vampire who drugged her, ready to hit him again if necessary. Her fear had morphed into anger, and she just wanted to hurt him, make him apologize, and take her away. She had never wanted to hurt someone so much in her life. She had violently reacted to Dr. Montgomery, thrown things at the woman, but this was different. It was survival, lashing out to protect herself even if she was not sure what she needed protection from.

Damien didn't answer at first. Just rubbed his hand along his jaw, moving it from side to side to assess the damage. Elora almost scoffed at the idea, highly doubting she did anything. She would be shocked if she did any damage, given what he was and what she wasn't. Finally, he smirked.

"That wasn't nice." Elora didn't respond to his opinion on her manners and instead repeated her own question, slowly, enunciating each word as if he didn't hear it the first time.

"I told you in the car. You're home. Now, I need you to get dressed so I can go get Killian."

"Who?" The name made the hair on the back of her neck stick up and goosebumps line her skin. She knew the name and tried to dig into her mind to discover its origin. Damien just tilted his head and narrowed his eyes.

"Let's not play that game. Now, there are clothes in the closet. A shower and a tub through that door. You should consider taking one." He got up off the bed and wandered over to the desk, leaning against it as he watched her. She didn't move but gripped the sheets instead.

"If you change clothes, there may be something in there more comfortable for you." His eyes drifted to the plunging neckline of the nightgown and her arms as he spoke. Elora squirmed and pulled her knees to her chest, forcing down the nightgown to make sure her legs were covered and that the rest of the scars were hidden. He didn't need to know they were there, didn't need more to stare at.

Damien watched her a moment longer, waiting to see if she would move before he turned and left the room. A lock clicked into place and Elora let out a breath she didn't realize she was holding, her chest deflating with the escape of air. He said he was going to get Killian, making it seem like she should know who that is. But she didn't. All she had were hazy memories of a man sitting in a chair before her, a man touching her shoulders and arms, followed by blood and pain. Not the remnants of memories of someone who would want her returned safe and sound.

Her scars began to itch and burn as she sat on the bed and considered her options. At the thought, she huffed a laugh. Options weren't something she currently had. The locked door and vampire guard made that very clear. There were no windows in the room. Only the bedroom and closet. A solid wall was behind the bed and the door was in front. Just another cell to keep her in. But at least her room at the hospital had contained a window, the day room had a wall of them.

Was it still daytime? How long had she been sedated? Her eyes roamed over the room, searching for a clock or anything to give her a sense of time.

With a reluctant sigh, she decided that she at least wanted to change clothes even if it wasn't her own, hoping that if she felt more comfortable, she could think a bit more clearly. All she knew was that she didn't want to be exposed when Killian, whoever that was, entered the room. Cautiously, she stood, planting her feet on the floor as she waited to see if the room would spin. When everything stayed in place and her legs remained under her body, she headed to the closet, fumbling for a light switch for only a moment before she turned it on. On the far wall was a full-length mirror, revealing exactly what she looked like, why Damien had said she needed a shower or bath even if the reflection was slightly warped. Not real glass, she realized.

Her crimson hair was a disaster of knots and tangles from the roots to the dead ends. Two eyes ringed with shadows stared back at her, dead and empty, and for a brief heartbeat she wasn't sure that the reflection was hers. The pale lines and puncture marks lined her skin, starting just below her jawline, traveling down her neck and onto her chest, disappearing below the neckline of the gown. And then down her arms to her wrists, where the heaviest concentration of them lay. She knew without looking there were more on her thighs.

Both sides of the closet were lined with clothes and drawers—pants, skirts, dresses, and jeans lined the walls while the drawers were full of undergarments, socks, and silk nightgowns. Shoes lined the floor near the mirror, everything from slippers to stiletto heels. Not a single shirt or dress was long-sleeved, and she had to wonder if it was intentional, if Damien had told them of her preference out of spite. He had said she would find something more comfortable, a taunt to a weakness she had mistakenly revealed.

"Prick," she muttered to the clothes, searching through them for whatever would cover the most. She found a red T-shirt with a high collar and some loose pants, similar to what she wore while in the hospital. The shirt didn't cover nearly enough, and she dug through the drawers, tossing clothing to the side before slamming them shut, frantically moving shirts and pants aside until a sharp exhale filled the room. A long-sleeved black cardigan. She pulled it on, smiling and closing her eyes as the fabric slid onto her, relishing the feel of the sleeves on her arms. Only then did she leave the closet and enter the bathroom, a gigantic room with a toilet, tub, shower, and sink covered in various bottles.

Elora grabbed the brush and started working through her hair, wincing at each tangle and knot as she forced the bristles through. As she finished one side, the hair now lying flat over her shoulder, the lock clicked once more, and the door opened. Her grip on the brush handle tightened as she glanced around for anything that could be useful, anything that could be a weapon beyond what she currently held.

Nothing. Whoever had set her room up had been careful, almost like they have experience keeping sharp objects away from people.

"Are you decent?" Damien's voice carried across the room, and she exited the bathroom, brush still in hand as she worked through the other side. A smug grin spread across his face as he took her in, and his smile grew wider when he spotted the sweater. He stepped further into the room, noting the brush in her hand, and moved over to the side, leaning against the desk, arms crossed over his broad chest. She tracked him as he moved, noting the redness on his jaw and cheekbone, letting a satisfied grin grace her lips as his own faltered just a bit.

Another body strolled into the room, their presence taking up every bit of space and air, leaving her feeling disconnected from everything. She hadn't noticed the other person, her focus too heavily latched onto Damien. The door closed and clicked shut, rendering Elora frozen in place with her eyes wide and lips parted and memories at war inside her mind. Brief images and scenes raced through. Not a single one remained long enough for her to understand them. A crying woman. A sneering man. Teeth and fangs. Blood. A lullaby. A sketchbook spattered with something red.

The vampire in front of her was older than Damien, but she knew it was impossible to tell. Age was difficult when it came to them, since the slightest sign of age took decades to manifest on the skin. This one seemed to be in his late thirties at the most. The stranger towered over her by several inches, taller than Damien. His white hair was brushed back away from his face, lying across his slim shoulders. Gray eyes stared out from the delicate features with a predator's intent. Where Damien was sharp jawlines and full lips, this vampire was soft with a small nose and his lips were thin. His features were almost boyish, she realized. The perfect disguise for the monster hiding underneath. Those thin lips stretched into a grin, gaze dark and greedy.

She knew this vampire, knew this look. And her body screamed at her to run.

"Hello, little rose." His voice grated against her ear, her skin, and she flinched, taking a step back from him, realization hitting her like a truck. Fear, icy and all-consuming, took over every inch of her body as she tried to shrink, make herself smaller somehow. Maybe if he couldn't see her, then he couldn't force her to stay. She could shrink to the size of a bug and scurry through gaps in the floor, finally making it out.

Memories rushed unbidden towards her and hit her with wave after wave of recollection. Of a woman on the floor screaming the first time that Elora said no. Of the agony followed by soft words and promises.

"Hello, father." Her own voice was tiny and for a moment she wasn't sure either one of them heard it despite the silence of the room. She struggled to understand how she could have forgotten his name and who he was, what he was to her. Damien didn't move as he watched her, the smile on his face gone as she took a step away from her father and the brush fell from her hand.

~ ~

CHAPTER 23

Elora

She took a breath with each step away from the vampire and tried desperately to quell the rising panic in the pit of her stomach. The word "father" sounded wrong against her mouth and her tongue rebelled even as she forced it out. The truth tasted bitter, like battery acid and betrayal all at once. Her mind settled onto the word, dragging forth minuscule flashes of their interactions.

Killian sat in the armchair and gestured for her to sit in the other one even as she backed away. His eyes lingered on the cardigan covering her before his expression turned to one of distaste. Instead of following his directions, she retreated until her back hit one of the bedposts, aware that this was nowhere near enough distance between them.

In the back of her mind was a growing knowledge of what the vampire would do to her. She shivered, her eyes never leaving his as they narrowed, jaw tightening with each passing second in which she didn't take the seat he offered. Killian's focus broke from her for only a moment and settled on Damien. In a single look, an entire conversation occurred between the two of them. Instantly, Damien was at her side, hand on her arm and fingers squeezing into her flesh. He dragged her to the chair in tense silence until he tossed her down into it with such force the entire thing shifted slightly.

Killian's eyes flashed to Damien, an amused yet irritated expression displayed on his face.

"Easy with her. She needs patience, Damien. Patience and care." Damien scoffed at Killian's honeyed words, but the vampire showed no signs he heard it, just casually looked over her features. His eyes shifted from her hair to her face to her neck, where they hesitated for just a moment before continuing. It was like being inspected for imperfections or flaws, forced under a magnifying glass as each piece was excised and dissected.

"He is very loyal to me. I saved him from a horrible situation and gave him the life and status he enjoys now." Damien inclined his head in a sign of submission, a demonstration of said loyalty. Elora wanted to scream that she didn't care about his loyal dog, that she wanted to know why she was dragged back, what he wanted from her. But he held up his hand as if to stop her questions before they began.

"We have plenty of time for questions. And I promise you can ask me any of the ones you have. But I have a couple I want to ask. May I?" His voice was smooth and warm, reminding her of the hot chocolate she would drink with Elizabeth during the winter. A comfort drink for the two of them before they moved onto coffee and lattes. But it wasn't comfort it inspired now.

"A question for a question. You ask one and then I ask one. No lying, no hiding information." Elora didn't expect him to agree, to concede to her demand, a game she had played before with Dr. Montgomery when answers were few and far between. Irritation flashed across his features so quickly she almost missed it. Killian's shoulder tensed, his hand flexed in his lap, and a warm smile that didn't reach his eyes was plastered on his face.

"Of course. Can I begin?" Elora only inclined her head in response and leaned back in the chair in an attempt to look at ease. She calmed her breathing and calmed her heart rate, knowing he could sense it, and hear the rapid nature of her pulse from the way his eyes kept darting to the vein along her neck. Their instincts were heightened beyond a human. Their sense of smell and hearing were enhanced to predatory levels.

"Is your room to your liking?" Her mouth fell open, and her carefully crafted response to why she ran away vanished from her lips. She had expected demands about her escape, the listing of names of those who were involved, and about how she ended up in a psychiatric hospital. Not one that made it seem like he cared. She swallowed, wishing desperately for something to drink.

"Yes, it is very nice." Killian's smile grew, revealing fangs, and she pushed herself further into the chair, resisting the urge to pull her legs underneath her.

"I'm glad to hear that. It is the same room you were in as a child, just updated for the young woman you have grown into." She nodded as she looked around the space and searched for any sign of her childhood. A toy, a doll, a crayon drawing. Anything.

"What do you plan on doing with me?" The question left her lips before she could stop it, cursing slightly at the impulsiveness of it. She had planned on asking about the caseworker, the poor woman dragged into this simply by being assigned her case. Elora had a guess about the woman condition, knew she was probably dead or close to it. Killian's brows knitted together as a sense of sadness, maybe disappointment, settled into his features.

"I don't plan on doing anything. I wanted my daughter home where I can care for her and keep her safe." The words rang hollow to her, as if he practiced the response and appearing hurt that she would even ask such a question. She stifled the urge to roll her eyes, her self-preservation barely overcoming her desire to show this vampire exactly what she thought of his answer. Not every memory had returned, and those that had were a jumbled mess lacking any sense of order or connection, but she knew that Killian was a liar and a manipulator. It didn't matter if he was somehow her father.

"Why are you so afraid of me, little rose?" There was hurt in his voice, and she shifted uncomfortably, debating telling the truth.

"We both know the reason. You more so than me. I have enough of my memories back to know to be afraid." Her voice wavered as she spoke, wishing she had more to say, a more concrete example to shout at him. He shook his head in disappointment and waved a hand before him, gesturing to her to ask her own question.

"What happened to my caseworker?" Her eyes roamed over Killian, searching for signs of violence or blood that would tell her anything. But he was perfectly composed, a crisp white button-up shirt and black slacks, hair slicked back without a single strand out of place. Not a drop of blood or wrinkle that indicated he did anything to her. Elora wasn't sure she truly cared about the caseworker. She had barely known the woman and spent most of that time annoyed with her, despite her kindness and enthusiasm about Elora's new life. It seemed wrong that she would become fodder for whatever this was.

Killian waved a hand dismissively. "She was used for food, fulfilling the only purpose humans really have." Her hands clenched into fists as she shoved them down by her sides, hiding them between her body and the sides of the chair.

"We are more than food, you bastard. We are more than things for you to play with and feed from." Her response was stronger than she had expected, and Killian quirked an eyebrow as his lips turned down, as if something disgusting had suddenly appeared before him. She felt Damien move closer, standing beside her chair with a hand on the back of it.

"We?" Killian chuckled darkly and shook his head. "Oh, little rose. It's adorable you think you are human. You are my daughter and are very special."

"You're a fucking liar. I don't feed. I don't have fangs."

"True, true. All very true. But it wasn't always the case, my dear. You used to feed and drain humans dry just like the rest of us." She sucked in a breath while harsh glimpses of her teeth in necks and wrists at a banquet table played and then vanished back into the void.

"That makes no sense! I haven't fed in years." Her voice cracked as she latched onto something, to anything that could explain away Killian's words, the images and sensations drawn forth by them.

"I'm aware and I am looking into that little hiccup currently." Finally, his warm façade broke and revealed an unflinching rage, a fury that would burn down worlds and shatter bones, drain humans and render them ash. She glanced away, unable to hold it.

"I don't understand," she whispered into her hands. "I don't remember enough." Killian sighed, exasperated by her words.

"You are not a human, but I suppose you're not really a vampire, either. At least, not a traditional one. Your mother and I managed to create something very special when we had you. She wanted a child so desperately, but traditional reproduction is basically impossible for a vampire." He shrugged slightly. "Science was involved. An altered form of artificial insemination, as the humans refer to it as, coupled with genetic manipulation."

There was too much to process there. Too much information to take in and she winced at the feeling of her nails as they dug into her palms, using the pressure and tinge of pain to center herself. One by one, she started picking through his words.

Not human but born a vampire. The first of her kind, as far as she knew. Abomination. Attacking Elizabeth rushed forward, a reminder that she had always known she wasn't human, but something else. Even when Elizabeth had claimed Elora turned her, she had held out some hope that it wasn't true, that someone else had gotten to her foster sister after that. The process was so much more complicated, requiring draining the human before sharing blood.

And her mother. Killian had mentioned her, but there was no warmth or fondness in his voice. There was a sterility to his words, something that made the relationship feel transactional. A woman's cries filled her ears, whimpers and shouts and screams of the word no, of commands not to touch her daughter. Elora shook her head softly, hoping to make them disappear only for them to be replaced by the sound of humming, the feeling of a brush in her hair, the sound of a feminine voice saying her name. Nothing tangible, all faded pieces.

"I'm an abomination. A science experiment. The result of a vampire playing at a god." She glared at him, hoping he could feel exactly how much she despised him. Instead, he just beamed as he gracefully rose from his chair and leaned towards her, cupping her cheeks in his hands.

"No. You, my precious daughter, are our future." His eyes moved to Damien at his place behind her chair. He nodded, his hands dropping from her face before he turned towards the door.

"Damien is going to be your best friend. He will make sure everything is taken care of, that you are taken care of." His hand settled on the door before he turned to her, a promise hidden in his eyes.

"I will see you very soon." She tried to swallow, but found her mouth was completely dry as she watched Killian leave, his words a threat that lingered in the room. Damien sighed deeply and dramatically, leaving her debating punching him again. Before she could properly weigh any pros and cons, he dropped into the chair Killian vacated and studied her.

"You seem happy about the arrangement, babysitter." She bitterly commented, observing his face as she finally drew her feet underneath her, relishing the way her body felt compact in the seat. The corners of his lips twitched as he watched the movement, the only sign of something happening behind the mask of indifference.

"It isn't what I would have picked as my next assignment. Watching over spoiled brats isn't exactly appealing." She shook her head before leaning back, resting against the back of the chair.

"Would you have preferred more stalking? More kidnapping?" His lips turned up just slightly at the end, as if she was amusing.

"I had hoped for something more physical, more violent." He jerked his head towards the bed. "There are books on your nightstand. I'm assuming that your father—"

"Do not. Call him. That." The malice that dripped from each word caught even her by surprise, and Damien's eyes widened just a bit before he shut his expression down once more. The label felt wrong, making her want to stick pencils through her ear drums so she never had to hear again. It was repulsive, a reminder of the fragments she needed to piece together.

"As I was saying, your father has more in his own rooms and will be happy to get you any that he does not currently own. Your wish is his command."

She flipped him off as she stood and walked back towards the bed, listening as he followed, steps heavy as the floor creaked under the force of each one. She wasn't sure exactly where she was going or what she was doing, seeking an escape from looking at him, hearing his voice as he purposely irritated her for no other reason than his own enjoyment. A hand gripped her wrist and twisted her body before her back hit the wall with a thud that caused a burst of air to escape from her lips. He stood in front of her, arms pinned to her side. A sarcastic smile played on his lips, one that betrayed the anger in his eyes as he looked at her like she was nothing more than a rock in his shoe, an annoyance to be removed and tossed aside.

The heat from his body radiated through the cardigan and the shirt beneath it, searing her flesh. His breath was hot against her skin as he studied her features and gripped both wrists together between their bodies. Bruises would be left behind in the shape of his fingers. She struggled slightly, twisting her body one way and then the other. A pointless endeavor. Each time she had hit him, she had the element of surprise, an underestimation of her abilities on his part. No such thing existed for her now. His smile grew, and she stopped, letting out a huff of frustration as muscle memory took over, a knowledge left over from years long since passed. She could picture herself in this very position, a different vampire in front of her, their face obscured by a fog, leaving only a flash of fangs and a sick smile.

"If you're going to bite me, just get on with it. I have better things to do, and it wouldn't be the first time one of you cornered me." She sneered as his face contorted in uncertainty. Elora turned her head to the side and closed her eyes, knowing exactly what was coming, bracing for the pain that always accompanied it. The hunger in his eyes was clear as his eyes darted along her face, trailing along her cheekbone and jawline, her lips and neck, the pulse just beneath her skin.

"Can we hurry this along?" She huffed as he stopped. None of them had ever hesitated before, always eager and desperate, tearing and ripping. His gaze lingered on the scars. A mixture of puncture wounds and long lines that started just below her ear and ended near her collarbone. An emptiness filled her, a hollowness that allowed her to escape, body rising above the room, entering a space where she felt nothing, heard nothing, saw nothing.

His hands loosened just a bit, but he didn't move. Elora opened her eyes, finally curious as to what was happening. There was something akin to disgust on his face, and her cheeks grew warm.

"Never. Fucking never." His words were a declaration, a vow made to both him and her. "I have standards."

She shrugged as much as she could with his body still pressed to her. "Too bad no one else does." He snarled, mouth opened to retort when her knee jerked up and hit the soft spot between his legs. His hands released her as he stepped away, groaning in agony and doubling over. As she stepped away and sauntered over to the bathroom, finally ready to take advantage of that bath, she heard his muttered curses.

"Spoiled fucking bitch." The door shut behind her as she left him to his rage and pain.

~ ~

CHAPTER 24

Damien

"**P**erfect. Right on time." Killian's voice filled the space, eclipsing the whimpers and faint cries that emanated from the center of the room. Damien allowed himself a disinterested glance towards the man strapped to the wooden chair with a plastic tarp underneath to protect the expensive rug. A human by the smell of the blood that slowly leaked out of the cuts along his thick brow and thin lips.

"Looks like you started without me," Killian grunted as he wiped his hands clean, scowling as he scrubbed his knuckles where the blood had dried. He grabbed a piece of ice from the bucket behind the bar and dragged it over the lingering gore. Water tinged with pink dripped to the floor before Killian rubbed the towel over his knuckles once again, and a small sound of satisfaction came from him as the blood finally disappeared.

"He wasn't cooperating with being tied up. I tried to explain we were waiting for someone, but he fought like a child." The look of utter disgust made the human wince. The ropes had already dug into his raw and bleeding skin. Damien took a moment to study the man, searching for weaknesses, for hints as to who he was and why Killian felt the need to bring his second-in-command in. Usually Damien dealt with threats: vampires who had forgotten who was in charge, who broke the Accords in ways that would get them caught, who were chosen to send a message to the other vampire families. Rarely was he brought in for humans. They were too easily broken, and Damien had a nasty habit of breaking them. Keeping them alive wasn't on his list of talents.

"Usual plan?" Damien shrugged off his leather jacket and removed the watch from his wrist, an ancient silver thing that only told the time. He never wanted anything that did more than that.

"Of course, but try to be gentler this time around. I have some questions that I need answers to. When I signal, do what you do best." Killian settled into a chair just outside the perimeter of the plastic tarp, drink in hand.

Damien crouched in front of their guest and lifted his dangling head with the very tip of his finger, a dark and cruel smirk on his face.

"Looks like we get to have fun." The human's eyes widened as he realized who was in front of him, who was voicing not-so-subtle threats. Killian's right hand. Torturer. Enforcer. They had many names for him, a reputation that had grown with each broken body, each dispatched problem.

"Okay. First question." Killian stared at the man and studied him to catch any subtle change of expression, any hint of a lie, any increase in his heart rate. Damien stood to the side with his hands clasped behind his back as he awaited the signal.

"What is the weapon the Resistance has developed?" The human shook his head as Killian sipped from his glass, face expectant as he watched the man before him.

"I don't know. I promise I don't. I was never trusted enough." A nod from Killian and Damien shifted into position, his fist meeting the soft flesh of the man's gut. The human let out a strangled grunt before sucking a breath. He would need to pull his next hit if the human was to survive long enough.

"We both know that's not true. I did my homework. Apparently, you didn't do your own. Or are you just trying to irritate me? I can promise you that is a very bad idea." Killian set his drink down, the glass making a soft clinking noise as it hit the side table.

"Let's see. Matthew Baker, correct? A cute four bedroom in the suburb. I can recite the address, if you like. But I have a feeling that isn't necessary. A wife and a daughter. Little Kayleen. Ten is such a fun age, but that is all beside the point. My interest is in the Matthew who works directly under Thorne, the so-called leader of your group. Now, are we done wasting my time?" The man's face paled with each word out of Killian's mouth. Damien noted how his hands had twitched as his wife and daughter were mentioned, at his placement in the hierarchy was revealed. Then the human shifted as his spine seemed to straighten, his expression hardening into something like defiance. Killian smirked as he noticed it, as well.

"Now, let me repeat the question and mind you, I will only do this once more. It won't be just you who pays the price. What is the weapon the Resistance has developed?"

"You can't threaten me with them. I know they are safe, somewhere you can't find them. We take care of our own." His words were forced between gritted teeth, the misplaced confidence almost admirable as he stared up at the head of the Ashcroft family.

"Interesting you should say that when I currently have eyes on your daughter at this moment. Honestly, Matt, there are better schools to send her to than Oakridge Elementary. It really is a bottom tier education."

"Lies." Another signal from Killian, a bored wave his hand.

This time Damien's fist hit the human's face, cracking against his jaw so hard he heard the impact, the sound clear in every corner of the room.

"A small girl, to be sure. I believe she is wearing a blue shirt with white flowers across the front and a white skirt. I am sorry to say that she has gotten it dirty. Grass stains. Difficult to get out from what I understand. Oh, and the cutest black shoes with the tiniest little heel on the back and a pink buckle. Adorable. Did she pick the outfit herself before school this morning?" Killian smiled broadly, both fangs on display in an obvious threat. Damien shifted, hands itching to get to work, to let out any of this aggression that built in that girl's presence.

But that was it. Damien was like stone as the man's entire body slumped, defeat clear in his expression. With the mention of his daughter, the human was willing to give them anything—his information, his loyalty, his soul. Damien rested his hand on Matthew's shoulder.

"You'll kill us, anyway." Killian grinned and leaned forward.

"We will kill you without a doubt. But talking will save your daughter and wife. You have my word." The man nodded and straightened, staring at the books in the background as if meeting their eyes was too much.

"It isn't perfected yet. There are missing elements we are still trying to acquire." He gave Killian a sideways glance that made Damien stand just a little closer to the human.

"The goal is to create a vaccine of sorts for humans, to help prevent the change no matter if they are willing or not. For now, we are testing something else. A repression medication for vampires. It would stop their need to drink blood, retract their fangs, and render them all but human." The man smiled, revealing bloodied teeth. Damien absorbed the man's words, the idea of repressing their hunger, their strength and heightened senses, the very essence of who they were as a sick feeling settled in his stomach.

"It would tame the monster within, give humans a fair shot at controlling their own lives, and stop us from being cattle for your kind." Killian nodded along with each word, listening intently as his face hardened.

"Where have you been testing this? The public? Captured vampires?" The man's grin widened, a knowing expression eradicating the fear and shame that had been there. Damien's body tensed, prepared for the consequences of whatever the man was going to say.

"Captured vampires, of course. There were also volunteers, people who turned that regret their decision and wanted another way of life. But there was also someone very special at a certain psychiatric hospital who given the medication starting the day she was admitted." The man shook his head, a chuckle sounding from busted lips. Damien's hands clenched into fists behind his back, the vision of the girl taking her medication every morning and night. There had always been a sardonic smile on her face directed at Viktor as she tipped them into her mouth and swallowed before lifting her tongue to prove she had taken them.

"Honestly, she was our most effective test subject." Damien felt the second the air changed, became charged with rage and hatred and violence. Killian snarled with his teeth bared in an animalistic display that made the man recoil, the self-satisfied expression gone in half a heartbeat. He stood and knelt in front of the human, resting his hands on his knees as he gave him a sad look, face full of faux regret.

"I am afraid I lied to you, Matthew. You tried to take my daughter, tried to render her as pathetic and pointless as yourself and every other human despite knowing how special she is. And that needs to be punished. Here is what will happen. You get to go downstairs to my cells where my vampires can feed on you, drain you to the brink of death, only to let you recover and do it all over again. And the whole time you will know not only did you sell out your people, but you also killed your daughter."

The man screamed curses and threats, promises of blood and retribution, of the end of vampires, of the battle to come, the war that would settle over the city until bodies lined the streets. Killian scoffed, disgust lining his usually soft features, turning him into every bit the monster the human accused him of being. He waved his hand one last time before turning towards his desk, attention suddenly focused somewhere else.

"Do what you do best but leave him alive. When you're done, deposit him in a cell. We will send someone else to dispose of the child." Damien cracked his neck in response as he stepped around the man and stood in front of him, teeth bared. He wasn't sure the violence waiting for the human was from Killian's orders or something else. Once more the girl appeared in his mind, the way she had faced him, the feel of her fist on his jaw, her body under his when she offered herself, each word that implied it was an action she knew all too well.

With only that thought in mind, along with a flurry of fists and screams and blood, Damien did what he does best.

CHAPTER 25

Elora

Much to her annoyance, when she walked out of the bathroom with nothing but a towel the next morning, Damien was waiting for her, reclining in one of the armchairs with too much ease, reading one of the books left on the nightstand. His comfort, the effortless way he moved through the room, felt unnatural. It was an irritation to add to the growing list. Despite its size, the room felt too small, like the walls were slowly closing in, a tiny inch at a time until she had to take multiple deep breaths to root herself back in reality. The memories were there, closer than ever, clumped together with no sense of time. At the hospital, there had been only whispers in the corners of her mind, waiting for her and reminding her they were there with rough prods and nightmares, the tiny echo of Killian's pet name. Easy enough to ignore, push aside, and bury down further.

Damien glanced up when he heard her exit the bathroom, eyes widening as he took in the towel, the water droplets on her scared skin before they flicked down to where her hands clutched the towel closed. A second passed and then another, neither one speaking until he cleared his throat, gesturing to the desk where a breakfast tray was waiting for her. The bed had been made while she showered and gave him a questioning look.

"Maid already came to straighten up. She will be back in a bit to get your tray." He turned back to the book while she entered the closet to find clothes, faced with the same options as the day before. Short-sleeved shirts and dresses with low necklines, as if someone wanted everything on display, as if her comfort didn't matter.

The cardigan was nowhere to be found, its spot in the closet where she left it last night empty. The maid had to have taken it for laundry and she cursed softly before she grabbed a long casual navy-blue dress, still short sleeved but with the highest neckline of the options. Holding back the trembling in her hands, she threw it on and searched one more time for anything long sleeved. A knit cover up. A winter jacket. Anything. She aggressively yanked the clothes one way and then the other repeatedly until she felt someone else enter the closet.

"Unhappy with the selection?" His tone was teasing, almost like they were friends or that he found the entire situation amusing. She just really wanted to hit him again.

"You know I am, asshole. Is this your doing? Your idea of fun?" He glared at her as she pushed past him, arms crossed over her chest as if it would hide anything. She could feel the burning of tears just along her lash line, waiting for the moment they were let loose.

I refuse to cry over this, she vowed and began her search on the floor. First around the bed before moving into the bathroom, hoping and praying that she was wrong. He entered the bathroom behind her and leaned against the sink, watching as she became more and more frantic as she opened cupboards and pushed the towels around. Maybe someone hid it, a sick idea of a joke. Finally, she sucked in a breath and fell to her knees, arms limp by her sides.

"You don't need to cover them up, you know. We all know they are there." She glanced up at him just long enough to see him shrug, as if this was nothing. As if the conversation and what was happening were nothing. Then again, he had made it clear that she was nothing, below his standards. She didn't really feel that she could argue he was wrong.

Defeated, she wandered back into the bedroom and sat in one of the armchairs, pulling her knees up to her chest and burying her face in her dress. What would even happen now? Just live each day in this room with Damien lurking in every corner?

Something soft landed on her shoulders and she lifted her head, flinching against the weight and touch of something foreign. She fingered the fabric before realizing it was a soft throw blanket she hadn't seen before. Not when she searched the room for weapons or again when she was attempting to find the sweater. She glanced over at Damien, prepared to thank him as good manners would dictate, but the self-satisfied grin on his face stopped any desire to do so. She refused to add to an already over inflated ego.

"Where am I?" She knew the question was rude and from the rise of his brows, he recognized it as well. Elora bent forward and wrapped the blanket and pulled it down around her before holding it closed.

"Your father's house. Ashcroft Tower, where all the vampires in this particular family reside." She let his answer wash over her for a moment while she tried to call forward what she remembered from before. Everyone knew of Ashcroft Tower, mostly as a spot for sightseeing and tourists. The sleek design and walls made of glass drew curious eyes and those obsessed with architecture. There had been school field trips to the Tower where a woman in a pencil skirt and blazer had given them a history lesson. No mention of vampires.

Vaguely, she remembered there being four vampire groups, each with their own head, who made sure the Accords were followed. Her eyes roamed around the room while her hands pulled the blanket closer around her, covering up any exposed skin that she could. So much of her memory was still blank, empty holes where knowledge was burned away.

She nodded and shifted, wrapping the blanket around her legs as well.

"Come eat. Your breakfast is getting cold." She glanced over at the tray, filled completely with eggs, bacon, and some types of potato. Off to the side was a bowl of fruit with two cups, one with a tea bag and the other filled with juice. She shook her head as her stomach curdled at the mere thought of food. With a soft shake of her head, she burrowed further into the chair and pulled the blanket towards her face. She knew she was acting like the child Damien accused her of being, but she couldn't make herself care. She heard him make a frustrated noise as his steps echoed in the room and she smiled slightly behind the soft fabric. With a sharp thud, Damien set the tray on the coffee table before her and knelt, holding onto either armrest, preventing her from escaping. Her eyes narrowed at him as he sighed and rolled his eyes.

"Eat."

"You watched me closely enough at the hospital to know I rarely eat breakfast, and I tend to have coffee."

"Look, personally, I don't care if you eat. Even if it would make Daddy very upset to know you are abstaining from food." He gave her a dark smile, as if he knew something she didn't.

"Well, in that case, I most definitely won't be eating." Damien shook his head, muttering something about being stubborn and the futility of it.

"That would be a shame considering if you don't eat, he doesn't eat." She shifted, not understanding as she watched his grin spread wider and wider at her growing confusion, and each and every line became etched into her features.

"He?" she asked him as he moved away, handing her a fork. Damien took the chair across from her and let his gaze return to her confused expression before moving to the blanket covering her scars and her legs drawn underneath her. Finally, he met her eyes once more. She didn't move. Instead, she leaned back in the chair and gripped the fork like it could protect her from him. His smile grew, displaying annoyingly perfect teeth and his two sharp canines.

"Viktor. If you don't eat, Viktor doesn't eat. Fairly simple, really. Didn't I mention this last night?" Elora shifted uncomfortably, meeting Damien's eyes unwavering, a coldness settling into her bones.

"Why would that matter to me? You know exactly how things were when I left, what he said." Damien nodded, as if he was considering her words.

"True. I will tell you that his response was brutal. Even I was taken by surprise by it, to be perfectly honest. But we both know that despite that, you won't let him be hurt just to spite your father."

"You don't know anything about me."

"I disagree, but that doesn't matter." He moved back and rested his ankle on his knee. "I guess he will waste away. He needs his strength, considering he is in one of the feeding cells, available to anyone who wants a little taste. Or more than a little."

Her reality shifted at Damien's words and the implication of them slammed into her, knocking the air from her chest. Instantaneously, she was no longer in control, her limbs operating under someone else's will, watching the scene in slow motion from the corner of the room where she was safe. With a snarl that didn't seem like it could come from her, she leapt over the coffee table, causing eggs and potatoes to spill over the rug and hardwood floor.

The fork was gripped in her fist, face contorted into something rabid and feral. There was an instant rush of satisfaction as she witnessed the surprise and panic flash across his features as she threw herself at him. All she could hear was a shout followed by a string of curses, but it sounded as if she was underwater, muffled and distant. For a brief moment, time stood still, the fork lodged in his flesh where his shoulder met his neck just below the wing of his moth tattoo. The scent of blood filled the room with its intoxicating appeal, along with the sound of her heartbeat against her chest, the sound of his doing the same.

Time returned to its steady movement as she flew across the room and collided with something hard, the sound reverberating off the walls. She groaned and cried out as her body hit the desk and she crumbled to the floor in a mess of tangled limbs. All she could do was close her eyes and force herself not to cry or even whimper as she tried to decide if anything felt broken.

"What the—" the voice entered the room as the door swung open, bouncing off the wall behind it. She knew she remembered it, but couldn't place it, her mind unable to focus on anything other than the pain that radiated through her body. She whimpered and rolled over onto her stomach in hopes of pushing herself up. Slowly, too slowly, she drew her legs under her, pushing herself to her knees despite her body remaining hunched over in agony.

"Deal with her first." Damien's command cut through the pounding in her head and hands grabbed her arms to haul her to her feet. The room spun and her legs buckled, sending her to the floor again where her knees cracked against the wood, sending another shockwave of pain through her.

"Pick her up! Move her to the bed." They did as Damien shouted, and one arm wrapped around her waist and the other under her legs, pulling her up so she leaned against them. She let out a sharp cry and felt the person holding her flinch. In a couple of short steps, they laid her on the bed, and she immediately rolled onto her side, arms wrapped around her torso as she tried to figure out where the pain was coming from.

The answer was everywhere. It was coming from everywhere.

"Are you okay?" The person leaned in close, the scent of mint mingling with the blood in the air, warm breath on her cheek as they bent over her. She could only groan in response, and they moved away, footsteps heavy as they approached the door.

"What the fuck happened?" The voice she only barely recognized was shouting, and Damien grunted. She tried to open her eyes even though her lids were heavy and refused to cooperate. Elora only wanted to know who it was, why the voice sounded so familiar.

"She stabbed me," Damien responded, disbelief lacing every word of his statement.

"With what? I thought there were no sharp objects."

"Apparently forks need to be added to the list." Silence enveloped the room as she embraced the immense pride in her chest due to the fact she had done damage to that asshole. He deserved it. Not just today, but every day since the hospital.

A brash laugh, free and completely unrestrained, suddenly filled the room, and she smiled. Whoever the other vampire was found this as amusing as she did.

"Not funny. It actually hurts." He seemed surprised by it, and of course, he was. Men and their egos could be bad enough. But vampires and their egos? That was something else entirely.

"I'm not disagreeing about the pain. But it is hilarious. I warned you about her and then you kept baiting her. Sounds like you did this yourself." The voice laughed once more and she let the sound envelop her, let it wrap her up so she could ignore the pain that was pulsing through every part of her. There was not a single nerve that wasn't screaming in agony.

"Fuck off, Lukas." The laughter stopped, but she could imagine the grin on their face, one that she could vaguely recall as though through a haze, the name a slight echo in her ear. The only sound was footsteps coming closer and closer before someone crouched beside the bed. Her back may face the wall, but she knew exactly who it was, could feel them with every fiber of her being.

"You should know you won't be punished for this. Killian's precious daughter would never be punished." She stilled at the closeness of his voice, and he leaned in closer, letting her feel the heat from his body, his breath on her bare skin with each word he said.

"But Viktor will be. And I will make sure you are there to see it all." With those parting words, he stood and tossed something on the bed in front of her. Two sets of steps exited the room, and she finally opened her eyes, wincing at the pain that shot through every bit of her as she tried to adjust her position into something slightly more comfortable.

In front of her, blurry from what was definitely a concussion, was a combination of silver and dark red in the vague shape of a fork.

~ ~

CHAPTER 26

Elora

The water was close to boiling as she sank into it, every bottle of liquid and salt and powder dumped in. Even with her foster family, she never had access to anything like this. Luxury items weren't possible when one person was a cook at a diner and the other worked as a janitor. But their life had been happy and comfortable. Never asking for more than they could afford or more than they were allowed. She winced at the memory of Elizabeth's disappointment as they walked away without chocolate to make a cake for her birthday, the price too far beyond what they earned. It would be the equivalent of two months of bus passes.

Elora's groans bounced off the tile as she reclined against the back of the tub, trying not to move. A knot of guilt erupted in her chest, and she could feel tears forming. Viktor was somewhere in this building, being used for who knows what. Would they really stab him? And with a fork? The idea seemed so asinine that she almost laughed. Instead, she sank beneath the water, letting her breath out as she simply floated there, flower petals just above her on the water's surface, wondering briefly what it would be like to stay beneath the surface.

It would solve nothing and everything at once. Killian would be denied his prize, along with whatever his plan was. He claimed to not have one and to only want his daughter back under his protection, but she knew without a doubt he was lying. The flashes of memory told her that much, at least. But she wouldn't really be better off somewhere else, and she wasn't sure she would be allowed to escape yet again. Elora had a feeling Dr. Montgomery would welcome her back with open arms, tutting her tongue when she told the doctor what had happened and what she had done. She would remind Elora to think about her actions and ask her if it had made her feel better. It's what she had said after Elora threw the paperweight at her when her release had been denied.

Elizabeth was obviously not an option. Unhinged and bloodthirsty by Elora's hand. The girl she had known roughly a year had dissolved, leaving behind something more akin to a beast. Obsessive and myopic in her thinking, her desires were for either ownership or revenge. Elora wasn't sure which one based on their limited and violent interaction.

She moaned softly as she resurfaced and let the water settle around her collarbones, the milky water covering the rest of her. For a moment, she could almost pretend her skin was flawless, pristine, and golden brown from time outdoors like it had been before. A sharp pain hit her chest as she yearned for sunlight, for the smell of trees and flowers and everything else that comes with it, for fresh air and the wind through her hair. It had been so long. Stale air that smelled of brick and garbage had been the closest she had gotten, and she doubted she would have the opportunity now.

Elora sank back down, running her fingers through her hair before coming back up, wincing when she noticed the milky white had turned faintly pink.

"I wasn't sure what you were doing down there." Her back is to him, but her arms quickly cover her chest, attempting to hide anything that may be on display. The water splashed against the sides of the tub as she jerked her arms around her, hoping the murkiness of the water covered anything else.

"Fuck off, Damien. Do you normally watch people in the bath?"

"Only the ones who stab me with forks, little rose."

"Don't call me that," she hissed back. The nickname, which is what she supposed it was at its core, tugged at something in her head, bringing it closer and closer to the surface, like a fisherman drawing in a net with their catch. She only knew she didn't want to see what it would eventually bring up. It could stay in the depths where it belonged.

Damien tutted in disappointment and entered the bathroom, resting against the sink and watching her.

"Would you prefer something else? Pet? Brat?"

"I'd prefer you not to talk to me." Elora lowered herself further into the water and ignored his smirk and watchful gaze. The way his eyes refused to move away from her. They lapsed into silence as the water cooled, and she shivered slightly. Still, he didn't move; he just allowed his eyes to wander over her face and water. Was he just going to stay there? Was this a battle of wills to see who would surrender first? She wasn't willing to play this game with him.

With a dramatic sigh, Elora stood, no longer content to deal with the cold water or his intense focus. With a single motion that she wished was just a tad bit more graceful, she pulled herself out of the water, using the edge of the tub to help her stand, her legs still weak and slightly wobbly. Without sparing him a single glance, she stepped out, dripping water on the floor, and reached for the towel waiting on the counter.

As she wrapped the towel around her body and cinched it tight just above her breasts, he cursed and left, admitting defeat in whatever this battle of wills was for.

"Get dressed. Your father wants to see you." His voice trailed in from the bedroom as she grabbed another towel for her hair, and her heart sank, her minor sense of victory squashed instantly.

"About what?" She tried to ask as casually as she could and very slowly walked into the closet, touching each item of clothing as she tried to postpone leaving the room.

"Just a nice little father-daughter chat. Nothing to worry about."

"So, not about you being stabbed?"

"He might mention it." She poked her head out of the closet door at him, a small smile playing on the corner of his lips. Elora couldn't decide if he was amused by her stabbing him or the scene that was coming. If it was the former, it would have been frustrating and an insult to their captor-captive relationship.

She grabbed a shirt and sweats, not paying attention to either one since it wouldn't matter and pulled them on. Damien tossed a bundle of fabric in her direction, and she caught it, holding it as a sense of uncertainty rushed through her. It made no sense that he would give her anything. She met his eyes as the question rested on her tongue.

"Just take it. Don't read too much into it." He strolled out of the room, leaving her holding the fabric in her hand. She held it up, extending it to see what it was she was holding. A long-sleeved sweater that was at least two sizes too big for her, lightweight but soft. She pushed her arms through the sleeves before pulling it over her head, barely wondering if maybe she should refuse it on principle. It pulled tight across her chest as she wrapped her arms around herself, enjoying the way her body disappeared beneath it. She took a moment to center herself as well as remind herself that nothing was on display as she inhaled and took in the woodsy cologne. It was his sweater, she realized with a start, and against her better judgment and without her permission, her limbs relaxed just a fraction before she followed him out.

CHAPTER 27

Elora

Elora knew without a doubt that she hated Killian's rooms more than her own, even just the sitting room she currently found herself in. The dark palette extended to everything—the large desk covered with papers and a laptop, the leather chair behind it, the three armchairs, and every piece of wood from the paneled walls to the end tables. The only exception to this ominous décor was the bar made of dark marble and glass in the corner. The mirrored shelves lining the wall were covered in bottle after bottle of something Elora knew nothing about.

She bundled into one of the chairs and declined the drink Killian pushed in her direction, relishing the flash of annoyance that appeared on his face. With a shrug, he set it on the table and reclined in his chair to study her. His eyes lingered on the sweater before they flicked to Damien, who stood in the corner.

"I have questions for you, daughter."

"I doubt I have answers, Killian." He flinched at her very deliberate use of his first name in the wake of his title for her.

"We will see about that." Her eyes traced over his face, searching for any hint of physical connection. His hair was almost silver as compared to her own crimson locks while his eyes were pale grey while hers were a dark green, the color of fir needles. She supposed they shared their softer features and wide eyes, but she had thicker lips than him. Maybe she simply took after her mother.

"Do you want to play your little game? Question for a question?" Killian's lips curled into a sneer, and she shook her head, rolling her eyes dramatically.

"I have nothing to ask you. Just start so we can get this over with."

"Fine." He shifted, taking a drink from something that looked distinctly like blood. "How did you run away last time?"

She sighed. "I honestly don't remember. I remember only a little, and your pet over there should have told you that. He stalked me long enough to know it."

"Then what do you remember?"

Her eyes darkened, pure malice and hate replacing the green. "You don't want me to answer that with people present. Unless they were part of it as well." Killian shook his head and raised his hand.

"Fair enough." He lifted his chin, as if considering his next question. "Your foster family, as you call them. How did you find them?"

Elora scrunched her brow. "I was left with them one day about a year or so before I ended up in the hospital. Just left there with a bag of clothes and no memories."

"Convenient," Damien's muttered comment reached her ear, and she snapped her eyes at him.

"Fuck off. Speak when you are spoken to, pet." Killian chuckled warmly at the exchange, amusement making him look almost human, almost like he wasn't a monster.

"It hurts to know you two don't like each other," Killian explained, eyes flicking between the two of them.

"That's what happens when one stalks and kidnaps the other," she responded as Damien huffed a laugh.

"On my orders, little rose. No need to hold a grudge against him for it." Elora said nothing as Damien snickered from his spot in the corner, enjoying the apparent immunity Killian was attempting to grant him. It didn't matter either way. There was no protection to be had.

"However, you do know it isn't very nice to stab people who are following orders, especially my orders. Maybe you should apologize to him." Killian's voice was smooth and calm as he looked down at his drink, the dark red liquid twirling in the cup before he took a sip. She shrugged, eyes moving between the two vampires.

"He's an asshole." Damien chuckled again from his corner, and she flipped him off, silencing him instantly.

"Little rose, we just discussed this. Plus, didn't he tell you what the consequences of your actions are?" She stiffened, regretting not just apologizing to him. It wasn't like they could prove she didn't mean it, that she would rather cut off a body part than truly feel remorse for hurting him in any way. The only drawback would be Damien holding it over her head for the rest of her time there.

But as angry as she was, Viktor didn't deserve to bear the brunt of any punishment that would be sent his way due to her. So, she held her tongue and played the role she had so many times when Dr. Montgomery threatened to increase her medication.

"Yes, he did. But it was conveniently not until after the fork was in his neck." Her voice was flat, not a single hint of the irritation that was there before. It was easy to turn off her emotions, to render herself an empty shell, to hide any sign of anger or frustration under a veneer of detachment and obedience. When she first came to the psychiatric hospital, she had been an open book, every thought and emotion on display for anyone to see. She couldn't stop it or put a mask on like the others could with such ease. Then, something had shifted, a growing sense of self-preservation to avoid extra medication and little trips to the green room, when the so-called delusions came into play.

Killian smiled and took another sip before gesturing to Damien, who stalked to the door, opening it wide to allow someone to enter. The second the body came into view, Elora let out a harsh cry. At the sight of the blood and ripped fabric, she no longer cared about the possible consequences of letting this response through. No longer cared about what Killian or Damien would do. Viktor's hair was matted and there was dry blood around his neck and exposed chest where his scrubs from the hospital were ripped open, revealing the cuts and bite marks that covered him. There was barely an inch of flesh that wasn't marred or covered in gore or wounds. If it wasn't for the two vampires holding him up by his arms, Viktor wouldn't have been able to enter the room at all.

It was clear they had bled him. The paleness of his once suntanned face revealed the extent of the damage. The two vampires dropped him into the open space next to where Killian was sitting across from Elora. Without a single moment of hesitation, she jumped to her feet and threw herself at him, wrapping her arms around his neck, tears stinging her eyes. Viktor didn't move, didn't even flinch at the contact. She opened her mouth to say his name, but a hand grabbed her arm and yanked her back, a snarl sound accompanying the harshness of the move. With a grunt, she swung around, hand balled into a fist, not caring who she was aiming for or who was touching her.

All she knew was that they needed to let her go, that she needed to get to Viktor, to apologize, to help him. No matter how they left things, he didn't deserve this. Her eyes met Damien's just as his other hand clutched her wrist, stopping her attempts to hit him. He laughed softly, a sound that basically begged for him to be stabbed again.

"I told you the girl had feelings for him." There was disgust in his voice, searing and dripping from each and every word.

"Sit down, daughter. Let's have a talk and then I will let you go to him." Killian sounded bored as Damien dragged her over, pushing her down into the chair.

"Then talk." She snarled, eyes not leaving Viktor, whose head was still hanging down against his chest as he knelt on the floor, hands bound in front of him. Killian laughed softly, and she finally forced her eyes from Viktor to him.

"We will need to work on your manners. Obviously, your time with the foster family and at the hospital was not very educational in that regard. So much time lost." He took another drink, draining the cup before he handed it off to Damien, who dutifully took it for a refill.

"We need to have a conversation about expectations, about your place here, about what happens if you break the rules. Understand?" She just nodded, eyes drifting back to Viktor. Killian made a disgusted sound before he muttered a thank you. Elora could only assume that Damien had finally brought his drink like the good dog he was.

"Look at me while we are having a conversation. If you look at the human again, I will have Damien beat him. Understood?" For the first time during the exchange, there was a coldness in Killian's voice, a breakthrough of everything he was hiding beneath his façade. She brought her attention back to him to see him swiftly shift into a smile that aimed to be warm and comforting but was anything but.

"Good. Now, first expectations. Damien tells me you are refusing to eat. That is hardly acceptable. If you do not eat, then Viktor doesn't eat. And since he will need his strength, that is not really fair to him. This goes for everything else. If you do not bathe, he doesn't bathe. If you do not sleep, he does not sleep. Understood?"

"Yes." Her hands were clenching and unclenching while her nails bit into her palms.

"Fantastic. Also, if you are violent in any way, either to Damien, me, or another individual in charge of you, Viktor will be punished. Speaking of which, Damien?"

Her breathing started coming faster and her heart raced as she watched Damien sigh heavily before pulling something from his pocket. He held it tight in his fist as he approached her. Her body ceased to work, blood seized in her veins, heart thrashing so fast it felt as if it had stopped. Damien held out his hand, a fork in his grasp. She understood exactly what they wanted from her, understood that they hadn't been lying, no matter how desperately she had hoped they were. But she hadn't thought she would be the one to do it, a cowardly hope to have when it was Viktor who would bear the punishment.

She could at least do it herself, save him from Damien's brutality and Killian's obvious hatred.

"Stab him in the neck. Aim for the same place as you hit Damien, or you will need to try again until you get it right." She lowered her head at Killian's words, tears threatening to spill once more.

"Stab him, or I'll have Damien do it. And he has a habit of breaking humans. Using a fork would surely add to his reputation. Your choice." She pulled her eyes from her hands and found Viktor awake, a dazed expression wandering across the room. Slowly, they moved from Killian to Damien, then finally to Elora, who held the fork in her hand. She knew they must have looked ridiculous, that she must have looked ridiculous, but that didn't keep the horror and regret from her face. His own eyes widened in surprise as he scanned her face before they carefully traveled over her features and body, as if searching for any injuries or signs of distress.

"Great. You've finally joined us!" She flinched as Killian's hands clapped together and his voice broke the silence, amusement tinged with a cold edge that made her want to take Viktor and run.

She could sense Killian wandering over to Viktor, his strides easy and almost lazy before he crouched next to him.

"Let's get him up to speed, my child. You do the honors." Viktor's eyebrows knitted together as he tried to decipher exactly what had happened, why they were both here. She threw her hands in the air in exasperation.

"What does it matter, Killian? Ask your loyal pet. He doesn't care about me, so this will accomplish nothing." Somewhere near her, Damien chuckled.

"I wouldn't say that. Besides, it isn't about his feelings for you. It's about your feelings for him, about your inability to leave him to someone else's mercy." She cringed at the truth in Damien's words, at the admittance that it didn't matter how he felt, only how she did. And she did care for Viktor. Ever since he took care of her after the first breakdown, changing the gauze, asking each time before he touched her because he saw her flinch. Ever since he made sure she got coffee in the morning and some squares of chocolate left behind in her room after horrible sessions with Dr. Montgomery.

Her voice was small, betraying the brokenness she felt, the lack of fight left. "Where should I start?"

Killian waved his hand through the air in a dismissive gesture. "How about just the highlights?"

She swallowed, wishing for a glass of water as her throat dried. With a deep breath, she knelt before him to look him in the eye as she repeated everything. Just the highlights.

"This is Killian, and you already know Damien. Killian is my father." She spat out the last word, furious that she had to give him the title at this moment. "I was brought here instead of the transition house when I was released. I didn't know they had taken you. Amy, the caseworker, is gone."

Her cheeks felt wet, traitorous tears finally running free. She took a deep breath, stealing a glance at Damien standing beside

Viktor. Damien's attention was fixed solely on her and her confessions, and she turned her focus back to Viktor, staring into his amber eyes, a color that reminded her of the bonfires they lit with her foster family.

"I attacked Damien, stabbed him with a fork. But I didn't know, Viktor. I didn't even know you were here or that they would use you like this." She broke, guilt and fury and shame ripping her apart into jagged pieces. She couldn't meet his eyes, couldn't bear to see the confusion or anger or hatred or whatever emotion would come with that type of confession. But the sound that came, the sound that filled the room and caused her focus to shift from her hands, was unhinged.

Laughter. Loud and boisterous. She had never heard him laugh like this. It had been small chuckles here and there when someone made a decent joke. But this was free and unrestrained and wild. She wanted to drown in it. The two vampires on either side of him stared as if Viktor was insane and maybe he was. Maybe draining his blood, letting him be fed on, revealing that an entire group of people actually do exist had been too much for him.

"Did you hurt him?" The question drew everyone's attention, from a sharp intake of breath from Elora to a small curse from Damien and silence from Killian.

Her lips curled into a small grin. "I sure as hell did." Viktor's eyes darted to vampire in question and nodded, as if affirming what he already knew to be true.

"I would expect nothing less." He beamed at her, face flush with pride and probably blood loss, but there was a glint in his eyes, giving him an almost feverish look.

"I'm supposed to stab you as a punishment, as a consequence. Again, I'm so sorry, Viktor. I didn't know."

"And if you don't do it, this asshole will?" He jerked his head towards Damien, who only shifted on his feet, hands flexing, as if hoping Elora would refuse and leave the job for him. She nodded, breath trapped in her throat as she tried to inhale, as she tried to understand exactly what was happening. He was supposed to be angry, supposed to call her horrible names and thrash against the ropes around his wrists, face contorted until it was unrecognizable. It was almost like this was a normal day for him as he rolled his shoulders as much as he could with his hands bound.

"Well, I would prefer you to do it, if that is okay with you." She shook her head as she started to back away. The weapon shook in her hand, the cold metal burning her skin as she wondered if she could get away with just stabbing Killian. But that would leave her with Damien and an entire building full of vampires to contend with. Not exactly the best odds for them.

"Do it, Elora. Don't worry about me." She glanced at Damien, who looked as confused as she felt, as if he had missed a crucial element of the exchange that explained Viktor's reaction. But wasn't this what they wanted to see? The struggle her feelings for him would cause. Or was it that it wasn't much of a punishment or consequence if he was willingly offering himself up like a sacrifice?

Elora rolled her shoulders back and turned her head one way and then the other as a sense of purpose flooded her body. The tears dried along with the trembling in her hands. She gripped the fork, welcoming the sting of the cold metal on her warm skin, and leaned forward to Viktor, who lifted his chin in defiance. Damien took a cautious step back, and she gave him an absolutely feral grin, enjoying the unrestrained concern on his face, the way he moved to protect himself and Killian if he needed to do so.

She had won this round, had won this power struggle, and they both knew it. Viktor met her eyes, a flash of fear and hesitation as he prepared for the pain he knew was coming.

"Hurry it up," Damien drawled, but she refused to shift her attention away from the warm face before her. With a smile that was more of a grimace, she raised her hand and brought the makeshift weapon down hard, hitting the same spot it had before with Damien. She took a moment to study her handiwork and compared it to what she had done to the vampire who was now watching just as closely. The fork was buried all the way to the end of the prongs, the handle sticking directly out from where it was imbedded in the space between his neck and shoulder.

Viktor didn't flinch, didn't move as she yanked it back out and threw it at Killian. It landed at his feet and Viktor's blood splattered on his expensive shoes. At some point, he had moved away from the two figures on the floor and stood near his chair instead. Blood began to pour from the wound and trailed down Viktor's collarbones and chest. The scent of it filled the room as her mouth watered and teeth ached at the smell.

Without a single thought, she wrapped her arms around his neck and pulled him close. She whispered over and over how sorry she was, how it was never her intention for this to happen, for him to be dragged into this. An intense warmth hit her forehead as Viktor's lips met her skin—forgiveness etched into the way he lingered there for a moment. She took a deep breath and inhaled the scent of him underneath the blood and sweat, took in the smell of something earthy, like trees and fresh air. As she exhaled, she shivered slightly and rested her head on his chest, not caring about the blood that was now on her cheek and shirt.

They were given a moment, just a brief second, before someone gripped the back of her sweater and pulled her away, tossing her across the room and back towards her chair. Elora's head bounced off the floor as Viktor shouted something that she couldn't make out, not with the vibration inside her skull. It was followed by the sound of flesh hitting flesh and then a body being dragged away.

She moved quickly, scrambling into a sitting position even as her head pounded, and the room tilted slightly. Killian stared down at her, eyes hard as they drilled into her own, daring her to say something. There would be consequences if she did. The truth of that was etched into the hard planes of his face where there was once softness. For once, she kept her mouth shut, opting to sneer up at him from her position on the floor.

He thought she was his, that she was his daughter in every sense of the word, a creature made in his image. He was wrong.

~ ~

CHAPTER 28

Damien

He locked the cell down after Lukas tossed Viktor onto the bed. It creaked under his weight as he landed on his stomach with a sharp exhale of breath. The beds weren't meant for someone as broad as him, more suited to young people who had been thoroughly weakened from consistent blood loss to people who had been brought in off the street half starved. It was honestly a wonder the bed had lasted as long as it had. It was a distinct possibility that Viktor would be sleeping on a mattress on the floor soon.

The room itself was the same as all the others—a bed, a sink, and a toilet behind a privacy screen. Each cell had three reinforced walls, and one made of shatterproof plexiglass that was meant to allow vampires to look in and pick their meal. Humans were taken for showers individually three times a week, more if the human was a popular choice. Their every need was taken care of since they were given food and shelter in exchange for their services.

The thought of Viktor sleeping on a mattress on the floor strangely brought Damien no joy or entertainment. A begrudged respect had grown in Killian's office. Even under Killian's watchful gaze, Viktor had been defiant until the moment he was dragged from the room. The kiss on her forehead had left both vampires furious. But it had been bold, a spit directly in Killian's face.

None of that had gone the way they had expected. In his mind, Damien had expected the girl to cry, to beg for Viktor's safety, requiring Damien to step in and finish the job. Viktor would rage against the punishment and blame the girl he had left in tears on the steps of the hospital for her role in it. Damien even expected harsh words, maybe even a curse or two, breaking her spoiled spirit once and for all. But no. Viktor had accepted it with a grin and a fucking kiss on her forehead. Not even a sound, a whimper, a sharp exhale of breath. Not until Damien had thrown the girl away from him, breaking her hold on him.

And the girl. She had taken the punishment without complaint, grabbing the fork from his hand and stabbing with only the slightest hesitation. After everything was done and Viktor had been dragged out, Killian had simply sent the girl back to her room, blood drying on her cheek and the shirt he had given her. Damien had never seen him so enraged, hands trembling and body shaking as he turned away from her, revulsion clear on his normally stoic face.

Viktor groaned as he rolled over from his stomach and sat up on the bed, glancing in Damien's direction as he watched him.

"That was all very touching." Viktor chuckled at Damien's observation before reclining back against the wall his bed was nestled against.

"I suppose so. Why are you still here?" Damien hesitated as the question bounced around in his head, the answer not quite apparent. Maybe he simply wanted to mess with the human, tease him about the dynamic. He took in the room as he considered his response, everything from the black-tiled floor and the black bed set. The privacy screen didn't seem like it would give much privacy due to its mesh-like quality. Damien leaned against a wall.

"I'm curious about the display, to be honest. On the one hand, it was all very sweet. But I heard what you said to her outside the hospital, your parting words to her when she asked about seeing you. Quite cold, Viktor." He let out a dramatic sigh. "Something just doesn't add up."

Viktor narrowed his eyes slightly before he schooled his expression. "It was for her own good. My job was done."

"How cryptic," Damien responded, trying to decipher any hint of what this human meant, what his words referred to. For some reason, Damien didn't believe it was simply a nurse releasing his charge. And even if it was, that had been cruelty. He had spent years growing close to her, gaining her trust and affection, only to toss her aside once she wasn't interesting anymore.

"You seem very interested in whatever is between us. I wonder why that is." Damien shifted, instantly on edge with the insinuation of his words. It was simply that their dynamic was intriguing, that there was obviously something going on between them that was problematic, to say the least. The drama of it was intoxicating.

"I love watching a tragedy in the making." He raised an eyebrow at Damien, not responding to the taunt. "Just know that if you pull that again, Killian will kill you."

Damien wasn't sure why he was warning the human about this, why he seemed to care about what happened when it really shouldn't matter.

"Hmm. Curious that he would kill over such a little thing, don't you think?"

"Killian would kill you just for fun, just because he was bored. Don't forget that part."

"I am aware of what Elora's father is capable of." There was malice in his tone, a hatred that festered with each and every word.

"I thought humans don't know about us. You all seemed to spend enough time trying to convince the girl she was crazy."

"Dr. Montgomery did. I never told Elora she was wrong. Not once." The admission was telling, and Damien latched onto it, understanding that somewhere in his history Viktor had experience with his kind. It was usually a family member killed by a rogue vampire or who took to the life a little too much, either becoming a donor to pay some debt or turning all together. He would have Lukas look more into it now that Viktor had become more interesting, more than a nurse who acted as a thorn in his side.

"And you know what Killian is capable of?" Viktor's eyes flashed, the first sign of anything other than boredom throughout the exchange.

"Yes, I do. And so do you. You've seen what he has done to those he claims to love, those he claims as his own."

"The girl?"

"Why do you call her that? What has she done to you?" Damien shrugged again. His opinion of her wasn't necessarily Viktor's business, but it wasn't a secret, either. Killian was aware of what he thought of her, and she knew as well. She may not know every detail, every motivation behind it, but she knew he despised her. Their forced interactions and her stabbing him had proven the animosity between the two of them.

"She's Killian's daughter and spoiled brat. Nothing more." It wasn't a real answer, but Viktor's eyes hardened all the same.

"Maybe by blood, by that's it. No one treats family like that." Damien gestured for Viktor to continue, his curiosity getting the better of him. Viktor sighed and closed his eyes for a moment.

"It isn't my story to tell. But you have seen firsthand what he has done. She may not remember it, but her body and her scars do." Viktor laid down on the paper-thin pillow and closed his eyes. A clear dismissal, and Damien struggled to pull himself under control at the sign of disrespect at the hands of a human.

He pushed off the wall and left, hitting the button for the elevator as he shifted from one foot to the other. It felt like an eternity before it finally arrived. No matter what he did, Viktor's words echoed in the hallway, following even when the elevator chimed and he got in, hitting the button for the blood bank floor. Without any interest or thought, Damien fed, choosing a young woman from the group who had been employed for this very reason. He didn't pick the ones who had been coerced into the job, those pulled from the streets where the options were to take the job or starve.

He briefly recognized the bland taste of the blood, metallic and lifeless, as he drank. Her breathless moans functioned only as background noise to the repeated assertion Killian's love was written on Elora's body, in each and every scar. Yet Killian only every appeared doting and loving, albeit a little possessive. But his daughter had been gone for years. It made sense that he would want her near, want her watched to make sure nothing like that happened again.

But there had been the dark look in his eyes, the predatory gleam when he tasted her blood. Damien shook his head and opened his door, letting out a breath as he locked it behind him. The blood from the human had done its job, satiating the gnawing feeling that came with hunger, but had done nothing else. In his early years as a vampire, blood had been intoxicating, euphoria is liquid form. It was what led to bloodlust among the young, especially those who don't have someone to help them through it, help them curb their thirst and learn to control it.

But that had changed. Blood and feeding were no longer enjoyable since the taste became bland and metallic, whereas there used to be distinct flavors based on who the humans were, where they had lived, what they had eaten. Feeding had become survival, a necessary requirement to stay alive. It was part of the growing unease among the vampire population, why so many were drawn to feeding directing from humans in hopes it would be different. While the blood may satiate hunger, it did nothing else. Many claimed they needed to feed more frequently when using the blood banks, but it didn't change the fact that feeding from humans was against the Accords and had led to the problem they were now dealing with — a human resistance.

Despite the room being dark when he returned, he could see well enough to drop his jacket on the chair at the desk. His room was simpler than others he had seen, especially Killian's and the girl's. Comparatively, Damien's room was empty, no paintings or random keepsakes. No books or family pictures. No trophies or personal touches at all. When he had been turned, there had been nothing to bring with him. Instead, the room housed only a chair, table, dresser, and desk he never used except to hold his random assortment of items that amounted to a jacket, watch, weapon, and cellphone.

It was well past one in the morning at this point. Speaking with Viktor and feeding at taken much longer than he had anticipated but he would still need to wake up soon to continue his babysitting duty. That was what it felt like: babysitting a twenty-five-year-old woman, almost twenty-six. He groaned at the thought, realizing it would mean some type of party or celebration. Killian never passed up a chance to display his power, influence, and wealth, and her birthday would make the perfect excuse. He would want to celebrate not just her birthday, but her return to the vampire family and her role as Killian's daughter. Rumors still spread like wildfire about exactly who she was, and this would put those to rest if Killian had his way.

The party would be a chore, yet another in the chronicle of dealing with her. He would need to follow her, make sure she didn't do anything embarrassing or stupid. There would be no drinking or feeding or anything else for Damien, as long as she was his responsibility. But Killian was content, happy even, and that had to be good enough.

Damien pulled off his shirt and threw it into the closet and onto the pile of clothes lying on the floor before he changed into a pair of linen pants meant for sleeping. A contented sigh sounded from his lips as he slid into bed, welcoming the feeling of cotton sheets against his skin. His preference for cotton had been met with sarcasm from Killian, who attributed it to Damien's so-called rustic upbringing, resulting in a nostalgic desire for them. At the time, Damien had thought it harsh, almost cruel to use his human life in such a way, a rude reminder of the life he was forced to live. But it was simple bluntness, as Damien had come to understand. Killian could be savage, murderous, and terrifying, but that was required. Any sign of weakness and everything would fall apart. So would anyone who was loyal to him.

Viktor had claimed the vampire was cruel, a key figure in the girl's scars. Laughable, really. He couldn't get the thought out of his head as the phone on his desk went off. With a muttered curse, Damien forced himself out from underneath the blanket and grabbed the phone, reading the text message from Lukas.

Noises from Elora's room. Check on it. Killian's orders.

"Fuck." With a roll of his eyes, Damien left the room, steps deliberately slow, careful not to slam the door in his anger. In a matter of moments, the elevator had gone up to her floor, and he paused outside her door.

Whimpers. Cries of something that may be pain. Without any more hesitation, he unlocked the door and entered, annoyed and curious more than anything. Because what he was feeling couldn't possibly be concern for her.

~ ~

CHAPTER 29

Elora

The blade stung as it pierced her skin and dragged along her forearm until there was a cut roughly a few inches long. The person who held the knife moved on and repeated the action on each arm and leg while she bled freely from each one. It was purposeful, bordering on ritualistic. Her arms ached from where they were chained to the bedposts and she squeezed her eyes shut, promising herself that she wouldn't cry out this time, that she wouldn't shed a single tear.

She wouldn't give them that satisfaction. None of them. Especially not him.

Elora could feel the pairs of eyes that watched her limbs where the blood was waiting, flowing in single lines down her skin and onto the sheets. She knew without a doubt they were waiting for permission; perfectly trained pets being held back from their treat by their master.

She stared at the ceiling and tried to lose herself in happy memories, lose herself anywhere that wasn't this room. But how could she when they were few and far between? She imagined the feel of the comb through her hair as her mother brushed it each night, the sound of her voice as she read to her. Elora couldn't recall her face, only her voice, the feel of her hands when she embraced her, the scent of lilies from her soap.

From the corner of the room where he sat, there was the sound of someone snapping their fingers, followed by low growls. The sound filled the room and sunk into her body as it reverberated amongst her bones. Her body tensed in response and prepared for what was coming. Without a moment's hesitation, hands and teeth and lips clamped down on her arms and legs, lapping and sucking at the wounds. It burned, like her body was on fire, combusting from the inside out. She closed her eyes, trying to shut out the sound of her blood being drained from her body, the sound of their moans as they took her in. A prize for their loyalty and blind obedience. She didn't cry out, didn't allow even the tiniest whimper to come from her as she clenched her jaw, lips tucked together firmly in a thin line.

Displays of pain, or weakness, only made it worse, throwing them into a frenzy that left her weaker than any other time.

A set of teeth sunk into her wrist and left the cut that had been made to spare her the pain of a bite. There were no thoughts in her mind, only a scream that echoed off the walls she had built up to protect herself in these moments. And there were so many.

The only sound in the room was of them feeding and the slight whimpers that escaped her lips, no matter how desperately she tried to keep them contained. Another bite, this time further up her thigh, hands grasping her leg as they pulled from her, over and over again. She cried out finally and was rewarded with a chuckle from the corner of the room where he sat.

Hands on her shoulder held her tight, finger digging in before shaking her, yanking her from where she laid on the bed. It made no sense since the chains held her firmly in place, not allowing her to move from her spot, move away from their desires. She thrashed, unable to move under their hands and teeth and her heart rate slowed down, finally drained as much as she was last time and the time before.

"Elora!" A voice called her name, one she knew but couldn't quite place. It didn't make sense. He didn't belong in this space, not at this moment.

"Wake up. Come on." Another jolt to her body and then arms were pulling her up from the mattress, violently shaking her.

Slowly, painfully, her eyes open, throat raw from where she was still crying out. The room was dark, save for a small light coming from the lamp on the nightstand beside her. Her breaths were forced pants, shallow and ineffective as she frantically searched her arms and legs for marks and bites, motions jerky and desperate. She shuddered as the residue of their fingers and teeth remained, their grips tight, teeth sharp. Elora swore her body was an inferno, radiating fire and heat, the cuffs still on her wrists and ankles.

Tears formed in her eyes as she searched the corners of the room for him, for Killian. For the first time she recognized him, could put a name to the face and the sound of his voice, his laughter. Each time it had been him, her father, sitting in the corner. He had watched them feed on her with his permission, like she was a reward for a job well done. The nightmares had plagued her during her time at the hospital, breaking through the nightly sedative to torture her in her sleep. She could only guess that being back in this room, being in his presence had brough it back, had allowed her to recognize that they were not simply nightmares, but fragments of memories, bits and pieces of the life she had forgotten and been shielded from. The protective barrier she had built up brick by brick had fallen away. Each word from his mouth, each singular second in his presence, the barrier chipped, letting it all come back. What had started as a drip, a single hint of memory, had transformed into an all-consuming flood that was drowning her.

She didn't want to remember.

"Elora, breathe." The hands on her arms let go of her as she jumped at the words, allowing her to jerk away, lashing out with her fists and feet. She didn't aim, didn't have the capacity to do anything but react, to hurt whoever was there. A scream ripped from her as the person muttered a soft curse, taking each hit as they found purchase. Her back hit the headboard, sending a wave of pain through her body. Her sharp cry filled the room and drowned out the other voice.

She froze as understanding raced through and her eyes opened to take in the figure on the bed beside her. Damien's hand tightly held onto her arm while the other cupped her jaw. His dark brown eyes stared at her as if searching her face for any sign that she was calm. There was something strange in his expression, a softness she had never seen as concern laced every feature. She could only think about how close they were, how she could feel his breath on her face as she inhaled and held her own before releasing it. The flecks of gold mixed in with chocolate brown seemed to gleam as she used him and his gaze to secure herself back in reality and away from memory turned into a nightmare. Slowly, so slowly, the feeling of those foreign hands and teeth disappeared and left her a trembling and crying mess on the silk sheets.

Neither of them said anything as her breathing evened out, and she nodded, giving him the permission he was waiting for to drop his hands to his sides. He shifted slightly and turned so he could see her better. Damien watched her every move, the rise and fall of her chest, the drying tears on her cheeks, the shaking of her fingers as she brushed a strand of hair away from her face. It was like he was waiting to see if she would break into a million pieces, and he would have to explain what happened. She wanted to scoff or say something about his concern for his own safety, should something happen to her. But there had been that softness in his eyes, the slight tinge of fear and concern as she calmed down.

Finally, Elora looked him over as the realization that he was in her room, comforting her after a nightmare had settled in. Red scratches and marks that would grow into bruises lined his cheeks and neck, even his bare chest. She paused, not even sure she was moving or breathing, as she traced the tattoos along his arms with her eyes. It was difficult to make out exactly what they were underneath the marks from her frenzied need to escape the nightmare that had followed her into reality. Her heart quickened once more as a new fear and panic raced through her.

"Please, please don't punish Viktor. I didn't know that was you. I didn't—" His eyes widened in disbelief as she plead for leniency, no matter how futile she knew it to be.

"Was it a nightmare?" His voice was like velvet, calm in a way she hadn't heard him speak. There was no edge to it or sneer like when he pushed her buttons or addressed her directly and acted as if she was beneath his notice, not worthy of his attention. This was almost comforting. Almost.

"Just one of many. Please, don't punish Viktor for this."

Damien's jaw flexed. "This can stay between us. No need for Killian to know or for Viktor to be punished."

"Don't tease me about this, Damien. Please." She hated herself for begging him, for her fear overruling her pride even as he winced.

"I'm not. I promise." She let out a harsh breath even as shock hit her. When she saw the marks on his face and bare chest, she had imagined him marching straight to Killian's rooms, dragging Viktor from wherever he was being held so he could be punished for her actions. She could picture Killian's disappointed yet manically excited face as he clicked his tongue at her, demanding something horrible in retaliation for breaking the rules.

"But there is a tiny condition. Tell me about your nightmare."

She rolled her eyes and scolded herself for not seeing there would be something, some condition to guarantee his silence.

Nothing came for free; no act of kindness was without strings attached. Elora crossed her arms over her chest and felt the silk of the nightgown, the same flimsy piece of fabric she always wore in her dreams. It was all part of the ritual—silk and blood. Her stomach rolled and bile rose in her throat at the thought. For a moment, it was silent as Damien disappeared into a different part of the room and returned with the small throw blanket in hand.

"Here. So you can cover up." She took it from his hand, grateful for him not touching her, and threw it around her shoulders, pulling it tight as if it would protect her from holding up her side of their bargain. She gave him a small nod that she hoped he understood as gratitude.

"I don't really remember it." She rationalized that this wasn't truly a lie but was more of a half-truth. There were gaps, just as there always were. This time, however, there were fewer of them with Killian's face and voice revealed and understood, latching onto memories long since dormant. She didn't remember anyone else in the dream, their faces obscured by a fog, rendering them unrecognizable. Plus, it was hard to know when you squeezed your eyes closed in hopes of escaping, in hopes of leaving your body so you didn't have to experience it, feel it in each nerve in your body.

"Tell me what you do remember." Elora scooted to the edge of the bed and let her legs hang off as she stared at her hands. She wasn't sure she could meet his eyes while she told him, while she exposed this part of herself to a vampire who hated her despite any comfort he offered now. He didn't deserve to know her shame, her self-hatred at her inability to fight, not just in the nightmares but in those moments as well. Not once had she fought, not once had she screamed or thrashed to try to protect herself. A part of knew it would have been stupid, that her self-blame and guilt were misplaced and irrational, that she had been a child. Killian always kept the leash tight, the chains strapping her to the bed while she was drugged into a strange state where she knew what was happening but was unable to fully move. Then, there were those who were used as collateral, who were punished if she fought.

Yes, rationally she knew that there was nothing she could have done. That the shame was unfounded. But her rational mind did not hold sway here as it left her to her darkest thoughts. Elora took a deep breath and held it, letting it out slowly as she clasped her hands together, praying it would stop the shaking.

"They aren't really nightmares, but memories. That is what I figured out while working with Dr. Montgomery. It's the way my repressed memories come forward. Or so she had told me during our sessions. I don't remember everything from my life before my foster family, but what I do remember comes out in the nightmares." She quickly glanced at him, reading his expression. Blank. Nothing was there to give her even the slightest hint of what he was thinking about her confession so far.

"This one was fairly standard." She shrugged, and he adjusted how he was sitting, turning more towards her.

"What happened first?" His attempt to encourage her to continue was successful as she felt the words rushing forward, demanding to be let free, demanding that someone, anyone, listen to them.

"I always wake up in this room. It's a little different. There are toys and dolls and books, but I just stare at the ceiling. There are lights up there, little lights my mother had added to the ceiling to look like stars." Elora smiled sadly at the thought and picked at the skin around her fingernails.

"I am chained to the bed, both arms and legs. There are cuts on them. I can always sense people in the room, but I can never see their faces. I know that there is someone watching from the corner and then someone gives a signal." Her voice broke, and she swallowed as she took a moment before continuing.

"They attack me, I suppose. Feeding from me, touching me. I can't move. I can't cry out or it will be worse. Usually, I wake up once my heart rate slows down in the dream." Elora wiped a tear from her cheek and shook her head as if this was nothing, as if she had told him her favorite meal or what her favorite movie was.

Damien didn't say anything, just took her hand, stopping her from picking at her cuticles. His thumb rubbed over her knuckles, and she watched the gesture as if it was the only thing worth seeing in the entire room. She could feel his gaze dissecting everything—her body language, the expression on her face, the trembling limbs, the tears. Elora didn't meet his eyes. She refused to see the revulsion and disgust that was bound to be there. Or even worse, a hunger that she had seen so many times before on the face of those in her dreams.

She didn't mention Killian as she decided to keep that name behind her teeth, terrified of ruining whatever this moment was. Damien's loyalty lied with him, but if she tried desperately enough, she could pretend otherwise.

"You should take a bath. You're covered in sweat. It will help." Elora nodded, not sure what else there was to say in response.

"I'll go run the water while you gather up some clothes. While you're in the bath, I'll get you some new sheets and a blanket." His grip on her hand tightened as he touched her chin and turned her face until she met his eyes.

"I'll stay here until you fall back asleep. Okay?"

"And Viktor won't be punished? I didn't mean to hit you, not this time." She gave him a small grin and hoped her words would come off as a joke between the two of them, as if her repeated violence was simply fun between friends. Damien pulled her hand and drew her to him. His arms wrapped around her, and she rested her head against his bare chest, suddenly aware of how gross she felt. The sweat clung to her skin and her hair was a tangled mess. The damp strands stuck to her face and exposed back along with the wet nightgown. Despite this, she refused to move, only prayed and hoped she could stay here and enjoy the strange safety she felt in his arms. Even if it was a lie and wouldn't last past tonight.

CHAPTER 30

Damien

He realized relatively quickly he wasn't sure he could keep her nightmares a secret from Killian, despite what he may have promised her. He had never tried to keep anything from him. And if he was honest, it was irritating that he was attempting to do so now. It felt like a betrayal against him, a slap in the face of everything Killian had done for him. He wanted to blame her for this and rail against her for dragging him into whatever last night had been. Yet her fear and panic, the shame and guilt he saw on her face forced him to stay his anger, to rethink things in a way that made him uneasy.

Her first thought had been of Killian, but not in the way Damien would have expected. He had been prepared to fetch Killian so he could comfort his daughter the way he had done. Killian would have been the one to hear about the rage inducing memory and Damien could only hope that he would seek out those who had hurt her. But her fear had been palpable, existing in the room at their feet like a living thing. And her second thought had been of the human, the piece of garbage who had turned her away once she was released and was no longer under his control. Something in his gut twisted at the thought of her begging for Viktor to be spared, as if Damien was cruel and wouldn't understand she had fully aware of what she was doing.

She had seemed so broken, shattered, and left in pieces. It was as if she had been attempting to glue herself back together by herself each time it occurred. He knew intimately how that left jagged edges and chips behind, something not quite whole, not quite the same.

And now, standing in Killian's office while he looked through the papers on his desk, he was uneasy. Not a hair out of place on Killian's head, nor was there a wrinkle in his crimson shirt, which was a shade so reminiscent of the girl's hair. His long fingers moved the papers around, face contorting with each new document as he scanned the contents. Some were placed to the left and were meant to be destroyed, and others to the right were meant to be filed away. Damien shifted uncomfortably, nerves taking over his normally calm and stoic demeanor whenever he was in the head vampire's presence. He had been summoned with Lukas left in his place to watch over the girl, something that also left a strange feeling in his chest. Finally, after what felt like hours, Killian glanced up from his paperwork and studied him, eyes holding a glint that could promise anything—violence or praise, a new mission or punishment.

"We are having a dinner party for my little rose. To welcome her home and celebrate her birthday. It will be a party to rejoice at the fact that all traces of the hospital are gone from her." Damien's eyebrows knitted together as he recalled the human they had questioned, whose daughter was already buried while her mother wept at her grave, left alive for this particular form of torture. The girl had been a test subject of sorts, given some type of repressive medication. None of it had made much sense to him at the time. It wasn't his job to understand.

"My doctors tell me that the medication in her system will be gone by Friday, so we will have the party on Saturday. A small gathering — just key members from the other vampire houses. It will be subdued, obviously." A small smile played on his lips as they both recalled what vampire parties normally included — unhinged feeding on humans, sex on the banquet tables, and the elimination of rivals or feuds.

"And what will you need from me?" Damien shoved his hands in the pockets of his jeans and waited, hoping he looked as at ease as he normally did.

"You will be by her side throughout the night. Protect her. There will be vampires there who may see her as a way to get to me, to force my hand. We have also had rumors of the Resistance leaping on any opportunity to cause problems."

"Of course." It was exactly as he had guessed last night before the nightmare had drawn him from his bed. Killian would want him to babysit her through her first event, her coming out party in a sense. He thought he would be irritated at the assigned job of shadowing her all night, standing at her side through the dancing and dinner. Damien believed he would be annoyed by the fact he wouldn't be able to take part in the more entertaining, if not debauched, portions of the night. Normally, he would feed, enjoying the human in every conceivable way as he did so.

For some reason, he didn't lament that loss as he waited for the irritation to manifest.

Killian nodded, as if his agreement was anything but a guarantee. It was a warranted assumption, considering Damien had never told him no, never turned down a job. The debt he owed the head vampire was too much for that. His mother had owed him too much for that, but not anymore.

"But I do have something for you to do tonight. I want you to get Dr. Montgomery's journals. I've recently learned that she keeps her patient notes in her own journals and does not add everything to her online files.

"That seems unorthodox."

"And illegal. My hope is there is some information in them that could prove useful in understanding my daughter and what was done to her, as well as more insight into this doctor who treated her. There is too much that doesn't fully add up."

It would explain the gaps in the girl's records, leaving him confused and frustrated by the obvious lack of detail on every page of patient notes. It had been the bare minimum—vague topics discussed in therapy, references to medications with no discussion of what they did or why she was taking them. Only the assertion of the girl's delusions and auditory hallucination, just enough to potentially keep her there. At the time, he had simply assumed it was human error, the result of a failing human-run establishment with little to no oversight.

"Do we know where she keeps them?"

"Her office. She doesn't necessarily hide them, according to my contact. They are on the bookshelves, disguised as medical texts."

"Simple, yet effective." His comment resulted in a soft laugh from Killian, the sound finally putting Damien at ease.

"Yes, I suppose so. I want those journals, Damien. I want to know about my daughter's time there, details on the damage they did." There was a pain in his voice that was hard to reconcile with the nightmares he heard about last night. She hadn't mentioned Killian directly, but there were references to permission being needed along with a figure in the corner.

"I'll get them. Who will watch her while I am gone for the night?"

"Lukas. I trust him with her." That much was obvious, since he was the one with her now. Damien considered for a moment warning Lukas about the nightmare, about what she may need from him if they came back. Lukas had been the one to tell him about the noises coming from her room. Hopefully, he wouldn't have questions since Damien hadn't told Killian, and he needed to make sure his withholding information didn't get back to him.

For a brief moment, he almost broke his promise to the girl. She was nothing to him, a mission he didn't want, a woman who threw away everything he had prayed for as a child. And Killian was her father. Didn't he deserve to know if his daughter was having such visceral nightmares? The words were on his tongue, but they refused to move, refused to be voiced into the space between them. The confession halted before he could give it life, an instinct screaming at him to be quiet, to keep his mouth shut, leaving Damien almost ashamed of the action.

Accompanied by a sharp pain in his chest, he understood that he was choosing the girl's secrets over Killian, resulting in his world tipping onto its side, contents displacing and spilling out. He wasn't entirely sure what shape they would take once he put them back together.

"Bring me the journals as soon as you return. I expect them by morning.

* * *

The grounds were dark and silent as Damien approached, jumping the iron fence with ease. His steps were silent on the grass as he avoided the gravel, unsure if there was any security patrolling the grounds at night. There hadn't been any guards that he knew about while he worked there, but that didn't mean that hadn't changed. But no lights turned on as he made his way closer, no flashlights illuminated the grounds as guards patrolled. It was as if the building was deserted, left to rot and fall into disrepair.

At the door, Damien pulled out the keycard he had taken from Viktor when he dragged the human back to the Tower, throwing him in a cell to be used to keep the girl in line. He supposed he could have simply had his own credentials reinstated, but it would have taken time that he didn't have. Killian had demanded the journals by the end of the night, so Viktor's keycard would have to work. Apparently, even after being gone from work for a week, he was still employed.

The door unlocked easily with a soft click. The door squeaked slightly as he pushed it open and searched for any sign of life. Nothing. The first floor was empty, giving it a haunting appearance. The paintings of previous and current board members stared down at him, judging and smug from their place on the wall. Damien kept his steps quick and easy as he followed the hallway to the stairway where lights showed through the window in the door. After a quick peek, he entered and raced up the stairs to the second floor, where the doctor's office and the journals stood waiting.

Honestly, it was depressingly easy to break into the psychiatric hospital with their security system, outdated by at least a decade, maybe closer to fifteen years. And then there was the complete lack of personnel. No nurses roamed the halls for bed checks or vitals as they did several times a night, waking up the patients to make sure they were still alive and healthy. There were no rogue doctors roaming the hallways, finalizing patient notes as he had seen them do before. He couldn't even make out noise in the kitchens, cleaning up from dinner before leaving for the night.

Instead, he strolled through the hallway until he came to her office door with its traditional key lock. As he crouched down to pick the lock, Damien glanced down the dark hallway one way and then the other, despite knowing that there were no humans nearby. He would be able to scent them, hear their heartbeat, the predator in him rising to the surface.

Did the good doctor just not trust technology? His thought was punctuated by the door unlocking, his skill gained in childhood working perfectly. Considering she didn't use keycard locks or added her patient notes to the online files, it would be a fair guess to make. Plus, he had broken in and made it to her office within fifteen minutes. Maybe she had a point with her refusal to use modern tech for security.

The door made no noise as he opened and shut it, leaving him in a darkness that hid nothing from him. Being able to see in the dark was a perk that would have been helpful before he turned and broke into stores to steal food. Heavy curtains covered the windows, something he noticed even during the day when he would bring the girl here. The only lights in the room came from various lamps along the walls and the one on her desk. It was so much like Killian's office—stifling shadows with sharp edges meant to make the visitor uncomfortable.

Everything was exactly as she had it the last time Damien was in there and he turned on the lamp on her desk, the one furthest from the door and window and least likely to draw attention. His night vision was good, but not perfect, and he couldn't afford to mess this up. At one end of the bookshelves, Damien began his search, fingers trailing along the spines, searching specifically for medical texts that look a little off. The font with strange shape, the cover soft, a lack of authors or publisher on the spine. Every few books, he took one off the shelf and flipped through the pages before shoving it back into its spot with a frustrated groan. It was taking longer than anticipated.

Finally, towards the middle of the bookshelves, he found them. Each one had a title along the spine that says *Diagnostic Criteria Manual* along with a tiny symbol at the bottom, something akin to a star, a small indicator that these were different from the others.

One by one, he pulled them out and glanced at the first page where the patient's name was listed. Not just Elora, but multiple patients over the course of the last five or so years. After the first four journals, Damien finally pulled one that he needed with Elora's name on the first page in cursive and tossed it on the desk before returning to his search, yielding two more.

Three journals with roughly 200 pages of notes on the girl.

He knew he should put them in the small bag he brought with him, toss them in and then leave, never turning past the first page where her name was listed along with the years covered in the journal. He knew that the notes were for Killian, that he didn't need to know the girl's history, that it shouldn't matter. But her screams and the way she spoke echoed in his ears, her tears and terror there each time he closed his eyes, replaying and replaying. A constant companion. Torture, pure and simple.

With hesitant fingers, Damien opened the first journal and flipped through the pages, searching for something, anything that could give him even the slightest bit of insight, settle the uneasy feeling that had made a home in his chest since that night. Each page brought snippets of information in lines of neat cursive writing that piqued his interest until he found himself sitting in the large leather chair, reading by the light of the single lamp he turned on.

Session 5: Elora

Elora reports more nightmares during which she is being fed from by vampires. She explains that there is a vampire sitting in the corner of the room who is in charge of the situation, granting permission to those who end up drinking her blood. She claims that these are not just nightmares, but memories. When I asserted that the vampires were not real, she became angry and lashed out, throwing the lamp at the wall. She had to be restrained, and I ordered her medication increased.

Her memories do seem to be coming back despite the suppression measures. The medication that keeps her hunger at bay seems to be working, as she has reported no symptoms that would lead us to believe she is experiencing any vampiric traits. It hurts to have to convince her that vampires are not real and use the attack on her foster sister as a means of doing so. But it is for her own safety.

"What the fuck?" His mutter was horrifically loud in the silent office and his eyes narrowed as he flipped forward a few more pages, searching for another entry like this one. The doctor, with all her displays of concern and disappointment and declarations that Elora was a danger to herself and others due to her delusions and hallucinations, had been lying the entire time. The justification seemed to be to keep the girl safe, but there was no explanation as to who she needed to be protected from.

Session 14: Elora

The medication seems to have improved not only her symptoms but also the nightmares. We have started working through her attack with her foster sister. Elora claims that she had no control over her body and her actions. She expresses a deep guilt and shame in her actions, explaining that it reminds her of her nightmares.

The biggest challenge for Elora going forward will be to work through her shame and guilt, both for what she did to her foster sister but also for what was done to her. She still refuses to discuss the scars.

We will need to continue to reinforce that vampires are part of her mind attempting to make sense of her guilt and shame. Hopefully, with time, she will come to believe it.

Session 56: Elora

She was not present for her appointment today due to being in the green room. The nurse's report claims she attacked a resident by jumping across the table and biting the male resident. She was able to bite his neck for only a moment before two nurses pulled her off and sedated her. She was then left in the green room until she woke up approximately an hour later, which was much quicker than it should have been. For her height and weight, a dose the size she was given should have sedated her for roughly 5 hours. I am concerned that the level of medication in her system will cease to be enough. I'm not sure how much higher we can go without doing long-term damage.

The resident she bit was taken to the infirmary, but his wound closed quickly, and he was moved into an observation room. It is possible her bite has done nothing and there will be no lasting effects. However, I am not sure we will be that lucky. This is why she cannot be allowed to leave and be found by her maker.

Session 103: Elora

Her release was denied again today, and she expressed nothing in our appointment. She refused to speak about it or anything else. Instead, I talked to her about the reasons why she hadn't been allowed to leave. She can't know that my input was a crucial factor in that decision. But she must remain here where I can monitor her. It is for both her safety and the safety of the public.

Once she returned to her room, she broke the mirror somehow. It was made of the same reflective sheet that the others were made out of. However, she was able to break it and used a piece to attempt suicide through two long cuts along her forearms, requiring over 25 stitches due to the length and depth of the wound. The details are being withheld from her file, per my request.

Was this the incident that Viktor had alluded to after her breakdown? Either way, the reference to her biting a resident was new information, a little kernel that would have made his job easier and quicker if it had been in her file. And yet, if Dr. Montgomery was aiming to keep her a secret, the vague notes made perfect sense. He flipped through the pages, searching for the name of the resident she had attacked, but there was nothing, as if the patient simply vanished. A job for Killian's team. The rest were notes about how she had become quiet and non-confrontational, which Dr. Montgomery, in all her years of education and practice, took as a positive sign. Damien knew it for what it was—a mask, a disguise for a woman who didn't feel like she had any power, any control.

With a deep breath, Damien shoved the journals into the bag and left the way he came in, still not finding a single soul and wondering if maybe now that the girl Dr. Montgomery wanted to protect so much was gone, security didn't matter as much.

CHAPTER 31

Elora

S he had expected Damien when she opened her door that morning; the knock jarring her from her book. He never knocked, just entered like this was his room, like his presence was desired and welcomed no matter where he was.

"Just a second." Her voice covered the sound of her moving the food on her tray around, hoping it looked like she had consumed something beyond the cup of coffee. When she finally did open it, she found the only other vampire she had met beyond Killian and Damien. Lukas was by far her favorite so far, but it wasn't as if the bar was set that high. As long as he was kind and treated her like she wasn't dirt, he would keep his place at the top.

She gave him a grin and stepped aside, gesturing for him to enter with a dramatic swing of her hand. Elora enjoyed his company. The vampire was fun, quick to laugh, and actually engaged her in conversation, and didn't sit silently in the corner with a scowl on his face.

"Looks like it is my turn again today. Unless you plan on breaking my nose?" His wide mouth somehow spread even wider as a genuine smile appeared on his face and she rolled her eyes at his comment, having forgotten about that.

"In my defense, you were kidnapping me and had knocked out my caseworker. I would think a broken nose was fairly earned." He laughed loudly before glancing back at the doors to Killian's rooms. She cocked an eyebrow at him as he shrugged and came inside, a wry grin on his face.

"Where is my normal jailor?" She tried to keep her voice casual, but he shook his head and smiled, offering a desk of cards.

"I heard you know how to play." The surprise must have shown on her face, as he chuckled. Damien had to have told him, yet she doubted he had mentioned she could barely play anything beyond Go-Fish.

"That is a bit generous. Technically, I know how to play the few games allowed at the hospital. Normally, I play solitaire since I didn't exactly make friends while I was there." His smile faltered just a bit before he brightened up, as if he were determined to make this as normal as possible—no talks of kidnapping or hospitals allowed.

"What can you play? Poker? Blackjack?" It was her turn to laugh, and she took a moment to enjoy the feeling, the eruption of a sound that she hadn't made in days or weeks.

"Oh no, those games weren't allowed. We played Go-fish or War, though that game was banned shortly after the great Card Game fight during my second year."

"War? I've never heard of that one." Her eyes went wide, and he scrunched his nose. She couldn't believe it, since she had thought it was a game most children were taught.

"Sit down and give me the cards. I'll teach you." With an exaggerated eye roll, he handed her the deck and pulled up an armchair before settling into the desk chair already there. She took her own seat across from him and made a show of taking the cards out of the sleeve and removing the Jokers.

"The game is simple. We split the deck and then we flip cards. Whoever has the higher card wins the hand and takes the cards. The person who manages to collect the full deck wins."

"That's it?" His face had taken on an expression of severe concentration, as if this was a life-or-death challenge he was determined to win. Elora snickered softly and started dividing the deck.

"That's it. How about we up the stakes?" Her question hung between them, suspicion lining his otherwise kind face.

"What type?"

"Nothing that could get you in trouble. If I win the round, I will ask you a question. If you win, you ask me one. I promise not to ask you to reveal anything too embarrassing." The corner of his mouth curved slightly, a hint that he probably believed he would certainly win. He had to know there was no strategy for this. It was a game of pure luck. A simple matter of who had the higher card.

"Deal. Who goes first?" His face was the very image of determination as he studied the set up closely.

"We both can, but honestly, it doesn't matter. It isn't like the top card is going to change if one of us hesitates for a moment." His eyes narrowed, like he was trying to decide if this was a method of cheating.

"We put them down at the same time. Agreed?" Elora giggled at the commanding tone.

"Agreed." And they began.

Elora flipped her first card as he flipped his—a king to his three. She chuckled and took them both, setting them in a pile off to the side. She watched as his face grew more serious, preparing for the next set. Elora groaned as she put down a six to his eight and he let out a triumphant noise, grabbing them and shifting in his seat. She won the next hand and then him once more. It wasn't long before they both ran out of cards and had to pick the pile they had been adding to, hers quite a bit thicker than his.

"This doesn't seem fair." There was a certain competitive streak to him that she hadn't anticipated but was thoroughly enjoying. Cards at the hospital had been played by a group of medicated and apathetic patients who had no real interest in winning. Playing against someone who actually wanted to win was thrilling.

She won the next three hands, and she grinned at the growing frustration on his face before he tossed down his last few cards, admitting defeat. With a glare that was more amusement than anything else, he leaned back in the chair and looked at her expectantly.

"What is your favorite season?" The laugh from him was so loud even she was worried Killian would hear it from his rooms or office.

"That's your question?" She nodded as she noted the disbelief in his tone, the suspicion that she had wasted her victory on such a mundane question, which she supposed was valid. She could have asked about Damien or Killian, or even about Viktor. The question could have gotten even more personal if she asked about how he turned, about why he turned, and whether he had a choice in the matter. But she didn't want to ask about any of that, didn't want to drag any of it into this tiny bubble he had helped her create through a simple game of cards.

"But it is so personal. How can I reveal something like that?" She shrugged softly.

"You don't have a choice. Losers answer questions." He scowled before lifting his eyes to the ceiling.

"Spring, I guess."

"Why?" she responded, despite knowing the answer. His grin widened.

"You need to win to find that out."

"Rude, but fine. If it is that embarrassing, I understand."

"We play by the rules, El. Your rules, I might add." She smirked at the nickname, never having one before that she liked, one that didn't make her skin itch or her heart freeze in dread or rage. It felt warm, like a hot bath. It was perfect.

She gestured for him to shuffle and pass out the cards, which he did without a single moment of hesitation. He won this round and rubbed his hand along his jaw, making a spectacle as he thought up a question. Her heart raced slightly as she realized the flaw in her game, that he could ask her anything. She made promises about the types of questions she would ask. He had done no such thing.

"What's your favorite food?" A slight breath escaped, and her body relaxed.

"Not a food necessarily, but a drink. Hot chocolate or a vanilla latte. They were my favorite when I lived with my foster family. My sister and I would get them once a week, a treat that we saved up for since it was expensive for us. And at the hospital, coffee was the best tasting thing they offered for breakfast. But I miss it so much."

She watched him wince slightly at the mention of her foster sister and former home. His sympathetic eyes burned with questions he wanted to ask but wouldn't. Elora looked down at the cards as she shuffled and distributed them once more. Bringing up the hospital and her foster family wasn't intentional, but that had been her life. Was she meant to sterilize for the comfort of others?

Lukas won the next round quickly, and she cursed softly, causing yet another laugh from the vampire. It wasn't that she was afraid of his questions anymore, but she simply did not enjoy losing. Maybe she had a bit of a competitive streak as well, despite never having a space for it to come out and play. Lukas's lips turned up as she surrendered her last few cards, and he gathered them up like winnings from gambling. Despite her best efforts, she grinned at the sound of his laugh, losing herself in the infectious nature. It seemed as if there was so little to laugh or even smile about, either now under Killian's control or before.

"Hmm, what do you enjoy doing? Like hobbies or anything like that?" Elora opened her mouth to explain that she had no hobbies, that life had been therapy, meals, and rerun TV shows, but she snapped her mouth shut, taking a moment to consider the question.

"Reading, I guess. I also liked sketching." Before the hospital, she almost added on to the end. From the sad smile on his face, he knew exactly what she had kept out of her response.

"Can I ask what you liked to read, or do I need to win another hand?" He smirked as she gave him a deadpanned look and leaned back in the chair.

"I will read anything. My foster family always teased me that I would even read a cookbook if it caught my attention. Fiction, memoirs, true crime, romance. It really didn't matter. It was about the escape for me." About avoiding memories and nightmares, about avoiding sleep and a slight hunger that never really went away. It had been a gnawing in her stomach, a burning in her throat that no amount of water could quench.

"I can understand that. I used to play sports for the same reason, but when I was turned, I wasn't able to really play anymore. The vampire advantage was too obvious." He winked, but there was no joy behind it. He truly had lost something he loved, like she had.

"There isn't a vampire sport league of some sort? You could all play basketball together or something?" He laughed again as she built up the courage for another question.

"No," He replies. "Unfortunately, I haven't found anyone willing to play human sports with me, no matter how fun they may be."

"Too bad." She shrugged. "Do you regret it? Turning?"

Lukas went unnaturally still as his eyes glazed over and she watched a million thoughts race through his mind, each one displayed in perfect detail on his face. He wasn't the empty slate that Damien was, a puzzle that Elora could never fully understand, could never guess at what was going on beyond his somewhat constant disdain for her. Lukas opened his mouth to answer as the door opened, dragging both of their focus to the figure strolling in, black shirt untucked and the sleeves pushed up to his elbows.

Damien stood in the doorway, hand on the knob as his eyes narrowed and his features stiffened. With a tension that felt almost physical, he took in the cards on the table and their casual demeanor. His eyes shifted between the two before they settled on Lukas.

"I'll take over for the night. You can go." Lukas stood, leaving the pack of cards behind. He threw a smirk at Elora over his shoulder, eyes twinkling once more, any trace of his reaction to her question gone.

"We can finish that conversation later." He winked and shut the door behind him. The loss of his energy and warmth was felt immediately as Elora's smile faded and a hardness settled into her eyes.

Damien took Lukas's seat and grabbed the pile of cards that had been left behind. His long fingers straightened the edges of the cards before shuffling, looking as uncomfortable as she felt as memories from the other night played in her mind. His voice had pulled her from the nightmare, his hand gripping her chin as he helped her breathe. Him holding her in his arms, running her a bath and staying until she fell asleep, sitting at the desk instead of the armchair.

"Making friends?"

"Jealous?" He huffed instead of answering.

"What were you playing?"

"War. Have you ever played? Lukas hadn't." He grinned, the gold in his eyes brighter than she remembered. Or maybe it was just that she now knew it was there.

"Of course. What kid doesn't know how?" His words felt like a barb at Lukas, and she rose to the occasion, eager to defend her new friend.

"Not every kid learns. I didn't until the hospital." It was a lie. She had learned the game long before then. Elora took the cards he dealt her even as he glared, eyes roaming over her face.

"Interesting you are defending him. I thought you were spoken for." She stiffened slightly at his insinuation, at the reference to Viktor and whatever was between them. They tossed their cards down, resulting in her having the winning hand—a nine to a four.

"Interesting you felt the need to insult him to begin with." Again, she won the hand with her queen against his jack. Damien didn't respond, just renewed his focus on the cards and game until she won. Unlike Lukas, he didn't surrender when he got down to his final few cards, and defeat was all but inevitable. No, he played until she took the very last card from his hand, as if there was a chance of him winning as long as he kept going.

"What did you talk about?" He watched closely as she shuffled and dealt the cards, grabbing them and straightening them as he waited for her answer.

"We asked each other questions and answered them depending on who won. I found out about his favorite season, and he found out about my hobbies and favorite food. Nothing to tell your master about." His eyes flashed, and he gave her a cruel smile.

"I won't tell daddy you're flirting with vampires that he personally turned. I happen to like Lukas and don't want him dead." Elora set her cards down and slid them over the table as confusion lined his face. A part of her didn't want him to know that he had hit something so painful, something that brought back the feel of teeth, of Killian giving the signal for the others to pounce like animals. She placed her hands in her lap and studied the desk, tracing the swirls of the wood, the tiniest imperfection.

"I think I'm done playing." Slowly, he gathered the cards in a pile and forced them back into their box before he reclined stiffly back in the chair, running his hand through his hair. He opened his mouth for a moment before closing, as if the words he was going to say were dead on his tongue. A single moment of silence stretched between them before he spoke.

"You should know someone will be here in the morning to fit you for a dress." He didn't look at her as he spoke and instead focused on something behind her.

"Am I allowed to ask what the dress is for?"

"A party. In your honor, of course."

"My birthday?" She had completely forgotten about it, hadn't bothered to count the days or keep track. It was difficult to celebrate another year alive sometimes. At the hospitals, birthdays were barely recognized. A dozen happy birthdays muttered during group therapy and a cupcake if the patient had a family who visited.

"Among other things. Your father wants to show you off and allow us all to celebrate your return." She flinched at the use of the title father being used for Killian, and Damien's eyes narrowed once more, the tiny bits of gold now gone.

"He is your father. Just because you are too spoiled and bitter to recognize him as such, doesn't take away from that fact." There was a venom to his voice, a barely hidden hatred that she couldn't understand, couldn't figure out where it came from.

Her blood rushed to her head, and she pressed her hands into the fabric of her pants, gripping the fabric in an effort to control herself, to control her emotions. Spoiled? Bitter? Was that what he truly thought of her? She took a deep breath and closed her eyes until hands relaxed.

"You may tell Killian," Elora emphasized the name and sneered as anger flashed on Damien's face, "that I will be awake and ready for my fitting."

Damien pushed himself to his feet, and the chair scooted behind him with a loud screech, the force almost knocking it to the ground. She laughed, loud and unafraid of any attention it may draw, and stared directly into his face as his hands twitched at his sides. After a moment, he stomped to the door, the key already in his hand.

He turned to her as he twirled the key between his fingers. An ancient-looking thing, like something from an old movie.

"I'll do that. Good night, little rose."

He closed the door quickly and the lock audibly clinked into place just as the lamp she had thrown at his head hit the wall.

CHAPTER 32

Elora

She was still eating breakfast that was made up of an egg scramble with cheese, bacon, and fruit when the seamstress arrived the next morning—or was attempting to eat breakfast. When she saw the food on the plate where every item was a sign of the position she found herself in, Elora knew she should have been ecstatic and grateful for every piece. But each bite felt like cardboard in her mouth and turned into a flavorless mush that never seemed to stay down or impact her hunger.

The hunger was constant, a never-ending sensation of starvation, ravenous as she forced bite after bite into her mouth. She grimaced as it turned to ash, and she forced herself to swallow. She consumed cup after cup of coffee, sweetening it with milk and an unholy amount of sugar, which added some flavor. As long as it washed away the taste of food from her mouth, even if it came back up only a bit later.

The seamstress, a small human woman with silver hair and a youthful face despite the crow's feet around her eyes, watched Elora wearily as she entered the room and set her bag on the desk. Was the woman aware that she was surrounded by vampires? Elora questioned as the seamstress's eyes took in the room. Was that the cause of her obvious unease? Or was it Damien who entered behind her?

Elora scowled at him, debating whether she could convince him that he didn't need to be there, that his presence was not necessary. But from the expression on his face, he looked like he would rather be anywhere else, and she wasn't going to help him escape this. Even if it did punish her in the process.

His attention traveled over the room, taking in the untouched breakfast tray before raising an eyebrow at her. Unknown to Damien, she had been disposing of most of her food, attempting to make it look like she had been eating so that Viktor wouldn't be punished because her body couldn't seem to accept anything. She threw up anything she managed to force down, running a bath or the shower to cover up the sound.

She fought the sudden urge to explain this to him, to yet again plead with him not to punish Viktor for her actions, to not withhold food from him. But a subtle shake of his head silenced her. It wasn't a conversation to have in front of the woman who was now taking pins and fabric from her bag.

"Is there a preference for fabric type? Color?" Her voice shook slightly as she laid out the various fabric samples. She had pushed up the sleeves of her dark blue dress that reached her black boots. The dress made her look younger, and Elora found herself questioning the woman's age.

Elora simply looked at Damien, doubting that she had any choice in the matter.

"White. Or a pale cream. A pale palette overall." Elora's eyes widened at Damien's response, as did the seamstress's.

"Not black or deep blue or something along those shades? It would suit her hair and coloring much better." The surprise in her voice was enough to overtake the shock, and Elora almost smiled. Some myths and expectations never seemed to die. Of course, the palette of the room probably didn't help. The sheets and rugs were black, and the furniture was made from dark wood. All a very uniform, if cliched, color palette.

"Killian's orders. And he had no preference for fabric. But he did have some design ideas to share with you. Sketches." Damien pulled a collection of folded-up papers from his back pocket and handed them to the seamstress, who simply looked through them.

"These are —."

"They are Killian's wishes. I'm sure you understand what that means." A hardness lined each word, and the seamstress nodded quickly.

"Of course. Now I need you to step outside. I must measure her. I will bring you back in once we start picking fabric and such." Damien hesitated, eyes moving between Elora and the seamstress. While she watched Damien, hands on her hips with impatience, Elora attempted to view the sketches that she had tossed down on the desk near the fabric samples, head angling one way and the other trying without luck to see anything.

"Sir, she will be nearly nude. Unless you wish—" Elora only heard the door click shut before the seamstress laughed softly and shot her a conspiratorial look, a sly smile on her small lips. Elora found herself grinning back.

"My name is Sarah, dear. Now, let's get those measurements. Please remove your clothing. Just to your undergarments, please."

Sarah turned around to find something in her bag, but more likely to give Elora a sense of privacy while she pulled her shirt and pants off, instantly crossing her arms over her chest. Everything was exposed and on display for this stranger's eyes and judgment—every scar and blemish on her pale skin. After a moment, Sarah twisted back around and let out a sharp exhale of breath before muttering what sounded like a prayer as her eyes raked over Elora's body.

Tears, unbidden and fierce, appeared in Elora's eyes as the old woman touched her arm, the calloused hand warm and comforting in a way she didn't realize she would ever feel again. Motherly, a protective gesture as Sarah tried to console her, to signal that she was there with her. Elora tried to look at the old woman and meet her eyes to see the reaction on her. Only concern awaited her as if the woman knew exactly how she got each and every scar.

"My dear girl." Sarah squeezed before letting go and shaking her head. "Let's get these done so you can dress."

Her movements were swift and methodical: arms, waist, bust, shoulders, along with others. She double and triple-checked each measurement before she wrote them down in the tiny notebook on the desk. She was careful around Elora's arms and chest, barely touching the skin as if it would disturb what was there. It was a kindness that Elora wasn't used to, that she wasn't sure she deserved while Viktor rotted in a cell somewhere in the Tower.

"You may dress. I got the measurements." Elora nodded and pulled her clothes back on, happy to be covered once more. After a final tug at the long sleeves, she came up beside the woman and touched the fabric samples one by one. She wasn't sure what they were called, only that she recognized the swatch of silk, the feeling of it suffocating and agonizing all at once. She would take whatever material the blankets at the hospital were made of before she willingly took silk.

"I am thinking of using either satin or chiffon. Do you have a preference?" She pulled one sample forward, placing it on the desk before grabbing another. Elora let her fingers rest on the options before she realized she probably wouldn't have too much choice in the matter. But maybe she could make a small request.

"Not silk. Please." The words came out more desperate than she had anticipated, but Sarah said nothing, just wrote something in her book.

"May I see the sketches?" The papers were folded once more, the actual design options hidden.

"No, you may not." The voice came not from Sarah, but from Damien, who had snuck back in, settling into one of the chairs.

"How did you know I wasn't naked anymore?" A small smile played on his lips as he placed his elbows on the armrests.

"I didn't." For a brief moment, Elora considered whether the seamstress's scissors would do more damage than the fork had, if she would be able to grab them before Damien realized what was happening.

"Killian would like the dress to be a surprise. A birthday gift for his daughter. Thank you, ma'am. I believe you have everything you need." Sarah inclined her head in response to the dismissal, obviously no longer at ease in the room. She began to gather her things, placing the fabric, pins, and other items into her bag.

"The dress should be ready Friday for final fittings. I will be back then." Damien nodded before sauntering over to the desk and picking up the sketches, unfolding them one by one, studying each one before he held one out to Sarah.

"I think this one will suit her best. But feel free to use your expertise." She gazed down at the sketch, her eyes taking in the various lines that Elora could only see a slight glimpse of.

"Am I allowed to make alterations to the sketches, add or subtract elements?" Her eyes hadn't left the sketch as her brows came together and her nose scrunched as if she smelled something foul.

"Only enough to make it suit her. Remember, it is Killian you are trying to please. Not the girl."

The girl. He never called her by her name, not outside the night he woke her from her nightmare. Even when talking with Killian, he had only referred to her by that. It was 'the girl' or 'little rose,' and both filled her with a cold rage. It was the same with the gown, an item to remind her she was a doll to be dressed up and displayed, paraded around like a prized pet. And at the end of the day, that was all she was to both of them.

Elora hugged the woman and Sarah gasped slightly in surprise before she wrapped her own arms around her client. Sarah said nothing, just untangled her arms from around Elora after a moment and left. The door shut softly as Elora simply stood in the middle of the room.

"Eat. Or Viktor doesn't eat." Elora flopped down into the chair with a dramatic sigh before she scowled at him and took a bite out of a piece of cold bacon, ignoring the nausea that came with it.

"Can I see him?" This seemed like a stupid question even as a flicker of surprise flashed on his face.

"You know the answer to that." Of course she did.

"How do I even know he is alive? That you haven't already killed him?" Elora knew on some level that they hadn't killed him, just as she knew that Viktor was a toy Killian was playing with, a way to force her best behavior. Damien sneered as she took another bite, only feeling the cold, congealed fat coating the bacon. She swallowed and desperately chugged down the coffee in an effort to force the food down and remove the taste from her mouth.

"You don't." She set the slice of bacon down and carefully wiped her hands on the napkin.

"Then I have no reason to eat. Maybe you can explain that to Killian."

"Are you saying you don't trust us to keep him alive just for you? I'm hurt. Truly." She gave him a feral grin and watched him shift slightly in his chair, muscles tense as he tracked every movement and shift in expression.

"I tend to not trust lapdogs. And your feelings are the least of my concerns."

"No, your concerns are on humans who toss you aside." She just chuckled at the comment, which was the only response Damien seemed to have whenever Viktor was brought up.

"That seems to bother you more than it does me." She stood and left the tray as she made her way to the bookshelf, choosing one of the limited options provided for her.

"Fine, pet. Finish the rest of that and I'll take you down there. But you only get ten minutes." Elora stifled a smile as she returned to her seat and shoved cold eggs into her mouth, chewing slowly and forcing herself to swallow with a quick drink of coffee. It was only once she had eaten every bit of food while Damien watched that she remembered she didn't know what state Viktor would be in when she finally got down there.

* * *

Elora hadn't realized her rooms were so far up in the Tower. The buttons in the elevator indicated there were thirteen floors, plus the lobby and garage. Her room, along with Killian's, was on the eleventh floor, the only ones there based on what she had seen. The hallway was short and had only two doors across from one another, the dark wood and polished silver doorknobs mixing in with various pieces of artwork, all initialed I.A. at the bottom.

"Killian's offices are just above this floor and below this are mostly rooms for vampires who belong to the Ashcroft family." Damien's explanation filled the silence as they waited for the elevator to arrive, as if he couldn't bear the quiet any better than she could.

"Was it always called the Ashcroft family?" He gave her a confused glance before squaring his shoulders, the movement making the dark green t-shirt stretch across his chest.

"No. This family always takes on the name of whoever is the leader. It has been known as the Ashcroft family for roughly a century at this point. Don't ask me what it was before. I don't know. It was before my time." She nodded as the elevator dinged open, and Damien let her enter first, watching closely as she stepped in and turned around to face him. He quickly followed behind her, pushed the button for the third floor, and waited as the doors closed.

"You said that this family changes its name based on the leader. Does that mean others don't?"

He scoffed slightly. "You don't need to pretend you don't remember anything. Not with me."

Elora's fingers curled into her palm, her nails sinking into her hand. Her memory was a void despite pieces coming back. Certain things were returning, even if it left her trembling and crying in the middle of the night. The memories brought with them sensations, reminders of what it was like to experience those moments—teeth and fingers and blood and laughter, all merging into a personal hell she never fully escaped from.

There was no music as they lapsed into silence, just the sound of their breathing. Elora was fairly certain he could hear her racing heart. She forced her words behind her lips, swallowing them before they could break free and ruin this visit for her. Instead, her mind conjured up image after image of the condition she would find Viktor in. Pale, body covered in bruises and bite marks, cuts where he had been bled, body ripped and broken beyond repair.

The doors slid open to reveal a long hallway with rooms on either side. The wall was broken up by large pieces of what looked like plexiglass that allowed them to see inside the rooms. It reminded her of the reptile exhibit at the zoo she had visited for a school trip. As she followed Damien down the hallway, she forced her eyes ahead of her, not glancing into the rooms. She could sense bodies in each cell and hear their moans and whimpers. The coppery scent of blood lingered in the air as her mouth began to salivate, the gnawing in her stomach stronger than ever.

The rooms all looked the same with the same style and furniture, and she had to concede they were much nicer than she had imagined. In her mind, she had pictured torture dungeons with little more than a bed and a hole in the corner. She shook her head slightly, scolding herself slightly. Killian would never allow his food to exist in squalor, and she should have known that.

Damien stopped and gestured to the room to their left, and she slowly turned her head. Just because the rooms themselves looked comfortable for the most part didn't mean that Viktor wouldn't be in a horrible state. A sharp exhale escaped her lips as she took in the sight before them. Viktor was sitting on the edge of the bed, arms resting on his knees as he stared at something on the floor. He hadn't noticed them, or maybe he had, and he didn't want to see her.

"You have a visitor." Damien broke the silence, taking away her ability to observe her friend without him seeing her. Viktor's eyes flicked up to them, first to Damien and then to Elora, mouth dropping open instantly.

"Okay, ten minutes start now." He leaned back against the wall as if he was preparing to watch his favorite film or show, like they were his entertainment for the week.

"I take it you're not going to leave?" Her words were sharp as the question left her mouth and he smiled, shaking his head. After a final glare in his direction, she sat in front of the plexiglass with her legs crossed before her. She motioned for Viktor to join her on the other side, pretending that there was something akin to privacy.

"Are you okay? Have they hurt you?" Elora knew the answer to her question. There were marks on his neck and on his exposed wrists. Then there was the bandage covering where she had stabbed him.

"Nothing too terrible. What about you?" She shook her head as she drank in the sound of his voice.

"No one has touched me." His eyes narrowed and raked over her skin, searching for any sign that she was lying.

"You look exhausted." Damien snorted at Viktor's observation. "Are you sleeping?"

She shook her head, staring at the bandage along his neck she couldn't seem to drag her eyes away from. "It's the nightmares, Viktor. They are back almost every night. I can't sleep. I'm having trouble eating. Everything tastes horrible, worse than the hospital, and you know how bad their food is."

"Are they giving you your medication?" His question surprised her. Why would the medication be his main concern?

"No, nothing since I got here." Viktor sat back slightly, moving away from the glass in a way that seemed easy, like it wasn't a calculated move. But she caught the shift in his expression, passing so quickly she second guessed what she saw. His gaze moved to Damien, who seemed very interested in the conversation.

"Is that the plan, then? To remove it from her system?" Damien raised one shoulder, either because he didn't want to answer or because he didn't know the answer. Elora's guess was on the former. Killian seemed to tell him everything.

"Why is it important? It's just nightmares, Viktor. I can deal with them." Her face contorted as she tried to understand the concern, the slight fear that took over his face. An intense expression shifted his features, sharpening his eyes and mouth as he watched her, surveying her like he was looking for something specific.

"It's not just nightmares. Everything is coming to the surface, Elora. Your memories, your urges, everything." He turned his attention to Damien as if he couldn't bear to look at her anymore.

"What are you talking about? Tell me, one of you." Damien shifted, shoving his hands in his pockets as he stared at something in Viktor's cell. He wouldn't even look at her, and neither would Viktor. "Now!"

"The medication Dr. Montgomery was giving you, the one you were on since your first day in the hospital, was meant to suppress your vampire urges, but it also made you sleep and stop the nightmares. It's why she had to up the dosage when you attacked that patient when you started dreaming again." Viktor leaned forward, hand pressed against the glass as if he wanted to reach for her, embrace her. As if it would make this any better.

"You knew. You knew this whole time." Her mind was racing, searching through every interaction they had for any indication that he had known, any hint that she had missed, not wanting to believe that not only had Dr. Montgomery lied to her, but so had Viktor. Elora forced her trembling hands into her lap, grasping at the fabric.

"At first, I only knew that your mediation was being used to suppress your urges to feed and make you sleep without dreaming. It could also help your brain keep your memories suppressed. That's all. Dr. Montgomery wouldn't give me any more details than that. She told me the rest after you attacked the patient." She could barely understand his words, her mind a jumbled whirlwind of thoughts and questions that made it nearly impossible to hear or understand anything.

"Why tell you about that in the first place?" Damien voiced the question, beating Elora to it.

"She noticed you were comfortable around me, that we were able to build a report. She thought it would be helpful for me to be informed and watch you a bit closer in case there needed to be a change in the dosage."

"She used you to control me. And you let her." He emphatically shook his head, eyes wide as his mouth opened to respond. Elora raised her hand, holding it in a gesture she hoped would shut him up. She didn't want to hear another word; didn't want to hear whatever excuse or rationale he was going to give her. Because the fact was simple—their friendship had been another case of being babysat. First Viktor, then Damien, and finally Lukas as the stand-in. It was just a continual stream of people who were meant to keep her in line and make sure she behaved how they wanted. For

Viktor, it was making sure she took her medication, didn't attack anyone, and that she didn't display any symptoms. For Damien and Lukas, it was making sure she did as Killian wished.

Her mouth moved as she struggled to form words or thoughts while Viktor glared at the vampire beside them, as if this entire situation was somehow Damien's fault, like the betrayal wasn't at his own hand.

"I guess that explains why you tossed her aside when she was released. Your job was done." She expected some type of sick amusement in Damien's voice, a vindication that this was the tragedy he thought it was. But there was only an icy calm, a barely restrained anger.

"Fuck you, Damien. You know that's not the case."

"Isn't it?" Her voice came out smaller than she had wanted and for a moment, she wasn't sure Viktor had heard her. Damien had; she could feel his attention on her once more as he watched the interaction.

"We were already getting close before Dr. Montgomery approached me and asked me to help her with you. The way she phrased it is you needed help; you were fragile in a way. And you had a history of not taking your medication and she was worried about the other residents and what would happen to them if the medication disappeared from your system completely. I already cared for you." He was rambling, spouting out excuse after excuse as if it would somehow erase what he did.

"Enough to lie to me. To let me keep thinking I was crazy because I knew vampires existed, enough to report about the private things I told you to a woman you knew I hated. A woman you knew liked to provoke me, liked to play on my guilt." She stood, unable to be near him anymore, unable to look at him and the panic there. He didn't think she would ever find out. He probably figured she would be released and disappear, and he would never see her again.

"I'm sorry, Elora. I was worried about you, and I just wanted you safe." Resignation, pure and utter defeat, laced each word.

She threw her arms up as looked around her and pointed at Damien. "Well, you and Dr. Montgomery failed at that. I am back in my own personal hell with the very monsters I was told didn't exist." She turned away from him, ignoring his pleas, and his repeats of her name.

"I think it's been ten minutes." She met Damien's eyes as she spoke and he nodded, betraying nothing as they walked away from the shouts coming from Viktor's mouth, the pleas that she come back and listen to him, that he could explain. Something tightened in her chest, something she tried desperately to block out. Tears formed in her eyes, and she straightened her posture before taking a deep breath, refusing to shed even a single one.

But it hurt. It was agony.

The elevator finally opened, and they stepped in while Damien pushed the button for her floor. Over and over, she reminded herself that she just had to make it to her room, and then she could fall apart.

CHAPTER 33

Damien

It was midday when Killian summoned Damien to the top floor, where preparations for the party were in full swing. Dozens of vampires and humans worked to set up a long banquet table in one room while Killian's newest assistant placed tiny cards with names on the table for the seating arrangement, placing one down and then moving it to another spot at Killian's direction.

In the ballroom, the columns that lined the walls were wrapped in lights and garlands of dark red flowers while new chandeliers hung from the ceiling. Roughly eight different marble statues lined the dance floor, four on either side, each one either a bust of Killian or the girl. Whoever had made them had done meticulous work. Each detail was etched into the marble almost perfectly. But the haunted look in the girl's eyes was missing, as were the scars along her chest and neck. Somehow, the bust's beauty was diminished because of it.

If Killian were to ask Damien's opinion on the décor, he would have said it was all over the top and unnecessary, even if it was meant to be a display of power and solidarity between father and daughter. At its core, it was also a demonstration of the possessiveness of a father over his child, an attempt to dissuade anyone who may pursue her for political or other reasons. The idea of someone approaching the girl rested uneasily in his stomach, along with a sense of dread and irritation that didn't make sense. It was on Killian's behalf, due to the vampire's orders to protect the girl and keep her safe. Some arrogant vampire trying to weasel his way into the girl's affections wasn't appropriate or even tolerable.

At least that is what Damien told himself.

Killian stood in the center of the ballroom, having left his assistant to finalize the place settings as Damien approached him. Despite being impeccably dressed, as usual, in a black tailored suit with a dark purple dress shirt underneath, he looked exhausted. His hair was pushed back away from his face, but strands were falling into his eyes and along his cheeks. His jaw was lined with uncharacteristic stubble, and dark circles hung under his eyes on his unusually pale face. Obvious signs of hunger and Damien had to wonder how long it had been since Killian had fed and why he was delaying it.

He was scrutinizing the placement of some lights along the ceiling, meant to mimic stars in some type of reference or homage to the girl's mother. Her mother was never mentioned, and there were no pictures of her anywhere. Damien had always assumed Killian mourned her too greatly, that the reminder was too much to bear.

"You needed me?"

"I wanted to discuss some security precautions for the party and then talk about my daughter. There are some potential issues we may need to address." Killian didn't look at him as he signaled for the lights to be shifted one way or the other. Damien waited for Killian to speak, not sure that moving the lights was making a difference, but decorating had never been a strong suit.

"As you know, there will be other vampire families at the party. Heads and second in command, as usual. We will also have humans there for anyone who wishes to take part."

"Do you think that is appropriate? Considering that the girl has never attended a vampire party, let alone seen a group feeding like that?" He waved his hand dismissively.

"She has attended some of the tamer ones before she left. And she will need to be part of vampire life, eventually. Take part in the duties of the family, obviously. Group feedings won't be too surprising."

Damien wasn't sure he wanted to admit that Killian was right. Besides, something about his words made his skin crawl. It isn't necessarily the thought of her witnessing the literal bloodbath that came with live feedings like this. Or even the possibility of public sex was also fairly common. However, the idea of her being involved in that caused something in him to twist uncomfortably.

No, it was the comment about group feelings not being a surprise. His focus instantly retreated back to the girl's nightmare, the chains she had described, and the person in the corner giving orders. Viktor had mentioned her memories returning, and she had said it wasn't a nightmare. Could the person in the corner have been --- No. Killian was her father, protective and possessive, but in a way that originated with wanting her safe now that she was back. Maybe one of the other vampire heads? Darian, maybe? He had always had a unique sadistic streak that extended to everyone, even his family, if rumors were to be believed.

"Am I to keep her from such activities?" Killian finally looked at him, eyes hard.

"Of course. No one touches her. But that brings up another concern." Damien nodded as both an acceptance of the order and also an encouragement to continue.

"Her medication. After reading through the journals that you gathered and talking to my own team, it is clear that her vampire traits were being suppressed, rendering her human. Now that the medication will be gone from her system, she may be experiencing some symptoms." Disgust lined each word, as if the idea of being cut off from his vampiric urges was the worst possible fate, as if he couldn't imagine her existing that way.

"You're saying she may need to start feeding?" Damien couldn't imagine she would respond well to that, considering her views on vampires, even after she found out she practically was one.

"Honestly, I am not sure. She is different, my little rose. I want you to be prepared, in case the blood stirs something for her, causing some urges to come to the surface. I have a little test ready for the dinner portion that will hopefully help us understand where we are at with her progression."

"Of course." Killian scanned one of the busts, fingers trailing along the rose crown that rested on its head. Red roses, so dark they were almost black, are intertwined together with green fabric, creating the vision of a queen, a goddess.

"Have you noticed anything different about her? Has she mentioned anything?" Damien almost laughed at the question, and if it had been anyone but Killian, he would have.

"I doubt she would tell me anything. She hates me and speaks to me only when necessary. I think she would rather stab me in the heart than tell me if something was wrong. I can ask Lukas. He has spent some time with her, and she seems to trust him somewhat." Damien ignored the rush of irritation he felt at the honesty of those words. He didn't want to think too much about why that would bother him.

"She is quite fierce, isn't she?" Killian seemed equally impressed and angry at the observation, as if he admired the trait, but also wished to cut it out of her to make her more pliable.

"She seems to be, yes." Damien's answer was true enough, and he ran his hand over the spot where she had stabbed him with a fork. A fork! Never in his time of working with Killian or even when he was on the streets before being turned had he been stabbed with a utensil.

She was a contradiction. When pushed, her fury was a sight to behold, even if he was usually on the other side of it. And yet, she so often retreated into herself, hiding behind humor or even pure silence. He didn't understand it or her. It was like he was missing a crucial piece and when asked about it, Viktor had been no help. He simply claimed it wasn't his story to tell.

"What about the human? Did she confide in him when you took her to see him?" Damien almost let the surprise show on his face, but from the smile on Killian's lips, he knew it was there. He had been a fool to think he could have taken her to see Viktor without Killian knowing about it. She hadn't been forbidden from seeing Viktor, but she hadn't been given permission. Damien ran his hand through his hair, noting to trim the shaved sides that were growing out, and picked his words carefully.

"She mentioned nightmares when they spoke. The human made it seem like the medication had helped keep her memories hidden and now they were returning."

"Hmm. I suppose that makes sense from what I have gathered from the journals." This tiny pill felt like a problem, but Killian didn't seem concerned about it. The man they had questioned had mentioned a weapon, one that was tested on someone at the hospital. A pill that could suppress vampire traits as well as memories? It seems like it could be useful, possibly for the Resistance in diminishing vampire numbers, even weakening them to eliminate them easily.

But maybe not. It would require time — time to build up a level in the vampire system and then time to suppress the memories, unless they simply killed the vampire right away. And if they wanted to use it for longer-term suppression, then it would require the vampire to take it every day. If it was ever going to be used as a weapon, it would be fairly ineffectual in its current form.

"Is there anyone in particular I should keep her away from?" If Damien could identify who the problems were, maybe it would be easier. Killian shrugged, studying one of the busts of himself.

"She can mingle, of course. Engage in small talk with anyone. Keep the conversations basic. I don't want too much detail about the hospital getting out, just that she was there due to some mental distress. Keep the details to a minimum. I think Darian will be the biggest concern. He knew her before she left. He was," Killian paused for a moment, searching for the correct phrasing, "close to her."

Darian was the head of the Ravenwell vampire family and was a confidant of Killian's at one point. From what Damien remembered, the two vampire heads had some type of argument, leading them to become distant and paranoid about each other. It had led to a feud that resulted in disputed territories and small fights in some of the poorer neighborhoods. Damien had been sent out numerous times to deal with those, dispatching many of Darian's best vampires. He was not a fan of his.

"I understand. That should be simple enough." Killian turned to him with a fierce expression that made his eyes seem brighter.

"Do not get complacent. Even if everyone else behaves, there is no guarantee she will. We will make sure to have some company to keep her under control." Viktor would be at the party then. But in what capacity? Part of the buffet for the vampire? A guest of honor in name only? Damien nodded as unease curled in his stomach.

"Now, go check on my daughter and make sure she is prepared for tomorrow night. I expect perfection, Damien. Don't let her disappoint me."

He wanted to ask more questions, about the journals, about the medication, about why she had left in the first place. Damien wanted to ask him about her mother, about the lights on the ceiling. But he stopped like he always did and held his tongue as Killian turned back to his assistant to demand more roses and ask about the humans being offered up at dinner.

Instead, he spun around and left the obnoxious display behind, trying to plan how to keep the girl safe from herself and her guests.

~ ~

CHAPTER 34

Elora

The dress fitting had been quick but uncomfortable despite Sarah's best efforts. Elora had been kept blindfolded during it, a piece of soft fabric tied around her eyes so she couldn't see the dress. It was clear that the woman was a master of her craft. There were little changes to be made, only a tightening here and a loosening there. True to her words, the gown contained no silk. Even if she couldn't see the dress, she could feel it, the exposure so immense she wanted to cover up with anything she could find.

"You look beautiful, honey. Gorgeous. Wear it like armor." Sarah had leaned in, and Elora could smell her perfume, something like cinnamon and vanilla. "Your scars are proof you survived. Don't let them diminish you."

At the woman's words, Elora had straightened and pushed her shoulders back. She had felt the words deep inside her, an echo that added steel to her spine that she could only hope would be there once the woman left, once Elora saw exactly how much was on display.

Damien appeared shortly after the seamstress had left, after she had curled into a chair with a book and the blanket Damien had left behind. The book itself was some fictional account of a war that was more of a romance than anything else. But it was diverting, allowing her to escape whatever her reality had become. And there was nothing else to do. Nowhere to visit, and no friends to come and keep her company. After getting only one-word responses from her, Damien had left, no doubt standing guard outside the door or something equally ridiculous.

Now, she wore the gown as she sat in front of a vanity mirror that had been brought in for the purpose of getting ready. The mirror was real, providing a reflection that wasn't distorted, highlighting each change to her appearance. Her crimson hair had grown since the hospital and there were dark circles under her eyes. But the dark green of her eyes was bright with hints of brown.

A young vampire Elora didn't know stood behind her, gathering her hair and arranging it in a way that resulted in a half-up and half-down style. The parts left down were curled into ringlets that felt warm on her exposed back. With a small smile on her face, the vampire turned Elora's chair to face her. The vampire was beautiful in a way that most were with her perfect skin, sky-blue eyes, and red lips. Elora wondered if it was lipstick or just part of what she was. What they were? Something in her mind rebelled at the idea even while another part accepted it, understanding that no matter how much she denied it, nothing would change.

The vampire in charge of making Elora presentable ran some black eyeliner along her lids and added just a hint of mascara before she covered her lips in red. She turned Elora back to the mirror, her face displaying a proud smile. Elora simply took in her reflection and resisted the urge to recoil, to smear the lipstick, to pull her hair out of its careful design. She knew she looked different, that she looked wrong even. Her skin was paler than usual, skin so light she could make out the veins along her arms while her eyes appeared dark, almost black instead of the normal dark green. But Elora smiled as she met the vampire's eyes, hoping she didn't notice the grimace and revulsion she was trying too hard to hide.

She had done beautiful work when she molded Elora into whatever Killian wanted her to be that night. It wasn't the vampire's fault that she hated it, hated herself.

"Let's see the whole picture." She took a step back and waited for Elora to stand and move away from the mirror so they could both take in everything at once.

The gown was beautiful — simple and almost basic in its design. The corset bodice was strapless and fell into layers of fabric once it hit her waist. The fabric used in the skirt was light and hung loosely from where it meets the corset. The whole gown was cream, and she was positive that it clashed horribly with how pale she had become. The only hint of color came with the pale pink that made up the boning and cups of the bodice, merging seamlessly with the cream in the skirt. Elora moved the skirts, twirling them slightly as she stood there, feeling their weight as she spun in a circle. There was a hidden slit in the skirt that showed entirely too much if she moved too freely, exposing her right leg up to her thigh. She made a mental note to be careful with each and every step she took.

The request for a cover-up of some sort was right on her lips, along with the desire to explain that there was too much showing. But it seemed like that was what Killian wanted with his design of the gowns. Had they all been like this, or had there been some with more coverage? Ones that would have covered her chest and arms. She stopped twirling as the skirts settled against her legs and she remembered that Damien had picked this design and claimed it would suit her best.

"Is everything okay?" The vampire in front of her looked scared as she studied Elora, and she made an effort to soften her expression.

"Of course. I'm sorry. You worked miracles. Thank you." Elora forced her voice to sound warm and was rewarded with the fear melting from the vampire's features, leaving her looking proud once more. She knelt and slipped a pair of heels on Elora's feet, a set of strappy heels that seemed to make her at least four inches taller and promised to hurt her at some point in the night.

Elora opened her mouth to ask for a different pair of shoes, hopefully, a pair that wouldn't cause her to fall on her face, when a knock sounded at the door. The vampire called for them to come in as she stood back up, hands on her hips and scanned Elora once more. Damien didn't hesitate before he entered, dressed unsurprisingly in a black suit, hair brushed back away from his face but still looking unruly. Elora couldn't help but take in a breath and curse how unfair it was that he was so gorgeous despite being an asshole.

The vampire standing beside her giggled slightly as Damien studied the two of them, eyes first wandering over the vampire's black skin-tight gown before they moved to Elora. She shifted awkwardly under his gaze and his brows furrowed together as if he cared, as if he hadn't picked this design out himself. With a deep breath, she stood taller, forcing her spine straight in an effort to embrace what Sarah had said during the fitting. Confidence. Beauty. Armor.

"So, were you correct?" Damien shook his head, as if he was far away and needed it to come back to reality.

"What?"

"You said this was the sketch that would suit me. Were you correct?" Elora braced herself for his response, knowing that she was pushing him even as something she couldn't read crossed his face. She wanted to irritate him, make him regret coming into this room, seeing her, and escorting her to this horrible party. It was all a display of power, an opportunity for Killian to show that he got his possession back. Damien smiled a full smile that lit up his face, making his eyes gleam slightly. He had never smiled like that before, not in front of her.

"Yes. Yes, I was." He didn't expand, but let his eyes move over her again, lingering on her chest, moving down her body then returning to her face. His own face was scrunched up, the smile gone. In a single moment, his usual disdain was back.

"And Rebekah, you look gorgeous as usual. Will you be attending as well, or is the dress for someone in particular?" A flirty grin graced his lips as the vampire beside Elora giggled once more. A knot formed in her stomach as she watched the exchange, trying her hardest to not roll her eyes.

"Yes, I will be attending." Her voice was breathy, like her dress was too tight and she couldn't breathe.

His grin grew wider. "I'm sure all eyes will be on you."

Elora brushed past him, beyond done with the obvious flirting and pretending she wasn't in the room. She scoffed as she opened the door and waited, trying to understand why the display bothered her. She just wanted to get it all done—the party, the dinner, and whatever else would be included. After it was all done, she could come back to her room and take a hot bath, wash away the feeling of everyone's eyes, and cover up once more.

Damien was instantly at her side, leaving the giggling vampire in the room, holding out his arm for her to take as if he were a gentleman. Silently, she took it, keeping her touch as light as possible.

"Jealous?" He grinned down at her, mimicking the question she had asked him after Lukas had been sent from her room.

"If that is your type, then I wish you the best of luck. I'll be happy to find an alternative company. Maybe Lukas will be there. He is always so much fun." She felt him tense, the muscles in his forearm tightening even as she smirked at the response.

"I'm sure he will be busy. He is quite popular." His voice was strained as he pushed the button for the elevator to take them up to the top floor. Her heart skipped a beat as she considered what was awaiting her.

"He will make time for me. We have gotten quite close." The elevator doors closed behind them, and Damien spun to her, dropping her arm as he backed her against the wall. She met the darkness in his eyes, defiant as she refused to look away, refusing to defer to him.

"You won't leave my side. Not for Lukas. Not for anyone." His focus shot to her lips before he met her eyes once more.

"Looks like I am not the jealous one." He leaned closer.

"I already told you once I have standards. And you do not meet them." He pushed himself back and straightened his jacket. "You are my problem tonight, and I'm going to keep you safe."

"I didn't realize a good time with Lukas was unsafe," Damien said nothing even as he stared forward, jaw clenched, and hands fisted at his sides. A chime rang out, and he grabbed her arm, once more placing it in the crook of his elbow before the doors opened. It was almost like the moment had never happened. Back in place was a blank mask that hid every thought or emotion that she wanted to see.

The two of them were met with music and voices as the doors opened to reveal a ballroom that was obviously over-decorated. At first, no one seemed to notice their arrival, and they wandered into the room. Elora's eyes darted around, taking in every detail from the lights on the ceiling to the statues that bore her face, crowned in wreaths of roses. At least a hundred individuals populated the area, some dancing in the middle of the room while others mingled along the edges. There were a number of servers who walked around the room with trays of drinks and small plates of food. From what Elora could see, it was a combination of vampires and humans, although the vampires vastly outnumbered their counterparts.

She allowed Damien to lead her over to the side where Killian stood talking to another vampire, an older man with reddish hair dressed in a simple black and white suit. He looked underdressed compared to Killian, who wore a textured black jacket with roses and vines running over it. The shirt beneath it was a deep red, the entire ensemble matching the palette of the decoration of busts and garlands placed around the room.

Killian noted their approach and nodded slightly at Damien even as his face brightened with a predatory smile. Elora could feel Damien's grip tighten as he glanced down at her and then back at Killian as his body stiffened.

"My darling, let me introduce you to a dear friend. This is Darian, the head of the Ravenwell vampire family. He actually knew you when you were younger." The meaning of Killian's words was not lost on her as Darian's gaze roamed over her. Elora squared her shoulders and smiled, bowing her head in deference that she knew Killian appreciated.

"It is nice to meet you." Elora didn't recognize the voice coming from her — calm, quiet, and submissive as she kept her eyes on the vampire before her.

Darian laughed loudly and inclined his head as well. "Do you not remember me? As I remember, we were friends." Elora's palms started to sweat as she tried to pull her hand from Damien's grip. Instead, his own tightened, keeping her in place.

"I am sorry, but I remember very little from my time here before. Plus, I was only a child at the time." Darian's smile grew wide, his fangs appearing like a threat.

"Yes, I apologize for that. Apparently, her time away has damaged her memories. But, from what I understand, they are starting to return." Killian and Darian shared a knowing look, and she backed away, finally freeing her hand from Damien.

"I would like to get a drink." Killian nodded his head at her words, as close to permission as she was going to get as the two vampire heads shared in their secret conversation that she knew, without a doubt, was about her.

Elora turned sharply, her skirt twirling as she stalked off, not sure where to even find a drink as she weaved through the various bodies along the edge of the dance area. With each step, she could hear the snippets of conversation, forcing her to recoil into herself, her shoulders slumping forward, head hanging as she stared at her feet.

Killian's plaything.

No, I heard that's his daughter.

I thought vampires tended to be sterile.

His scientists, and money, were able to help in the process.

Did you see the scars? How shameful. To display to the world that you allow that.

Her hands fidgeted at her sides as she frantically searched for one of the humans with a tray, finally spotting one and yanking the drink to her mouth, consuming it all in a single swallow before searching for another. Her eyes frantically scanned the room, refusing to stay locked onto one of the dozens of pairs that stared at her in either fascination or disgust. Women in elegant gowns that displayed less flesh than her own lined the walls, whispering behind gloved hands as their eyes met her own. Men stood beside them, dressed in tailored suits and tuxedos, each with a sneer on their lips and a hungry gleam in their eyes.

Another human wandered by with a tray of glasses balanced on his hand. There was something strange about the blankness of his expression, the emptiness in his eyes as he made his way through the room. Elora grabbed another drink, leaving the empty glass on the tray as the human moved on. The liquid was thick and sweet as she took her time sipping it this time, letting it warm her stomach until her skin flushed slightly. She had never drunk anything like this before, nothing beyond a sip of wine at certain family gatherings while with her foster family. Or when she and Elizabeth had drunk an entire stolen bottle of wine.

"What are you thinking?" Damien's hand was wrapped abruptly around her upper arm, and she tried once more to pull away and escape once again into the crowd, but his grip was too strong.

"I was thinking I was thirsty," she hissed, trying once more to move away from him.

"You are to stay with me tonight. It's your father's orders." She took a drink to distract herself before she could do anything stupid, like tossing the contents of the cup in his face.

"I'm sure I'll be fine. Go on and entertain yourself. You don't need to be tied to your master's spoiled daughter the whole night." Damien growled slightly and pulled her further away from the dance floor and released her arm, crossing his own over his chest.

"As much as I would like to leave you here to survive on your own, I can't and won't. I have too much respect for your father. So, we will walk around and mingle. We will make small talk and then we will attend dinner. And then, finally, I can escort you back to your room and be done with you for the night." Not a single thought went through her mind as she finished her drink and thrust the cup at him. Surprised, he grabbed it and watched as she turned away and dashed away.

Rage and fear and despair all merged together under her skin as she raced away from him and into the dancers in the center of the room. They paid little attention to her, their eyes on one another as if the music coming from somewhere in the room held them in a spell. She weaved through them all, careful not to touch anyone as she headed towards the other side where there were fewer people to watch and judge and whisper. She wouldn't force herself on him, wouldn't force him to be in her company even if it hurt something in her to know she was such a burden to him.

She let out a slight cry as a hand grabbed her biceps before it dragged and pulled her behind them into a curtained area away from the crowd. The space was dark, lit only by the small lights wrapped in the garland that hung from the ceiling. The music was muffled slightly, leaving her own harsh breaths audible. She spun, fully prepared to release every ounce of frustration and anger on Damien with a slap to his perfect face. He would deserve it for touching her, for dragging her in here, for his cruel words.

The face before was familiar in a way that made her take a step back—first one and then another until the wall was flush against her back, the surface cold against her exposed skin. The vampire before her appeared young, like Damien and Lukas. His long black hair reached past his shoulders and hung limply around his face, framing his strangely bright eyes and highlighting the glint that made her heart stop and hands sweat.

She knew his face, had seen it over and over again in her nightmares. She knew the feel of the fangs he was currently displaying with his smile, the feel of his hands that were clutching her arms. His fingers began to move as she froze in place. Each one idly trailed over her collarbones before they moved down her arm and then back up, tracing each scar. With a soft whimper, she shifted to the side and inched towards the curtains that were blocking them both from view. Through the gap, she could make out the dancing figures and the humans wandering with their trays of drinks. He moved with her, adjusting himself so he was blocking any chance of leaving.

And it didn't matter. She stood there, trapped in not only this moment but every memory where she was cornered like this. Once again, she was chained, held in place by something less tangible than metal, but no less strong. The music had disappeared, leaving only an echoing silence that enveloped them both.

"I think you remember me. Don't you?" She swallowed as his silky-smooth voice washed over her. No answer left her lips, as she was unsure if she could even speak. He leaned in close, his mouth touching the shell of her ear before he inhaled deeply. Inside, she screamed at her feet to move, at her hands to push him away, for her mouth to shout or scream or call for help. But she was stuck, thrust back into a moment she couldn't seem to get back out of.

"I have to say I missed you, missed the taste of you. Nothing else really compares. Killian was right about that." His fingers trailed up her neck to her jaw, forcing her head to the side as she gathered her skirts into her fists. Her screams reverberated inside her head, bouncing around without ever finding footing, without ever becoming real. Instead, a soft whimper escaped, and she could feel his grin.

Elora shook her head, but his grip tightened, fingers digging into her chin as he forced her head to the side. She tried to breathe, to make herself come back to her body, to regain control. But each breath was shallower than the last, coming in short bursts as if her lungs couldn't remember how to do it. Her head was swimming, and she felt her body weaken as oxygen deprivation took over.

She couldn't swallow and there was too much noise in the silence, echoing and echoing and echoing until she wanted to scream and cover her ears. The dress was too tight, the fabric suddenly burning and itchy against her skin. His tongue touched her neck, languidly moving from her collarbone to her jaw, and a small noise escaped her lips. He grinned against her skin; his canines sharp against her flesh.

"What's happening here, love?" She exhaled sharply at the sound of Damien's voice, but the vampire in front of her didn't move, just trailed his hand up and down her arm as he answered Damien.

"Not your concern. Move on." She could feel his breath as he spoke, followed by his tongue as he took another taste.

"I wasn't speaking to you, Jonas." Damien was quiet for a brief moment, waiting for Elora to respond. But words were a foreign concept.

"Please," she whispered, praying Damien understood her.

"Again, not your concern." Jonas's voice had taken on a cold edge that dampened the huskiness that was there only a moment ago.

"Actually, it is my concern. Let her go. I don't think the lady seems very interested." Damien's voice was low, a promise of violence she had never heard before.

"Trust me, Damien. I know exactly what our little rose is interested in." In a blur of movement and snarls, Damien grabbed Jonas by the neck and pulled him back, squeezing until Jonas let out a cry of pain. One swift punch to the stomach and Jonas doubled over, cursing and gasping for breath.

Elora tried to explain to herself that the hands were gone, but her skin burned at each point where he had touched her. She squeezed her eyes shut as she listened to Damien force the vampire to leave. Slowly, she took a breath and held it, just as Damien had shown her before.

"Leave Jonas, or you won't survive long enough to attend dinner." The other vampire cursed Damien once more, and she felt her body relax as his footsteps retreated and the music seemed to return.

She crumbled and fell to her knees as she struggled to follow Damien's instructions. Her fingers formed claws as she reached for her skin, hoping to tear away any trace of his touch.

"Stop, you need to breathe. You can't do this right now." Damien's words reached her, but only barely. It was almost as if he was speaking from another room, the sound muffled and garbled by the wall between them.

"I'm trying," she muttered as she followed his instructions from the night he had forced her from her nightmare.

"Look at me. Please." The desperation in his voice drew her from the panic that had hijacked her senses, and her eyes moved to his own, widening at the fear and anxiety she saw there as he knelt before her.

Once more, she nodded and released the skirt clutched in her fists. Slowly, so slowly, the panic retreated as he touched her arms hesitantly, his fingers almost hovering above her skin as he rubbed them up and down. A part of her wanted to scream at him not to touch her, but the feeling was comforting and anchored her in reality. It was earnest and quiet, not bringing forward any memories of pain or blood.

Damien drew her to him, holding her tightly in his arms as he waited for her to finish returning to herself. After a few moments, she did just that, and her body went limp in his embrace. Neither of them moved, despite knowing that the panic had passed. But she absorbed his touch, breathing in deeply the smell of his cologne and shampoo, and a soft shudder traveled down her body. He didn't move away or flinch as he held her tight against him, his cheek resting on top of her head, careful not to disturb the intricate placement of her hair.

"Thank you," she whispered into his shirt, and she felt him tense. On a certain level, she knew she shouldn't find comfort in his embrace, shouldn't see this moment as anything but him calming her down for Killian, making her presentable once more. His disdain for her had been made abundantly clear, and she doubted this moment would change anything. But she wanted for just one more moment to pretend that he didn't hate her, that she didn't want to stab him any time he came too close, that Killian wasn't waiting just beyond the curtain.

A bell rang out in the dining room, followed by Killian's voice inviting everyone to the dinner table. Just like that, her single moment of pretending was over.

~ ~

CHAPTER 35

Elora

Damien stood in front of her as she tried to readjust her dress and erase any mark of what had happened. His mouth turned down slightly as he watched her, using his thumb to fix a smudge of her lipstick, brushing the underside of her bottom lip. A shot of electricity rushed through her, one that she desperately tried to ignore by giving him a tiny sardonic smile.

"How do I look?" He didn't answer at first as he straightened and pulled at the bottom of his jacket. Only once his own appearance was restored does he look at her, gaze slowly trailing over her dress, her hair, her face. His eyes flashed, darkening slightly as he took her in. She knew the skirt was creased from where she had gripped it and that there was a small tear in the bodice near the neckline. Her arms bore red marks from where Jonas's fingers had dug in, where her own nail had sunk in an attempt to bring her back to reality.

"Perfect." He held out his arm once more and escorted her to the dining room, joining the group that was making their way through the large doors. The dining room was just as overdecorated with garlands, lights, and chandeliers. The banquet table took up the majority of the room, the dark wood covered partially by a black runner embroidered with flowers lying along the middle. Bouquets and candles made up the centerpieces while gold-edged plates and utensils sat at each place setting. There were lines of humans waiting along the walls, hands clasped behind their backs and eyes straight ahead.

As they made their way into the room, Damien escorted her to her seat, the chair directly to the left of Killian, who sat at the head. To his right was Darian, while another vampire, a young woman with silver hair and black eyes, sat beside him, disgust clear on her face as she watched Elora take her seat. Vampires and humans alike took their places at the table, some pausing for moment to double-check the name on the small card before each chair. Elora searched the faces for any hint of familiarity, but only recognized Jonas at the end of the table, a red spot on his cheekbone and along his jaw. His eyes met hers and he ran his tongue over his fangs while a wicked smile played on his lips.

Damien sat beside her—her guard in his correct place. She would never admit to him that he was right, that she needed protection here. He would only make a smug comment and remind her of it constantly, something that felt akin to teasing now. She wanted to believe that something had shifted between them, moving from obvious hatred to someone more neutral at the very least.

A young human came up beside her and sat a plate of food down while another filled her glass with the same wine as before. Roasted vegetables, mashed potatoes, and some type of roasted bird were arranged perfectly. The smell reached her, and her stomach churned, nausea causing vomit to rise in her throat. She knew she wouldn't be eating anything, not without embarrassing herself and Killian by extension. She turned her attention from the meal in front of her and eyed the table, her attention snagged by the fact not everyone was being given a plate. Maybe only a third of the guests that were sitting at the table had a plate before them. Dread and familiarity clutched her tightly as she hoped with everything in her that her fear was unfounded.

A fork hit a glass, and Killian stood from his spot at the head of the table. The room went silent instantly, all attention given to the leader of the Ashcroft vampire family. Her own focus went to him as she listened intently, making sure she behaved accordingly. She wasn't sure if Damien would tell him what happened, report how she ran off and was cornered by another vampire, allowing herself to get very close to being fed on. Or maybe Jonas would complain about what was denied to him, what he felt he was entitled to. Elora didn't want to risk Killian's wrath, not with Viktor still under his control.

"Thank you everyone for joining us. Tonight, we are celebrating a very important young woman. I know there are rumors about who and what she is. And while I find these rumors distasteful, I do understand that they stem from the secrecy that surrounds her. Elora is my daughter who has recently been returned to me. She was forced to spend years with humans who took her to hurt us, to hurt me." Killian turned and smiled down at her, a warmth on his face that went no further than his lips. Elora kept her face blank, not reacting to the lie that she had been taken by the humans. But she supposed admitting your own daughter ran away was not quite the show of strength he would want.

"As some of you know, Elora was nothing short of a miracle. Her mother and I tried for a long time for a child. It is rare, if not impossible, for vampires to reproduce beyond turning humans. Indeed, there is no record of such a thing occurring. But it is not impossible. Through modern science, we were able to conceive."

Applause broke out at the table before going silent again.

"Her birth and very existence is a gift in more ways than one. I was granted a wonderful child who can carry on not only the Ashcroft family name but also the Corvin one. A child who is more resilient and stronger than even the oldest among us." A rumble of shock and whispers erupted, but Killian raised his hand.

"Her mother was the human sister of the current Corvin family head — Silas."

Elora frantically searched among the vampires who sat at the table, looking for one who could confirm this. Maybe Silas himself. But she was only met with expressions of anger and fear, maybe even greed, a desire to own and control. If she didn't have a target on her back before, she most certainly did now. Especially with Killian's declaration of her being stronger than any of them sitting at the table. She could almost hear their wheels turning, considering all the ways they could use her to achieve whatever goals they had.

"Silas can, of course, confirm this, but he unfortunately could not make the party to meet his niece. He does, however, send his well wishes." Killian left the words hanging for a moment, giving the guests an opportunity to question him and comment in some way. Only a fool would do that, and his expression made that clear enough.

"Fantastic. Now, my wonderful guests, let us eat." Killian sat back down and gestured to the figures huddled along the wall. Each one took a hesitant step and then another, acutely aware that they were the prey in this room of predators. She could see their shaking hands, the fear in their eyes, the way they recoiled from every movement and noise.

The sound of snarls filled the room as one by one the humans were pulled into the laps of the vampires near them. They did not fight; instead, they willingly melted into their arms as the vampires stroked their cheeks, their jaw, and their necks as if all their fear was forgotten. Fangs sank into flesh and moans rang out across the room even as Elora gasped, trying not to cry out at the sight. It wasn't compulsion or forced as she had expected, but willing submission no matter what hesitation they had shown at first.

She had known this was coming somehow, had seen vampire parties that descended into feeding and more. Shards of memories flashed before her eyes, of large parties like these where everyone fed before bodies were removed and replaced, a consequence of those who could not control their thirst. Moans and cries of pain had mingled with the orchestra music, and she had sunk into her chair, holding onto a doll in an elaborate gown that matched the one she wore. Another flash of memory, of lying on a table, limbs spread out like a verifiable feast.

She shuddered and reached for her drink, trying to drown out the memories and the sounds of feeding erupting all around her. Elora let the liquid linger on her tongue before she swallowed and closed her eyes for a moment, setting the glass back down before she moved to stand. A hand grasped her and gently pulled her back down into the chair. She didn't fight Damien's unspoken command.

"I am tired. I would like to go back to my room." She met Killian's eyes, who gestured to someone behind him.

"I am sorry, my dear. But you can't yet. You haven't eaten." Elora pursed her lips together and tried not to glare at him.

"I don't really have an appetite." For days now, food had had no appeal even as her stomach growled and it felt like her body was consuming itself, the gnawing growing more intense every day. With a soft sigh, she grabbed her fork and pushed around the vegetables like a petulant child.

"Hmm, that is too bad. That means your little friend doesn't get to eat either. In fact, why don't we just dispose of him altogether? If you aren't concerned about his well-being, after all." He jerked his head off to the side and she turned in the direction he indicated, inhaling sharply as she spotted Viktor being escorted into the room. Eyes darted to him, watching him hungrily despite the human already in their arms.

She twisted back to Killian, shaking her head. "Please. Please don't." Killian smiled softly as the two escorts stood behind him, Viktor held tightly between them.

"I am just concerned about you, daughter." Elora looked down at her plate and swallowed as she speared what she thought was a potato and hoped she could eat it. A bite. One piece. Anything. She lifted it to her mouth, the smell of it forcing bile into her throat. She didn't even get the piece into her mouth before she gagged slightly and dropped the fork as Killian chuckled.

He knew, she realized with a start. Someone had told him about her conversation with Viktor and it was one of two people—Viktor or Damien and she knew exactly who she would place her bet on. She darted a quick glare at the vampire who was seated beside her, his eyes focused on Killian, who nodded to someone behind her. One of the servers stood beside her, wedging himself between her and Damien. His stance was stiff as he rolled up the sleeves of his white button-up shirt and held out his arm. The skin was riddled with pale scars, a mirror image of her own. Her eyes moved between Killian and the young man, her heart racing against the corset bodice of her gown.

With a quick and graceful movement, Damien took the knife reserved for her food and quickly made a small slice across the human's forearm and held her empty wine glass beneath it. The blood poured into the crystal glass as its smell filled the air and merged with the rest. It was a strange mixture of scents, blood, and perfume, each with a unique twist to them. Some were sweet, like candy or chocolate, while others were more natural, more like the forest or flowers.

She could feel it as each pair of eyes at the table locked onto the scene, taking it in with a curiosity that felt like perverse voyeurism in its finest form. Elora shrunk slightly, her spine curving as she recoiled into herself, hoping to disappear into her gown. She wanted to run, to retreat, to push her chair out and flee the room even as the coppery scent forced her hand to reach out and take the glass from him. Just like the night with Elizabeth, she no longer felt completely in control. Pure instinct drove each movement, drove the way her mouth salivated at the smell that came from the glass in her hand.

She took a deep shuddering breath as she brought the glass to her lips, silently begging herself to set it down, to throw it away, to deny this moment, this desire. It was an acknowledgment of the change occurring, what Viktor hinted at when they met. She couldn't meet his gaze even though she knew he was watching, could feel his eyes on her. Elora could only imagine the revulsion on this face, etched into every feature.

The blood was warm as she took her first drink, letting it slip past her lips. Her entire body jolted, and she took another swallow, then another, and another until the glass was empty. She barely managed to stop herself from licking the remnants from the crystal. Quietly, she waited for the repulsion to hit her, for it to come back up and spill out over the banquet table, staining the white tablecloth red. But it didn't.

Instead, euphoria ripped through her body, each limb and nerve alive and burning in the most glorious way as it worked its way through her system. She felt awake, more than ever before, as if she had slept for days and woken completely rested. It was perfection, as close to paradise as she could get. A moan escaped her lips and her back arched.

Applause broke out, starting with Killian before moving down the table as the rest of the guests abandoned their own meals for a moment to celebrate, a symbol of her acceptance into the vampire family as Killian's daughter. At the sound, she sat back in her chair and stared at the ceiling as she allowed herself to enjoy this feeling of being perfectly satiated, of feeling whole once more. It was a high, like the ones she had heard people at the hospital describe. Those in rehabilitation for drugs, whose addiction had led to violence and mental health issues, their voices had been laced with regret and longing as they walked through memory after memory.

"And this, my wonderful guests, is the true celebration!" Killian's voice traveled over the room, quieting the applause as everyone stared at him with rapt attention. "My daughter had been kept weak by the humans who took her, using a new tool to suppress her power and her hunger. Tonight, we celebrate that she is once again fully herself, once again a true daughter of mine."

The crowd cheered once more and Damien shifted beside her, startling her from her post-blood haze, his own applause suspiciously absent amidst the rest of the room. She wondered briefly if the haze, the euphoria happened every time or if it was the result of it being the first time since the medication left her system. She didn't remember feeding before Elizabeth, didn't remember this level of pleasure at the blood hitting her system. Maybe she had simply been given blood before she left Killian, like a child being given their meals already cooked. Killian was still speaking, but she did understand a word he said. Something about taking this tool away from humans and their growing disobedience.

She turned to Viktor, still standing with his escort behind Killian. His brown eyes were trained on her, dark with something she couldn't quite decipher. In her mind, she expected disgust, anger, or hatred. He had been correct in backing away from her the other day, the way he had shifted away from the glass dividing them. Tears pooled in her eyes as they watched each other, neither looking away, seeking comfort in one another. And then his lips mouthed a single message, the movement almost imperceptible: *It's okay.*

Elora huffed a laugh because it wasn't. Nothing about this was okay. She was exactly what Viktor feared she was, exactly what Killian wanted her to be. At her core, Elora had become her father's daughter and from the pure elation on Killian's face, he knew it as well as she did.

"Good girl, little rose. Very good. Would you like more?"

She shook her head even as she listened to the light laughter lingering throughout the table.

"Tsk, tsk. I doubt you got your fill. You must be starving. Refill her cup, please." The server beside her was somehow still standing, the napkin around his arm stained red and dripping. Elora struggled to understand how he was still conscious, how he was still there beside her, waiting to fulfill his purpose. Damien removed the fabric and refilled her glass before handing it back to her.

She wanted to dump it out, throw it in Killian's face, but the scent was undeniable, irresistible, and she found herself consuming it instantly. The bliss hit her once more, and she was sure another moan escaped her lips as she savored the taste. Damien squirmed and wrapped the napkin back around the server's wound before the human was taken away from the table. She didn't remember it being like this when she drank from Elizabeth, didn't remember there being this sense of utter completeness, of becoming whole. Maybe she was too young at the time. Maybe she simply blocked out how enjoyable it had been, like a memory she locked away.

"Damien, I think it is time for her to return to her rooms. You do not need to stay with her and are welcome to return to the party should you like to." Killian turned his head slightly to the side and gestured to the two vampires on either side of Viktor. One of them knelt beside the vampire head and bent down, listening intently as Killian gave him an order. Elora strained to hear what it was but gave up when she could only hear the conversations erupting all around her.

With as much grace as she could muster, Elora finally stood. She tried her hardest to ignore every pair of eyes that watched her as if something was fundamentally different about her. Some part of her core molded into something else. And on a certain level, Elora supposed it had. Her true nature had been revealed and brought to the surface. She ran her tongue over her teeth, feeling for any sign of physical change. Nothing. No sharpened canines, no fangs. Her steps were steady as she left the table and exited into the ballroom, heading towards the elevator with Damien a few paces behind her. She could feel his silent presence, taking comfort in it after the predatory gazes of everyone in that room.

Killian had been less than forthcoming about the details of what she was, only mentioning genetic alterations as the key to her conception. But what genes were altered and how? What would the consequence be? He had said she was stronger and more resilient, but in what ways? And there was what Jonas had said in the shadowy corner of the ballroom. That he had missed her blood, that nothing else had been the same.

It was too much. Too many questions, too many changes, and she found herself longing for the hospital as she pushed the button on the elevator and stepped in with Damien at her side. The hospital had been predictable, the routine clear, no surprises despite the issues with Dr. Montgomery. But there had been no life-shattering revelations, no existential crises that left her feeling unhinged and unanchored.

The elevator chimed, and she walked off, hands already on the corset ties, struggling to pull them free from behind her back. She grunted as Damien opened the door for her, silent as he stepped to the side so she could enter.

"Would you like some help?" His voice was low, husky as he took a step towards her, watching as she nodded and dropped her hands to her sides. Her breath was shaky as he gripped the ribbons, loosening the corset until the gown hung on her figure. Neither of them moved, his hands resting on her hips, and she forced herself not to lean into his touch, to not lean back onto him.

"Thank you," She whispered as his hands dropped from her body and he took a step back. The only sound she heard was the door opening once more and closing, leaving her in silence. Her whirling thoughts and questions were all crashing into one another, neither lasting long enough to fully consider. She licked her lips, taking in the blood left behind. Her entire body eased as she dropped the gown and left it behind and ran a bath of water hot enough to burn the skin off her bones. After grabbing a long shirt with the familiar scent of Damien's cologne, she washed away the makeup and feel of the stares on her from a night of exposure in more ways than one.

CHAPTER 36

Damien

The more debauched portion of the dinner was in full effect by the time he returned from escorting the girl to her room. Bodies joined with other bodies on the banquet table or in the various chairs. The room was filled with the scent of blood and sweat, moans and cries that filtered out into the hallway. Damien could hear it even as he stepped back out of the elevator and he almost turned back around, not wanting to take part in this particular set of activities.

But he knew Killian expected him to return, and he said exactly that when he said Damien didn't need to stay with her once she was back. And yet, he had almost stayed, had been unable to remove his hand from her side, simply stared at her exposed back that was riddled with scars. There was no part of her that wasn't marked in some way and a part of him wanted to stand guard outside her room while another part wanted to hold her. He had seen her shaking, seen the horror on her face at the glass of blood, seen the way her gaze shot to that asshole Viktor, as if she expected to see revulsion.

Damien had only seen perfection, broken pieces put back together in a way that left it breathtaking and otherworldly, something people wrote poetry about. Revulsion was the last thing anyone should see when they looked at her.

As he left, he considered finding Lukas to ask him to take his place standing guard. But even as the thought entered his mind, he spotted his friend very much engaged with a human towards the end of the table, kneeling between her legs, her head thrown back in either pain or pleasure or both. It depended on what Lukas wanted for her, what he catered his bite towards. They could make their bite pleasurable or painful, depending on what they wanted the human to feel.

No, the girl would be safe. Jonas was still here in the room, engaged in conversation with Killian and Darian at the head of the table. All three of them leaned in close together as if they wanted to be sure no one would overhear whatever they were discussing. For some reason, it put him on edge. Jonas had attacked the girl and Darian had acted strangely as well when introduced to her, referencing how well he had known her before. Just as Jonas had.

Damien shook his head and remained by the banquet room door, leaning against the frame, hoping desperately that Killian would dismiss him soon. But as Killian stood and moved away from the two vampires, Damien realized that was not what would happen.

"My office." He nodded at the command and followed Killian from the room, down the elevator, and into his office. Killian said nothing the entire time, even as the symphony of moans and cries and music faded away, disappearing entirely once the elevator doors closed. Damien studied the way Killian's hands were shoved into his pockets, the way his jaw was clenched, and his eyes were dark. A combination that did not bode well for anyone involved.

Killian poured himself a drink and sat at his desk, smiling broadly. "You did good. Despite the whole situation with Jonas, you kept her out of trouble."

Damien quirked an eyebrow. "Jonas told you what happened?"

"He tried to tattle on you, thinking I would be on his side. Obviously, I was not. Don't worry. He won't touch her again without permission." Damien noted that he didn't say whose permission, whether that be his or Elora's.

"Good to hear. It seemed to rattle her." Her disheveled gown and torn bodice appeared once more. The sight of Jonas with his teeth at her throat caused Damien to move his hands behind his back to hide the way they clenched into fists.

"Oh? She seemed well put together when you two sat for dinner." Damien shrugged, wondering if her father hadn't seen the state of her gown, the slightly smeared lipstick, the handprints on her arms, or the bits of hair that had come free.

"She is good at collecting herself. She is stronger than she looks." Killian stopped moving for a moment, the glass in his hand halting midway to his mouth before taking another sip.

"That may be the first nice thing you have said about my daughter, Damien. I am curious about the change of heart." The words were casual, yet the tone was anything but.

"Not a compliment or change of heart. Just an observation." Killian nodded slightly before lapsing into silence, which spread between them as he remained standing by the door. With a final sip, Killian finished his drink and reclined back in the leather chair.

"I am having a nightcap taken up to her soon. I want you to deliver it and make sure she drinks it. I am worried that she didn't consume enough, especially now that the fucking medication is out of her system." It was the words of a caring father, a concerned vampire who knew the hunger that came with being freshly turned. At the core of it all, that was what she was despite being born a vampire, the only one of her kind.

"A nightcap?"

"Just some blood. She will start drinking some with her meals if she still wants to eat human garbage. However, after her reaction tonight, I doubt that will be a concern. You will be in charge of making sure she feeds. Understood?"

"She is just as likely to throw it in my face as to drink it, Killian." Damien could picture it — handing her the glass followed by the flash of anger on her face that always showed when he was in her presence, then it would splash in his face.

Killian huffed a laugh. "That may be true, but she is your responsibility. Simply remind her of that useless human she cares about." He spat the word. Viktor was a reminder of his daughter's past life and existence, of the fact she thought she was human until a little bit ago.

"Of course. Is she going to feed directly from a human, or am I getting blood from the collection rooms?" Damien wasn't sure he wanted to be the one to bring a human to her to feed from. Her reaction would more than likely be volatile or extreme, either aimed at him or the human. Newly turned could have trouble handling their bloodlust, turning frenzied in a matter of seconds.

"Collection rooms for now. I don't want her feeding from a source until we get a better grasp on her urges and hunger."

"Understood."

"Good. And Damien, make sure she drinks it. I can't have her weakening herself out of spite."

Damien nodded and turned, leaving Killian sitting there with the strangest smile on his face, a combination of hunger and triumph.

* * *

Damien didn't recognize the male vampire that stood outside the girl's room holding a bottle and a wine glass. He had expected one of the workers from the collection rooms, dressed in their usual white uniform that was very similar to the scrubs worn at the psychiatric hospital. With narrowed eyes, Damien looked him over as he approached, trying to note anything in case he needed to find him later—brown hair and darker skin, almost as tall as Damien, but lanky with long, thin limbs.

The vampire didn't say anything, simply thrust the glass and bottle into Damien's hands before spinning around, practically running back to the elevator. For a moment, Damien questioned whether his obvious fear was from threats Killian may have made or of himself. He had made a reputation for himself by taking care of Killian's dirty work and violence wasn't an odd behavior within the walls of the Tower where attacks against one another for the sake of a minor insults weren't unheard of.

Damien knocked and waited a brief moment before entering, figuring he had given her enough time to cover up if necessary. The thought of her being in a state of undress forced him to pause as he opened the door, brought on by a desire to give her the privacy she was so often denied. She had been exposed enough tonight. The room was silent, and he spotted the gown in a pile on the floor where she discarded it after he left. There was a splash of water from the bathroom and Damien set the bottle and glass on the desk before taking a seat to wait for her.

He could only imagine how she felt now that the whole ordeal was over. Between Jonas, the whispers, and consuming blood for the first time in years, the night must have been exhausting. And he had heard the whispers, the rumors even after Killian made his announcement about who she was. The gossip was vile and more than once he had to stop himself from intervening, from dragging vampire after vampire before the girl to make them apologize and beg her forgiveness.

And still, a tiny shred of guilt was lodged in his chest at his role in the choice of gown. There had been others that had covered a bit more with translucent sleeves or thin lace over the bodice. He had chosen it because he knew it would be stunning on her, and would present her as Killian's daughter, which was what the vampire had wanted. And he had been correct. When he saw her in the gown, her hair pulled away from her face, her eyes lined in black, any ability to speak had disappeared. It wasn't until they were in the ballroom that he realized exactly how horrible his mistake had been. He hadn't considered the other vampires in attendance or what they would say or do.

Damien had noted the way she sought a cover-up of some sort, the barely restrained anger in her expression when he saw her. She saw the scars as something to be ashamed of, something to be hidden. The comments he had heard, and she had heard as well, had only confirmed her own opinion despite them all being so horrifically wrong.

The water began to drain, and he heard her groan as she stepped out of the tub, probably wrapping a towel around her body and another around her hair as she so often did. As she stepped out, Damien's assumptions about the towels were proven correct. Her eyes met his. Once the surprise had worn off, she glared at him as if it would make him burst into flames.

"So, you are creepy as well as an asshole. Good to know." He tracked her as she moved to the closet, closing the door slightly as she dressed. Damien didn't respond, swallowing back the retort on his tongue despite wanting so desperately to verbally spare with her, to throw insults and sarcastic comments back and forth like some type of toxic game where there were no winners. He enjoyed seeing the frustration on her face, the way her lips curled, and the tiniest lines appeared between her brows when she was most certainly considering hitting him. It proved she hadn't fallen into that dark place she retreated to when everything became too much. Instead, he needed her to cooperate and drink Killian's gift. And pissing her off wasn't going to help that.

She came back out dressed in one of the shirts he had left in her closet and a pair of sweats, her long hair damp. Damien hadn't told her he had brought a small pile of large shirts for her — long-sleeved with high collars — just left them in there, along with the rest of the clothes. There were traces of makeup from the night, mascara and eyeliner under her eyes, and the red lipstick smudged into a light pink, giving her a haunted look.

"I brought a gift," he informed her and gestured to the glass. She froze in place, eyes locked on the items waiting there.

"I don't want anything from you." He groaned at her words, remembering that he had warned Killian about this. He should have sent Lukas, since she seemed to like him. Finding them playing cards and her enjoying his company had bothered him, and still bothered him. It was the ease she had with him, the way her smile came easily, and how her laugh was light and almost gentle. The sound of the two of them left him irritated, which hadn't helped the conversation that had come after Lukas had left the room.

"Good thing it isn't from me." Her eyes narrowed.

"I don't want anything from him either." Damien moved his shoulders in something like a shrug before he poured the liquid in the bottle into the wine glass. The smell hit them both, and he watched as she shuddered and inhaled the aroma. The blood was fresh, probably harvested within the last couple of hours. Only the best for Killian's daughter, while the rest of them made do with what there was. The coppery tang of the blood mingled with something else, something natural—the woods or trees. Pine, maybe. He had never spent much time outside the city despite his mother always talking about camping or hiking, her favorite activities from childhood. But it never happened either because there was no money, or a client didn't show up. Just another promise out of reach.

"Just drink it. Now that you are feeding, you need to keep yourself from getting too hungry. It can become a problem." She hesitated, watching him. "The sooner you drink it, the sooner I leave."

And that had done it. The magic words that made him realize she wanted him gone from the room so desperately, she would adhere to Killian's request. He tried to ignore how his chest tightened, how it hurt for her to despise his company. A part of him wanted to stay and ask her stupid questions like those she and Lukas asked each other.

She let out a deep sigh and grabbed the glass, finishing it in three swallows, wincing each time as if it tasted bad. With how fresh it was, the blood should have been amazing. No, Damien was certain it wasn't the taste, but what it represented for her.

Her hatred for Killian made little sense to him. He understood her anger at being dragged back, kidnapped as she liked to say. But was this really worse than that hospital? Worse than that horrible psychiatrist? A flush of irritation raced through him, reminding him once again that she had the world handed to her, presented on a silver tray. Killian had given her everything—his precious daughter, a miracle, as he had always explained every single chance he was given. And she had run away and hurt dozens in the process. The pile of vampire bodies at her feet knew no limit. Everyone who allowed her to run away and every vampire who failed to bring her back were publicly executed to make an example.

"Good girl," Damien sneered as she set the glass down, the sound startling in the otherwise quiet room. She just flipped him off, but it didn't hold the same malice as it usually did. Instead, it felt empty, like a muscle memory that had no thought behind it.

His expression disappeared as she perched on the edge of the bed and wrapped her arms around herself. He wanted to ask her what she thought of the party, of the changes she was undergoing. He wanted to ask if she was okay after everything, ask if she needed anything. It was the only reason he was still here, still hesitating in her room.

"You can leave now." He exhaled at her command and stood, not looking at her as he shut the door behind him.

CHAPTER 37

Elora

She regretted her words as soon as the door closed, and the lock clicked into place. The room was suddenly too big, too quiet as she scooted back on the mattress and pulled her knees to her chest. The party and Killian's gift had left her broken, cracks forming as she heard every word from dinner repeated as if she was still there. Jonas's assertion about her blood brought back too many memories, each one worse than the one before. And then there was Darian, who had put her on edge, her body screaming at her to run, to get as far away as possible. Killian had said that the vampire had known her before she left and she was inclined to believe him, knowing exactly what that entailed. She wondered how many of the scars could be attributed to him.

She pushed herself back onto the bed until she hit the headboard. Only then did she rest her head on her knees and wished she could call Damien back or send for Lukas. Someone to talk to, someone to distract her with card games or discussions about books or sports or other normal things that weren't her blood and vampires in general. Exhaustion, deep and undeniable, worked its way through her as her eyes grew heavy and a familiar warmth hit her limbs.

Sedation. Her thoughts started to slow down, forming and then disappearing. It was a sluggish feeling, and her thoughts felt trapped in ice, unable to lend her even an ounce of coherence. She moved and clawed towards the edge of the bed as her vision began to darken around the edges. The panic in her chest grew as she fell forward off the bed, crying out as her head bounced off the wood. The sound of her voice was disconnected, like it didn't come from her.

Reality was separating, leaving her in a strange void where time was lost and only empty spots in her memory were left.

Her heart raced as she pulled herself towards the door, fingers and nails digging into the wood, each movement growing weaker and weaker.

Get out of here. Hide. Now. The thoughts repeated as a scream that echoed in the empty chamber of her head. Already she could feel what was to come, a reminder of what would happen if she didn't hide. The door opened softly, and someone entered, their footsteps slow and easy as they wandered further into the room and crouched in front of her.

"Now, now, this is unnecessary." His voice was easy, almost amused, as he reached out and ran his fingers through her hair.

"Please. No." Elora's voice came out broken, almost a whisper as the sedative took a stronger hold. She could barely see, only shapes and shadows. Killian clucked his tongue and stood, stepping back from her as she listened to another set of footsteps enter the room — these lighter and hesitant.

"Get her ready. I've waited long enough." She tried to cry out, to scream, to beg them not to touch her, to hide her. She tried to call out for Damien, for Lukas, for anyone who would help her as she began to drown. But she couldn't. Instead, everything went dark.

* * *

Everything hurt, even parts of her body she didn't know could hurt were screaming in agony. Her head was pounding, and each breath felt like fire. Slowly, she opened her eyes before she squeezed them shut as the light from the bedside lamp flooded her vision. She groaned and then opened them once more, blinking slowly as she allowed them to become acclimated to the light.

What happened?

She remembered the party and then Damien escorting her back to her room, his hands on her back as he loosened her dress. She hadn't drunk anything other than a little wine and the blood. The reminder caused a bit of bile to rise in her throat. This wasn't a hangover; at least she didn't think so. After returning, she had taken a bath to wash away the feeling of Jonas's hands, the searing gaze of every vampire in that room. Then —

Nothing. Nothing after that.

She sat up, wincing as the thin blanket and nightgown pulled at her skin, snagging on something. With a hiss, she fell back onto the bed and craned her neck to check over her body. Elora inhaled sharply as she took in the blood covering her skin, leaving only bits of flesh visible. The silk nightgown she didn't remember putting on was ripped down the front and up the side. Only one thin strap held the entire garment up, since the other was gone.

Her brows furrowed together as she recalled the feel of the long shirt she had put on after her bath. Instantly, her heart leaped into her throat as flashes came back, hitting her like punches to the stomach. Hands. Fingers. Teeth. A burning sensation throughout her body and agony before everything went black. She had screamed and cried out until her throat was raw before succumbing to the darkness.

With a whimper, Elora sat up, leaning against the headboard for a moment while she took a breath. Each movement was like moving through heavy snow, like she was weighed down. Panic was coursing through her as she took in the cuts, long and deep along her arms and legs. She could feel more along her chest but couldn't see them and could only guess that maybe that was for the best.

What if they come back?

The thought came unbidden to collide with her panic and create a storm that threatened to destroy her, leaving her trembling as she tried to stand. Each step was shaky, and she held onto the bed as she moved, gripping anything she could reach for dear life until she made it to the door. It felt so much further than before. Her hands shook uncontrollably as she turned the handle, praying and hoping that it was unlocked.

It clicked, and she pulled the door open, peering out and finding no one standing guard. A part of her thought that Lukas would be there, taking the night shift for Damien since he had been in charge at the party. But no one was there, only an empty hallway full of paintings and statues.

She left the door open as she moved, leaning heavily against the wall, her labored breaths the only sound. Each step towards the elevator took every ounce of strength she had left. It was as if her knees would buckle at any moment, and she would collapse and have to crawl her way to wherever she was going. With a start, she realized she had never settled on where to go, had only been motivated by a desperate need to escape the room, to leave the blood-soaked bed behind.

Damien. His room. Only his name repeated in her head as she moved.

Despite everything, there was only one place where she would inexplicably feel safe, and she knew it even if she didn't understand it. Damien would do what needed to be done, even if he hated her. Unless he had been a part of it, unless he had been there and watched it happen as Killian's trusted lapdog. Her finger hesitated on the button that would take her down to the floor where his room was located, hovering slightly as she considered the possibility of him being involved. Of his teeth in her skin, her flesh under his control as she lay unconscious. It didn't feel right. Damien had made it clear he had standards, and she wasn't up to them.

He had said he would never feed from her, never lower himself in that way. With that thought as comfort, she finally pushed the button and leaned heavily against the wall as the elevator went down one floor before opening with a chime. For a moment, she wasn't sure she would make it out of the elevator, let alone down the hall. Her legs shook, and each step felt like she had run miles.

This is a bad idea. Elora pushed away the thought. No, it was the only option. There was no one else.

She glanced down the long hallway that had doors to at least a dozen rooms on either side. Lukas had explained that his room was the first one on the right and that Damien's was across from it. A smirk had played on his lips as he explained their rooms were beneath hers and Killian's because of their status and their loyalty to Killian. It had taken every ounce of restraint to not scream at him, to not tell him every horrible thing that Killian had done. Lukas was loyal to the head vampire and owed his place in the Tower to him. She may have liked Lukas, may have enjoyed his company and easy laughter, his jokes and willingness to talk to her like she was normal, but she could never forget where his true loyalty lay.

Elora knocked on Damien's door before she sunk to her knees as the last of her strength left her, each ounce spent on the way there. There were sounds coming from the other side of the door, but she couldn't make them out. She exhaled at the knowledge he was at least in there and raised her arm, grabbing the door handle, hoping with every part of her that wasn't locked.

To her immense relief, it turned, and she pushed it open before collapsing.

~ ~

CHAPTER 38

Damien

He didn't remember the name of the human in his lap, only that his teeth were in her neck and her blood was doing little for him. She moaned as he drew from her, already regretting his decision to opt for a live feeding instead of a collection bottle from the refrigerators. He had thought some physical interaction would help the hollowness he felt when he left the girl's room when she had demanded he leave. But it was doing nothing.

The door creaked open softly, the sound drawing not only his attention but his annoyance. Damien removed his fangs from the human who gave a slight whimper at the loss and prepared to punish whoever was stupid enough to come in without permission. Only the crumbled figure on the floor crowned with crimson hair gave him pause before he tossed the human from his lap and leaped to his feet. His heart raced as he rushed towards her and crouched in a single movement. He cursed as he took her in and eyed the bites and cuts covering her arms and legs. Her hair was matted and tangled from blood and her nightgown was hanging low along her back. It wasn't what she was wearing when he was sent from her room. His hands hovered above her body for a moment as he struggled to grasp the sight of her battered form.

As easily as possible, he turned her over onto her back and hissed as he scanned her face. Pale, paler than he had ever seen her, and scrunched up in pain despite being unconscious. Her neck was the worst. Not a single spot of skin wasn't covered in blood. He could barely make out where the wounds were underneath it all. With the gentlest of touches, not sure he should move her, he lifted her into his arms, ignoring how the nightgown started to fall in its current state.

"Out. Leave." The human didn't hesitate, just rushed out the door, letting it slam shut behind her. Somewhere in his mind, he knew he would need to follow up with the human and make sure her mouth stayed shut about what she saw tonight. Killian would kill him if he knew the girl came to him like this.

He laid her on his bed, careful not to touch her more than necessary, then sat beside her, trying to figure out what to do. Normally, he was the perfect person to have in an emergency, a cold figure who could take care of what needed to be done without any issues. But seeing her in this state had any semblance of control or thought gone from his mind, unable to even decide what to do next.

Damien regarded her carefully, noting the emptiness of her face before brushing aside a strand of hair. At first, she looked simply peaceful with the softness of her lips and the way her eyebrows now rested easily, usually drawn together in irritation or annoyance. The pain was gone from her expression, leaving nothing behind. It wasn't peace, but a hollowness, an absence of everything that was her. Even in sleep, he had always been able to see her, the slight changes in expressions as she dreamed the night he stayed in her room. This felt unnatural. She didn't move an inch other than the steady rise and fall of her chest, the only indication she was alive.

Should I wake her up?

Something horrific had happened. Someone hurt her. Blood rushed through him as he struggled to keep his temper in check. That fuck Jonas. Damien knew it was him. There was no question. But was all this from him? It seemed so unlikely, but Jonas had been unhinged at the party, willing to force himself on her despite there being dozens of people around. Maybe Darian? There had been something in the way he looked at her when they had been introduced.

He tore his eyes away from her and grabbed his phone from the nightstand, sending a quick message to Lukas, the only person he trusted to look into this.

My room. Now.

Damien tossed the phone back onto the nightstand, not bothering or needing to wait for a response before gathering a wet cloth from the bathroom sink with a bowl of water. Slowly, with the lightest of touches, he started to wash away the blood, rinsing the cloth as he went, only managing to clean one arm before needing to replace the water.

How long would she sleep? Did she need blood? Water? As he started to wash the blood from her neck, she stirred, whimpering as her face contorted in pain.

"Please, don't. Please." Damien closed his eyes and clenched his jaw as her pleading ruptured something in him. The girl before him wasn't who he thought she was, not the spoiled brat who threw away her gifts and protection. He needed to know why she ran in the first place, even if he doubted that she would be the one to tell him anything. And he didn't want to ask her, didn't want to make her reopen those wounds, especially not now. He would find Dr. Montgomery and demand information about her history. If that didn't work, there was also Viktor, who could be encouraged to talk even if she ended up hating him for it.

Someone knew something.

"Not again. Please, not again." Damien dropped the cloth onto the nightstand, realizing that she was reliving whatever happened, that whoever had been in that room was still torturing her, even in her sleep. His fingers touched her arm gingerly, only enough to make her aware of his presence.

"Elora. Wake up." She whimpered again and tried to curl into herself, her head ducking down to her chest as she attempted to roll over. Gently, he grabbed her arm, holding her in place. He needed her to not turn away from him, needed her to wake up and escape whatever hell she was currently stuck in.

"No, don't touch me!" Her voice broke the silence as she started thrashing and he gripped both of her arms, terrified of what she would do to protect herself.

He shouted her name once more before letting go, allowing her to fall back on the bed as her eyes finally started opening. Her green eyes, a color so rich it seemed impossible, darted around the room as she struggled to orient herself.

"You are in my room. You came here before collapsing." His words were soft, barely above a whisper, but she nodded and met his eyes as he knelt next to the bed. Slowly, the fear ebbed away from her face as each feature softened and tears gathered in her eyes. With a grimace, she sat up and rested against the pillow and headboard. He gathered his hands into fists just below the mattress so she couldn't see the rage lingering under his skin. He wanted to reach out, brush away each tear that now ran down her face, and pull her into his embrace to stop the shaking. She didn't look at him, but instead let her eyes roam around the room, over each piece of furniture, each empty shelf.

"I'm sorry." Her voice came out as a small broken sound that made him want to annihilate whoever caused it. He wanted to throw something, break everything that he could get his hands on if it meant making sure he never heard it again. The apology made no sense. There was nothing she would ever need to apologize for.

Damien shook his head before remembering she hadn't looked at him. "You don't need to do that. You've done nothing to apologize for."

For a moment, she didn't answer, just wrapped her arms over her chest as if trying to disappear into thin air. The nightgown was destroyed, one strap completely torn from the fabric where the entire top portion had been ripped. He pulled the thick blanket up from the foot of the bed and over her, covering her up to her shoulders. She flinched at the movement, and he sat back on his heels, giving her space even though he forced himself not to pull her into his arms.

Finally—finally, she looked at him, eyes glistening yet blank, the pain too deeply etched into her core to be seen on the surface. He let his hand move towards her slowly and brushed away a tear as it fell down her cheek.

"I'm sorry," she repeated. "I didn't know where to go." He nodded, giving her space to speak despite the dozens of questions rampaging through his mind. Instead of asking all of them, he settled on one.

"What can I do?" His words were calmer than he felt. She shook her head, brows knitting together as if she was struggling with a thought. Damien crawled a bit closer, the wood of the floor pushing into his knees, and he had to suppress a hiss of pain.

"Can we get you cleaned up?" She recoiled slightly away from him, arms tightening around herself.

"I won't touch you unless you need help. Unless you ask me to. Okay?" She nodded and let him take away the blanket before she crawled off the bed. She swayed slightly and paused. Damien stood beside her, ready in case she started to fall, every inch of him screaming to help her to prevent any more pain.

Step by step, she made it to the bathroom and stood in the doorway like she was unsure of what came next. The nightgown was hanging off her frame, allowing him to see more of the damage. Bruises were starting to bloom along her ribs and shoulders, and his fingernails dug into his palms. She was a vampire now, or something akin to it. Bruises of this magnitude would require brute force, the kind that would kill a human.

He squeezed by her, making sure he didn't touch her, and ran her a bath, keeping the water hot but not enough to burn. After a quick gesture towards the tub, Damien averted his gaze, busying himself by grabbing towels from the cabinet near the sink. A faint whimper reached his ears, and he stared straight ahead at the wall, towels clutched tightly in his grip.

"I need help." Again, that fucking voice. Broken, not a hint of her fire. He swallowed and turned to see her struggling with the nightgown. Her arm wouldn't rise high enough to ease the strap off. Whether it was broken, or she was just too drained to lift her limbs, he wasn't sure.

With slow, measured steps, he moved towards her and raised his hands to the remaining strap of the nightgown, easing it down her body. Tiny cries of pain escaped her lips, and he flinched each time the fabric was pulled from the dried blood and wounds. Her entire body trembled as he took her hand, helping her balance as she lifted one leg and then the other. All the while, he stared at the wall while she sank beneath the water, and it turned a brownish color as the blood started to rinse off. He grabbed her some soap and shampoo, cursing himself for always buying the cheaper options.

"I'm going to find you clothes."

Her response was instantaneous, panic and fear echoing throughout the room as she reached for him. She flinched as the cuts twisted and opened from the movement. "No! Don't leave me."

Damien knelt beside the tub and cupped her cheek, relishing the way she didn't flinch or recoil. Slowly, he watched the panic leave her eyes. "I locked the door, Elora. I'm just grabbing you something from my bedroom. I'm not leaving. Okay? I'll be right through that door."

She hesitated before nodding, eyes darting to the door that he would be walking through as soon as she gave him permission. He gave her a small smile, hoping to comfort her as he stood and left. As he searched through his clothes, he listened for her, listened to each whimper and small cry as she soaked in the water. He finally chose a large, long-sleeved sweatshirt and the smallest pair of sweats he had before returning to the bathroom to look for any medical supplies. Usually, he kept a small pharmacy in case missions for Killian went bad and he needed Lukas to patch him up a little bit. Vampires had accelerated healing, but some things took longer to heal than others- like stab wounds. Or deep incisions for bloodletting.

After digging through the towels and half-empty bottles under his sink, he found a small bundle of gauze and medical tape and turned back to her. Her eyes were closed, and she didn't seem to have moved since he left.

"You need to wash, love. We need to make sure your wounds are clean." His words were gentle as her eyes opened, and she reached for the soap. Slowly, she ran it along her arms, wincing whenever she went over a particularly deep cut. He simply studied the tiles along the floor, suddenly noticing how the red and cream tiles alternated in an illogical pattern.

"Damien. My hair. Can you—" she trailed off and tears formed in her eyes again. In an instant, he was at her side, the bottle of shampoo in his hand.

"Of course." She lowered into the water, wetting her hair before sitting back up. He poured some of the liquid onto her head and started gently working it through her scalp where there seemed to be the most blood. It would probably take more than one wash to get all of it out.

She winced in certain spots, and he forced his touch to be softer. They had to have pulled her hair, tightened their grip, and yanked. As he rinsed the first round of shampoo, chunks were left in his hand, long strands of her striking red hair. He took a deep breath, willing himself to push the fury deeper inside. This was not the time for that to show. Once more, he added shampoo and worked it through. This time she didn't wince, just eased against the edge of the tub and water splashed to the floor as he rinsed it once more, finally satisfied that nothing remained.

"Are you ready to get out?" He made sure to lean back away from her, moving so that he couldn't see her body or the water anymore.

"Yes." She sounded exhausted, and he wondered exactly how much was taken from her, how drained she was from whatever they had done.

"I'm going to go into the bedroom so you can get out." She nodded, and he set the towels down on the counter nearest the tub. For a few moments, he could only sit on the bed and listen as the water sloshed, and she got out of the tub. He listened to her footsteps on the tile as she moved through the room, hesitant, as if she wasn't sure she could stand. Finally, she exited the bathroom. One towel was wrapped around her body while the other was wrapped around her hair. She leaned heavily on the frame as she studied him, eyes empty and lifeless.

All he knew was that he was going to kill whoever did this, whether Killian sanctioned it or not. He would repay them for each cut, each bite, each handful of hair ripped from her head.

"Your clothes are here." He gestured to the bundle at the foot of the bed. "I'll turn away while you dress."

She nodded and grabbed the shirt, each movement mechanical as she struggled to pull it down over her head. He cringed as a defeated sigh escaped her lips and he turned towards her and helped her with her shirt—one arm at a time, careful of the cuts and bites on her body. It fell to her thighs, the high collar covering everything while the sleeves hung over her hands. He studied the various cuts once more as the shirt covered her up. They were healing, but it was clear some of them would scar again. He held up the pants, but she shook her head.

"No. It hurts too much." He nodded, and they stood there, and silence settled between them.

"I can't go back in there. I can't." She stared at the floor, at the rug that covered the wood. "I can find somewhere—"

"You can sleep in here." Hesitantly, he placed his hand on her arm and led her over to the bed, helping her in before pulling the blanket up. The towel in her hair had come loose, and he gently removed it, letting her damp locks spill out over the pillow like a puddle of blood. He thought he heard her murmur a "thank you" even as her eyes closed and her knees pulled up to her chest, making herself as small as possible. It was something he noticed she did, even at the hospital, tucking her feet under her and pulling them towards her. It was as if she thought if she took up as little space as possible, she would be safe.

But she wasn't, and he didn't want to face how much of that may be his fault. Softly, he whispered good night as she let out a shuddering breath, clutching the blanket like it was the only thing keeping her grounded.

A knock sounded at the door, and his gaze darted to the sleeping vampire in his bed. But she didn't move, breathing softly with her lips parted slightly. Damien moved through the room with careful steps and pulled the door open slowly, unsure if the hinges would make noise. He had never cared to notice before. Lukas stood on the other side of the door in a long shirt and cotton pants, confusion clear on his face. His hair was a mess as it hung loosely around his shoulders. From the look on Lukas's face, Damien must be a mess as well. With a quick glance back at her, Damien stepped out but kept the door slightly open in case she made even the slightest noise.

"What is it?" Lukas tried to look around him through the cracked door, but Damien shifted, blocking his view. "Oh, I see." A small smile played on his lips while Damien's hardened into a line.

"No. Not that. I need you to do something for me. It needs to stay between us."

"Of course. What is it?"

"No one, Lukas. Not even Killian." He nodded as his expression grew grim. Damien would never ask him to keep Killian in the dark, never ask him to keep a secret from their head vampire. But Lukas was always more loyal to Damien, something he should have reciprocated but didn't. His loyalty had always been to the vampire who saw something in Damien, something worth saving when his life had been given to pay a fucking debt.

"Go to Elora's room. Something happened. Look for anything weird, out of the ordinary." He had spent time there with her and would notice anything strange or different.

"You got it." He turned to leave, no questions asked. Damien had known there wouldn't be when he asked him here. Lukas was more than his second, as Killian referred to him. They had been turned around at the same time, only a year or so apart. Lukas had been tuned first and had helped Damien adjust to the changes, helping him feed and learn the rules of living in the Tower. Damien trusted him without question. If Damien asked Lukas to keep this quiet, he would.

He closed the door and sat in one of the armchairs as he ran his fingers through his hair. Nothing about this made sense. She was meant to be protected as Killian's daughter, the entire reason she had been dragged back here, but she had been attacked. There were no other words for it. The wounds and bruises made it clear. Had Killian known about this? Is that what Jonas had meant by he knew Elora better than anyone else did? His hands itched to find Jonas, to demand answers to every single question that raced through his mind, forcing him to question things he never would have before her. Killian had to have known. The look between him and Darian had implied as much.

And he had berated her, insulted her over and over again because she refused to claim him as her father. Of course, she didn't. Piece after piece fell into place as his body tensed from the need to find Jonas, to find Darain, to make them regret even looking in her direction. And if Killian was involved, then he deserved something else, something that would make what Damien had done to others look like gentleness. It had started before she left or ran away or whatever had happened. She had been a child.

A soft knock on the door forced him out of his thoughts and he opened it, knowing exactly who was there. He tensed instantly at the distress in Lukas's eyes and carved into his face.

"Damien—" He faltered; gaze once more moving behind him before Damien could block her.

"What? What did you find, Lukas?"

He swallowed and met Damien's gaze again. "I should come in for this." He looked pointedly down the hallway where the doors to the other rooms were, where other vampires may or may not be sleeping. He moved aside, pointing to the bathroom to try to keep the bedroom as silent as possible. Lukas followed his lead without a word, hesitating only once as his focus lingered on Elora in Damien's bed. Her breathing was easy, her face soft and peaceful. The blanket covered her body, but from the look on Lukas's face, he had an idea of who lay beneath it. He whispered a curse and shook his head before they both entered the bathroom and closed the door just a bit before speaking.

"Chains. Attached to the bed posts. Arms and legs. And the sheets — fuck Damien. The sheets were covered in blood."

Damien took a breath, steady and easy, as he opened and closed his hand.

"Any hints of who was there?"

Lukas shook his head. "Not really. There were traces of scents, but nothing I could isolate. It was mostly blood. It is bad, Damien. There were others" — again, he faltered, and Damien considered punching him for hesitating. He was holding on by a thread, a single thread that could snap at any minute. Lukas must have seen something on Damien's face because he started backing away.

"Clean up the mess. Don't tell anyone." His words cut through the room, sharp and cold, as he gave Lukas the orders. Vaguely, Damien realized this may be a bad idea, that Killian would have already sent someone. But he couldn't focus on anything but the woman in his bed and each and every injury on her body. Couldn't focus on anything but erasing it from her room and then finding out who needed to die.

"What are we going to do about this?" His horror had turned to rage and if Damien wasn't so far in his own fury, he would have commented on it. Lukas had grown to care for her, between broken noses and card games he had come to like her.

Instead, Damien just shook his head. "We can talk in the morning."

A whimper came from the room, and he turned away, waving his hand in what he hoped was a dismissal. Slowly, he reached the bed once more, not sure if it was a nightmare or if she had woken up. As he got closer, he met her eyes, open but only just.

"Can you — can you sleep here, please?" He nodded before going to the other side of the bed and lying down, settling on top of the blankets. He felt it as she rolled over and faced him, but he stared at the ceiling, willing his thoughts to calm and the tension to finally leave his body.

"Damien." He turned his head slightly. "Thank you." He turned his head to look at her, taking in the exhausted expression, the hollowness of her eyes, the bruises along her cheekbones. He shook his head.

"No need, love. None at all." For a moment, he saw something dart across her face, surprise or something like it. He had called her love. Not her name or any nickname, but love. And it had felt so right to do so, the word coming off his tongue with such ease he hadn't realized he had done it. She scooted closer, and he froze, even as her head rested on his chest, and he breathed in the smell of his cheap shampoo. Her breathing evened out as she fell back into what he hoped was a dreamless sleep. After what seemed like hours, Damien fell into nightmares of blood staining her pale skin red and a mangled body held by silver chains.

CHAPTER 39

Elora

The room was dark when she finally woke up and nestled deeper into the thick blankets, enjoying the feeling of something that wasn't silk against her skin. It took her a moment to realize that this was not her room, not her bed. She darted up as last night came back in waves—the party, Damien's visit to her room, the blood, the visitors, and coming to this room once she woke.

The drugged blood. Damien had given it to her and claimed it was a gift from Killian meant to help her with her hunger now that she was fully a vampire again. Had Damien known what he was giving her? Had he left her gift wrapped for what came later?

She glanced down, eyes moving over her arms and legs, taking in the healing flesh. Damien had helped her clean up after collapsing at his door, had washed her hair, and helped her change. Had it been guilt? Or was he cleaning up Killian's mess like he always did? She had heard the vampires talking during the party. As much as she was a topic of conversation, so was he. Killian's right-hand vampire took care of problems that popped up, removing any hint of dissent, any threat, or disrespect.

She was sure that included cleaning up after Killian's activities, as well as his favorites.

Elora pushed the blankets from her legs and stood, barely registering the fact the long shirt she wore did not belong to her. She remembered Damien pulling the shirt over her head when she couldn't raise her arm and recalled refusing pants because it hurt too much to move her legs. She held onto the mattress and then the bedpost as the room shifted slightly. Her stomach was a gnawing mess, the feeling akin to it trying to consume itself as she tried to moisten her mouth. It was so dry, and she was so hungry.

You need blood. Her rational mind knew this and could recognize the truth in it. If she had been drained as much as she thought, then she needed quite a bit of blood to even be able to function properly.

She winced slightly as she walked towards the chairs, hoping to sit for a moment and figure out what she was doing, and where she was going to go. All she knew was she refused to stay in Damien's room, refused to sleep in his bed again. She pulled on the soft pants that were left on the desk and realized that she also couldn't go back to her room. The very thought of being in there again made her nauseous, made the fingers reappear on her skin. But what would Killian do if he found her here? His possessiveness over her was immeasurable, but he obviously had no trouble sharing as long as his permission was granted, as long as he was present.

As she pulled the pants up over her hips and fell back into the chair, the door opened to reveal Damien with a tray that held two cups and a bottle. She jumped up and retreated slightly at the sight of the bottle, the smooth insulated silver the same as the one from last night. The items in his hand were quickly placed on the table and forgotten as he rushed towards her, concern that was strange to see in the light of day lining his face.

"You shouldn't be up yet, Elora." There was a slight edge to his voice, like he was angry she was still there or that she was there at all. Of course he would be. But her name; he had said her name, the sound of it on his lips utter perfection even as she scowled at him.

"I'm fine." He just chuckled softly and shook his head as he poured the blood in the bottle into the two glasses.

"Come sit down and drink this. You lost a lot of blood last night." Which meant he knew what happened. She wondered if she had told him or if he had guessed. Either way, she didn't move. On the one hand, he was right about her not being up, since her legs didn't feel like they could hold her much longer. On the other hand, she didn't trust the drink he was currently offering.

She perched on the edge of the bed, legs dangling as she pulled the sleeves of the shirt down over wrists and hands. Damien nodded and grabbed the glass before slowly moving towards her, like he was afraid she would run. Only once he was in front of her did he extend the glass in an offering.

Elora didn't take it, only stared at it.

"You need to feed, Elora. You need to replenish what you lost." A darkness crept through her at his words, and she narrowed her eyes. She retreated into it as her body shut down, every emotion locked itself behind a wall and she turned into something cold.

"What I lost? What I lost, Damien? Is that what you think happened? That I misplaced it?" Her voice was soft and calm. It was emotionless, and she watched Damien's nostrils flare as his face paled.

"That's not what I meant, and you know it." He let his arm dangle down to his side and held the cup by the rim.

"Do I? Because do you know what I remember? I remember you bringing me blood just like this. Only that blood had been drugged. I was drugged." Her voice rose despite trying to keep it under control, to not let him see how many cracks were there.

Something she couldn't really read flashed in his eyes before he took a drink from the glass and handed it back to her.

"Drink. Then we can talk." She knocked it from his hand, the glass shattering on the floor. She thought she heard him curse, but couldn't concentrate on anything, couldn't focus enough to even see straight or discern anything intelligible.

"Damn it! You need to feed, Elora!"

"That's what you said last night, too! You said I needed to drink it, that it was important, that it was necessary since I was so new to this state. Did you know? Did you know!?" She knew she was yelling now and even as she told herself to stop, her voice rose higher and higher.

"No. I didn't know." She could hear the resignation in his voice, the sound of someone who knew they had lost. She should stop, shut up, and leave him with his guilt.

"Let me guess. Killian ordered you to give it to me and you asked no questions." She sneered at him. Her mouth twisted in disgust as she took in the defeated expression.

"He said you needed to feed, that you needed to drink some since the medication was gone from your system. I remember what it was like when I first turned. The thirst can be overwhelming." His voice was quiet as he watched her, for once allowing every emotion to play across his face—the guilt, the regret, the rage.

She cackled in response and savored the way he flinched at the sound.

"You did this to me. Just as much as they did. I hope you know that." His face contorted in anger as he took a step towards her. Despite every part of her wanting to stand her ground, she backed away. One step and then another until she was trapped between him and the wall. There was nowhere to go. The bed was on one side and the wall to the other. Her options were limited, and she wasn't sure she had the strength to make it across the bed. As if hearing her thoughts, he stood off to the side and gestured towards the door, the message clear.

"I've asked Lukas to watch you today, since his company is more preferable." The door opened and Lukas took a step in, a smile tight on his face as he ran his hand through his loose hair, leaving it resting along his collar. He must have heard everything from where he was and she winced, not sure she wanted yet another person to know what had happened. She didn't respond to Damien, refusing to even glance in his direction as she followed Lukas back to her room.

***

They had been standing silently in front of her door for an hour. Or many ten minutes? She wasn't sure. Lukas simply stood beside her, waiting for her to make the first move. But she couldn't. Her hand wouldn't reach out for the handle, her body wouldn't move towards the door. She shook her head and stared at the marble flooring.

"I don't know if I can."

"If it helps, I cleaned everything. All traces are gone. I promise." She nodded, unsure how to explain that it was simply the room itself, what it represented, what it reminded her of. Unsure how to react to the fact he knew everything, knew what had happened, had seen the aftermath, she shook her head.

And still, Damien had sent her back. Her presence was so terrible to him when she wasn't pliant, wasn't a disaster where he could play the hero.

"Can I see Viktor? Please?" Lukas sighed deeply and shifted on his feet, probably weighing his options.

"If I take you to see him, can we try to go inside after?" She latched onto his arm, his shocked eyes moving instantly to the place where she was touching him.

"Of course. I promise." He inclined his head before patting her hand, his touch hesitant as if he were unsure if he should.

Then, it was only a matter of minutes before she found herself in front of Viktor's cell where he was sitting on the floor, head against the wall with his eyes shut.

"Viktor," her words were a whisper, unsure if he was asleep. His eyes jerked open and found her, widening as he took in her appearance. It's only now she realized she should have fixed herself before she left Damien's room, combed her hair, and dressed more appropriately. At least what she was wearing hid the majority of the wounds.

Viktor moved next to the plexiglass, pressing his hand against it as she put her own against his and gave him a soft smile.

"I'm sorry, Viktor. For getting angry before." He frowned as his brows furrowed in confusion before his eyes moved to Lukas, standing a little way down the hall. Elora was sure he could hear every word that they said, but she could appreciate him giving them the illusion of privacy. It was more than Damien had done.

"Don't. Don't ever apologize for that. I deserved it." She sighed and nodded as she tracked the healing bites on his arms and neck, all in various stages of healing. None of them looked recent from what she saw. He had changed from what he wore the night of the party, now dressed in a black outfit that reminded her of scrubs.

"What happened, Elora?" He gestured to what she imagined was a cut along her face and another along her neck. She hadn't been able to look at herself in the mirror, so she could only guess what he was seeing.

She swallowed and took a breath, begging her body to stop trembling. "I—"

"It happened again? What happened before?" She didn't speak. She didn't need to. Viktor understood without her needing to explain because he knew her and her past. Even if it was because Dr. Montgomery had shared things with him without her knowledge, at this moment she couldn't be angry about it. And she couldn't be angry at him. Dr. Montgomery had been the one to share everything, to draw him into her scheme, to constantly lie to her, to tell her it was all in her head.

She watched as his features, normally so easy and comforting, contorted in fury, a terrifying fire burning in his eyes before he jumped to his feet and began pacing in the space that was too small for him.

"Viktor, please," she pleaded with him, tone desperate and exhausted all at the same time, and his shoulders slumped slightly as he stopped his movement and stared down at her. There was something hard underneath the concern and fear, something she wanted desperately to understand.

"We need you to get out of here, Elora. Do you understand? You can't stay here. He will keep hurting you, letting people hurt you."

"I know. But I don't remember how I got out last time and this time I have a guard at all times." They lowered their voices, hoping that Lukas wouldn't be able to hear them. Would he report back to Damien? To Killian? Elora wanted to trust him, but she didn't know him beyond the fact he was horrible at card games.

"Don't worry about that. We will get you out. Understand? I need you to be strong a little longer." Tears formed in her eyes, and she glanced over to where Lukas was studying the paneling on the walls.

"Okay." Her words were nothing more than a whisper from someone who refused to let themselves hope.

"Promise me?" Viktor pushed closer to the plexiglass, desperation lining each and every contour of his face.

"I promise." She wanted to tell him that it wasn't worth getting her out, that she wasn't worth whatever consequences would come with it. Killian would never let her go again, not now that he had her back. She had been lucky the first time around and she knew that. All she could remember from her escape was a large figure carrying her out of the Tower, and plush rooms in a large house before being left with the foster family.

Frustration flooded her body as she tried to remember, some part of her knowing there was a crucial piece missing, something that would be revealed if she could just remember.

"We need to go." Lukas's tone was apologetic as he neared them, the illusion of privacy over.

"No," she whispered, her eyes on Viktor, who simply held her gaze.

"Look, Killian will kill me and him if we are caught. Let's go." Viktor nodded in agreement before moving away from the plexiglass.

"We will get you out. You are worth more than this." She didn't say anything, not trusting her words or her reaction. She knew Lukas was right, that Killian wouldn't hesitate to kill either one of them, but it felt wrong to leave Viktor here. They may not be feeding directly from him, but there was a single puncture wound in the crooks of both of his arms from where they were draining him.

She stood and followed Lukas to the elevator, where she was reminded that she now had to fulfill her side of the bargain and go back to her room.

CHAPTER 40

Damien

Dr. Montgomery wasn't at the hospital today. After a quick phone call asking to speak with her, the nurse at the reception desk informed him that she had taken a personal day. Damien had planned on cornering her in her office to demand answers about Elora's past. But he supposed that location didn't matter as long as he got what he wanted. And so, with an extra phone call to Lukas, he had the address to her fancy condo in one of the better neighborhoods.

The drive to her had been quick since she was fairly close to the Tower, only twenty minutes. It could have been quicker if the traffic had been better, but there was a demonstration of some sort. A protest about food prices and restrictions. These had become more common in the last few months, probably courtesy of the Resistance. They were fanning these fires, encouraging the unrest among the population caused by governmental control.

Or, more truthfully, by the vampire families and the Accords that left rules and expectations in place to make sure vampires were fed while keeping the human population safe. The Resistance argued that the vampires broke the Accords first, since they started feeding directly from humans, both those who were willing and unwilling. While they were correct, their reaction felt over the top, extreme in its violence. Piles of vampire bodies had been set on fire in public spaces, parks, or city squares. A few weeks before Elora had been removed from the hospital, there had been a pyre of vampires outside the Tower, resulting in Killian flying into a murderous rage, screaming and demanding the heads of the humans who were to blame. They had been easy to find, eager to claim their handiwork. And they proudly defended it until they were drained dry, bodies disposed of in the incinerator without ceremony.

He circled the condo building three times, looking for an alternative way inside other than the front door where a man sat in the lobby to greet visitors. The condo number on the address indicated the third floor, and he searched the building carefully before spotting his way in. A fire escape was near one of the windows to an apartment he was sure was hers. After letting out a deep sigh, he got out of the car and ran through his plan once more. He recited the practiced questions that he needed answers to over and over in his head, knowing that he may not deserve them, but that they were necessary.

A large part of him was drowning in guilt. Damien knew the role he had played in everything, knew he gave Elora the laced blood, put her in a position to be beaten and used. Shame and self-hatred were overwhelming as he entered the alleyway, marveling for a moment over how ridiculously clean it was. The pavement was swept, trash contained, and not in bags tossed against the walls. It took only a moment to climb up to the third floor, and he shook his head in disappointment as he eyed the large open window and quietly ducked inside.

His gaze wandered over the large open space. There was no division between the kitchen, living room, and dining area. And the room itself was pristine. The marble counter gleamed and the metal appliances were spotless. Not a single fingerprint to be found. Either the doctor was a bit of a neat freak, or she employed a cleaner. The decor was the opposite of her office. Minimal and bright. The tall windows had no curtains or coverings, letting the light in. Every piece of furniture was made of either a light brown wood or pale fabric. It reminded him of the model homes he had snuck into as a kid to sleep.

For a moment, he was worried he had the wrong place. Then he caught her scent — a mixture of rosemary and something more floral — coming from the room to the right. As he moved closer, footsteps silent on the white carpet, he could hear her voice as she spoke with someone on the phone.

"You don't understand. She is in danger. I have it on good authority she is being abused." She paused, listening to whoever was speaking. "Yes, like before." Another pause.

"No, my journals were taken from my office."

Damien stepped through the doorway and leaned against the wall, waiting for her to notice his presence. It took only a moment, and her eyes widened slightly in fear. A smile stretched across his face as he gave her a little wave. It always brought him a touch of amusement when their fear coated the room, permeating every inch of space. And this human deserved it after everything she had done, all the lies she had told. After convincing Elora that she was insane and then drugging her.

"We will figure it out. I know that." Her voice had gone sharp, irritated either by his presence or by the other person on the phone. More than likely, a mixture of the two. She muttered an "okay" and then hung up, turning her attention to Damien.

"Have a seat. I am assuming you are here to make some type of demand?" He raised a brow at her response before he did as she suggested. He reclined back in the chair, resting his ankle on his knee as he studied her. It was odd to see her outside of her professional attire. Her hair was loosely pulled back into a knot at the base of her neck, and she wasn't wearing her normal make-up. It almost made her look younger than she normally did.

"What does your master want?" Damien hid his surprise that she knew about Killian. He knew that she had an idea that someone had hurt Elora in her past, but never guessed the doctor would know that. This could make things either easier or more difficult.

"I'm not here on his orders, Dr. Montgomery. I have some questions for you about your previous patient."

"Call me Denise. I assume that telling you I can't discuss her with you would mean nothing?" He smiled and inclined his head as she sighed and sat back. She seemed to have been expecting him, had prepared for this conversation or some version of it.

"I suppose I owe Elora an apology. I told her that you weren't a problem. She wanted to get rid of you, you know. Asked Viktor to look into you. Said there was something not right." Well, that answered that question. Even if Elora had known what he was, she hadn't known who he had been working for.

"I kept that girl safe for years, kept her out of that monster's hands."

Damien chuckled. "A vampire is hardly a monster. Simply another version of creation." A better one, as Killian would argue.

"I didn't say vampire. I said monster. Killian is a monster." Her words were cutting, hitting deeper than he thought they would. She knew something, something that he either didn't or that he refused to acknowledge.

"Why?" Damien had really hoped that Killian's name wouldn't come up, that he hadn't been involved. But that hope was rapidly dying as he sat across from this woman who had taken care of Elora, even if it meant gaslighting her along with the suppression of her true nature.

"Elora never talked about it directly. She honestly couldn't. You are aware of her memory loss? I know you read her file and took my journals, so you know quite a bit. Under hypnosis, she was able to remember some things. But she grew violent during those therapy treatments, and we abandoned them after a few sessions." Her hand reached for a small scar on her temple and rubbed it almost absentmindedly.

"Did you record those in your journals? I don't remember seeing it."

She nodded. "Yes. During those sessions, she discussed horrific abuse. She was restrained, chained to a bed, and used. The earliest memory she recalled during our limited sessions before we stopped was twelve years old, but I had a feeling it went further back, started earlier than that." Denise shuddered and took a deep breath before continuing.

"It was Killian. She described him in each memory, even said his name a few times, though she never remembered when she came to after. Sometimes he watched, and sometimes he was an active participant. They fed from her mostly, but there were other things involved. Things I will not name, but you are creative. I'm sure you can figure it out." Her voice was hard, her eyes murderous.

"And I had her safe. It was not the best situation, but I was working towards getting her out of the city. And you took her back." Damien went completely still at her words as the shame and guilt rose again. She was right. He had taken her back. But he hadn't known, had only seen a father who wanted his daughter back. Had only seen a spoiled child who had been given everything and then thrown it away in a fit of pointless rebellion.

He had been a fool and now her pain and blood were on his hands.

Damien shifted slightly before speaking, wanting to throw blame at her feet, at her denial of every memory Elora had. "Maybe if I had known earlier, things would have been different. Maybe if her files had been complete, I would have known, and we could have worked together." She scoffed, waving a hand dismissively before giving him a look that screamed that she thought he was a child and an unintelligent one at that.

"Normally, I wouldn't even address something so asinine. But her current situation is partially your fault, so I will. Her files were not complete for one reason: keeping her hidden. Two interested parties were searching for her. Killian, as head of the vampire family, has access to unlimited technology and money. It would have been easy to find her, especially once he bought off most of the hospital board members. So, no. Her files were kept incomplete because that information couldn't be out there for anyone to find." She stared at him. Her eyes pierced him in a way that made him want to shift in his seat and hide behind something. It was as if she was seeing everything he had ever kept hidden. She leaned forward slightly before speaking.

"And would it have mattered in the end? Would you have gone against your master's orders to bring his daughter back?" Damien wanted to say yes. He would have given up his very soul to be able to say yes, but he couldn't. He wasn't sure it would be the truth and knew she would see that instantly. She gave him a sad smile before leaning back.

"I thought so." A satisfied smile curled around her lips. "How did you find her, anyway? Was it a nurse who tipped you off?"

"Ryan. The nurse who attacked her. He had tasted her blood and contacted me. The rest, you know." He saw her face fall for just a moment, and he savored the guilt on her face as it matched his own.

"You said two interested parties. Who's the other?" Denise shook her head and didn't respond before asking her own question.

"Has he hurt her yet?" He didn't answer, couldn't answer, but that seemed to be enough for her. She slammed her hand on the desk and stood, marching over to the window as she became lost in her thoughts. Damien fell into his own as they both waited for the other to speak. Lukas had mentioned the sheets, something other than blood. A wave of nausea hit him with such force he almost vomited on her expensive rug.

"If Killian didn't send you, why are you here? You took her back to him." She didn't say it, not again, but the insinuation was clear. He had taken her back and had followed orders without question. And now he was here without his knowledge.

He considered her question for a moment, knew that the answer was that he had wanted proof that it wasn't Killian, that he could reasonably get permission to go after Jonas and Darian.

"I don't know. She was hurt last night after a party thrown in her honor." He laughed bitterly at the idea of it being for her. It was a celebration, that part was true. But it was a celebration that the medication was gone from her system, that she was worth feeding from again. Suddenly, Killian's dark circles and pale complexion made sense. He hadn't been feeding because he had been waiting patiently for her blood to be ready.

"She came to my room. She said she didn't know where else to go. She was — she was covered in cuts and bites. They drained her. Sedated her first but drained her." He didn't say that he was the one to drug her. The words wouldn't form on his tongue. Even if he hadn't known, it was still agony to consider it, to give voice to what he had done.

"And they will do it again. And again." Damien flinched at the truth in her words. He knew that, knew that there was something about her, something about her blood that Killian craved. Something that Killian had created.

"Why? She is his daughter." His words were quiet and for a moment she didn't answer, as if she was weighing each part of her response. Either she didn't know, or she wasn't sure she should tell him. He couldn't blame her if it was the latter. He wouldn't trust him either.

"Killian doesn't see her as a daughter. Maybe he did at first. Who knows? From what I understand, he seemed to want a child with Iris, Elora's mother. But something changed over the years, as Elora matured. Something about her blood. He got a taste of it and realized how different she was and what those differences meant. At least he thinks he does."

"What differences?" Damien sat up straighter, hoping beyond anything that he would finally get some answers to the question at the center of all of this.

Denise turned away from the window and stared at him with that searching look he had seen so many times when she interacted with Elora. Now he understood how uncomfortable it had made her, why she had squirmed and shifted and fidgeted. It was like being put on display, forced onto a pedestal while she took each piece and studied it one by one.

"I don't think he ever really wanted a child despite what the rumors say. He was just appeasing Iris and took advantage of the situation. It's why he designed her the way he did. Enhanced her. Elora's blood is more potent, making her a valuable commodity for Killian. If he can create more of her, then he can corner the market with a new blood source and even eventually replace humans. But it is more than that. She is more than that."

He laughed bitterly. "Of course she is."

Denise raised a brow before continuing. "Elora's blood could be harnessed for multiple reasons. For feeding, as Killian wants. But it could do so much more. It's what I was researching when you took her from me."

"So, you were researching what? A cure? A weapon?" Her eyes narrowed, recognizing that he was the very thing a cure or weapon would be used against.

"I don't think we need to discuss that. My research is my own." She returned to her chair, easing into it as if they were discussing the weather or something equally mundane.

"What do you know about the Accords?" Damien was startled by the question and the fact this was not exactly where he saw this conversation going. He considered the brief education he got once he was turned, something that had felt very similar to on-the-job training.

"They were started after a deadly fight between humans and vampires. Vampires were overpopulating, and the humans were dwindling quickly, which meant we were running out of food sources. The vampire heads meet with some humans, local government or something like that, and set up what became known as the Accords." She nodded along as if he was a student reciting their lesson.

"Which are? What exactly do they cover?" He rolled his eyes at her leading questions, annoyed slightly at the entire conversation.

"That vampires will not feed directly from humans. Vampires will only use blood banks and will remain secret in return for the human population being controlled in order to create a consistent food source. Basically, we can't feed directly from humans, either willing or not." He gave her a dark grin.

"But we both know it doesn't work that way. A lot of humans willingly take jobs as blood sources, allowing vampires to feed from them for money." She gave him a deadpan look, one that silently asked if he really was that stupid.

"Willingly? Like how willingly you were turned? Like how your mother was a source?" No matter how much practice he had in keeping his face blank, in keeping his emotions under control, he had not been prepared for her words. Even as he tried to figure out how she could have possibly known, she grinned. She knew exactly what type of point she made, and what type of hit she managed to land.

"The point here, Damien, is that she is a commodity to Killian. She is the means to a new breed of vampire that doubles as food, not held by the same standards listed by the Accords. Imagine —

an Elora in every vampire household; collection banks that house only those turned by her and those like her. Humans rendered obsolete, removed from the equation. And Killian exclusively benefits from all of it, the power and money unlimited. The other vampire families will have to bow to his whim if they wish to be able to feed at all. And he will keep the original, feed from her, and share her as he sees fit."

His hands curled into fists at the thought of even a single repeat of last night, let alone an entire lifetime, until eventually she was drained completely. Killian would eventually grow tired of her. Damien had seen the frustration each time she fought against Killian, even in the smallest amounts. It would only be a matter of time. And then there was the eradication of the humans, a slow process that would leave Killian in charge of everything. Did he care about humans and their fate? Damien wasn't sure he did. What he cared about was her, protecting her and keeping her away from Killian.

Fuck. When had his loyalties switched? When had he come to care about her enough to defy the one who made him? He wanted to say it was last night as he took care of her, washed her hair, and slept beside her so she would feel safe. Or was it when he saw her in that dress? Maybe it was the moment she stabbed him with a fork — wholly defiant and fierce, despite believing he could kill her.

Damien stood, not sure what else to say. He knew that he had more questions, but the only thought in his head was getting back to the Tower and planning. He would drag Lukas along with him, since he knew without a doubt his friend would want to help.

"You can't save her." It was as if Denise read his mind, a horrifically unsettling feeling. "Not as long as she stays there. As long as she is under Killian's control, there is no hope for her."

Damien sat back down, registering her words even as a deep sense of foreboding took over. She was right. He could fight Killian, try to protect her, and make sure no one touched her again. He could kill Jonas slowly, let him bleed out before letting him heal, only to start over again. But it would be pointless. Killian would kill him, remove Damien as an obstacle without any issue, and continue with his plans.

"Then what do we do?" Denise smiled and rested her chin on her interlaced fingers. Damien had a feeling he had said exactly what she expected, and that she had seen more than he had wanted her to.

~ ~

CHAPTER 41

Damien

The apartment building in front of Damien and Lukas was old and run-down. The brick was chipped and the railing along the stairs leading to the front entrance was rusted and barely hanging on. There were multiple broken windows with pieces of cardboard covering up the holes. Only the top floors of the tall building looked relatively new as the windows were intact due to their height. The two vampires weren't sure what they were looking for and knew only that Killian said there were credible rumors that this was another Resistance lair that he needed them to gather intel on before shutting it down.

Damien had taken the job without question, even as he fought the urge to tell Killian to pick someone else. He hadn't wanted to leave Elora alone without someone he trusted with her. Initially, he had suggested Lukas stay behind, but Killian had insisted that he take him in case backup was needed. A part of Damien wanted to believe Killian's explanation, but he knew it was so she would be alone, and it killed him to know that. His stomach churned at the thought of her there now with no one to intercede should Killian bring back his favorites.

You took her back. Denise Montgomery's voice echoed in his head and ensured that his guilt didn't leave but rooted itself in every part of his body. Not only had he taken her back, but he also had hand-delivered her the night of the party.

"Is she doing okay?" His question broke the silence as he and Lukas watched the building from their hiding place in the opposite building across the street—a warehouse that currently housed hundreds of boxes and crates.

"You would know if you had gone to see her instead of ordering me to watch her," Lukas snapped sharply before settling onto one of the crates with his eyes trained on the front door across the street.

Damien's head twisted to Lukas, who kept his eyes on the target. At least Lukas seemed able to focus. He hadn't been to see her since the morning after the party, almost three days ago. Damien wanted to say that he was giving her space and trying to let her heal as much as she could after everything. But the truth was that he was a coward. The truth was that he didn't want to face her anger after she figured out that he had given her the drugged blood. He hadn't known it was tainted, but the blame still lied with him.

"It's better if I don't. Trust me." This time, it was Lukas who lost focus as his eyes revealed something Damien couldn't quite read.

"Bullshit, Damien. She needs—" Damien cut him off. He didn't want to hear what Lukas had to say about what he thought she needed and repeated the question.

"How is she?" Damien watched his jaw move as Lukas's eyes moved slowly between him and the apartment building across the street. Lukas shook his head and looked back to the apartment building, keeping track as an elderly woman—human, from what he could tell—entered with a bag of groceries in her arms.

"What do you think? She doesn't talk. She won't play cards no matter what I offer her. She either sits in a chair reading or takes a bath. Her skin is always red when she comes out, like the water is boiling, and she scrubbed herself raw. It's—it's bad." Lukas ran his fingers through his hair and blew out a breath before continuing.

"She asks about you sometimes. It's the only time she does talk. Asks where you are, why I am in charge of her now." Lukas let the words hang between them. Damien's heart stopped for a moment as he imagined her haunted expression and the ashes in her eyes where there used to be such an inferno. It had been so fierce it could have burned the world into nothing if she wanted.

"Has anyone been to see her?" It was his worst fear. It was the first thought in his head when he woke and the only one present as he lay in bed.

"Not that I know of. I am dismissed shortly after she feeds at night and don't come back until morning." Damien grunted.

"Why haven't you been there? Killian's orders?" Lukas and Damien both tracked a young kid who appeared from an alley near the building and watched as he greeted his friend.

"Has she mentioned anything about what happened?" Damien wanted her to talk to someone, and Lukas was the best option. He could control his anger better and could make her laugh or smile at the very least.

"No. Like I said, she hasn't said a word since I took her to see Viktor." He said this so nonchalantly that for a second Damien thought maybe he didn't hear his friend correctly.

"You did what?" He hadn't told Damien about this, and the frustration was clear in his voice. Lukas shifted slightly before gesturing to a window towards the top of the building where someone had opened the curtains to reveal a man in khakis and a t-shirt. His hair was cut short, almost to the scalp, and there was a knife strapped to his belt. Damien watched as he walked through the apartment and disappeared wherever there were no windows.

"She wouldn't go back inside her room. She was terrified, and just stood in front of it for twenty minutes before begging me to take her to him."

"How did that go?" Damien had a basic idea based on what he knew of their relationship.

Lukas shrugged. "He made a show of vowing to get her out there. I don't think he knew I could hear them."

Damien huffed a laugh. That was exactly how he thought it would go. Maybe Viktor would be useful. Dr. Montgomery had helped put together a plan to get her out—a basic plan, more of an outline than anything else. She had her role in it, and he had his. Viktor could be a valuable part.

Damien took a deep breath as he watched as a group of humans wandered up to the door and entered the building. A few minutes later, he spotted them in the same room as the man in khakis. It looked like Killian's intel was correct. There was definitely something going on here, but whether it was worth the time and effort was a different conversation. It could just be a group of knife enthusiasts getting together to look over their collection.

"There was something strange about the whole conversation, though. I don't trust him. There is something off." Damien nodded at Lukas's words and gestured for him to continue as they watched the apartment windows.

"He kept saying that 'we' will get her out. Not 'he' will get her out. That she was worth more than what Killian wanted her for."

"She is worth more than that." Lukas sighed and ran his hand down his face at Damien's response.

"Not the point, and you know that I agree. Never mind. I'm just paranoid when it comes to her now, I guess." They both lapsed into silence.

"Are you going to see her once we get back?" Damien shook his head and debated whether to try to get into the building.

He couldn't think about her right now or about what seeing her would mean.

"Are you just leaving her, then? Fuck, Damien, I know you don't like her, but no one deserves what she has been through. She doesn't deserve for you to toss her aside when she has no one." Damien's hand grabbed his friend's shirt collar before he realized what he was doing and pulled Lukas close, as his eyes widened in surprise.

"No. I'm getting her out. We are getting her out." Damien let him go and turned back to the apartment building and the now-closed curtains.

"Shit," Damien muttered before searching the street below to see if anyone managed to leave while he was preoccupied.

He could feel Lukas watching him and the way his eyes drilled into the side of his face as Damien actively refused to return his gaze. That reaction was over the top, and they both knew it. He had never let on to Lukas that he didn't hate her or that his feelings had become somewhat complicated when it came to her. And he was sure refusing to see her after that night didn't help the perspective. But Lukas had to understand that they couldn't risk Killian growing suspicious, had to understand that the vampire was too possessive and too observant when it came to Elora. And if they wanted to get her out from under Killian's control, they needed to be careful.

"Is there a plan, or are we just going for it?" Damien gave him a dirty look as he finally tore his eyes from the group that had gathered at the entrance to the apartment building. and stood as they prepared to leave.

"There is a sketch of a plan. Just the highlights." Damien jerked his head towards the door as they left.

"Perfect. My kind of plan." Lukas grinned back. It was the first one since Damien had left Elora with him that morning and didn't come back.

"Let's check that apartment. I think Killian's intel was right." Lukas nodded, and they left their hiding spot before entering the apartment building and traveling up to the fifth floor. There were four apartments per floor and based on the window placement, it was easy to figure out which one they needed.

The inside of the building was just as dated as the outside. The wallpaper was yellow and peeling away, exposing what was underneath. There were stains and discoloration where paintings used to hang in the hallways and the carpet was torn apart to reveal the flooring. The overwhelming smell of mold and smoke lingered in the air and the only sound was a crying baby somewhere in the bowels of the building.

Checking the hallway, Damien knelt in front of the door and started to pick the lock, which finally clicked after a few moments, and he pushed it open.

"I need you to teach me how to do that." Lukas's voice was low as they entered and each of them took a side as they searched for anyone who may have stayed behind.

The apartment itself looked ancient, like it hadn't been updated in decades. The counters were covered in something that looked sticky, and the cabinet doors in the kitchen were hanging where the hinges were broken. The carpet seemed to radiate an odor that implied it hadn't been cleaned and tiny creatures may live in it. The little furniture present was destroyed, either the fabric was ripped, or the leg of the coffee table was cracked. It reminded Damien of the houses they lived in growing up when he was just happy to have somewhere to sleep.

"I tried, remember. It was a disaster." Damien started down the one hallway, noting the discolored spots on the wall where pictures hung once, while Lukas checked the kitchen and living room. There were only two bedrooms and a bathroom. Damien checked the bathroom, only to see that it was missing the sink before checking one of the bedrooms, which was empty.

"No one out here. And that's not fair. You are a horrible teacher." Damien chuckled lightly at the comment before opening the last door. A bedroom, or that's probably what it was intended for. Once pastel pink was now discolored into something more orange than anything else. The carpet, thick beneath his boots, was a tan color, though it may have been white once. It was an old room, either unused or ignored for it to get this bad. He opened the closet, checking for anyone hiding in the jackets hanging there.

"Lukas." Damien listened to Lukas's footsteps in the hallway as he stared at the only thing in the room besides a large table covered in papers. A symbol was painted on the wall — a black rose with a stake through the middle. Not very subtle or original as far as Resistance symbols are concerned. Honestly, it was a little on the nose.

"Well, that's new." Damien nodded at Lukas's comment and took a picture of it with his phone before moving to the table to look through the papers. Most of it was basic information that they had found in the hideouts before – the names of the vampire families and the important people within each one along with their locations. He noted that the Corvin location was still unknown, even to this group. Piece by piece, Damien took a picture of everything. He didn't want to give Killian any reason to think he missed something important.

Damien moved the papers around until he spotted an unnamed file. Everything else on the desk was loose, as if didn't matter, so why was this information in its own file? He opened it, and his heart skipped a beat as he stared down at a photo of Elora from the night of the party. She was looking over her shoulder as if someone was calling her name. Behind her, Damien could make out the roses and lights of the ballroom, along with the shadows in her eyes, the hesitation and fear she was desperately trying to mask as they walked in side by side. Someone had infiltrated the

Tower, and Killian was going to be pissed, cutting down anyone and everyone until he found the culprit. Or until Damien did.

Damien moved the picture to see the rest of the file only to find more. Dozens of them went back years. Some were from the hospital, while others were from her time with her foster family. Photos of Elora and Elizabeth in a coffee shop, bright smiles on both faces as they clutched the cups in their hands. Elora's cheeks were red from the cold, but her face looked alive in a way that Damien had never seen. Another photo of the two of them in front of school, both dressed in jeans and a T-shirt. Elora's crimson hair was in a braid that lay across her shoulder, hiding the worst of the scars.

It was odd seeing a younger version of her even though the scars still peeked out from under the neckline of her shirt. Others were of her at a park while another was in front of a diner with two people who Damien assumed were her foster parents. Along with the pictures were lists of locations and years—where she lived, where she went to school, and even where she got coffee and went grocery shopping. There was information for the hospital—passwords and notes that made no sense. Coded messages from someone inside the ward and suddenly Denise's words rushed back.

More than one interested party.

Elora's blood could be harnessed for multiple purposes.

My research is my own.

Is that what was happening here? Were they planning on taking her to harvest her blood, or did they simply want to use her as collateral in their fight against vampires? If that was the case, why Killian's daughter? He wasn't the only vampire head with people close to him, people who could be used for leverage. And the human Matthew had said they were missing a key piece to their weapon. Was she it?

Damien closed the file and tucked it under his arm before he made his way back to the door and signaled to Lukas that it was time to leave. The doctor was right, and all this did cement the fact he needed to get her somewhere safe, somewhere she couldn't be used.

~ ~

CHAPTER 42

Elora

The vampire who came in the door after Lukas left for the night was dressed head to toe in white. Her black hair was cut into a pixie style and her brown eyes were empty as she casually made her way to the bed where Elora lay. Lukas had given her a nod and wished her a good night before locking the door behind him. He had glanced back only once with concern on his face. She knew she should at least smile at him to try to ease his worry, but she couldn't make herself do it.

"Who are—" She held a single finger to her lips as she set her bag on the foot of the bed and handed Elora a piece of paper with two sentences on it. The penmanship was harsh, but simple, like they were gripping the pen too tightly as they wrote.

Let her do what she needs to without a fight. Remember who will pay the price if you don't.
-K

Elora had simply nodded and handed the note back to her waiting hand. She gestured for Elora to sit up as she started pulling various items from her bag and setting them on the nightstand. A box of latex gloves, a syringe, alcohol pads, and a large collection bottle similar to the one that came once a day for her to share with Lukas. It seemed that he was the one in charge of her now, since Damien couldn't be bothered to see her.

She moved to the side of the bed and sat along the edge before rolling up Elora's sleeve to her biceps, exposing the crook of her arm. Elora sighed and let her head fall back, ignoring the confused look on the vampire's face. She could have explained that this was just a blood collection and that it could have been worse. But no words, no fighting. Just silent obedience.

Elora barely registered the slight pain as the needle entered her arm. But she watched her blood drain into the bottle, quickly filling before the vampire took another from her bag and allowed that one to fill as well. It was a strange and almost unreal feeling to watch it exit her body without the use of teeth or the burning sensation that always came with it before the sedation took over completely. After a few moments, the vampire pulled the needle from her arm and covered the hole with a band-aid, a completely unnecessary move since it would be healed in a matter of minutes. Elora tracked her movements as she put the bottles into the bag and headed towards the door, careful not to make a single noise as she shut it.

And for the past week, it became a ritual. It was something she could expect to happen every night once Lukas had retreated back to his rooms. Each night, the same vampire came and collected her blood. The first night it was two bottles, the next it was three, and then two. There wasn't necessarily a pattern to how much was taken. Only that one night would be a larger amount, followed by smaller amounts, before being given the night off.

Maybe the point was to make sure she didn't become too weak or drained. She rationalized that Killian wouldn't want his favorite food source to grow too sickly to provide for him. And that was what she was. A food source. A blood bag. Not a daughter, not someone precious to be protected or taken care of. Viktor wanted her to be strong, to hold on, but she wasn't sure she could. What she knew was that she couldn't take another night of being chained to her bed, drained and touched.

The day she had been left alone while Lukas and Damien were sent on a mission was the last time Killian had personally visited her. She remembered the majority of what happened, even if parts of it were now blurry, even if she didn't want to. No sedative this time. Killian had declared he wanted her submission, had wanted her willingness and silence. But she had fought violently with nails and fists and screams that amounted to nothing. Each time her fist hit his face, she felt a surge of pride that she had finally fought back against him. Yet, it didn't matter in the end. She found herself overpowered and chained in the same spot, only this time he cleaned up himself afterward, satiated and content from his private feeding.

With soft words meant to be comforting, Killian had led her to the shower and removed the nightgown. Something in her told her she should refuse him, recoil from his touch, and lock herself in the closet until he left. But she was so exhausted, had nothing left to give. Killian had washed her hair like she was a child, whispering promises for the future and apologies for the pain. When he had left, eyes heavy and bright from her blood, she had vomited until there was nothing left in her and then vomited more.

It didn't matter anymore. Nothing did.

"Good morning, El!" Lukas's voice rang out as he entered with a tray balanced in his hand. His hair was braided back away from his face and a mischievous grin lined his lips as he turned so, she couldn't see what was actually on the tray. She sat up from her spot on the bed and pulled down her sleeves to cover the bruises in the crooks of her arms, leftover souvenirs from her nightly visits. Killian hadn't come back for a private feeding, and Elora wondered if the collection bottles were meant to stop that. Maybe somewhere in him, Killian knew what he had been doing was wrong.

She walked over to the desk and stared at the tray there: the two wine glasses, the collection bottle, and the last item—a takeout cup from a coffee shop. Elora glanced up at him with confusion lining her face.

"Take a drink." She narrowed her eyes and considered the last time she blindly drank something a vampire had handed her. But it was Lukas, and it wasn't blood this time. Slowly, she grabbed the paper cup and let herself enjoy the heat radiating through the protective sleeve around it. She inhaled slowly and savored the scent of vanilla and coffee as a smile stretched across her face. It was the first one since the night of the party.

It was a vanilla latte. Her favorite type, just like she had told him. She took a small taste and held it on her tongue as her eyes closed in pure bliss. It was exactly how she remembered. Better than that. She swallowed and opened her mouth, searching for the words she wanted to say. She wanted to thank him, not just for this, but for everything else. But words failed her by staying lodged in her mind and refusing to cooperate.

Without a thought, she set the cup down and leaped forward. Her arms wrapped around his massive chest, and she buried her face in his shirt, inhaling his scent. He went completely still for a moment as his hands hesitated and hovered above her before he wrapped them around her and rested his chin on the top of her head. He held her even as she trembled and shook, even as she closed her eyes and let a few tears slide down her cheeks.

Finally, she drew away and instantly missed the warmth of him and the security in his embrace. She groaned slightly as she sat at the table and clutched the latte to her chest. He smiled at her before sitting and leaning back.

"Wait a minute. Drink this before the coffee."

"Are you bribing me to feed?" She raised a brow and smirked at him as he chuckled in response.

"You could call it that." She rolled her eyes dramatically and nodded as he started pouring out the blood into the two glasses. Despite their embrace only a moment ago, Elora still watched him as he drank first and waited a couple of minutes, as if it would tell her if it were drugged. Finally, she drank it in two swallows in her desperation to get it over with. Blood only brought on memories. There was no more euphoria like there had been at the banquet or rush of completeness and perfection like that night. Now, it only brought back the feeling of something crawling under her skin and her hand went to her neck, where she traced the newest scars that were still pink.

"How are you, El?" His words were cautious, as if he was afraid that he would break some kind of spell that was holding them in this moment. She shrugged and sat back, holding the coffee in her hand. What was she supposed to say? That she was broken? That any semblance of who she was had been eradicated in a single night? Any lingering remnants ripped from her the day Killian came to feed and then drained her each time the vampire in white came to visit?

"I'm fine." Her words were a whisper, and she saw the way his mouth twisted, the way his body tensed slightly, as if the lie lingering between them had struck him like a slap to the face.

"We both know that's not true." He was quiet for a moment before he shifted in his seat so he could lean towards her. "I'm worried, El." She nodded, once again speechless in the shadow of his concern and his desire to help her. But what if he reported back to Damien what she said? Or to Killian?

"It'll be fine, Lukas. I promise. I've survived this all before." She gave him a sad smile. It was the kind that was meant to tell him that the conversation was over and nothing else would be said.

"You know, when I was younger, I had a sister. She was about a year younger than me. Lily was her name. She was the opposite of me in some ways. I was an athlete and made friends with everyone and anyone. She was quiet, but popular with the art and theater kids, even though she also did sports. Honestly, she was a part of everything to the point I always wondered how she managed it. Typical sibling dynamics, almost cliché, in a way." Elora pulled her legs under her in the chair and took a drink of her coffee. Lukas smiled at the thought. His eyes were distant as he spoke.

"She was fierce and fiery when she wanted to be. Fought with the school for money for their production one year to have better sets on stage. I remember wanting to be like her, wanting to stay by her side, so maybe some of her boldness would rub off on me. I played sports and did well in school, but she was beyond that." She noted the use of past tense and frowned behind her coffee cup.

"We found her in the lake near our cabin in the mountains. Her letter to the family only said she was depressed and that she couldn't do it anymore. And that she was sorry." He stopped for a moment as his face scrunched with concentration and emotion. He rubbed his hand along his jaw before starting again.

"The letter to me said she was tired, that she was exhausted down to the very bones of her body, down to the very fiber of her being. She was so tired of fighting her mind every day, begging it to cooperate and not scream at her to jump in front of a truck. She was tired of convincing herself to stay alive. She said it was a constant battle against her own mind to keep herself alive and she was done fighting it." He met Elora's eyes as his own shone with tears and shared memories.

"I know you're tired, Elora. You don't have to fight it alone." He reached out and pulled her hand into his. He squeezed it tightly before letting it drop back into her lap. She expected him to give her another grin or make a joke like he always did. But he only stood and grabbed the tray before locking the door behind him as he left.

~ ~

CHAPTER 43

Damien

Denise set the small bottle on the counter and leaned back. Her face was the very image of distrust and trepidation as she eyed it for a moment longer and focused on the powder as if counting each tiny grain that made up the whole. Her eyes shifted to Lukas and Damien standing on the other side of her kitchen table. Her gaze was dark and assessing in the bright lights that hung above them. Like the last time Damien was here, the kitchen itself was so spotless it looked like no one actually lived there or had ever set foot inside.

Damien reached out towards the bottle and wrapped his fingers around the key to everything. The plan depended on two things—this tiny bottle and Elora's rage. The powder was easy enough with Denise's assistance. It was a special concoction developed by the Resistance and was basically a stronger version of what was given to Elora while at the hospital. To be extra careful, it was also laced with a powerful sedative. It was Elora who was the potential snag in the plan, since her fierceness had diminished and was almost gone entirely since that night. It was like looking at a hollow shell where her very essence had been ripped out through a jagged wound.

It broke him to see it, and he knew that Lukas felt the same. The guilt ate them both alive as it feasted on each thought and regret that plagued them hour by hour, minute by minute. Her accusation rang in his ear whenever he had a silent moment. All he saw was the image of her collapsed on his floor with all the blood and torn skin. She had been drained and left to pull herself back together. He had been terrified by the rage that coursed through his veins, the almost overwhelming desire to hunt down those who had hurt her and do worse. Even now, the fantasy was always with him, silently planning how he would bleed them dry over and over, remove the skin from the hands that touched her, and yank out the teeth that fed from her. By the end, there would be nothing, but bones left behind.

But she had needed him at that moment. She had come to him and there was a sense of satisfaction in that. She hadn't gone to Lukas, no matter how close they had become.

"I have a question." Lukas's rough voice tore through the silence.

"The plan is clear." Denise's response was curt, as if Lukas was a subordinate that the hospital. It was a tone meant to shut him up.

"I know the plan. My question is why you are helping with all this? You were testing this drug on her for the Resistance." Lukas's gaze was all paranoia and distrust as he searched for lies in each line of her face.

"My reasons are my own." The words echoed something she had said to Damien about how her research was her own. But he couldn't deny the validity of Lukas's concern.

"You worked with the Resistance, though. I saw their file on her. It was full of pictures of her from childhood, dates, and addresses of each place she had lived. She is more than your test subject." Denise sighed at Damien's accusation and leaned forward to rest her forearms on the marble counter.

"Yes, I worked with them. Past tense is an important distinction here." She gave Lukas a pointed look. "To answer your question, I have mistakes to make up for and whether you believe me or not, I care about what happens to her. It's part of why I fell out of favor with those in power."

"Mistakes?" Damien could guess exactly what she was referring to, but he wanted to hear her say it. He wanted to hear her admit to the torture she had put Elora through with each moment of gaslighting, of convincing her she was insane.

"I spent my time with her convincing her she was mentally ill, that her memories were manifestations of her guilt. I used the darkest part of her against her in an effort to keep her safe. But that failed thanks to you two." Damien flinched and from his peripheral, he saw Lukas do the same. Of course, she would end her confession with a reminder of their own role.

"Safe from Killian?" Damien could hear his friend putting pieces together and trying to understand the rationale. She nodded.

"Among others." Lukas placed his palms flat on the table and leaned towards her. His jaw tightened and fingers bent into claws as if they could pierce through the counter.

"Such as?" His voice was low and deadly as he demanded answers. She raised her brow but didn't move.

"Are all vampires this stupid or just ones who were athletes before turning?" Lukas jerked back and Damien shook his head. This was not helping, even if he had his own questions. For right now, they just needed to get her out. There would be time for answers later. And if she tried to betray them, she could easily be dealt with.

"That sounds like someone who doesn't want to answer."

"The Resistance wants her, obviously."

"Her blood?" Damien interjected, before Lukas could respond. He finally understood what the human he had interrogated meant by the missing element. "They need it to finalize the weapon." For once, Denise looked surprised and leaned back.

"At least one of you is well informed. I'm assuming you used creative tactics to gather information from someone in the group." Damien didn't confirm or deny, but it was an answer for her either way.

"If you try to turn her over to them, I will kill you." Lukas's promise lingered in the room and the two glared at each other.

"Yes, yes. I'm sure you will. But I have no intention of turning her over. My time with them is long since passed, I assure you."

"And why is that?" Damien's curiosity got the better of him as he asked his question. She shrugged before her features softened and she glanced away to seemingly stare at the vase on the counter.

"Our goals were no longer aligned. I wanted her safe. They wanted her to be utilized, no matter the cost."

"And the cost?"

"Her life. They need her blood, but even then, it would be a series of tests and experiments as they fine-tuned and finalized the weapon. She would survive at first. They would take blood and let her heal up before repeating the process. Eventually, they would end up pushing too far, draining too much." She sighed and ran a hand along her neck. "I couldn't doom her to that and did everything I could to keep her protected under my watch."

Again, the unspoken ending to her explanation was his own role in ending that. But what would have that life looked like? Forever taking the medication, attending group therapy for issues she didn't actually have, individual sessions where Denise would play-act as a psychiatrist and convince Elora that her memories weren't real? It was a different kind of hell than the one she was currently in, but a hell, nonetheless. Denise claimed she had planned to get Elora out of the city but had given no details and he had no way to know if that was true.

Neither Lukas nor Damien said a word in response. There was nothing to say. There was no comfort to give, no lies to tell to try to make her feel better about any of it. They each had to sit with their own guilt for what they had done. Damien lifted the bottle and stared at the powder inside, noting the way it seemed to almost shine under the lights of the kitchen.

"How does it work?" They had discussed the larger points of the plan—that the powder would be given to Killian, that Elora would need to attack Damien in order to get them all in a single room, that Killian wouldn't walk out of that room, that they would all meet in the garage to make their escape to the safe house Lukas had set up only a few days ago. Damien hadn't seen the place, but knew it was an apartment that had been left empty for quite a while. Lukas had signed a rental contract under a fake name and gave the manager six months' worth of rent in cash, who didn't ask any questions after that.

"Pour it into his drink and stir. After that, he just needs to finish it off."

"How long until it takes effect?" Damien was trying to figure out the timing to keep any damage to a minimum. He would need to give it to him early enough that it would start working before Elora was forced to hurt anyone.

"Depends on how quickly he consumes it. Drink it slowly and it will take longer. Down the drink in a single swallow and its effects are much quicker. But you are still looking at roughly seven to ten minutes." Damien considered this alongside his timeline. It might not be fast enough, and his pulse quickened. This could be a problem. If Killian figured out what was going on, he could retaliate before the drug could work, killing them all before finally succumbing.

"But I have an idea, since I can see the hesitation on your face." She gave him a sideways glance. "You should work on that."

"What idea?" Damien forced the words out. He wouldn't admit to her that it was because of Elora that he had less control over his expressions, that something about her rendered him vulnerable in every possible way.

"My plan would make the lead-up more effective and would help it take effect much quicker." Damien looked at her expectantly and waited for whatever her master plan was. He had no doubt that her contribution would be crucial, that it would prove more useful than anything he or Lukas came up with.

A slow smile appeared on her face. "I want to be there when you get her out."

"No. That is just an extra complication, and you can't exactly be trusted." Lukas's denial was swift and vicious, but she didn't react. Instead, she only shrugged and waited.

"Deal. Tell us."

"Start giving it to him now. Small doses, nothing that would make him suspicious. Just a pinch in his drinks will do. Or a bit more in a bottle." She paused, considering the next move.

"I'm assuming he is draining her? Hoarding her blood?" Damien nodded slowly. He didn't know for a fact, but it seemed likely. "Well, that works in our favor. Put it in the blood since odds are he drinks it routinely, most likely every night, if my guess is correct."

"And this does what exactly?" Lukas had cringed visibly when Denise mentioned the bottle of Elora's blood, as if the idea of drinking from her was the most repulsive thought he could have. Damien knew his friend would rather starve than feed from her, no matter how tempting her blood was meant to be.

Denise sighed, as if explaining this was beneath her. "It builds up a level in his system, weakening him a bit before the moment you give him the rest. If he is already weak, then hypothetically it will work faster, giving you a better timeline."

Damien and Lukas both nodded, ignoring her reference to this hypothetically working. It would have to. Drugging Killian was the best, and possibly the only, chance at this. It was either it worked or both he and Lukas would be killed. The consequences for Elora would be much worse. No other words were exchanged. Denise would be waiting with the car, prepared in case Elora needed to be sedated or calmed down. The fact Damien needed to goad her into a rage could be devastating and catastrophic if they weren't care-ful. The doctor would be able to help with that.

"I don't like this. There are too many people involved who can be a problem." Lukas's voice overwhelmed the horrible elevator music as they left Denise's condo. Damien knew Lukas had a point. It was a concern he also had.

"I know. But there is no other choice. If necessary, we remove the problems when the time comes." Lukas nodded as he shoved his hands into his pocket.

"She asked about you again." Damien felt his heart constrict. A part of him wanted Lukas to keep that to himself. It was torture. And yet, it was hope that she didn't despise him as much as he thought she did. Things had shifted after her nightmare and pro-gressed from there. The night she came to his room had been the moment he knew nothing would be the same, the moment his en-tire world turned inside out.

"And what did you say?"

"That you were busy with work for Killian. She wants to know why you've been avoiding her." Damien shook his head as they stepped out of the elevator and headed to the car parked across the street. The lobby was full of vases of flowers of every vari-ety—bouquets of daises and tulips with baby breath. The scent was overwhelming, pushing out anything and everything else. The young man at the desk inclined his head to both of them as they left, face disinterested as he tracked their movements.

"I'm not —" Damien stopped his lie before he got too far. Lukas would know he was lying and was probably already waiting for it to pass his lips. "I can't handle seeing her. It's selfish and I know that, so don't feel the need to tell me."

"What happened that night?" Lukas had never asked. He had only taken care of her and tried to drag her back from whatever darkness she was currently sinking into.

"I —" Damien shook his head. "I gave her drugged blood at Killian's request. It is my fault she was left in that room like a sacrificial offering to him and whoever else he brought with him. And the vacant look in her eyes is a reminder of my own fuck up." Lukas didn't comment or call him out for his actions. Instead, he grabbed Damien's shoulder and squeezed before getting into the car with the tiny bottle of powder hidden deep in Damien's pocket.

~ ~

CHAPTER 44

Elora

She had read the same paragraph three times by the time the door opened that morning. The tray entered first, followed by Damien. Elora sat up a little straighter, surprised by the fact it wasn't Lukas, as it had been for the past week. She hadn't seen Damien since she had woken up in his bed. Elora placed the book on the coffee table and watched Damien as he moved into the room and set the tray on the table. As she chewed on her cuticle, the skin ripping slightly and drawing blood, Damien gestured to the bottle and glasses as if he had brought an amazing gift. She said nothing. Just stood and walked to the desk before sinking into the chair. Each movement was stiff and mechanical. Empty, so very empty.

"I brought breakfast." She inclined her head at his words while ignoring the underlying concern in his tone.

"Thank you." Quietly, she waited for him to pour it, as Lukas always did. He hesitated only a moment before doing so and handed her a glass before pouring his own. She simply drank one sip, then two before finishing the glass and setting it back on the tray.

"Have you enjoyed Lukas's company?"

"Yes. He has been kind." A sardonic grin quirked at his lips, but it didn't reach the rest of his face, which held only anxiety.

"Only kind? Most women, vampires and humans, say he is more than that."

She raised a brow at his comment and let the implication settle between them. He was trying to get a reaction from her, and she refused to give him one. Instead, he studied her and traced each movement, including the way she held the glass, and the way she stood and went to the bathroom to prepare a bath. The blood never failed to bring back the sense of hand and teeth, the two irrevocably intertwined with one another. Would she ever be able to feed without reliving it? Or was this simply her new reality?

She turned on the water in the tub so that only hot water poured from the facet. Steam filled the room and fogged the mirrors above the sink. She wanted it to burn. She wanted it to hurt.

"That seems like a bad idea." Damien's voice came from the doorway where he stood observing her. Elora glanced at him over her shoulder before taking off her clothes — first the shirt, then the rest. Instantly, he was at her side with his hand around her arm in a tight grip as he bent down. She could feel his breath on the shell of her ear.

"This won't solve anything." She nodded, but not in agreement. It was submission in its purest form. Instead, she wrenched her arm away from him and shut off the water. Elora closed her eyes and did not flinch as the hot water burned her arm. Without a word, she pulled the plug and drained the water.

Damien let out a sigh as he turned from her and left the bathroom. For a moment, she listened to see if he would leave and allow her to continue her routine. Why couldn't it be Lukas here? He never asked questions but allowed her to do what she felt she needed. He may not have understood, but he accepted that it wasn't his place to stop her. Damien never got that lesson. Being Killian's pet had given him a sense of entitlement and ownership over her and what she did. How long until he was invited into her room along with the others? Would he even agree? Would his vow to never feed from her hold true if Killian invited him?

The door never opened as the water finished draining. Instead of the hot bath she wanted, she followed Damien out of the bathroom without bothering to cover up. He saw everything that night in his room when he cleaned up after Killian's mess.

"Lukas will be taking over for me for the rest of the day." She pulled a shirt over her head without bothering to check the sleeves or what it looked like. Then she slipped on a pair of shorts she found in one of the drawers. There were new scars there, and she spent a moment counting them.

One. Two. Three. Four. Five.

Five new scars along her thighs.

"Elora?"

She exited the closet and sat in her chair before pulling the same book she had been reading for over a week into her lap. She hadn't made it past the first chapter.

"Thank you for telling me." The words on the page didn't make sense. She could recognize the letters individually but couldn't seem to piece them together enough to understand what was being said. Something about a dragon, she thought as the door finally opened and closed.

* * *

Lukas pulled out the deck of cards as soon as she drank her meal. As much as she hated the taste and the memories it triggered, she couldn't deny the satisfaction that came with it. The blood always tasted familiar. It was the same each time as if it came from the same person. But it went beyond simple consistency. It tasted like pine and oranges, like something she knew in a previous life.

"Play with me? Any game you want." She kept her gaze on the cup as she sat it down.

"Any game?" She wasn't sure why she was giving in and speaking once more. Maybe she was tired of seeing the obvious pain on his face each time she refused him. Maybe she just wanted to hear him laugh again. Not hearing it felt wrong, almost like a part of him was shut off while in this room.

Elora could practically feel the smile that carved across his face and the light in his eyes that seemed to radiate as he shuffled the cards. His hair was down today, and she realized she preferred it this way. It framed his face in a way that made him look even younger, if that was possible. He already couldn't look more than twenty-four or so.

"Any game. Even that one stupid game that requires no skill." She smirked despite herself, enjoying the tiniest bit of herself that wanted to feel something.

"Let's play Go-Fish, another game requiring very little skill." He laughed softly, like he was afraid that if he was too eager, she would retreat back into herself.

"I actually know that game. Should we do a truth for a truth?" He glanced up at her as he started passing out the cards and she picked each one up, holding them in her hand.

"If you want to." She didn't care if they played with those stakes and wasn't even sure what she could offer him should she lose. What else was left for them to know? His shoulders tensed again as they began the first game.

"You go first." She studied his smile. It was genuine, but strained as he took in her appearance. She knew how she looked—dark circles under her eyes, and bruises along her neck and arms. Like a corpse. She looked like a corpse, and maybe she was one.

"Got any threes?" She grunted in frustration and handed over a card.

"How about any sixes?" Elora shook her head, and he frowned slightly, drawing a card from the deck.

"Any fives?" She asked, and he shook his head without bothering to hide the victory in even the smallest win. His eyes were bright as he watched her once more draw a card. He must have been incredibly competitive before turning.

"Where has Damien been?" She took a moment to note the hint of surprise on his face.

"Doing work for Killian. Any queens?" Elora chuckled before shaking her head. Of course, it was Killian.

"What type of work? Any eights?" He shook his head at her request and ran a hand over his jaw and over to the back of his neck.

"Problems with humans. There have been attacks on vampires. Damien is looking into it. Any kings?" She shook her head and considered his words even as she asked if he had any threes, which he did. A small grin graced her lips as her collection of matches grew.

"The Resistance, right?" Lukas didn't look shocked this time and only nodded in confirmation. He cursed slightly as she finally won the rounds with almost double the number of matches. She straightened her back and waited, considering what she could ask or demand from him.

Elora sighed and chewed the inside of her cheek. "Why is he avoiding me?" The words sounded horrifically weak, like she was seeking his attention or something else. She sounded like a woman who didn't know when she wasn't wanted. Her feelings for him were complicated at best. All at the same time, Damien was safety and comfort as well as cruel and harsh. Lukas let out a long breath as he gathered up the cards and began to shuffle.

"I don't think even he knows the answer to that. I'm not sure he realizes he is doing it." Elora had expected him to deny that Damien was avoiding her, to defend his friend's actions. It wasn't that she needed him to confirm it, but hearing Lukas's answer was like a piece of ice in her chest. She had known it but could ignore it and pretend that it wasn't necessarily happening.

Lukas dealt the cards and quickly won this hand. He gave her a shy smile as he gathered the cards into his hands. "Tell me an embarrassing secret." He winked at her as the words left his lips.

The question was strangely complicated and straightforward at the same time. Everything that some people would consider embarrassing had just been a part of her life at certain points. Instead, she thought through what would make him react, filtering through dozens of options before at the perfect one.

"I've never played a single sport."

Elora watched his eyes widened to the point it was comical, just as she knew they would.

"Never?"

She shrugged. "When I was with my foster family, the opportunity never came. We went to school and came home. I didn't have any friends other than Elizabeth and she was never interested in sports either. And then, the hospital didn't exactly have the equipment for anything."

"Sports were a lifeline for me growing up. I can't even imagine never playing." She gave him a puzzled look in hopes he would continue. Other than telling her about his sister, Lukas never talked about himself. Neither did Damien. It was a fact that left her feeling more and more like a specimen kept behind glass, all her secrets and facts listed on a plaque next to her cage for all to see.

"Baseball was my favorite. I played for my school and would have played at whatever university I went to. But that never happened. Instead, I ended up turned into a vampire and working with Damien."

Damien. Not Killian.

"Which one of you turned first?" It was a question she didn't expect him to answer, especially since she hadn't won another round of the game.

"Me, but only by a year or so. I was only twenty-four when I turned, and Damien was twenty-three. I helped him through the transition. Then he worked his way through the ranks, so to say."

She said nothing. She didn't want to talk about Damien or Killian or what rising through the ranks entailed. She was pretty sure she could guess.

"I wish I could play someday."

"Maybe you could. I would teach you, including all my tricks of the trade."

She gave him a small smile as she stood. It was exhausting to pretend with him, even if she didn't want to. He had to know that it wouldn't happen and that the whole idea was a dream without any basis in reality. He had to know, just as much as she did, that she wouldn't ever leave this place, wouldn't ever be outside of Killian's reach again. She had walked through escape plan after escape plan. But none of them ended well, especially not with her perpetually weakened and drained.

Nevertheless, she appreciated the hope he was trying to give her by offering it up in a pretty box wrapped in a satin ribbon. Only it would be empty once she opened it. There would be nothing to take out and hold, to envelop herself with, no way to save her. She entered the bathroom and finally filled the tub with the scalding hot water she was denied earlier.

CHAPTER 45

Damien

No matter how much Damien hoped he had, Lukas hadn't exaggerated. He knew his friend had been telling the truth, but seeing it was something entirely different. It had been agony to watch her move through the room. There had been no sarcastic remarks in response to anything he said, no response to his insinuation about Lukas, no reaction to him stopping her attempt to hurt herself with a bath that bordered on boiling. He still couldn't believe her skin hadn't broken out in blisters when she reached in to let the water out.

She hadn't even said a word when she took her clothes off. She hadn't demanded that he leave or had called him a creep for following her. Most disturbingly, she didn't try to cover herself. It wasn't that he wanted her to be ashamed, but there had been a silent submission to her actions. It didn't matter to her anymore. It felt like nothing did and that alone was terrifying, leaving him with a pit in his stomach that threatened to overtake his entire being.

I'm going to kill him.

The thought should have shocked him, and he knew that. It should have left him feeling conflicted or guilty. Killian had made him and given him everything he wanted or needed. After his father had traded him in to be a blood source to pay his own debt, Killian had taken him under his wing. The head of the Ashcroft vampires had seen something in him and gave him a choice. All he had to do was to settle the debt—a life for a life. As soon as he pulled the blade from his father's heart, Killian turned him and offered to take care of his mother, promising she would never work as a source again. It wasn't Killian's fault she had passed only a couple of years later.

Yet, instead of feeling conflicted over this shift in loyalty, it simply gave him a sense of purpose, something to focus on other than the way she had collapsed at his door, and the sheer emptiness in her eyes when she watched everything around her.

He didn't want to leave her again, even if it was in Lukas's care. But there was someone he needed to speak to, someone who could be useful. Lukas had overheard him and Elora as he vowed to help her escape. If he meant that, and Damien had no doubt that he did, Viktor would be useful as a key player in a plan that had finally come together. Denise had her part. Lukas had his. And now Viktor would find out what his role was.

Viktor sat up straight as Damien strolled up to his cell. His steps were purposefully slow and leisurely. Damien didn't want him to see how tightly he was coiled; how close he was to snapping. He needed to play this as easily as possible and give away nothing while still convincing Viktor to help. He wasn't sure the human would agree if he knew the truth.

"You let them hurt her." Damien reigned in a flinch despite knowing it would begin this way. Lukas had filled him in on Viktor's reaction to seeing Elora. He was only glad that she had healed some before she came down. Damien wasn't sure the cell would have held him if he had seen her that night, human or not.

"Not intentionally. And it will not happen again." An eyebrow raised as Viktor studied him and absorbed his response. Damien gave him a moment to consider it, to decide if he wanted to listen or if this was all going to be pointless.

"And how will that happen?" Damien took a few steps towards the cell and leaned on his shoulder against it, so his back faced the camera he knew was aimed down the hallway. He had scolded himself for forgetting it was there when he brought Elora down here the first time. Irritation and arrogance had led to his misstep, and it was one he wasn't going to repeat now.

He lowered his voice just enough to make sure Viktor could still hear him. "I plan on getting her out, taking her away from here."

"Why? You've always hated her." The distrust and paranoia were clear in his tone, and Damien accepted it, knowing it was warranted after everything.

"I have a deep-seated interest in getting her out of here. That's all you need to know." Damien watched as Viktor filled in his own blanks. He knew that whatever he was coming up with was horrible, rendering Damien the villain in whatever this story was.

"What happens once we get her out? Where does she go from there?"

"The plan is to take her to a safe house until we find somewhere more permanent." His eyes narrowed slightly as he chewed on his cheek. The motion was fascinating to watch as the wheels behind Viktor's eyes turned.

"I want to stay with her. If she gets out, so do I. I'm not leaving her again, not with you." Damien shrugged as if this was nothing.

"Even though she is one of us? Even though she will need to drink human blood? Are you going to offer yourself up?" The questions were cruel, and Damien knew that, but his curiosity about the limits of their dynamic was more important to him now. Viktor had kissed her forehead after she stabbed him, promising it was okay as he watched her drink blood at the party. Did it truly not matter to him what she was? It was difficult to believe, but she seemed to inspire loyalty. Lukas was a testament to that. Damien was as well.

Viktor didn't say anything and held Damien's gaze whose expression didn't change even the smallest amount, despite the growing pain in his chest.

"Whatever you want. I wouldn't dream of breaking you two up." Damien moved his hand into his jacket pocket as his fist tightened. That was exactly what he wanted to do. He wanted the human out of the picture, but it wasn't his choice. It was hers, even if every instinct told him Viktor was a problem.

"What do I need to do?" Damien smirked and enjoyed the way Viktor bristled at the sight.

"Nothing. Truly nothing. Just allow everything to happen. It's better if you don't know the details. I need your reactions to be real."

He opened his mouth like he was going to ask questions and demand the details Damien just said he wasn't going to give him. Damien raised an eyebrow, as if daring him to do so. Instead, he closed his mouth and nodded as his face settled into a look of determination. And Damien wanted nothing more than to shatter his jaw and leave him behind.

* * *

The file Damien found at the apartment building was sitting on Killian's desk as he paced the room and shoved his hand through his hair every so often. Damien could only watch from his spot in one of the armchairs. This was not something that you interrupted and survived.

Damien had watched as Killian flipped through the pages and paused only to take in each picture of Elora. With each image, each piece of paper that held information about her whereabouts and activities for the years she was gone, Killian's body had tensed, muscles tightening as a rage Damien knew all too well overtook him. Better than anyone, Damien understood the reaction since his own had been similar, albeit for different reasons. Killian was protecting his assets, his property. The thought made Damien want to break something.

"Fuck! How did we not know, Damien? How did they find her? Who took the pictures?" His voice echoed throughout the room, and Damien resisted the urge to back away. He knew Killian would be beyond pissed when he saw the pictures from the party. Someone had gotten in, seen her, taken photos of her, and then turned them over to the Resistance, a group determined to remove vampires from power. Whether that was through a violent coup or simple eradication, Damien wasn't sure.

He didn't say anything. Killian didn't expect an answer unless it was Damien serving that person to him on a silver platter.

"Since childhood! Ever since she left here. How did they even know she existed? We kept her a secret."

Damien waited as Killian's pacing slowed. His hands now hung limply by his sides as the initial fury left him. Instead, there was a determined and cold rage left behind. It was more dangerous than anything else.

"What do they want with her?" His voice had lowered as he calmed and leaned against the desk, hands gripping the edge so tightly his knuckles were white.

"I'm not sure. There was nothing in the papers or files about that. My guess is she is a way to get to you, or the Corvin vampire family, since she could technically be considered an heir." The Corvin family was a bit more archaic and believed that the ruling of the vampires should be done by those turned by someone connected to the original bloodline. They named heirs who took over either when the current head died or when they stepped down.

Other families believed that the most powerful should be in charge, which was how Killian came to power. He had challenged the previous vampire head and won without a single injury. No one contested the win or challenged him since.

Killian hummed as he considered Damien's explanation. "That makes sense, not that it makes it any better. They want her as collateral, leverage."

"That's my theory based on what I've found so far."

"I want you to continue looking into this. Find out the identity of every person you saw at the apartment. Then I want answers, Damien. I want answers and then I want the threat eliminated. Do you understand?" He nodded without bothering to explain that he had already started working on tracking down the various humans who had been in that room. The first few were easy since the neighbors had known exactly who they were. There were still three more to find, but at least he had addresses for the ones who had spent the most time there.

If his other plan worked, Damien wouldn't have to tell Killian anything. He would still find out exactly what was going on, but for himself and for her. Killian had forfeited his right to know anything about Elora the moment he touched her all those years ago.

"How is my daughter? I heard she had been a bit morose of late." His tone shifted to something akin to sweetness and warmth. Damien adjusted the sleeve of his jacket to hide how he had tensed at the change in topic.

"She has been quiet from what I understand. I've had Lukas looking after her while I follow up on leads from the apartment."

"Are you so eager to not be in her presence? I thought your sentiments towards her had changed." Damien held Killian's gaze as he watched him and waited for the slightest flicker of movement in his features, even as Damien tried his best to look disinterested.

"All she wants is to read garbage novels and play cards. It's boring when I have other work that can be done. And she seems to enjoy Lukas's company."

"I didn't put Lukas in charge of her, Damien. I did not give you permission to pawn her off on someone else." There was an edge to his tone and a coldness to his words. He could only wonder how he was expected to track down the Resistance members who had gotten the photos of her while also spending time with her as Killian wanted.

"I apologize." The words felt like ash in his mouth as his anger burned every last bit of patience he had left for this conversation.

"You'll send Lukas for any recon you need to be done. When he manages to find someone of interest to us, then you have permission to leave her. I need you to protect what's mine. Am I understood?" Damien bristled at the wording — protect what's his. He tightened his jaw to prevent himself from making the mistake of screaming that she wasn't his, that she didn't belong to anyone.

"Understood." Damien nodded as he headed to the door, wondering exactly what it would feel like to rip his throat out.

CHAPTER 46

Damien

Lukas was standing outside her door, leaning against the wall with his arms crossed as Damien approached. It is strange to see the vampire frowning, but it had become a permanent state during the last week or so. It was Elora, or what had been done to her, and Damien knew that. Lukas was more open about his anger and desire to see everyone who touched her destroyed. It's why he had to be kept away from Killian. Lukas's face would reveal every inner thought and urge. Usually, it was refreshing to see someone, vampire or human, who didn't wear a mask.

In this case, it was a liability. He winced slightly as Damien stopped in front of him. If possible, Lukas's frown grew deeper as he ran his hand through his hair.

"What?" Dozens of scenarios raced through Damien's head. Was she okay? Had something happened while he was gone?

"You should know something. I haven't really told you, but—" He hesitated as he watched Damien's brows narrow and his jaw tighten.

He let out his breath. "Your suspicion was correct. Someone has been draining her. I noticed it a few days ago. She's been tired, more so than normal. And there was a bandage on her arm. I saw it today before she managed to take it off. I think she's been hiding it."

Another pause and Damien waited. "And she was visited at some point. I think it was when we were at that apartment. When I came back, I could smell her blood in the room. I tried to talk with her, but she won't talk about any of that. She barely talks at all."

Damien cursed as his hands flexed at his sides and reminded himself not to punch his only ally in this.

"And why are you just now telling me?" Damien's voice was low and calm.

"What were you going to do, Damien? Demand that it stop? March in Killian's office and tell him not to take any more from her? I didn't tell you because there was nothing for you to do and it would just piss you off."

"Then why tell me now?" He nearly shouted at Lukas. His frustration was mostly because Lukas was right, and Damien knew it. Putting a stop to the blood collection was exactly what he would want to do, despite the fact it wouldn't end well. Killian would try to kill him, and he wasn't sure he could take him on his own. Hence why they needed Denise.

"She's weak. Physically, I mean. I watched her today. Dizziness when she stands and sleeps throughout the day. It's why I'm out here. I didn't think she would appreciate me watching her sleep." He tried to grin as if this was a joke or something humorous and not her health they were talking about.

Damien huffed a laugh. No, she really wouldn't. But that was before the night she showed up in his room. Since then, she hadn't fought anything, hadn't said anything. He doubted she would say anything now. Which presented a slight hiccup in his plan, one he would have to try to remedy. The key pieces were there, but it all rested with her. And he was running out of time. She seemed to fall further and further into herself with each day. How long until she was gone?

"Got it. Anything else?" Damien prepares himself to go into her room and face what he would find there. She still hadn't said anything about his part in her sedation other than that morning.

"I've gotten her to talk a couple of times now. I got her to play cards this afternoon after you left. We only played a couple of games, and she talked a bit. Nothing like before, but small victories." Damien nodded. That was potentially a good sign.

"Do you think—" Lukas knew exactly what he was going to ask, exactly what he had hoped this meant.

"No. I think she's getting worse. Honestly, I think she's given up. And who wouldn't at this point?"

Guilt grabbed him in a chokehold, and he flinched. So much of this could be placed at his feet simply because he was following orders, simply because he didn't pay attention to what was going on right in front of him. But he had seen what he had wanted to see. And now she was paying for that.

"Tomorrow, Lukas." He nodded before moving towards the elevator. She only had to make it through one more night.

Damien's hands trembled as he turned the handle and entered the room. It was dark, with only a lamp by the bed creating any light. He could make out her figure curled up on top of the blankets with her knees pulled tight to her chest. She looked small there in the massive bed that could easily fit multiple people. At first, he hesitated. Her chest rose and fell as if she was asleep until he noticed the light reflecting in her eyes as she stared at the wall.

He walked to the bed and rested against the post as he forced his expression to display something closer to apathy or boredom, like this was all a formality, like his chest wasn't squeezing at the sight of her so diminished.

"Have you had dinner?" His voice sounded horrendously loud in the perfectly silent room.

"No." He almost didn't hear her, and he had to stop himself from moving closer, to sit near her and touch her arm, her cheek.

"I'll have someone bring something." Damien turned away from her, unable to stand there anymore. All he wanted was for her to fight him, to argue with him. He wanted her to call him an asshole or a creep. Hell, he would take her throwing something at him—a lamp, a pillow, anything.

"Damien?" He stilled and took a breath.

"Yes?"

"Why do you hate me?" For a moment, he couldn't speak, couldn't formulate words or thoughts. There was such defeat in her voice, such vulnerability in the question itself. He wanted to pull her into his arms and tell her that he doesn't, not anymore.

Silence settled over the room and wrapped them both in its embrace while he searched for words that he couldn't tell her, not now, not right before he needed to rely on her hatred of him. Or what was left of it.

"Don't worry about answering. It doesn't matter anymore." He turned to her as her words repeated in his head. He watched as she pulled herself from the bed, moved sluggishly and slowly, and made her way to the bathroom. Another bath, he assumed. Damien listened as she closed the door, and the water turned on before ordering her dinner from the collection rooms.

I'm an asshole, was all he could think as the water turned off and he heard the sound of her getting in. In another life, he would distract her with stories from his childhood. Not the sad ones where they stole food, but the ones where he did stupid and embarrassing things. She would laugh and the sound of it would be like a balm for his tattered soul. He would ask her about her foster sister, about going to school, about anything other than Killian, and everything he did. He wanted to know her inside and out, wanted to know all the stupid, pointless things that people wanted to know. But all he could think was that he wanted so much but deserved so little. Not from her.

A knock broke through his thoughts, and he grabbed the tray from the vampire waiting before kicking the door shut behind him. Damien was already setting the tray down and pouring the blood into the glass just as she exited the bathroom, already dressed in a long shirt—his shirt from the night she was attacked. A strange sense of pride hit him as he watched her curl up in a chair and arrange the throw blanket over her legs.

He noted the new scars there, still slightly pink against her pale skin. If they weren't taking blood each night, she would be fully healed, and the scars would blend in with the rest of her. But it was difficult to heal when you were being drained, when your strength was being sapped for someone else's use. Was Killian keeping the blood for himself, drinking that instead of feeding directly from her? Damien supposed the other option was that he was selling it or giving it away to those who have something of equal value to give him in return.

Damien hands her a glass filled to the rim. She shot a quick glance at him and then the cup. With a performative roll of his eyes, he took a quick sip before handing it back to her, knowing exactly what she expected, what she feared he would do. To her, Damien was Killian's pet as much as she was. He was sent to do the dirty work while she existed as a plaything. Thankfully, she took the glass, and he sank back into the chair while trying desperately not to watch her as she finished it in two quick swallows.

He tracked the way her eyes closed, and her lips curled in disgust. His eyes lingered on the line of red along her lips. The effect it had on her was baffling and captivating to watch, even if she suppressed it. Her tongue traced the line of her lips, removing any lingering blood.

"Do you always watch people like this?" Damien jerked back as he tried to force his features into an expression of disinterest, an easy nonchalance.

"Only when I have a vested interest in making sure they finish their food." Her eyes narrowed and his heart jumped a bit. A reaction—it was at least a reaction.

"I thought you only cared when it was drugged, and you were following orders." He shifted slightly to hide the flinch.

"Should we discuss that?" This question did not fit with the plan and certainly did not work towards tomorrow or what needed to happen. But he couldn't stop it. He had felt the words leave his mouth before he could stop them. She sighed and closed her eyes for a moment, as if this whole conversation was pointless and exhausting.

"What would be the point, Damien? I would remind you of the role you played; you would remind me that you didn't know, and that Killian only asked you to give me the blood. I would tell you it doesn't matter because you are his little pet, following every command and whim like a well-trained dog. You would get angry, call me spoiled, or something worse. And it will fall apart from there until one of us leaves, or you get stabbed." She turned back to the blanket on her lap, playing with the stitching along the side.

"I'll tell you that I want to blame you but can't. I'll tell you that I want to hate you even now but can't make myself do it even when you goad me and force me to become the worst version of myself possible. And I won't tell you because it won't matter, because nothing matters anymore." She stood and left the sitting area before curling onto the bed with only the throw blanket to cover her. He didn't move. He only sat there, frozen in place by her confession. For a moment, he didn't move because if he did, then they would move on from this single space in time where she didn't despise him, and he could pretend that she knew he didn't despise her either. This strangely horrific and toxic and perfect moment would cease to exist. Instead, they would continue, and everything would revert to her hating him and him hating himself.

~ ~

CHAPTER 47

Elora

The gnawing in her stomach grew stronger and louder with each passing minute. Breakfast had never come that morning and her desperation for it was its own living entity, resting directly beside her, whispering how delicious blood would be, how much she needed it. The night before the female vampire who never told Elora her name had taken three collection bottles, leaving her exhausted, drained beyond belief. She had flinched as Elora slumped over while her blood was siphoned out. Elora could only watch the internal struggle that ensued — whether to help her sit up or to leave her alone. The vampire had decided on the latter and let her sink into the bed as she grew weaker and weaker. Elora supposed it didn't matter and within moments, she had passed out as the ordeal ended. The vampire removed the needle from her arm and collected her materials, leaving just as silently as she had arrived.

At first, Elora thought she may have slept through breakfast and that Lukas had decided not to wake her up. Her concept of time was based solely on the clock on her nightstand, where it currently said it was almost two in the afternoon. But usually, there would be something waiting for her, a bottle with a glass on a tray sitting on her desk. Nothing was there now.

Elora curled up in her bed and pulled the blankets over her, considering whether she could just go back to sleep.

"Hungry?" Damien's voice filled the room, and she quickly sat up. It felt like thousands of spiders were crawling all over her, both inside and outside of her body. It was a direct result of the hunger currently creating a merciless storm in her chest, every emotion and thought sharpened and closer to the surface. The gnawing in her stomach was torture as she followed each of his movements while he set the collection bottle down along with a wineglass. It felt like withdrawals, like what the recovering addicts described in group therapy.

"If you want to feed, you will need to come here." Her eyes narrowed as she wished he would burst into flames. She didn't want to deal with him, not after her question yesterday and a confession that she couldn't make herself regret.

"Where's Lukas?" Elora allowed herself to enjoy the way his face contorted for a split second before quickly resuming its usual sneer.

"Miss him? Well, I'm in charge today. Daddy says it's my turn again." She snarled at him, a sound she had never made before. He chuckled and shook his head before patting one armchair and sitting in the other. Slowly, she made her way towards him, feeling like there was a game being played here, but no one had told her the rules.

"I'll let everyone know that Lukas is off limits. There will be a lot of disappointed vampires. As I said before, he is very popular." He winked at her before handing her the wineglass now filled with blood. The smell captured her attention and focus as it became the only thing she wanted, the only thing that truly existed in this room.

"In that case, be sure to send him later tonight. I have some free time." She watched the muscles in his jaw tick, the way his eyes hardened for only a moment, a slight glimpse of who he actually was. For a moment, she held the glass to her lips and tensed at the way Damien seemed so at ease while a mischievous smile played on his lips. It was the type of smile that would normally make her feel violent, but she didn't feel anything. Only the slightest twinge of irritation, barely enough to register as existing.

She took a sip while searching for any hints that it was dosed again. Only the same taste of pine and oranges. It must be the same blood every time, or did all blood simply taste the same? She didn't remember if the server at the party had tasted like this, had been too distracted by the monumental shift in her existence.

Elora swallowed the rest, ignoring the returning sense of fingers on her skin. The churning in her stomach had dulled, but the ache was still there. Missing blood that morning had been worse than she thought possible, especially with how much had been drained the night before. It was overwhelming. She held out the glass to Damien and let him refill it, that horrendously handsome grin still plastered on his face. A bit more irritation found its way to the surface as she glared at him, and his smile only widened. What was so fucking funny?

"Tasty?" He set the now empty bottle on the table and sat back, resting his ankle on his knee.

"Obviously. Do you always ask stupid questions?" For the first time in weeks, she felt something other than the void that had replaced everything inside of her, something other than pure numbness.

"I'm only asking because that blood is special just for you. No one else drinks it. It even has its own area in the collection rooms. Did you know that?" Unease swirled in her core as she tried to drink the rest of what was in the glass.

"Let me guess. Drugged? How predictable of you, Damien. Disappointing, to be honest," His smile faltered for just a moment, a flash of what looked like hurt. Her grip on the glass tightened as the smile returned and he leaned forward, elbows resting on his knees and fingers interlaced under his chin. His dark eyes twinkled, the amber flakes seeming to glow with the intensity of his gaze as she took another drink. Damien's attention never left her face and tracked each minuscule movement as she finished off the glass, savoring the way she now felt satiated, felt complete once more.

"It's Viktor's, you know. The blood. Daddy thought you would enjoy it." Her breathing stilled as her eyes moved between the collection bottle and the glass in her hand. Thoughts raced through her mind. Viktor's blood. They had been giving her his blood. It was why there were no new wounds when she saw him, only a bandage in the crook of his arm. She knew it felt familiar, that she had known that scent and taste. It reminded her of home, of safety. Now she understood why.

"Just a special gift for you, little rose." Blood rushed to her ears as her body became unbearably hot. Damien's words enclosed her in their grip, squeezing until breathing hurt and burned with each gulp of air she took. The entire room disappeared, leaving him sitting across from her, perfectly at ease even as everything inside her fell apart.

Snap.

The stem of the glass broke in half, and she felt the pieces of it slice into her hand. It was like every time she lost herself in her rage, each time she found herself with a makeshift weapon in her hand turning her into some force of nature bent only on pain and revenge. Thoughts exited her mind instantly, and there was no more rationality to be had. Her heart was racing too fast, so hard that she wondered if it would crack her ribs even as her vision narrowed on the only person in that room that mattered. She moved quicker than she knew she could and lunged at Damien, the stem of the glass in her hand.

She felt the moment she landed on him, with her knees digging into his thighs as one of her hands forced him back against the chair. She didn't even bother looking at his face, his expression. It didn't matter what she would find there. Her eyes were on the broken piece of glass, feeling it enter his chest, every inch of it as it moved through flesh and muscle. A cry erupted from her mouth, a primal scream of anger and rage. Damien grunted and cursed, though it seemed to lack any vitriol that she would have expected. Elora faced him finally as her fingers gripped his jaw to force him to look at her, forcing him to witness what he and Killian had turned her into. He didn't throw her off of him, didn't push her away, or force her off his lap even as a feral grin carved itself across her face. She didn't fly across the room like the last time she stabbed him, but instead fell to the ground, weak with every bit of energy spent. She had nothing left.

Damien stood as his fingers gingerly touched the spot where the broken wine glass protruded from his chest and glanced at the blood soaking through his pale blue T-shirt. She smirked as the spot grew, as he stared in disbelief at his red-tipped fingers. With a grunt, he moved on top of her, his legs holding her in place as he straddled her frame. With one hand, he held her wrists together and forced her hands above her head.

"That wasn't very nice. Is that how you treat everyone who gives you a gift?" She spat at him, smiling as it coated his cheek. He chuckled before leaning down close. She could feel it as his chest pushed into hers, his breath on her face, the heat from his body.

"You'll regret that," he whispered, though there was no malice in it, only detachment, before he called out for Lukas.

Viktor. With a sudden jolt now that her brain and body were connected and back under her control, she cursed at her own stupidity, her own inability not to react to someone who wanted exactly that. She eyed the broken glass stem protruding from Damien's chest, near his sternum, and she swallowed thickly. He was right. She would regret this, already did. She knew who would pay the price for this and it wouldn't be her.

"Now wine glasses are off the table as well?" Lukas's voice filtered into the room, and she squirmed, trying to work her way out from underneath Damien. His grip tightened on her wrists, and she whimpered slightly at the pain.

"The list just seems to be growing. Soon all she will be allowed is plastic cups, like the kind kids use." The two vampires laughed slightly at the joke. She craned her neck to find Lukas standing off to the side, his face uncharacteristically blank. Her eyes started to sting as she realized she was on the verge of crying in front of both of them. Lukas wasn't a friend, but she hadn't thought he was cruel.

It shouldn't have hurt like this. The coldness overtook her, every emotion, every hurt, every desire to survive past this moment bleeding from her, soaking through to the floor beneath her. She gave Lukas one more glance, one more pleading look before giving over completely, understanding what had to happen.

"Are you going to behave?" Damien's voice broke through her thoughts.

"Fuck you." She didn't look at him, just kept her eyes on Lukas, who seemed disinterested in the whole exchange.

"Daddy wouldn't like that, and I have standards. Are you going to stab me again or can I let you up?" She went limp at his response. No, Killian wouldn't like that, not without his permission, not without being able to watch. Tears started pouring over, streaming down her cheeks and into her hair that pooled around her head.

"Let me up and then get out." Damien nodded, apparently out of sarcastic remarks.

"Lukas, clean up the glass. We wouldn't want her to have any extra weapons." She didn't bother asking where he was going. It would be a quick trip to remove the glass from his chest before reporting to Killian.

She said a silent apology to Viktor as Damien released her hands and stood up, moving quickly to the door. With a final look at her, Damien simply smirked as she scrambled back, not caring about the glass digging into her legs and feet as she moved. Her back hit the bed, and she sat up, pulling her knees in and squeezing them to her like they were her salvation, and waited. There was nothing else to do.

CHAPTER 48

Elora

"I thought you were my friend." It sounded childish even as the words left her mouth. "I thought it was only Damien and Killian who were that cruel."

She watched him pause slightly, fingers hovering above a rather large piece of glass. Somehow, his betrayal was worse. Somehow, she had come to see him as a safe place. She had been a fool.

Lukas didn't say a word as he knelt to pick up the rest of the broken pieces of glass, gingerly placing each shard in the trashcan. He moved around her, careful not to get too close, as if he thought he was the next target of her rage. Did he not realize she had nothing left? No more fights. No more fury.

She knew the next steps to this: Killian's office, Viktor, and blood. Viktor wouldn't survive a weapon to his chest, the stem to a glass, or otherwise. A plan started to formulate as she watched Lukas gather up the last of the pieces before he rested against the wall, arms crossed over his chest. His eyes were burning a hole in the floor as he refused to even glance in her direction. A heavy silence fell over the room.

Elora had made the same mistake as she did at the hospital. She had believed that spending time with someone and engaging in fun conversation equated to friendship, to someone caring. She knew Damien liked to play with her, helping her recover one day and then baiting her with malice the next. But she had thought Lukas had come to at least enjoy her company, at least enough to not want to see her hurt. She scolded herself for having been stupid in more than one way, but it wouldn't matter for much longer. It was time to test exactly how valuable she was. There were so many holes in this plan, so many pieces she hadn't bothered to think through.

Hours passed, or maybe less, before the door finally opened and Damien strolled in completely at ease, that horrible arrogance never clearer than in this moment. He had changed his shirt and there was no indication that the wound was bandaged or if it had healed enough to not need it.

"Time to go, sweetheart." Damien smiled at her before nodding to Lukas, who moved swiftly towards her and grabbed her arms.

"I won't run, you idiot. That's not necessary," Elora snarled at Lukas, who simply stared directly ahead, his features hard in a way that felt unnatural. She shouldn't miss his smile.

"Not taking any risks. You're not exactly known for being stable."

"I'm what you and Killian have made me." Her words hung in the air between them. No response from either vampire as she steeled herself for what was coming, what would be required of her if she submitted like every time before.

Her heart seized for just a moment as her breathing started to become shallower. She closed her eyes and inhaled deeply before holding it. As she exhaled, she stood straighter and forced herself to look directly in front of her—not at Damien, not at Lukas. She forced the panic and fear down. They wouldn't get that response from her. Not this time.

One step and then another before she exited the room and stopped, waiting for them to direct her, unsure of the setting for the upcoming scene.

"This way," Lukas directed her toward the elevator as Damien pushed the buttons. The short ride was painfully quiet. It seemed they had no desire to speak to her or even look at her as they escorted her to her fate. She told herself that everything was going to be okay and that her plan would work.

And if it didn't? Well, then she supposed everything would truly be okay.

Damien knocked on the door to Killian's office. The desk where there was usually a secretary was empty. The less of a potential audience the better, she supposed.

"Come in." Killian's voice rang out from beyond the door, and she shuddered, knowing what was coming. Will Viktor already be in there? Bound and waiting to be punished for her?

Elora pushed the thought from her head as Damien opened the door and let Lukas escort her through, forcing her to sit in one of the armchairs. Her eyes scanned the room, finding only Killian leaning against his desk. He looked disheveled, like he hadn't slept in days or even weeks, and his hair hung loose by his shoulder in a wild mess. His shirt was partially unbuttoned, sleeves were rolled up to his elbow, revealing tattooed forearms—a vine with thorns and flowers on both, mirror images of each other. His slacks, usually perfectly pressed, were wrinkled like he had worn them for days.

She fought a smile from her lips, enjoying his haggard appearance. It warmed something inside her to see him at least partially broken down. Damien nodded at Killian before strolling over to the personal bar in the corner of the room, no doubt preparing his drink for the show that was to come. Elora noted without taking her eyes off Killian that Lukas had left, probably now tasked with retrieving Viktor. On the floor to her right, directly between her chair and the one Killian usually sat in during these little meetings, was a large tarp that spanned most of the space.

"I'm disappointed, daughter. I thought you had learned last time to behave." Killian even sounded exhausted. There was none of the usual arrogance or amusement in his voice, only disinterest. She shrugged as he picked up his glass from the desk behind him and took a drink, allowing a small smile on his lips as he swallowed.

"Maybe if you had better babysitters for me, this wouldn't happen. Your quality of vampires seems to be slipping." Her eyes flicked to Damien for just a moment before returning to Killian, who huffed slightly. Maybe a laugh, maybe not.

"Oh, little rose. We can't just stab people who anger us." There was amusement in his voice, even a bit of pride. She wanted to remind him he was known for killing those who irritated him, and that her behavior was exactly what one would expect with him in charge.

"Well, we will have to agree to disagree." Killian stiffened at her words. Was he expecting her to apologize and beg, agree to never hurt his second in command again? Elora almost snorted a laugh at the thought. No, he wouldn't be that stupid.

"He deserved it. I only wish I managed to do more damage." Damien straightened a bit at her declaration, eyes focused on Killian and his drink.

"You know the consequences, daughter. Viktor will be the one to pay the price." Exhaustion, pure and beautiful, laced each word. She breathed it in and filled herself with it as if it were the very elixir of life. It was better than blood.

She nodded at him, slowly and deliberately. "So, you have said."

His eyes narrowed as he finished his drink and handed the glass to Damien, who took it without a single glance at her. Usually by now, there would be at least one sneer, one disgusted smirk. Now, there was nothing.

"Has your concern for the human decreased so much now that you have returned to your true nature? Now that you need to drink blood?" Killian ran his hand along the stubble on his jaw and waited.

"It is interesting just how much my concern for Viktor bothers you."

"You are debasing yourself, daughter. And the thought makes me sick." She shrugged at Killian's declaration and the venom in each word.

"If I am so debased, why do you keep me around?" He stilled at her question, and she took the opportunity to answer for him. "Is it because of what you take from me? What you allow others to take from me?"

"Quiet." His command was low, almost impossible to hear. But the violence was present in the way his eyes darkened, the way his mouth thinned into a line across his exhausted features.

Damien said nothing during the exchange and poured another drink into the glass. The door beside her opened and Lukas entered with Viktor standing tall beside him. Viktor was roughly the same size as Lukas, both tall and broad. He had been dressed for the occasion in a new white T-shirt and jeans. They had even given him back his boots and his hair has been combed back from his face, longer and resting along his brow. Healed cuts and bite marks lined his neck and arms, thin pale lines along his tanned skin.

Your personal blood bag, a voice inside her whispered and she turned away from him, ashamed that she had been feeding from him. Even if she hadn't known it was him, she had still been feeding from someone—a daughter, a wife, a son, a husband. A person with a family and a life who deserved more than what Killian gave them, if he gave them anything at all.

Elora had heard rumors that he employed humans to provide blood, but the conditions were poor and there was no way out of the arrangement. He would lure people off the streets with promises of food and a roof over their heads and even had other humans vouch for him to make recruitment easier. She was sure it sounded like a dream, a miracle with Killian as the saint who granted it. The dark secret was that if he grew tired of you or you grew too weak, then he disposed of you.

None of them lasted long, from what she had learned—months at the most. She had benefited from that and only now cared because it was Viktor, someone she knew and cared about.

Killian picked something long and shiny from his desk before moving towards her.

"The rules were clear." He said nothing else before placing the knife, a long thin blade that was familiar in a way that made her skin crawl, on the table. With a slight wave of his hand at the weapon, he walked away and returned to his place at his desk.

"Yes, they were," she replied and picked up the knife, glancing briefly at Viktor, who was now kneeling in the middle of the room. His gaze was fixed not on Killian but on Damien, who was watching everything with a detached boredom. Elora closed her eyes before opening them and testing the tip of the blade by running her finger down the edge. She gave it a detached assessment as the skin there opened and blood pooled in a stream of tiny droplets. The smell filled the room, metallic but dark and rich. An irresistible scent, and she observed Killian close his eyes as he took a deep breath and inhaled.

"But that won't be happening, Killian." She watched as he flinched at the sound of his name on her lips, and she grinned. "You see, I figured something out."

"And that is?" Each word sounded as if it was being forced from his lips as his jaw clenched.

"All of this is to keep me controlled because you can't lose me again. I'm too important. Whether it's because of my blood or just your ridiculous need to control everyone and everything, I'm not sure. And to be perfectly honest, I don't care." She said each word carefully to make sure Killian and everyone else in that room understood what she was saying, and what was going to happen.

Killian took another drink and watched her carefully over the rim of his glass. His lips were tinged red as he lowered the glass. Blood. Her blood, more than likely, and her stomach turned at the sight despite the smile that grew wider on her face.

"But I'm not letting that happen anymore." She raised the knife to her neck, making sure the point was pressed deep enough to draw a little blood. "He goes free, unharmed, and left alone, or I die."

Elora ignored the cry from Viktor, who had started to crawl towards her before Lukas gripped his shoulder and held him in place. She kept her eyes focused on Killian, whose expression had erupted with rage, as if he hoped to scare her into dropping the knife and submitting yet again.

"If I release him, let him go without any strings attached, as you demand, then what? What happens then?" Killian's voice was deadly as he took another long sip from the glass.

She took a deep breath. She had prepared for this. "Other than my dropping the knife before he is gone, I'll do what you say—give blood, feed from humans, whatever you want."

"And without my collateral, how do I make sure that happens?" Ice dripped from each word as she kept the blade steady against her skin, never wavering. He would not win this and would not sway her.

"Don't you trust your only daughter?" She gave him a sickly-sweet smile. It was the one that she would give Dr. Montgomery whenever she claimed Elora made progress by lying once again.

"As much as it pains me to say, daughter, no, I don't. Want me to tell you what I think your plan is?" He took a step forward and drained the rest of the glass before setting it down. She could sense Damien off to the side, watching as this all played out, ready to do whatever was needed for his master. Viktor hadn't said a word since the demand left her lips, but she could hear his harsh breathing.

Elora only waited.

"I don't think you plan on surviving this, which is utterly heartbreaking. I think you plan on getting this human," he spat the word like it was a disgusting taste in his mouth, "out of here and then slitting your throat, hoping it will be deep enough that the blood loss will kill you before you can heal."

"No!" Viktor's voice finally rang out, and she glanced over at him. She could only hope that her expression was blank and that he wouldn't see the utter defeat in her eyes. Killian was right. She had already made the decision not to leave this room alive. They wouldn't touch her again, wouldn't chain her up, and use her for their own purposes.

"It helps that I've been kept fairly weak," she admitted with a shrug, as if it didn't matter that he figured it out. And honestly, she wasn't sure it changed anything. Her plan stayed the same. If he came any closer to trying and stopping her, she would act. If he didn't release Viktor or ordered Lukas to kill him, she would act. It didn't matter what Killian's next move was, because hers remained the same. And from the murderous gleam in his eyes, she knew he realized that.

Another step. Then another before his face contorted and confusion raced through his features. With a trembling hand, he gripped the back of the chair in front of him and tried to steady himself. His pale eyes frantically searched the room, moving rapidly from her to Lukas to Damien, who stood behind him. There was panic on his face as his fingers dug into the leather of the chair. She took a step back. Was this a ploy? A way to get close enough to grab the knife from her?

"Finally." Damien's voice crashed through the room, but she couldn't look away from Killian, who had slumped down to the tarp that had been laid out for Viktor, a pleading expression on his face as he met Elora's assessing gaze.

~ ~

CHAPTER 49

Damien

"I thought you said it wouldn't take that long." Damien shook his head and shrugged as he stared down at the vampire collapsed on the floor. He didn't look at Elora. He couldn't meet her eyes right now, even though he knew she had to be confused. The paranoia was practically radiating from her, filling the room along with the scent of her blood. Killian was right. It was unique, almost irresistible.

"What? What is going on?" Killian's words were labored, as if it was taking every ounce of strength to force them out. His focus shifted around the room before spotting Damien and Killian's trembling hand reached out for his second-in-command. A soft shake of his head was the only action before Damien crouched down in front of him. His dark hair fell onto his forehead as he studied the vampire in front of him. Blood had started to trail from Killian's eyes like tears. From her spot in the middle of the room, Elora didn't move or remove the blade from her neck as she tracked the scene in front of her.

Damien said nothing. He just reared back his fist and swung forward. The sound was audible as it collided with Killian's jaw. And then again and again. Blood coated his knuckles with each hit.

Rage and guilt and shame swelled under Damien's skin, forcing a snarl from his mouth as he relished each and every hit. He finally stood to his full height and stepped back to stare down at Killian with disgust on his face, committing the scene of the vampire bleeding on the floor to memory.

"I don't owe you an explanation, Killian. Instead, I will only say you know what you did, what you were continuing to do. It ends now." Killian spat at Damien's feet, and the bloody mess landed in front of his boots.

"I fucking made you. I created you and you betray me for that?" Killian's head jerked in Elora's direction even as he leaned against the chair with his arms limp by his side. A line of red trickled from the corner of his mouth and from his nose, but Damien wasn't sure if it came from his beating or from the powder Denise gave them to use.

"And I thank you for that," Damien smirked cruelly at the pathetic body on the floor before turning to Elora. "He is yours if you want. Or I can take care of it."

Elora met his gaze with her eyes narrowed, as if trying to figure out if this was a trick. She took a step back and Damien cursed silently. They didn't have time for this. His eyes lingered on her face along with the blade still at her neck, even as her hands started to shake.

"Elora, you need to decide. I won't take away your chance for revenge, but you need to decide so we can leave." She shook her head and backed away once more. Her grip tightened on the knife and pushed harder until she drew more blood. He took a step forward with his hand stretched out to stop her, but hesitated. She had been fully prepared to die and now wasn't sure what was happening. If he could have, Damien would have told her to plan and explained everything to her.

"No, it's a trick. You're working together to get me to let my guard down, then you will drag me back to the room and chain me up." Damien took another step towards her. His entire body flinched as she pushed the knife deeper. There was an awe to what he witnessed. There was a strength in her desire to save herself. She was fully prepared to make sure she never went back there and never felt the metal on her wrists and ankles. He understood her fear and the paranoia that laced each move she made, but it was only a matter of time before someone came to find Killian. Damien met Lukas's eyes in a silent plea for him to help, to say anything to sway her.

Elora's gaze focused on Killian. His labored breathing was the only sound in the room as his eyes struggled to stay open. His fingers twitched by his thigh as his other hand rose slightly, as if he were reaching for her.

"I'm not. I promise. Please, I can explain, but you need to decide so we can get out of here." Damien's words were pleading and desperate, and for a moment, it looked like she almost believed him. Elora cackled, the sound growing louder and shriller as she took in the panicked confusion on Damien's face as his eyes moved to Lukas.

"Please." But she shook her head.

"You're good, Damien. I almost believed you. Just like I believed you when you took care of me, washed the blood from my skin, and dressed my wounds. But that is your whole game, and you learned from the best."

She shot a look down at Killian, who seemed to be fighting with everything he had to stay awake.

"He did the same thing. Cleaned my wounds, whispered promises and comforting words, and tucked me into bed. Did he teach you how to do it?" Damien felt his chest hollow out as if every organ was ripped from him and left behind only an empty space. This was what she thought of him, of his actions, and it hurt more than anything.

"Elora, listen to him. He's telling the truth. We are getting you out." Her focus followed the voice and found Viktor where he stood beside Lukas. Both of them watched her like she was a rabid animal, and they weren't sure what she would do next. Her eyes narrowed as if trying to understand what was happening and how it all was working together. Viktor held up his hands in a placating gesture and took a cautious step towards her. Damien let out a sharp exhale as the knife moved away from her neck while the wound bled down her neck and onto her shirt.

"You're working with him?" She gestured to Damien without bothering to hide her disdain.

"It was necessary. We just want to get you out. Let us do that."

"And Killian? What about him?"

"Like I said, he is yours if you want him. If not, I have a few ideas. But we need to hurry." Damien's voice was tense, and she glanced over at him where he still stood next to Killian's form. The vampire sat on the floor and leaned against the chair. His breathing was labored and harsh, and his eyes were closed as if he was asleep. With each breath, everyone in the room could hear his chest rattle.

"Don't rush her!" Viktor's harsh words rang out and Damien twisted towards him with his impatience clear on his face.

"We don't have time! Killian's guards will be back, and we need to go by then." Viktor started to say something in response to Damien's explanation.

"I want him." Her voice was quiet at first, as if she was testing out the words on her tongue. Each figure in the room went silent, even as a proud smile curled onto Damien's lips. There she was. There was the fierceness and the cold fire that fueled each and every move she made and every word she said. It was beautiful to witness.

"I want him." Her voice was louder this time, as if she had just realized that this was exactly what she wanted. Damien bowed and stepped aside before gesturing at the figure on the floor. She hesitated only a moment before she moved in front of Killian and knelt to study his face. Gently, she brushed the loose strands of hair away from his face and kissed his forehead. Damien was enraptured by the scene. He was unable to look away or stop the swelling of pride and something darker in his chest. His only regret was that Killian was not fully away, that they wouldn't get to see the surprise in his eyes, and the way life would seep away from him as his eyes went vacant and his breathing finally stopped.

She lined the knife up at his neck with the tip of the blade aimed directly over his pulse.

"Elora," Damien whispered her name, and almost recoiled from the smile stretching across her face. The strange gentleness was gone and replaced with something terrifyingly cruel. As much as Damien wanted to watch her take her time with Killian, they did not have time for games. Finally, she pressed the blade against the spot where his pulse would be, ready to plunge the blade into the spot —

Voices erupted in the hallway. Orders and demands filtered into the room, and they all froze. Damien's body tensed as he glanced between Lukas and Viktor. Both of them were staring with wide eyes in the direction of the noises. There was no more time for her to play with her prey.

"Hurry up or let me do it. We aren't leaving him alive." She nodded and adjusted her position before driving the knife into Killian's flesh. For only a heartbeat, she kept the knife buried to the hilt before ripping it out with a guttural noise.

Damien's focus was locked on the goddess of vengeance before him. She didn't wince or even blink as Killian's blood hit her face and covered her in a crimson that almost matched her hair that laid wild over her shoulders. A brutal grin carved into her face as her tongue brushed over her lips and licked away the liquid there. Blood rushed from the wound and poured down his neck and onto his chest. Killian didn't move. His expression didn't change. Peace. It looked like he was having the most wonderful dream, and all Damien could think was that he didn't deserve that type of end. He almost regretted using such a large dose, even if it was necessary. Killian should at least be conscious through this.

Her snarl echoed in the silent room as she raised the knife again and plunged it into his chest before ripping it out with jerky motions. Damien knew she was no longer in control. That dark side he had seen only a few times had taken over. She had become a conduit for every moment of fury and anguish since childhood. Again and again, the knife flashed down in a glint of silver and crimson. Blood spattered the furniture, walls, and floor. Every single item in the room was covered in flashes of red.

Damien grabbed her wrist, stopping her progress, and she let out a whimper before she allowed him to take the knife. Her body trembled and her eyes were glassy as she looked up at him. He felt her shake as she tried to stand and steady her harsh breaths. She didn't look down at Killian's body or at the rips in his shirt that revealed just how many stab wounds were in his chest and neck. And even with that, it was still better than he had deserved. A swifter death than he had earned.

"Enough," he whispered and moved his hand to her own, ignoring the blood that now covered his own hand as well.

"No!" she cried out. "It will never be enough." Her head dropped to her chest as blood pooled underneath her, soaking into the dress that hung from her frame. The draining had done more than made her weak. It had diminished her physically, and he felt her bones protruding through her flesh. How much longer would she have survived Killian's greed?

Damien lifted her into his arms with one arm under her legs and the other around her back to hold her close to his chest. Her dress was soaked through, and he could feel it through his own shirt and against his skin. He ignored the way she leaned against him and sank against his body in complete surrender, exhausted by the execution administered by her hand.

"I know, love. I know," he whispered against her head as it rested against his shoulder and placed a soft kiss on her forehead. She shuddered at the contact, and he wanted to think it was because she understood now. Maybe she now understood that he didn't hate her as she believed he did, that everything he did was for her. Every word he said, every cruel revelation, every sneer, and every smile had been done to get to this point.

"Lukas, the backdoor. You go first, then Viktor. I'll follow." Lukas nodded before moving towards the back of the room. Damien could hear Viktor's mumblings about how he should be carrying Elora. He ignored him since she was in his arms, and she would remain there no matter what.

~ ~

CHAPTER 50

Damien

The fact that Killian's paranoia had worked to their benefit tonight was Damien's only thought as they moved through the room and ignored the blood covering almost every surface. He always had a back entrance, usually used for secret meetings or to get rid of evidence. The one in his office was hidden behind his desk, near the bookshelf that held a miniature replica of the Tower, leading to his private feeding rooms and elevator. It was a safety precaution in case he was ever attacked by another vampire family or human rebel group. Damien doubted he thought the threat would come from within his own family, specifically from him or Elora.

And if it weren't for the vampire currently in his arms, he would still be Killian's perfect guard, the loyal dog obeying every order without question. He didn't regret Killian turning him despite the reason behind it, despite what he had to do to earn a place within the family. He didn't even regret the work Killian gave him, the missions he had completed for him, the lives he had ended. The only thing he regretted was not believing her and not seeing what was before his eyes the entire time.

It was why he made sure she was given the option to end Killian herself. Damien had known she would want it, would want to face him and make him bleed like he had done to her. It wasn't lost on Damien that if given the time, the process would have been drawn out for hours. The smile on her face had promised as much. It was only the interruption outside the office that had stopped her.

And it had felt like an honor to watch her take the knife she had so easily turned on herself and destroy Killian. The blood had splattered across her face and chest in a way that made Damien want to kneel before her and pledge his loyalty. The question was whether she would forgive him for what he had to do and say to get her to Killian's office, and what his role in the plan was.

Even if she was in his arms, head resting against his chest, he knew she was angry, or would be once she had her strength again. She would need to feed and then they would need to talk. He would need to explain and hope she understood. Plus, Damien had his own anger to contend with. She had been willing to die at that moment. He had seen it in her face as she faced down Killian, not a hint of fear or hesitation in her eyes. Killian had been correct. She had gone into that room with no intention of coming out alive. Another moment or two and it would have all gone very differently.

His heart squeezed slightly at the thought, at the image of her slashed throat and her blood gushing out, her body lifeless on the floor. He shook his head and forced the image away. She was okay. Safe and currently in his arms.

The staircase was dark as they traveled down each flight. They were moving slower than Damien would have liked, but Viktor couldn't see in the dark, and the light from his phone only provided so much for him. It didn't matter. They only needed to make it down a few more flights before they got to Killian's private elevator that would take them to the garage.

"Here." Lukas's voice was quiet as he pushed open the door just a bit to look out into the hallway that would take them to Killian's elevator. After a moment of tense silence, he glanced back at Damien and nodded before walking through. Damien listened to the heavy steps as Viktor followed Lukas, followed by him and Elora.

The hallway, short with a few doors on either side, was empty as they quickly but quietly made their way to the end where the elevator waited. No paintings lined the walls, no statues or tapestries or ridiculous art. It was designed to be an escape route, not to match the rest of the Tower's aesthetic. Damien adjusted Elora in his arms and felt her grip on her shirt tighten slightly as he did so. Lukas hit the button that would take them to the parking garage where a car was waiting. The second half of Denise's part.

It took a moment before the elevator arrived and they piled in. Lukas pushed the button for the garage, and they settled into an uncomfortable silence. All he could hear was Elora breathing, soft and easy, as her head rested on his shoulder. Without a thought, Damien once more pressed his lips to her hair and inhaled the scent of her floral shampoo that was mingling with the almost overwhelming smell of blood.

Damien shifted slightly and pulled his lips away from her even as Viktor's glare drilled into his face. For a moment, Damien glanced in his direction, noting the violence in his eyes, and imagined that if the human could kill him at this moment, he would without any hesitation. Lukas darted a glance at Damien, waiting for the slightest hint of violence, the slightest indication he needed to step in.

The elevator came to a stop, and he nodded at Lukas, who positioned himself in front of him and Elora as the doors slid open. The two of them searched the garage and spotted the car parked a few feet away. Slowly, first Lukas, then Viktor, and finally him with Elora exited the elevator while his eyes roamed over the space. Lukas drew the gun from his waistband. There shouldn't be anyone down here, not in Killian's private area where he stored the vehicles he never drove. In the whole time Damien worked for him, he had never seen him leave the Tower. Everyone came to him, either willingly or not.

"Where's Denise?" Lukas whispered as they surveyed the garage one more time, trying to see if anyone was hiding. There were plenty of hiding places—behind cars, behind pillars that held up the entire building.

Damien shook his head as he looked over the car, a basic four-door that didn't draw attention. Denise was supposed to meet them here and be ready to assist with Elora as necessary. He hadn't been sure what state she would be in and had wanted to prepare for any outcome, including Elora being hurt or needing to be sedated. The thought of her being put unconscious made him hold her a little tighter and his grip adjusted to hold her just a bit closer. Damien glanced down at her to find her eyes open, but empty, as if she wasn't taking in anything going on around her.

As they inched closer, both Lukas and Damien smelled it—blood.

Damien spotted the shoes first—a pair of tan flats that led up to a pair of jeans as he rounded the car, moving towards the driver's side. Denise's body lay there with a bullet hole in her forehead and Damien cursed. Her eyes were wide open in surprise and her mouth was contorted into what was probably a scream before she was shot. The driver's side door was open and there were three packs in the back seat, one for Lukas, Elora, and him. Damien hadn't told her Viktor would be coming with them, and she hadn't asked about him.

"You can't take her. We need her." The voice echoed in the garage. The space was suddenly too large and small all at once. Damien perked up but couldn't seem to tear his eyes away from the body in front of him. He felt Elora shift in his arms as she tried to see whatever had caused him to curse. He lowered his head towards her.

"Don't look, love." Elora sucked in a breath and then nodded despite the fact it was clear she had already seen her former psychiatrist. Damien took a moment to brush his lips across her forehead in a futile attempt to comfort her.

"Give her to me, Damien." Viktor's command mingled with the footsteps moving closer.

"And if I don't?" Elora stiffened in Damien's grasp, but he held her tight.

"No one needs to die here. There are enough Resistance members here to take care of you and your friend." There was a hardness to his voice, a commanding tone that Damien had never heard from him. Suddenly, he was not Viktor the nurse or even Viktor the irritating potential lover. No, he was a Resistance member, a spy, and a betrayer. Damien knew Elora realized that just as he did. Her grip tightened and her heartbeat quickened.

"Why do you want her? I thought you cared about her." Damien felt her flinch at his words. For a moment, he regretted them. He didn't want her hurt, not by Killian, not by Viktor, and not by him. She squirmed in his arms as she tried to get loose from his grip.

"She is a weapon. My responsibility. I told you that." He heard her hiss and then a fist collided with his face, forcing his grasp on her to loosen enough that she could free herself.

"You asshole! You lying piece of —" Her voice cut off abruptly and Damien followed her gaze to Viktor where he stood with Lukas, a gun pressed to his temple. Roughly six other humans surround them, each one armed. Lukas's gaze was locked on Elora. The resignation was clear on his face. He was willing to die for her, to make sure she didn't end up with anyone else who wanted to use her.

"Why?" Damien flinched at the way her voice broke on the word and her hands balled into fists at her sides. Viktor turned his gaze to her and scanned her ripped and torn blood-splattered dress that revealed every scar and puncture wound along her neck and arms. There wasn't even the slightest hint of regret in his assessing gaze. It was cold and calculating in a way that was so strange on a face that had only looked at her with affection.

"Your blood's the key. Dr. Montgomery had been working on it, harnessing it as a weapon. They want to wipe us out and you will make sure that doesn't happen." She choked back a sob and stood straighter as her body turned to steel. Damien stepped up beside her as she stared down at the human she thought was her friend and thought loved her.

"Then why kill her?" Damien gestured at Denise's body as Viktor shrugged.

"She wanted out, realized exactly what it would take to use her." In other words, Denise came to love the vampire who started as her patient and specimen but became something more.

"Is she worth your friend's life?" The question was aimed at Damien, but three voices rang out in response.

"Yes."

"Yes."

"No."

Lukas and Damien's affirmations versus her denial. He watched as Lukas gave her a smile full of warmth with a tinge of sadness. They had become so close so quickly. Lukas had taken care of her from the moment they sedated her in that gas station parking lot, carefully positioning her body to make sure she would be safe on the ride over to the Tower. He had talked to her, played games with her, coaxed her out of a chasm so deep no one else could reach her. He had seen the woman that she was, not who Damien assumed she was. Damien met his friend's eyes once more, knowing this was probably the last time he would see the bright amber that always seemed to gleam with amusement.

"I'm sorry, El." She let out a sob and fell to her knees as Viktor's brows furrowed together.

And then time accelerated, and each movement became a blur as Lukas spun and grabbed Viktor by the throat. A harsh growl erupted from him as he bared his fangs and tore into Viktor's shoulder. A howl of pain echoed off the concrete walls and half of the humans drew their weapons and rushed towards Lukas while the others raced towards Elora and Damien.

Damien grabbed her arm and yanked her towards him as she screamed Lukas's name, screamed at Damien to save him. She fought him every step of the way, throwing herself at Lukas as he battled Viktor and another human. His grip tightened to the point where he was sure it would bruise and he hated himself for it, hated himself for the way her voice cracked and went raw from the damage she was doing to herself.

"Fucking let me go!" Elora turned towards him. Her face was a vision of rage and anguish as she swung to hit him again. Damien dodged her hit, grabbed her other wrist and held it tight even as she continued to fight. Even with being drained and expending all her energy on Killian, Elora was beyond strong, and he struggled to keep her in his grasp.

"Lukas!" Her voice rang out over the sound of punches and commands and howls of pain. She jerked her arm and swung to hit him once more as her own cries joined the cacophony echoing in the garage. Not once did she stop trying to turn back towards Lukas, didn't stop trying to get to him. She would hate him for this. Any hope he had of explaining everything disappeared in a single moment.

Gunshots rang out as Damien ducked and grabbed the keys from Denise's curled-up hand. They hadn't thought to take them from her after her execution, so convinced that they would be easily disposed of, that Elora would go with them.

If Viktor had simply asked Elora, would she have gone?

Damien shoved Elora into the driver's seat and pushed her over as he entered beside her. Her eyes never left the fight happening behind them as she scrambled into the backseat. She pressed her hand against the glass and pounded.

"Please! Please, not him." She flinched as a series of gunshots went off. Damien ducked down even as he turned the key, and the car started easily. She screamed Lukas's name once more as he slammed it into gear and spared a single glance out the back window. Maybe he had subdued the humans and was ready to follow them? It was the two of them who delivered Elora here. Damien had wanted it to be both of them who left with her.

"Fuck." Damien's voice broke as he watched his friend through the rearview mirror. There was too much blood, the wounds too many. Around him were three unmoving bodies, and Damien felt a rush of pride that he was able to take them with him. Viktor stood beside him, bleeding heavily from a wound on his chest and another on his face—a jagged gash that started at his temple and ended just above his lips, traveling over his cheek and down the bridge of his nose. His one eye was already swelling, and his lip was busted.

"Come on!" Elora's voice rang out and drew the attention of both Lukas and Viktor. She frantically gestured for him and urged him to run, to get in the car and leave with them. For a moment, a single brief moment barely more than a heartbeat, it seemed like that was exactly what he would do.

Viktor met Elora's eyes as her cries continued and the remaining humans gathered around the two of them. Lukas was focused on her with silent acceptance and nodded. The human took the opportunity, and his foot struck out to collide with the side of Lukas's knee. With a devastating cry of pain, Lukas crashed to the ground. His cry mingled with Elora's screams as both sounds pierced Damien's ears. He turned in the car and watched out the back windows instead of the rearview mirror as Viktor pulled his gun out and leveled it against Lukas's forehead. He heard Elora's cries, her screams, her whimpers as she begged and pleaded.

"Please Viktor. If you ever cared about me, then let him go." She sniffed and ran her hand down the rear window. Damien wanted to tell her that Viktor couldn't hear her, that the car would forever contain every plea that escaped her mouth. Her fingers sank into the leather of the back seat as tears streamed down her face.

Lukas locked eyes with Damien through the window and nodded. The message between the two of them was clear, and he returned the gesture. Damien finally tore his attention away, no longer able to see his friend on his knees before that coward of a human. He wasn't sure he would be able to drive away if he saw anything else. Without a word, he slammed on the gas as a single gunshot rang out. He was too far away to hear his friend's body hit the ground.

~ ~

EPILOGUE

Viktor

He had never gone down to the maximum-security ward at the hospital. During his time working there, he had never had a reason, and it wasn't the type of place that one visited during their off time. His focus had been on Elora, per the orders of the Resistance and Denise until she fell out of favor. She was the perfect example of why you couldn't allow yourself to care about your mission, and Elora had been her mission.

Now, she was Viktor's mission.

The clean-up at the garage had taken hours. Removing the bodies and getting out without drawing attention to themselves had been a bit more difficult than he had expected. They had left the vampire's body behind as a tribute to what they had been able to accomplish, even if the main goal had been a failure. And there were the bandages, the stitches, the washing away of blood as he prepared for this next step. No one in the Tower had played their part correctly. Elora was never meant to kill Killian, though that change had been beneficial. One vampire head down and only three more to go.

No, Elora was supposed to escape with him, leaving Damien and Lukas dead. But somehow, that prick Damien had weaseled his way into her trust, maybe even her affections. He should have seen this coming when she started drinking blood. He had just hoped he had laid enough groundwork that she would turn to him and trust him beyond anyone else.

And now, here he was in the basement of the hospital, bandaged and sore from the fight, to pursue another avenue, another potential option for the Resistance. Elizabeth was a problem, but maybe she could be useful to them.

A sharp ringing sound echoed through the hallway as he made his way towards the metal door. The walls were the same sickly shade of cream as the rest of the building, but down here it seemed to take on a yellowish tint under the fluorescent lights. The linoleum floor was chipped and there were gouge marks that broke up the tan and white pattern.

Viktor listened to the click as the door unlocked and he pulled it open, wincing at the smell that assaulted his senses. Urine and feces and unwashed bodies. The maximum-security ward was little more than a prison, a space to put people and forget about them until it was time for whatever therapy they were subjected to.

He warily studied her appearance but did not move closer than just inside the doorway of her cell. She was given medication for the suppression of her urges like Elora was, but her file also stated she was routinely attacking nurses and other patients. Each time the dose was raised until she was now being given an astronomical amount, far above what was considered a safe dosage. Was it because she was turned by Elora? The Resistance had used this medication on other vampires before as a way to subdue them and gain information, but never on a vampire created by her.

Elizabeth was dressed in what once had been a set of standard-issued dark blue scrubs, but the pants were ripped and torn, and the shirt was missing an entire sleeve. She wasn't wearing any socks or shoes as she reclined on the mattress. Viktor noted that she didn't have a frame for it and wondered if she had used it as a weapon, hence its absence.

Her arms were under her head and her blond hair was matted as she stared at the ceiling while humming softly to herself. The dirt around her neck made her scars stand out like a beacon, pale slices of flesh among the filth.

"It's not polite to stare." Her voice was bright, almost girlish, and he cleared his throat to begin the prepared speech that he had practiced on the drive over. She was useful and necessary, and returning without her would present a very real problem considering he was already going to be out of favor for losing Elora.

Her foster sister would need to work as a consolation prize for now.

"Looks like they have been taking care of you." Viktor tried to make sure his tone was easy and conversational. He watched a smile spread across her face, revealing her fangs that looked like they had been filed down slightly.

"Excellent care. Are you here to take me to therapy? It has been a while, and I do miss it." She sat up slightly and stretched out, like a cat waking from a nap. A slight moan escaped her lips as she sniffed the air. Her eyes landed on him, all predator who now recognized their prey.

Viktor cursed silently and forced himself not to take a step back, to not give up ground. "Not therapy. But I am here to take you somewhere, should you want to go." She sat up the rest of the way and crossed her legs in front of her. Not once did she look away, simply stared at him, eyes flicking over his face in an unnerving assessment.

"And where would you take me?" She leaned forward, resting her arms on her thighs, face pinched in confusion or curiosity or both.

"With me. To see some people who want to work with you, want to help you." He stood a bit straighter and clasped his hands behind his back.

"Why would they want to do that?" Viktor considered her question, thinking through his prepared answer.

"We need your help with your sister. She has disappeared again, and we need to find her." For a moment, he worried that he had said the wrong thing, and that mentioning Elora had been the wrong approach. Their relationship was one of violence and obsession, of guilt and longing.

Elizabeth was fixated on her sister, making her the only topic of conversation in every therapy session. He had skimmed the therapy notes before coming down. To Elizabeth, Elora was simultaneously a goddess and a demon, a curse and a blessing, a savior and a punisher. She seemed to fluctuate between wanting to love her and wanting to drain her, that same addiction that seemed to plague anyone who drank from Elora.

At the end of the day, Elizabeth seemed to simply want Elora, wanted all of her to herself to do with as she pleased.

But he watched as the smile grew impossibly wider and her eyes seemed to glow. She stood and clapped her hands before jumping up and down like an excited schoolgirl who had been given a present. He reached out his hand and ignored the stench that grew stronger as she stepped towards him.

"Will you help us?" His question was pointless. From the gleam in her pale blue eyes and the twisted grin on her face, he knew exactly what her answer was.

"Of course. I miss my sister very much." She giggled, and he almost winced at how horribly wrong the sound was in this space. Finally, she took his hand, and he could feel the grime and dirt on her palm. She squeezed softly as she pushed past him, and he couldn't help but wonder if this was a mistake and he had made a deal with the devil.

ACKNOWLEDGEMENTS

I've tried to write this three times now and it keeps coming back to a very simple thank you to my partner, my daughter, and my cats. Thank you to my partner for his support even before he knew what I was doing. Thank you to my daughter for keeping me humble and forcing me to take breaks to watch reality television together. And thank you to my cats for being quiet, but judgmental company while I wrote.

Finally, thank you to the readers. I appreciate your support and can only hope you enjoyed the book and the characters I created. Hopefully, I will see you again for the sequel.

ABOUT THE AUTHOR

Misty Thomas is a writer, educator, mother, partner, and cat mom. When she isn't teaching or writing, she can be found drinking an unholy amount of coffee and finding new hobbies that don't last very long. She currently resides in New Mexico with her family.